AF335631

The Miracle Revolution

mark landau

Published by
First Edition Design Publishing
Sarasota, Florida USA

The Miracle Revolution
Copyright ©2016 Mark Landau

ISBN 978-1506-903-01-9 HC/CL
ISBN 978-1506-903-00-2 PBK
ISBN 978-1506-903-02-6 Digital

LCCN 2016953970

October 2016

Published and Distributed by
First Edition Design Publishing, Inc.
P.O. Box 20217, Sarasota, FL 34276-3217
www.firsteditiondesignpublishing.com

Disclaimers – Contains adult language and situations

Library of Congress Cataloging-in-Publication Data
Landau, Mark
  The Miracle Revolution/
 written by Mark Landau.
   p. cm.
  ISBN 978-1506-903-01-9 hc. ISBN 978-1506-903-00-2 pbk. ISBN 978-1506-903-02-6 digital.

1. FICTION / Adventure. 2. /Erotica/General. 3. / Paranormal.

T3745

www.mark-landau.com

Other books by Mark Landau

What We Can Do

The Love and Forgiveness Meditation

I Love You and Forgive You:
A True Self-Healing Tool and the Life Around It

Archetypes, Election, Evolution:
America's Denial of Democracy

This is dedicated to The Miracle Revolution.
Read *What We Can Do* and do the meditation with me.
The more we do it together, the more we manifest
miracles and renew the world.

I'd like to acknowledge Bruce MacLaren for offering to
edit, for all his suggestions, for writing the foreword and
for being my friend.

Foreword

This is a book like no other I can remember reading. It is an allegory, which Dictionary.com defines as "a representation of an abstract or spiritual meaning through concrete or material forms; figurative treatment of one subject under the guise of another." Exactly so. It is an entertaining, erotic, spiritual, rollicking good time of a simple sci-fi story that will probably provoke you, turn you on (or off) and possibly, if you let it, gently remind you of values long since buried in the cynicism of the 21st century western world. The Miracle Revolution (TMR) is a fantasy about healing the world and the realization of dreams that western societies have long since abandoned or never even dreamed. And it is a love story.

The love story told here is more than a little unconventional. I could say it's remarkable and about more than the human expression of love. In a way consistent with many spiritual disciplines, the love of TMR is divinely inspired and supported by highly evolved Extra Terrestrials who are sent to heal planet earth and its unique style of insanity. They are the promulgators of powerful abilities, which allow healing that could not otherwise take place. They are vehicles of divine love, a constructive power like no other. Love can wash over everything and there is joy in that washing. Whether this happens or not is a function of choices each of us makes.

In encountering some of the characters' choices, it is likely that readers will respond with their unique values, learning and experience to understand or be repelled. I encourage every reader to observe their own reactions and discover, if they can, the source of those reactions and whether the other values presented allow them to pale in comparison or disappear altogether.

It is this kind of personal examination that throughout the ages has been supported by the practice of meditation in all its many forms. The Dalai Lama has been credited with saying, "If every eight year old in the world is taught meditation, we will eliminate violence from the world within one generation." TMR offers one meditation developed and used by the author, which invokes two of the most powerful energies in human life. It is a gift from Mark to his readers.

The original title of this book was *Wish Fulfillment*, which is fully manifest throughout. It's fun to see one's hopes and dreams, many unconscious, pop on the page as a reminder of what we may have given up. It could even act as a first step in evaporating our cynicism, like discovering that Nisargadatta's current of energy and Christianity's Holy Spirit are alive in each of us to move us toward our own healing.

In any final analysis, TMR presents a simple, compelling story about what our lives could be, how they could feel and what they could accomplish. Its primary value is in opening and touching us so that we can rediscover what we may have always wanted. It is a far out treatise on divine and human love and surrender, sex and tantra. It may broaden your boundaries about what life is or can be about or it may offend your sensibilities. I think it will entertain you with a story about how the world could be, even without science fiction and fantasy.

Bruce MacLaren
Taos, New Mexico
September 6, 2016

Preface

I believe that life on Earth has evolved in long, excruciatingly slow periods of foundation building followed by rare, spectacular quantum leaps forward.

I believe that human evolution progresses similarly.

I believe that we are coming to the edge of a plateau where we are poised to take such a leap or not, to embrace a magnificent step forward or postpone it and tumble down the cliff to continue sideways in the trench for another two to ten millennia.

I believe that those of us, over the eons, who have believed in, longed for and tried to live something better have added to a cumulative cloud of influence that will someday buoy us up into our next higher form of functioning.

I believe we are in the throes of deciding if we are ready for that someday now.

And forgive me dear reader, I believe that larger and larger numbers of us incorporating a regular practice of meditation into our daily lives, especially one that carries the healing energies of love and forgiveness, could help us embrace it sooner instead of later.

I'm calling this ongoing but uncertain transformation The Miracle Revolution because if it truly happens it will bring about innumerable small and large miracles and transfigure life on Earth into something far more miraculous than it already is.

In what I hope is a unique, creative way, it's what this book is about.

Perhaps it's only me indulging in my idiosyncrasies and will touch few.

Perhaps, somehow, it will reach out and strike a larger chord.

Why has it taken this form?

God only knows.

Could it possibly be divine orchestration?

Can I explain myself to you?

Better not try.

Or better yet, if you have any interest, read *I Love You and Forgive You*. It does somewhat try.

If you read this book, I thank you.

If you grok it I love you.

If you don't read or grok it I still love you.

Maybe slow down for the reading.

Enjoy whatever in it you may find to enjoy.

Milk it for all it may be worth.

Maybe think about the universe in a grain of sand, the mustard seed that is so very small and yields such great, billowy clouds of yellow flower and green leaf, and of God in the smallest of things.

Maybe, if you find anything in this book you like, reread the dedication and take it to heart. Or reread it now and take it to heart.

I know there are things herein that will be hard going for some of you.

Perhaps if you stick with it, the payoff will be worth it.

If they're too hard or boring, perhaps skim ahead just a little.

I leave them in for those they are meant for.

May it find them.

You are so very precious.

If you only knew.

Our true preciousness is deeply elusive.

We may think we know it but haven't yet found it in its deepest, truest place.

Thank you, bless you, I love you.

May we love and forgive ourselves and all that is.

May we come to appreciate the value of doing this.

May we experience the grace and miracle of living it, the cleansed re-sanctification that healing can bestow, the resurrection of mature, divine innocence.

m

Santa Fe, NM

August 27, 2016

Chapter 1

And the Beginnings of Love

Eva Dunn was twenty-three. The Dunn part was easy. The Eva wasn't. So she'd say, "Not *EE*vuh or AYvuh, *EH*vuh. Like *nevuh*." And for those who persisted in getting it wrong where it seemed to matter, she'd say, "You know the male name Evan? Think of that without the n."

Her two names together lent themselves all too well to innuendo. Lord knows she'd been razzed, especially since she was drop dead gorgeous and had been since she was twelve. Everywhere she went men drooled and hit on her. What protected her was that she despised them. They were walking hormones. She wanted more than flesh and drive. She was impervious to virility. She wanted something intangible, some kind of substance, gravitas, a depth and breadth she had never seen. She'd had a few flings to see what it was like and get some experience. But they were soon killed by boredom and she had mostly been on her own. She was fine with that. Better alone than with any of these nothings. She had mastered the art of circumvention. Sometimes she called it circumcision. Cutting men off at the pass.

Her father's ancestry was English/Irish, her mother's Slovenian. She had thick, luxuriant, light brown hair; startlingly clear, piercing blue eyes; clear, light skin; a fine nose and bones; perfect teeth and the very best curves.

She had grown up in Madison, Wisconsin, and had completed her Bachelors and Masters there in Interior Design.

Her relations with her parents, both UW professors, were good. But she didn't feel that attached to either. The same was true with her older brother and younger sister. So as soon as she graduated, she moved to New York.

She had already gotten a job with the small, upscale Village Design House and soon found a nice, little, one-bedroom walkup in the East Village. Things came easily to her. Everything went swimmingly.

She loved New York and felt completely at home there. A lot of the ethnic men were louder and more brazen in their hoots and whistles than she was used to. But she knew how to ignore them and carry herself like a queen. She also got a permit and carried a small Beretta Pico in her purse.

Soon after starting at VDH, she became fast friends with Rosalyn, one of her co-workers, a thirty-nine year old New York Jew who embodied the best instead of the worst a Jewish American Princess could be. She was bright, attractive and sardonic with a glint in her eye and a sharp sense of humor. She was magnetically drawn to Eva, attracted to her. Sometimes she'd have fantasies about her that inspired self-love. She was normally quite heterosexual but Eva was something else altogether. And she was falling in love with her.

But about six months into Eva's tenure at the firm, Rosalyn's six-year-old daughter, Brie, was diagnosed with bone cancer. This changed everything and began a huge transformation in her. Brie's sudden affliction and possible mortality were killing her. She took a leave of absence and they moved into The Ronald McDonald House. It was a live-in cancer support facility for parents and their stricken children. Rosalyn had divorced her husband three years ago and he had moved to California.

So Eva took a Tuesday afternoon off and went to visit her there. It was heartbreaking. All the children, many of them bald from chemo and radiation. The parents quietly loving and hurting. You could feel the pain. But it was good they had each other for support.

Eva had never been afraid of death. She had never understood all the hoopla. It seemed to her a most integral part in the order of things. And she knew in a way she couldn't justify to anyone that it wasn't the end. It was a doorway, the next obvious step. She could understand the pain of seeing loved ones suffer and decline, of losing them. But she also knew that nothing was ever lost, that they were always still somehow there and that they were not other than she, that, on the ultimate level of existence, all was really one. She wanted to go up to them all, shake them and tell them that death was OK. It was nothing to be afraid of. But of course, she couldn't. She especially couldn't say that to Rosalyn. What a thing to say! But that didn't stop her from wanting to.

She thought she'd stay the afternoon but after a few hours the pain impelled her out the door.

As soon as she got outside, she gasped for air. As soon as she hit the sidewalk, she felt him.

He was a number of blocks down moving towards her. Her sense of him was palpable. She knew the presence she felt was male. And she knew it was what she'd always been looking for. It was breathtaking in its serene vastness. There was nothing presumptuous about it. It simply was—larger by far than any presence she had ever felt.

She slowed her pace as she walked west on 73rd. She forced herself to breathe, remain calm, bring all her awareness online to sense, feel, see. She drank in his proximity, his diminishing distance, the slight giddiness his depth and breadth brought forth in her. Her curiosity grew. What would he look like? Would he have a wife and child in tow? Would he be a centenarian?

She had crossed First Avenue and Second and was halfway down the block towards Third when she saw him. She knew immediately it was him. The sight of the man and the sense of his presence clicked into coalescence. She was thrilled. A sense of jubilation, excitement and empowerment shot through her entire body. She was now distinctly more than she had been a moment before.

He was older but not impossibly old. She had always been looking for an older man. He seemed about fifty. A few streaks of greyish white distinguished his dark hair. His features were very strong. He was definitely handsome but it wasn't his good looks that struck you. It was the strength of the chiseled planes of his face. He seemed like a living sculpture. His gate and carriage were graceful but bespoke power. He had a foreign air, decidedly European.

She impaled him with her eyes. He seemed to be sensing her, looking for her, gauging her soul as well. Their eyes met briefly as they passed. There was a jolt of recognition but not in the normal way. They knew they had never seen each other. And something else shifted deep within her.

There was no hitch in his stride. They passed each other and he continued onward. She about faced and followed a few paces behind. She knew she couldn't lose sight of him. Two such chances would not occur.

She hung back when they stopped at the light at Second and followed when the light turned. She was both in tow and had him hooked. She wasn't going to lose this one.

Towards the middle of the next block was a building she had passed and couldn't help but notice. It had three large flags waving in the breeze above its two-door entrance. One said 'Bohemian National Hall.' The other was a national flag she wasn't sure of, a blue triangle covering the inner angles of one white and one red rectangle. She wasn't sure, either, what country to assign 'Bohemian' to. The slang meaning arose and gave her a chuckle as she became certain he would turn into this building. It had a restaurant on the ground floor. But she knew it was more than a restaurant and meeting hall. There was something official here. It had the feel of a consulate.

She quickened her pace to draw closer to him. And when he turned left she followed behind. She could be quite bold when it suited her. She had greater trust in her inner knowing than most, that still, small gyroscope within that gave her the sense of the rightness or wrongness of things, their potential importance. But a thing like this had never happened before.

He stopped abruptly before the entrance and turned to face her. They could both tell they were both delighted.

"I can't tell you how glad and honored I am that you're here. You're a miracle," he enunciated beautifully with a slight accent. "We're about to leave US jurisdiction and enter Czech territory. Will you accompany me?"

"Thank you. *I'd* be honored. Lead on," she replied.

"Ah," he said moving to her side, changing his direction and courteously taking her arm, which she allowed. "But I said 'accompany.' It wouldn't be right for you to follow me like a servant. I should follow you like a queen. But let's enter as intimate equals. That will cause the greatest stir."

He smiled.

She smiled.

And the beginnings of love entered the building along with them.

Chapter 2

More Than Cosmic

"**M**y name is Gabriel Jelinek," he said as they stepped into the elevator and he gracefully turned them around. This caused her breast to gently jostle his arm, sending a warm thrill through both of them.

"And mine is Eva Dunn," she replied as he punched a button.

"D u n n?"

"Yes."

"Eva Dunn. So I had to wait till my fiftieth year to meet you?" he half asked.

She smiled, "I guess so."

She loved the way he gave her the information she wanted without her having to ask.

"J e l i n e k?"

"Yes," he smiled.

The elevator door opened.

They were in an open area connected to several offices.

The receptionist was stunning. She was a bit older than Eva, perhaps thirty-two. Her beauty was classic and timeless but it had a hard edge. The way she narrowed her eyes at the sight of Eva and Gabriel arm in arm spoke volumes. She had set her cap on him and had gotten nowhere. But Eva knew that this woman could be her friend.

"Alena, this is Eva, Eva, Alena."

"How do you do," Alena smiled.

"Pleased to meet you," Eva returned.

Slightly frosty with a hint of truce.

Gabriel guided her into his office.

He seemed to be the Consul-General.

"You're the Czech Consul-General for New York?"

"Yes."

"Pleased to meet *you*, sir."

"And I, you. So very pleased. What do you do?"

"Interior design."

"Ah, I could use your services."

"I'm at your disposal."

"Would that include dinner?"

"Yes, that would be lovely."

"Excellent. Thank you. French, Thai or Vegan?"

"Thai."

"Beautiful. I'm thrilled."

They paused to gaze in each other's eyes.

Something shifted and she felt a small, sudden lurch. She knew they had entered deeper terrain. But there was something more here, a sense of something unknown that could pull the rug out from under everything she thought she knew.

"I should warn you," he said quite lovingly. "If you continue following me, you could plunge down a mighty, glorious rabbit hole."

"That sounds both ominous and exciting."

"Let's say radically exciting."

"In a good way?"

"I would say in a most miraculous way. I know of others who feel differently."

"Can you tell me more?"

"I can and will but not here and now. There are things I must attend to. I will tell you as much as I know over dinner. But I will give you an out. Would you mind if I asked you to find your way out and return at five-thirty? If you don't I will know that you changed your mind."

"How could I with such an intriguing puzzle?"

"Some people could."

"Yes, well if I were that type of person it would probably be better if I did."

"Precisely."

They savored another few moments of gazing upon one another.

"I wouldn't mind in the least. You didn't exactly prearrange this time to entertain me. I'll see you at five-thirty."

"Wonderful," he said rising out of his chair. "You have enriched my afternoon chores beyond words."

She could feel how truly he meant it. It stirred her heart and loins as she arose. In a subtle, beautiful way, their bodies responded to each other in kind. He took her hand and drew it to his lips.

"I'm enchanted by you, dear Eva, thank you for finding me."

"And I by you. You're so very welcome."

Her cheeks and body slightly flushed. She swiveled on her feet and left his office.

After, "Bye, Alena," she was out of sight.

He sat for a few moments not doing a thing.

Then he got busy.

Eva knew how she would fill the time—as she had planned.

She marveled on her way back how everything was different, how something so wonderful had happened for her and something so terrible for Rosalyn.

When she got to Brie's room at Ronald McDonald, it was empty.

She hunted them down in one of the common areas. Brie was playing some elaborate board game on the floor with two other children as a few parents watched.

Rosalyn looked up, surprised.

"I was sure you were gone."

"I was. I met someone."

"You're kidding. You just left. How could you meet someone? Where?"

"I felt him off in the distance as soon as I hit the sidewalk. I didn't see him till I was close to Third."

"No."

"Yes."

"That sounds cosmic."

"More than cosmic."

"Let's find somewhere quiet. I want to know everything."

They went to a small sitting area. No one was there.

"Shit, Eva, I've been wanting to bed you myself."

"I know, my love. I'm sorry. This takes precedence for now."

"Of course."

"Maybe down the road we could do a ménage à trois or just the two of us. But for now, it's just him and me. If you and I did do something and then had a falling out, work could become terrible."

"I know, I know. Ever the practical one. So did you confront him on the sidewalk?"

"No. Our eyes met and something happened to me. I think he had sensed me coming as well. He kept right on walking and I turned and followed."

"Wow."

"Yeah."

"And then?"

"Then I knew where he was going and decided to follow him in."

"And where was that?"

"That funny building with the flags in the next block."

"The Bohemian Theater?"

"Yes, but the Czech Consulate is there as well."

"And he works there."

"Yes, he's the Czech Consul-General for New York."

Roz paused.

"He's older."

"Yes."

"How old?

"Fifty."

"Eva, that's more than twice your age!"

"I know. I've always wanted an older man."

"But that old?"

"Why not?"

"You know what comes next. Because when you're forty, he'll be sixty-seven."

"So what? Let's leave that for the future. I think it's a done deal."

"Already?"

"Already. I'm a different woman. And he's my man."

"Wow, instantaneous. As the world turns."

"Sometimes in the blink of an eye."

"So you followed him into the building?"

"No. He turned on the stoop and called me a miracle. He took my arm to escort me in. He told me I was entering Czech territory."

"And then he blurted his age?"

"No, he gave me his name in the elevator. And I gave him mine. Then he said, 'So I had to wait till I was fifty to meet you?'"

"He sounds good."

"He's amazing. I've never felt such a presence. And he tells me what I want to know before I ask. He has a slight accent but his English is world class. He's a total gem."

"Do I get to meet him?"

"Oh yes. I don't know when. I'm going back at five-thirty. He's taking me to dinner. I'd invite you but it's too soon. Let me have dinner with him first."

"Of course, darling, if and when the time is right."

"It will be. You're my best friend. I've never seriously considered being with a woman till you. I seem to want people older than me. I'd love to hear your impressions."

"Thank you, love, I'm glad it's been mutual. Too bad it's chopped now. It's funny we don't talk of it till a man appears."

"Yes. But we would have gotten to it soon. This just brought it to a head."

"And tonight you'll be giving head."

"Now Roz," Eva chuckled, "let's not descend beyond the basement."

"Sorry, I'm just jealous. On both counts. You get to be with a charmer and someone else gets to be with you."

"I know, dear. But maybe it'll take the edge off, knowing it's not going to happen for now. Our friendship is precious to me. Let's not endanger it."

"Of course not. That's most important. Who knows what it would have been like? I've never been with a woman, either."

"Probably lovely at first. But could it last?"

"Who knows? But even if not we'd still be friends."

"Probably, but feelings get hurt. What if we'd gone deep and then I'd met Gabriel?"

"Hmm, I see your point. Gabriel. Is he angelic?"

"He is, but very masculine. Gracefully masculine."

"He sounds intriguing."

"Totally. But let's leave our door open. I'd like to see what it's like, especially with you. But you've got your hands full, too."

Rosalyn paused and her countenance darkened.

"Yes, my poor, little darling. It's killing me."

"I know. What can I do?"

"I don't know. Just hang with me from time to time and uplift me with your wonderful news. I'm delighted for you."

"Thank you, sweetie. Let's go back and watch her."

They spent the rest of the afternoon playing the board game with three precious, bald children.

Chapter 3

A Completely Different Place

At five-thirty Eva waltzed into the elevator in the Bohemian National Hall.

Alena was still there.

"Go right in, dear," she smiled, all hint of frostiness gone.

Eva gave her a 'thank you' and her best smile back.

Gabriel sat at his computer.

He looked up and smiled quite radiantly.

"Have a seat. Just a moment, please."

She took the time to study his face and bearing.

Simple, graceful and regal all at once.

A moment became three.

She was quite content to devour the sight of him.

But as she did, something began to arise within her from her subconscious mind, something curious that she couldn't pinpoint, something odd, even not quite right. And then she had it. His skin. It was flawless—impossibly perfect. She searched for a mole, an irregularity. She could find none. She had never seen such skin.

Finally he did something definitive, sighed and turned to her.

"The cares of statehood?"

"Yes, not so bad. Mostly prosaic."

"Work does have that side, doesn't it?"

"Indeed, but now you're here to fill my evening and the prosaic has fled into my computer. Do you mind eating this early?"

"Not at all, I'm famished. I didn't have lunch."

"Excellent," he said, rising. "Shall we?"

She rose, too, and they walked out of his office.

They both said "Bye, Alena," simultaneously as they passed her.

This gave them all a chuckle and Alena said, "Bye, bye, enjoy."

"She seems nice," Eva remarked in the elevator.

"She is, a thoughtful, lovely woman."

"But not for you."

"No, not for me. I believe I've just met the woman for me. I hope I get to take her in my arms before the night is done."

"I hope so, too."

He took her arm and walked her out of the building then west to the end of the block. They crossed the street and turned right up Second. And there they were at Up Thai in less than two minutes.

"That was easy."

"Yes, it's lovely here and the food is quite good."

And to Eva's discerning eye, it was. All wood and lanterns and nice and quiet at this early hour. It had a sweet, casual intimacy. Gabriel led them to a table in the corner and they sat.

"Eva Dunn. Eva Dunn. You must have been teased. But what a great gift and treasure you are. Tell me of yourself."

"Not much to tell. And, yes, I was teased. I'm twenty-three. I've been in New York about six months. I grew up in Madison, Wisconsin. Both my parents are professors at the university. I have two siblings. I'm into aesthetics and design. I have a good job. I have a nice little apartment. Both are in the Village. I have one good friend. Design stores and clients get me around the city. Life is good."

"Is that what brought you to my neck of the woods?"

"No."

Pause.

"Rather not say?"

"I went to Ronald McDonald."

"Oh no! You know a child with cancer?"

"Yes, dear six-year-old Brie, my friend's daughter."

"How tragic!"

"Yes."

Silence, as Eva looked down, her eyes just starting to tear.

More silence as he looked at her with compassion.

"Perhaps we can help."

She looked up, startled. There was something odd in the way he said 'we.'

"I can't imagine how, besides what they're doing already."

"I know. We'll get to that. It's part of the rabbit hole."

"We're not there yet?"

"No, it takes some easing into. You seem close with your friend."

"Yes, Rosalyn. I love her dearly. We were both thinking of intimacy before Brie was diagnosed and you showed up. Neither of us has ever been with a woman. I would say she's more particularly attracted to me. But I am to her as well. We never spoke of it till this afternoon. So there, that's quite a bit more about me."

"Thank you, dear Eva. I'm thrilled you shared that with me. It makes me love you all the more."

At this point, a lovely, oriental waitress arrived at their table to give them menus. They looked at them, spoke of the dishes, decided and ordered.

"So you're high IQ?"

"High enough. My mother's an Astrophysicist and my father a Philosopher. I could have followed in their footsteps but I had no interest. Tell me about you."

"I was born in Ostrava, the second largest city in the Czech Republic. It's in the northeast corner near the border of Poland. It's a coal and steel town but it has some culture, too. I very much fell in love with and married a woman when I was in my twenties. We had a blissful two years before she was diagnosed with cancer. It took her very quickly. I've been alone ever since. I had a few affairs that lasted a few months. No one really interested me. I started working for the state and then studied and applied for the diplomatic corps. I wanted to come to New York. And here I am."

"No children?"

"No children."

"I'm sorry, that must have been hard."

"Yes, thank you. It was. But how is it that you're unattached? You must know how gorgeous you are."

"Thank *you*. I'm quite aware of the affect I have on men. But, you see, I despise them."

"You don't have compassion for them?"

"Sometimes, but rarely. Mostly I just despise them."

"But you don't despise me."

"No, I don't."

"Why is that?"

"Because you're different."

"How so?"

"You have the most astonishing presence I've ever experienced. I felt you from three blocks away."

"You're very perceptive. You feel energy?"

"I guess so. The insubstantial... No, that's not the right word. The subtle, the inherent... Inner substance is more important to me than the surface of things. Did you perceive me coming?"

"Yes, but not from that far. I became aware of you before I saw you, but only a minute or two. It could be predestination. We were meant to meet and we could sense it. We have a connection that we could feel, something momentous."

"That could be part of it but it's not all."

"No, you're right. It's not. Perhaps we're ready to speak of what I've been alluding to."

"I certainly am."

"OK."

They were silent for a moment as he seemed to prepare. She saw him grow somewhat distant then return more fully than ever.

Then he spoke slowly and deliberately, "About a year ago, a young man studying to be in the Czech diplomatic corps went camping in the woods with his girlfriend. They ran into a few members of a seemingly totally benevolent, extra-terrestrial civilization."

She looked at him for a moment and then burst out laughing.

He laughed with her, unstintingly.

When their laughter subsided, she said, "We'll that's about the last thing I expected to hear you say."

"I know. How does one say such a thing besides simply to say it?"

"And you're serious?"

"Totally."

"Why Czechoslovakia? Why not Russia or the US or all of us simultaneously?"

"They say it needs to happen very quietly, organically, person by person at first. They say it'll be a while before it's time to go public."

"But why the Czech Republic? Are they anywhere else as well?"

"No, only there. And we don't know why. Perhaps because we try to bridge the east and the west and we're a small, quiet country. They've never told us why they chose us. Maybe because no one would think something life changing would happen there."

"That could describe a lot of places."

"True."

"You haven't asked?"

"I haven't. And if anyone else has no answer has come to me."

"Have you had direct contact?"

"Yes."

"Truly?"

"Yes."

"What do they look like?"

"Here they've taken human form but not quite human, more like humanoid robot."

"And there?"

"They're energy beings. They're made of light."

"Like angels?"

"I guess."

"Are they religious?"

"They're here to heal us."

"You're kidding."

"No."

"They healed you?"

"Quite definitely. That's part of what you feel in my presence."

"So you had help."

"Yes."

"Forgive me. This is all a bit hard to swallow."

"I know."

"But they haven't healed Alena."

"No."

"Why not?"

"She isn't ready. She hasn't agreed. She's attached to her beliefs. She hasn't developed the trust. She has fears, religious fears."

"Oh."

"Yes."

"You're totally serious."

"Yes."

"Rabbit hole indeed."

"Yes."

"Or else you're a total loon."

"Yes."

She looked at him appraisingly for several moments.

"You're not a loon."

"No."

"When do I get to meet them?"

"Whenever you like."

"Tonight?"

"It takes a day to arrange."

"That's all?"

"That's all."

"Obviously this isn't top secret."

"No, it's not. They do want it to grow quietly. But they put no restrictions on us. They trust in the divine orchestration of things."

"They *are* angels."

"Maybe, but they have advanced technology as well."

"And you think they can cure Brie?"

"I know they can. They've cured quite a number of people of all kinds of things, mental and physical. You come out quite whole and sound in body and mind. People with lost limbs or deformities come out perfect."

"And that's why your skin is so perfect?"

"Yes, it wasn't before. I had moles and spots like everyone else."

"Come out?"

"Of being in their chamber in their presence."

"That's it?"

"Yes, though the experience itself is stunning beyond comprehension. It takes around two hours. Just seeing them changes one. Just seeing someone they've healed changes one. You were changed by our first glance. You perceived that, yes?"

"Yes."

"But they need the chamber to heal everything."

Pause.

"So I'll start meeting more people with presence like yours?"

"Yes, but this is different. We're uniquely made for each other. We've fallen in love. I didn't fall in love with any of them. I couldn't. If Alena would allow herself to be healed, I wouldn't fall in love with her either. It's you I was meant to fall in love with."

"And you know the same will be true for me?"

"No. But I almost know. I can't know for sure but I'm certain. This is more than it could be with just about anyone else."

"That's what *I* thought."

"And I believe you will continue to do so."

"Jesus, a man I not only don't despise but am completely captivated by and ET angels who can cure and perfect everyone in the world. Quite a day."

"Yes, and a woman I'm in love with at first sight. And for the first time since I was her age. Quite I day."

"Do they talk about Jesus or the second coming or anything like that?"

"No, but some people do. And others talk of the ascension or other beliefs this seems to fulfill. Alena has mentioned Satan."

"And you?"

"I explained it to you as I accept it. Foreknowledge takes on the dress and character of many times, peoples and nations. But I know this is of God. In a way it's like the rapture only better. It's all inclusive. And we get to stay here."

Pause.

"Well put."

"Thank you. I've thought about it."

Again, they looked into each other's eyes as the food came and was placed before them. Eva was momentarily distracted by the beauty of the waitress. Then they talked and ate.

"So you're sure they can heal Brie."

"Yes."

"And I can tell Rosalyn about this?"

"Yes."

"And anyone else I want?"

"Yes."

"How simple and obvious!"

"Yes," he smiled, definitely loving her.

"About how many people in New York have gone into the chamber?"

"Several hundred."

"Several hundred in a year, that's all?"

"Yes."

"All told by you or someone you've told?"

"Pretty much. They did direct me to several individuals working in the diplomatic corps, mostly from African and Near Eastern countries and one from Tonga."

"High level?"

"Mostly no."

"Are they monitoring us?"

"No, I don't think so, at least not individually. They just seem to want to get things going in certain places. Then they somehow find someone they deem appropriate."

"And in your country?"

"Several thousand."

"And around the world?"

"About six thousand so far."

"I would have thought it would spread like wildfire. At this rate it'll take forever!"

"No. At some critical point when there's a solid foundation, they'll speed things up. They can create chambers for millions of people at a time. Right now they're using one small chamber in rural Bohemia. It can hold about ten people. Usually they only do one person. They have to build up slowly. The human race is still too unstable. If it came out now in too big a way, people would go crazy. Slowly and gently for now. Then more rapidly."

"Have they told anyone where they're from?"

"They have some kind of world in the Alcyone cluster. It's part of the Pleiades in the Taurus constellation."

"I want to go tomorrow."

He laughed. "That's why I love you. Alena has known for a year. She's still not ready. Perhaps you'll tip the scales for her. It took me several days to adjust to the idea, to summon up the courage, to be ready to relinquish my smallness."

"I've despised smallness all my life, my own and other's. And Rosalyn and Brie are kicking me in the ass. I love aesthetics and perfection. I'd do it just to get rid of my moles. I'm ready. So tomorrow?"

"I can see you are. But it can't be tomorrow. You'll have to wait till the next day. I can email a colleague tonight but it's around midnight there now. He'll get it in the morning and arrange it for Thursday."

"What about emergencies?"

"They don't believe in emergencies."

"But it could be life or death."

"Divine orchestration. If they're meant to go in the chamber, they'll survive and go. If not, they'll die and not go."

"They talk of divine orchestration?"

"They remind us of it all the time."

"Good. I like that. So they don't resurrect the dead."

"No. Not yet, though they probably could."

"They couldn't do it more instantly?"

"Probably, but they've chosen this way. Perhaps they want to give people time to prepare or change their minds. They take things slowly. They're in no hurry. The royal pace of the elephant."

"They use that phrase?"

"No, I do."

"So you've talked with them."

"Yes, but very little."

"I'm getting a little giddy."

"I know, it's giddifying. Would you like dessert?"

"I don't think so. I don't want a sugar rush on top of this. Thank you so much. This was delicious. But the conversation has been something else."

"Coffee, tea, anything?"

"Maybe just some after dinner juice or dessert wine so we can linger here. Will you have something?"

"We could share a dessert wine but juice sounds better to me. I don't drink much since my healing."

He motioned the waitress over.

Each time Eva looked at her she was more smitten.

"What's going on with me?" she thought to herself.

"Do you have tropical juices?"

"Yes. We have guava juice, passion fruit juice and mango purée."

Eva was enjoying their engagement.

"Can I have an equal mixture of all three?"

"I'm sure they can do that."

"Beautiful, that's what I'll have. No ice."

"And you?" the waitress asked looking to Gabriel.

"I'll have the same."

It soon came and they sat sipping as they continued.

"This is delicious, too. So one small chamber in the woods of your country. How do I get there?"

"They can create a portal anywhere to anywhere. You walk through a doorway filled with light and you're there."

"Handy. I always wanted to teleport. So I don't need my passport."

"No."

"Will this portal be where you work or will they just create one at your place or mine?"

"They like using a prearranged place. It's the door to the utility room in the basement of our building."

"So I'm to come there the day after tomorrow."

"Yes."

"What time?"

"I don't know yet. I'll let you know tomorrow. Early morning most likely."

"And you won't chop me into pieces when you have me in your power in the basement of your building in Czech territory?"

"No. What a terrible waste that would be."

"And you're not really one of them, you of the impossibly perfect skin?"

"No, I'm not."

They sat and sipped, beaming at one another.

When they were done, he paid.

"Will you come with me to my place?"

"You betcha."

"Lovely, thank you, shall we?"

"Yes, let's."

They walked out and stood on the sidewalk.

"It's about eight blocks from here. Would you prefer to walk or take a cab?"

"Let's walk. It's lovely out."

He took her arm, turned them right and walked her to 72nd Street. Then right and west down the long, inter-avenue blocks towards Central Park.

They were content to walk New York's upper east side in silence with new, wonder, love-filled eyes. They easily found a pace that suited them both.

"How nice," she thought. "I wonder if he's right on Fifth."

And, indeed, he was. He turned her left when they got there and into a lovely, modern, doorman building just north of 71st. 900 Fifth Avenue. The doorman greeted him by first name and he responded in kind.

"That's casual," Eva remarked as they got in the elevator.

"Yes, like I like it. It took me a long time to get him to do that."

"I'm sure. It's unusual for buildings like this. The Czech Republic must pay their Consuls quite well."

"Nowhere near this well. I get an opulent ET stipend."

"You're kidding!"

"No. They bought me this condo. They want those helping them to live well. They simply augment my bank account when there's something to be done or gotten or when I need it."

"Gee, they heal you and make you rich."

"Only those who work with them."

"How long have you been with the consulate here?"

"Five years."

"So you moved here a year ago?"

"Yes."

"It's nice to come up in the world."

"Yes, indeed."

"Especially for such a good cause."

"The best there is or ever has been."

"God, if only all this is true!"

"In two days you'll know it is."

"Well if it's not, it's the best come on I've ever heard."

"And if it is the world will soon be a completely different place."

"I guess so."

Chapter 4

They Slept Like Babies

They left the elevator on the eighteenth floor, one below the highest.

The door lock was a keypad combination.

"Three, seven, four, seven, three," he said slowly, as he visibly punched in the numbers. "I love palindromes."

"Oh, me too!"

"In this one, three and four make seven and it starts with the lowest, goes to the highest and the middle is in the middle. Please memorize it and feel totally free to come and go at will. You can pop in any time announced or unannounced, day or night, me here or not. Mi casa es tu casa, quite literally I hope."

"Why thank you. It'll be nice to have such an elegant second home."

"From my side you have it."

It was grand and spacious with a huge bay window overlooking the park. A long set of armless couches were lined up beneath it. She walked up to them and gazed out the window.

"Make yourself at home. I'll boot up and email Cyril."

"Your colleague in Czechoslovakia?"

"Yes, the young man I told you about. The first to be healed. He became their coordinator for the world."

"They didn't heal his girlfriend?"

"Sorry, yes they did. One of the first two to be healed."

He pecked her on the cheek and left her to gaze.

She was still gazing when he returned.

"What did you say?"

"One for tomorrow."

"That's it?"

"Yes."

"Have you sent any homeless?"

"Yes, three."

"Only three in a year."

"Yes. They do want us to go slowly. Some people we're inspired to approach. Most we're not. Ultimately, this is a rescue mission. But we're not in the rescue stage. We carefully choose a few here and there for now. You'll be surprised at how few you tell. When they kick into high gear, they'll probably just take over. It's like they're carefully building a bridge between us and them."

"I guess I can see that. Most people would just laugh in your face. I laughed in your face, but not 'just.' We had something going that made me take you seriously. But, God Gabriel, you have it made. You could have a different woman up here every night."

"Perhaps, but like I said, no interest. Along with healing you get a certain kind of maturity. The things that drove you don't drive you anymore or not as insistently. Long before the healing I had come to the point where nothing would do but the real thing. I had that with Lada. I've been content to hold out for it. The few affairs I had didn't fulfill me. I have my prosaic work. I have my higher calling. I have my private life. That's more than sufficient."

"Until now."

"Until now. This is the real thing."

"How can we know? Is this false confidence? Will it lead to a fall?"

"I don't think it will, darling. I believe we can know. One just knows such things."

She turned towards him and looked him in the eye.

"Very well, I'm yours, at least for tonight. One step at a time. Please don't get me pregnant. I'm probably ovulating."

"Let's take our chances. I refuse to use a rubber with you. I don't even have one. If you get pregnant and don't want it they'll dissolve it for you."

"That's astonishing!"

"They're astonishing. It's all astonishing."

"They'll put me in the chamber to abort a fetus?"

"They wouldn't call it that, but no. They don't need the chamber for that. They've dissolved five pregnancies that I know of. They believe in the sacredness of life. They don't think a child should come in unless it's totally wanted. They're pro-choice. And it's very gentle on the woman. There's no trauma, though she may grieve it."

"Wow, the Christians wouldn't like that."

"Not certain ones."

"God, am I gullible or trusting or in love or what? OK, you win. I want you to. I want the same thing. But I'm not quite ready. Please give me a tour. I feel slightly drunk."

"Me too, dear. Besides the outlandishness of talking about them, it's our proximity and the immanence of what's to come."

"Literally, I hope."

"I don't think that's false confidence."

He took her hand and led her through his apartment. The large living room with a variety of couches, easy chairs and ottomans, an ample dining area with a beautiful, unique, octagonal table, a spectacular, spacious kitchen with a marble top island cabinet and it's own breakfast table and chairs, three bedrooms, two bathrooms and an office.

It was all gorgeous. He'd gotten nice furniture but it was still a little sparse.

"You did a good job. I could flush it out a little."

"Please do when you're so inspired. Make it ours."

"A lot of space for one man."

"I put up diplomatic people sometimes. But they guided me here. They wanted me to have this place, though I don't know why. I haven't made much use of it."

"Well I'm awfully glad you have it."

The master bathroom was something else.

She shut him out and took a pee.

And then the master bedroom.

"Shall I light some candles?"

"Please."

"Would you like a robe?"

"No, I think I'll just get naked."

"Divine. You're OK my doing the same?"

"Quite."

He lit the candles and turned off the lights. They got undressed and hung their clothes in his huge, walk-in closet.

They stood and looked at each other for several moments.

His form was strong, shapely and fit. His perfect skin glowed preternaturally in the candlelight. He was beautiful. Her body began to respond.

"You work out."

"Yes. I like to keep fit. You're beauty is breaking my heart."

"Good. Let it break, let it break completely."

They stepped into each other's arms.

Their lovemaking was wondrous—long, conscious, tender and strong.

They both came rather spectacularly, first she, then he.

They slept like babies.

Chapter 5

Life Is Magical

His alarm went off at 6:30.

They groaned and grunted, untangled and re-embraced.

"Mmmm," she murmured, "have I died and gone to heaven?"

"No, you're still living. You've both walked into heaven and brought it with you. Forgive me, darling, I have to go to work."

"Really? You can't just call in sick?"

"Really, it's better that I don't. There truly are things I must take care of today. You?"

"I only scheduled things for this afternoon. I thought I might be a basket case after Ronald McDonald."

"Why don't you sleep in?"

"Perhaps I will or at least take a long bath."

"Shall I make you breakfast?"

"Oh yes, I'll get up and eat with you and then see what's what."

"Do you want the bathroom first or should I? You know there are two if you want your own."

"Do you think we've heard from Cyril?"

"Oh yes. I'll boot up. You use the bathroom."

She got up naked and didn't bother closing the door. He loved it.

He went to his office, turned on his computer, went to his closet, threw on his pajamas, grabbed his robe, went back to his office, got the info and went to the bathroom to find her using his toothbrush.

"Didn't think you'd mind," she slurred through the gloop in her mouth.

"Of course not. Everything I have is yours."

"That robe for me?"

"Yes, unless you want something more substantial."

"No, that's perfect. I can let it fall open and flash my breasts at you."

"Marvelous, please do."

"So what time?"

"Eight in the morning. It'll be two there."

"Great, in just over twenty-four hours."

"Yes."

"And it really is everything you say it is?"

"Yes."

"Can I sleep here tonight?"

"Of course, I'd love it," he beamed. "Can I piss or should I go elsewhere?"

"Please, feel free. I'd love to see you piss."

He did. She watched him languidly while she finished brushing her teeth. The first stream came out to the side nearly missing the bowl. Then it became straight and strong. She was mildly surprised by how much she loved his genitals.

"That can happen. Dried semen and prostatic fluid."

"I see. The mysteries of the post-coital male. Quite endearing. I like you vulnerable, dear."

He flushed the toilet.

"I'll make us breakfast and do everything later."

"I'll finish up here and come help you."

"Great."

They cooked and ate. He showered, shaved and dressed. He got her cell number and called it so his would be in her phone. Then he left.

She took her long, hot bath and dressed. Then she stood staring at the park quite some time thinking of everything that had been said, had happened and might still be to come.

"How could it be?"

"How could it not be?"

Then she went home.

Their day flew by.

Gabriel called her and they arranged another dinner out, vegan this time. They would meet at his place first.

She packed a little bag, hailed a cab and was there by five-thirty, before him.

The doorman took one look at her and asked, "Are you Ms. Dunn?"

"Yes I am. Jack, wasn't it?"

"Yes, pleased to meet you. Mr. Jelinek called to let me know you'd be coming. Please go right in."

"Thank you. I hope we'll be on a first name basis, too."

"Whenever you're ready, ma'am."

"How about now?"

"Thank you, Eva. Please let me know if there's anything I can do for you. I'm a bit of a concierge, too."

"Thank you, Jack, you're a gem."

He'd even gotten 'Eva' right.

Gabriel was a gem, too.

He soon arrived and changed into more casual clothing.

They held each other in a long embrace and went down and waited while Jack hailed a cab.

He took her to Candle 79.

It was fabulous.

They didn't talk a lot. Mostly chit chat. The impending event made them both somewhat introspective.

They did have dessert.

"So tomorrow I'm transformed."

"Yes. You only become your very best self. All the little and big things that used to pester and diminish you are gone. You'll love it."

"How could it be so good?"

"How could it not?"

"I thought these identical words this morning before leaving your place."

"Life is magical. We've just never been able to truly live it."

They took a cab home.

They made wonderful love.

They slept like babies.

The alarm awakened them at 6:30.

They showered and ate together.

They were in Czech territory by 7:45.

They went to his office and sat.

No one else had arrived yet.

"Will you come with me?"

"Just to introduce you. Then I'll come back. Once you're in the chamber there's nothing for me to do there."

"I feel quite odd."

"Yes, it's definitely surreal. One hasn't much by way of experience to compare it to."

"I didn't feel frightened till now. I was mostly curious and excited."

"One can't help but be afraid. It's the unknown. Is there anything I can do?"

"Let's stand, please hold me."

He held her for a few minutes. Then she disengaged and sat down.

"Actually, let's go downstairs."

Alena was arriving as they left his office.

She gave Eva a startled look.

"You're going already?"

"Yes, a friend's child is dying. But I want to."

"I'll pray for you."

"Thank you."

They took the elevator to the basement.

Chapter 6

There Is No Separation

They stepped out into a hallway and Gabriel guided her to the right. It was a typical, old, New York building basement, power rooms, storage rooms, quite unglamorous.

Around the corner was the open door to the utility room.

There was nothing else back there but a black man in his sixties, just slightly grizzled, standing next to it. He wore a janitor's uniform.

He had serene, beautiful eyes and a mighty presence.

And his skin was perfect.

She looked more closely.

"He makes himself smaller with a slouch and a two day growth," she thought to herself.

"Jimmy, this is Eva, Eva, Jimmy, our maintenance man."

"Hi Jimmy, I see you've been through that door."

"Yes, ma'am, quite early on. They needed a gate keeper and there I was."

"How lucky for you."

"Yes indeed, ma'am. The greatest luck there is. Forgive me, but you certainly are a great beauty."

"Why thank you, Jimmy, I hope soon to be much more."

"You already are but that will happen too."

"Thank you for the reassurance."

"My pleasure, ma'am. It's a mighty day."

"Yes it is."

They still had a few moments.

She looked to Gabriel.

"Tell me where I'm going."

"The Bohemian Forest."

"How appropriate."

"Yes. It has one of the oldest mountain ranges in Europe and overlaps the German border. It's near the confluence of three rivers, the Vydra, the Kremelyna and the Otava."

"So I'll be in the wilds."

"Yes."

There was a flutter in the doorframe and the space filled with a shimmering light. Nothing could be seen through it. It gave no information but was somehow inviting.

"Shall we?" Gabriel asked, extending his arm doorward.

She looked at him and he gave a reassuring nod.

She turned and walked through the light.

And there she was in a beautiful, old forest in the warm afternoon light of an early summer day.

She laughed in delight.

Gabriel came through behind her.

She looked at him with a twinkle in her eye.

"Well, so far you haven't been lying."

"How could I?"

He nodded to the right.

Two beings walked towards them.

They appeared human.

They appeared not.

They had both an odd, mechanical aspect to them and an angelic one.

Their presence was staggering, far beyond Gabriel's and Jimmy's. But it was also uplifting, divine, loving. You loved them and they loved you.

You would say they were both men but also androgynous.

"May I ask you questions?" Eva blurted out.

"Yes," one of them answered in a melodious, half feminine, half masculine voice.

"Can you look more human than this?"

"Yes, we can blend in when necessary."

"Can you give me answers directly to my mind? Are we limited to speaking?"

She immediately knew the answer and more.

She could feel them as one in her awareness waiting to answer any question she might ask.

She stood entranced.

She thought the question, "Why here, why the Czech Republic?"

She received an onslaught of knowledge and images so rich in content it was almost overwhelming. But she loved it. She craved it. She devoured it.

As the data poured in, her questions arose.

All were answered as if a living story were being delivered directly to her mind and senses.

Loosely translated it amounted to this.

We don't consider nations.

We like this forest, these mountains.

We especially like the songs these rivers sing.

We were drawn here.

We didn't sample other places.
Our home is a star.
No water, air or earth.
Only plasma.
But there are rivers in the plasma. And they sing.
All the plasma sings but the rivers have their own special songs.
We are plasma beings, energy beings living in the plasma, in plasma villages, in plasma cities, in solitary plasma places.
The songs of these rivers remind us of the songs of our rivers.
And rivers of energy flow through this spot. They are part of our work. When there is no human to heal, we sing to them, we heal them.
There is only one being in your star. Almost all stars are the stellar bodies of a single light being. Few stars are the home of light civilizations.
We don't consider religions or history or who may have lived more God or less. Only God now and the work of bringing everything back to God. God is what we all are, what everything is when relieved of everything that is not God. We help dissolve not God.
Almost no one asks us like you. They are all concerned with what will happen, their fear and uncertainty, our strangeness.
Only three of the eight thousand, four hundred and fifty-nine invited us into their minds. It must happen before. After, there is too much wonder to question. And we send them back at the time of completion. Few are as ready as you.
We are not concerned with time. Only what we need to intersect with your world, to keep these appointments.
We are not concerned with the future. It is unknown.
We do not know when acceleration will be.
When readiness arrives.
We do not guess God's plan. We do God's work.
We are moved by God from within.
We are God moving from within.
There is no separation.
There is no difference.
Only in what we can know.
Come to the door when you wish.
Find Jimmy.
The door will lead you to one of us.
This is only for the three who have asked.
This is for you when you are ready.
There is no holding back.
We give everything you can receive.
Readiness is here.

Chapter 7
When Readiness Arrives

All this and more came to her.

She had no idea how long it had taken.

She looked around.

Gabriel was gone.

They led her to a very large tree.

It had a big, cave-like hole at its base.

It fluttered and steps led down to a dimly lit chamber.

That was definitely the best word for it.

As Gabriel had said, it was large enough for about ten people.

It was not quite square and not quite rectangular with no sharp corners, edges or angles. The walls, ceiling and floor seemed half metal, half light. They were a uniform but shifting golden color shot with highlights of red, light yellow and white. And there were momentary hints of all the other colors and every gradation between. They gave the chamber its light. There was nothing inside that she could perceive. It was definitely otherworldly.

She was drawn to stand in the middle.

The two robot bodies disappeared. Two amorphous forms of light were in the chamber with her.

Then it began.

She felt a ripple run through her.

Then she felt as if every cell of her body, every molecule, every atom, every subatomic particle and quark were on fire, only the fire was somehow cool and pristine, celestial and divine. It was a different continuum than hot/cold, but she couldn't say what the continuum was.

But it was vital.

So very charged and vital.

She was filled with divine energy light. And it was bathing every part and particle of her existence.

So many things were going through her mind.

So many images flying through her inner vision.

Children, peoples, animals, mountains, histories, migrations, worlds, lives and beings.

It was as if a trillion movies or lifetimes were unfolding every second and the weight of all the universes was slowing being lifted from her body.

Waves of energy, waves of light, waves of vitality cascaded through her non-stop for eternities.

She was aware of multiple levels, each one with a world of activity.

Vast, eternal stillness; cosmic, celestial universes; embryonic, childhood unfoldments; all the evolutionary strands of this and other worlds.

She was living an infinity of different everythings, on, on and on, as every wave and fiber of her body and being were undergoing different levels of electrification, inspiration, purification, eradication.

She was being stripped of everything and being given everything in infinitude every nanosecond.

She felt like God. She felt like nothing. She felt like a zygote in a womb. She felt like a flaming star, the wing of a butterfly, everything and anything she could and couldn't conceive.

She became aware of her breath. She was breathing in all the stars of the galaxy and they were cool and pristine.

She couldn't weep or speak or move, nor did she need to.

She was undergoing an infinite number of living universes exploding into being, contracting into nothingness and exploding again in no time flat.

At one point it felt like all the prisons in the universe had unified to become one impossible infinite wall that could never be broken.

Then it shattered and disappeared.

It all went on for an eternity of eternities.

Then it was over and she was standing outside the utility door blinking at Gabriel and Jimmy.

She couldn't speak.

No word would do.

No word would come.

She stepped into Gabriel's arms and grasped him tightly for many moments.

Finally she disengaged and looked at Gabriel, then Jimmy, then back to Gabriel.

She didn't know what to do next.

"It's alright. There are no words. I've arranged an early lunch. You'll soon start noticing your hunger. May I lead you for the moment?"

She nodded. She felt pre-verbal, like an infant. Only she could stand and walk.

He took her hand and led her to the elevator.

She tried to wave goodbye to Jimmy.

She couldn't.

The elevator came and they were lifted to the ground floor.

He walked her outside.

She gasped.

The stark beauty of the air and sunlight were almost painful.

He led her west to the corner and left on Second.

She looked around in wonder.

Everything seemed brilliant and new.

"Speech will return very soon," he said, "then hunger."

She was starting to feel the hunger already.

"Walking helps."

She did feel like she was getting her bearings again.

They crossed Seventy-Second and he led her into the Trend Diner at the end of the block.

She felt a rush of excitement as she was beginning to feel famished.

"First supper," she managed.

"Yes," he said. "Everything is brand new."

He secured them a booth away from the few parties. It was ten-thirteen, right between breakfast and lunch.

"Tell me when you're ready to talk."

"I think I am. I just don't know what to say."

"I totally understand. I just have questions. But they can wait till you're ready."

"I think I'm ready."

"What happened back there? I mean before the chamber. It's like you went into a trance. I couldn't believe your questions. They were so obvious and brilliant. I didn't have the wherewithal to really ask them anything when I went. My mind was racing about what would come next and what it would be like and how strange yet familiar it was. It seemed obvious to me that they answered your second one by speaking directly to your mind. Then you became immobile and they sent me back."

"Oh yes, that. So much happened in the chamber I almost forgot about that. It was amazing. It was far more than them speaking in my mind. They downloaded a world of information, images and experiences. They kept answering every question I had as it came up, not in words but in direct experience. They said there were only three of us out of 8,459 who were ready to ask and invite them into our minds. They said I could go back and receive more anytime I wanted."

He looked at her, dumbstruck.

"What a miracle you are!"

"What a miracle all this is! What a miracle that I had to leave Ronald McDonald so that I could meet you! What a miracle divine orchestration can be when it really kicks in! God, Gabriel. God, God, God. God is really back! I can't believe it and I've just gone through it! I feel like I want to shout it from the rooftops!"

"There you're not alone. We all feel that at first. But if we try, we can't. You'll soon find your stride with that. But being one of only three to have the presence of mind to tap into them in the face of it all... I salute you, dear Eva. You're even more than I've begun to comprehend. Can you tell me what you learned?"

"Oh yes, but there's so much. I couldn't possibly communicate it all. I'll do the best I can. Actually, I can probably give you the main points. I just can't begin to describe the direct experience of it."

"Whatever you can, darling. It'll all be perfect."

The waiter came with menus.

They looked at them and Eva laughed. The list was quite extensive.

"OK," Eva said, "let me do this first. I'm famished."

They ordered and Gabriel looked at her expectantly.

"They're plasma beings. They live in a star. The star has rivers, cities, villages and wilds of plasma. They don't give a hoot about nations or boundaries. They don't give a hoot about religions or history or what figure might have said what God-filled or not so God-filled thing. They don't give a hoot about when they'll accelerate. Actually, that's not right. They don't give a hoot about knowing the future. That's more like it. They say, 'When readiness arrives.' All they care about is doing God's work and that comes to them from within. They leave it all to God's will and timing. They don't second-guess. They were drawn to the old Bohemian forests and mountains and, especially, the songs the rivers sing. It reminds them of the songs of their plasma rivers.

But there's more than that. There are rivers of energy flowing through the earth, along its surface and around it. That place is a node, a power spot. When they're not healing people, they're healing those rivers of energy."

He laughed and smiled and loved her.

She went on to tell him everything she could of what she had learned.

"I can't wait to go back. Only three of us get to. They say to find Jimmy whenever I want. But I really can't wait to speak with Rosalyn."

"She may not go immediately."

"Oh, with Brie at her back, it won't take her long."

"Probably not."

"Does Jimmy have a cell phone?"

"Yes."

"Could you use mine to call him?"

"Of course."

She pulled it from her purse and Gabriel dialed the number.

She took the phone back and put it to her ear.

"Hello?"

"Hello, Jimmy?"

"Yes."

"This is Eva, I just went through."

"Yes, I know."

"Jimmy, they told me I could come through anytime, that I should just come and find you."

"Yes, they gave me that knowledge. I'm here Monday through Friday, eight to five."

"Great, I mostly wanted Gabriel to punch your number into my phone. Thank you. You'll probably see me soon."

"My pleasure, I'll be here."

She hung up and saved his number under 'Jimmy.'

Then she beamed at Gabriel as the food came.

They ate, they talked, they laughed, they loved.

Eva's first mouthful was a miracle of tastes, sensations and smells. The mélange in her mouth as it transformed with each bite and mixed with her mouth water gave her more gustatory pleasure than she'd ever experienced. She had to alternate speaking with silent eating. She was thanking God with each subsequent explosion of delight.

Finally, her divine meal came to its last mouthful.

When her savoring seemed complete, Gabriel asked her about the evening and spending the night.

"Let's give us a breather," she answered. "I want to get with Rosalyn. If I change my mind I'll call you. Otherwise I'll call you tomorrow."

"OK, now don't forget me."

"Ha," she replied, "not likely. I love you, Gabriel Jelinek. You're mine."

"Yes I am. And my home is yours as well. Please come back soon."

"I will. Don't worry, dear. Very soon. Why don't you go back to work? I want to call Roz. Let me get this meal. It's cheap and you've been getting everything."

"OK, but remember my stipend. It covers everything I need."

"I know. I'll let you wine me and dine me to your heart's content, though probably not much wine."

He leaned forward and kissed her lips, then arose and was gone.

"How wonderful," she thought, "a man who can just leave."

She was in heaven.

She marveled at how she felt, empty and full, light and thrilled all at the same time. She really did feel like all her baggage was gone. Her body felt like divine air, healthier than a human body could feel.

"So this is life."

She pulled out her compact and checked her face. Her mole and dark spots were gone. And so were the holes in her earlobes. She knew they wouldn't return.

She rang Roz.

Roz answered, "Hi darling."

"Hi, sweetheart, are you at RM?"

"Yes."

"I need to speak with you. Can I come by?"

"Sure."

"I'm nearby. I'll see you in a few."

"Great, love you."

"Love you too."

Chapter 8

Maybe You're the Accelerator

Eva walked the sidewalk elated. Everything was gorgeous. Everyone was beautiful.

She could see the grunge, the tiredness, the weight on the people. She could see their ugliness. But she could see their inner beauty like never before.

She looked at them as they walked by and some looked back.

Uncharacteristically, she looked them right in the eye. She could feel the change in the ones who reciprocated.

They walked by lighter and freer than they'd been before.

She entered the cancer home and went straight to Brie's room.

Brie and Roz were there.

Neither looked well.

Roz looked a little older and care worn.

She looked up and into Eva's eyes.

Her eyebrows raised and the shift occurred deep within her.

"Holy shit, Eva, that man has lit you up like a Christmas tree."

"It's not only him. We need to talk."

"Brie dear, I won't be long."

They made their way back to the small sitting area.

It was empty.

"Fasten your seat belt, Roz."

"OK."

"There's something happening in the world that's beyond comprehension."

"OK," a little more slowly and hesitantly.

"Take a deep breath."

"OK," and she did.

"I've just been completely healed by super advanced, divine ETs. All my baggage is gone. They can heal Brie. I guarantee it."

Roz just looked at her.

"I'm trying to compute what you said."

"Do you want me to repeat it?"

"No. Brie is worse."

"I know. They can heal her."

"Did he slip you acid? Are you off your rocker?"

"No, I can prove it or begin to prove it."

Moments ticked by as they simply looked at each other.

"Well you look sane and better than I've ever seen you. And you always did look rather spectacular. But there is something more about you. You look divine."

"Yes, that's part of it. Something happened deep inside when you looked in my eyes. Did you feel it?"

"Yes, now that you mention it. Something did shift, get lighter, even though Brie's decline is decimating me."

"That's a tiny part of all this. Eventually, they'll heal us all."

"Isn't there something about too good to be true?"

"That was before. They've changed all that. God has changed all that."

"Uh oh."

"I know. But believe me, I haven't gotten religion. Look at my skin. Notice anything?"

'The mole is gone. And not only that. It's utterly perfect!"

"They heal everything, Roz. Look at my earlobes. They were pierced."

Roz looked for a moment and digested this.

"Well, I would lie down in front of a bus if it would save Brie."

"I know."

"And you seem cogent."

"I am, more cogent than I've ever been."

"Your earlobes and skin are pretty impressive. Is that your proof?"

"Come with me to the Czech building. We'll go to the basement and meet an angelic, black caretaker. He'll open the door to the utility room. The doorway will flutter and fill with opaque light. I'll walk through the light and disappear. I won't be in the utility room or anywhere you can see. I'll be in the Bohemian Forest or God knows where. I'll be gone for a little while then I'll reappear before your eyes in front of the door."

"Well that would change my belief system, though it almost sounds like a parlor trick."

"That's the best I can do. You have to experience it for yourself. They'll heal you and Brie at the same time. The doctors won't save Brie, Roz. She'll die. This will completely heal her of everything including all that shit they've been pumping into her. You and her together."

"If I begin to take this seriously it raises a million questions."

"I'll give you all my time. I'll tell you everything I can. But the earliest it can be done is one or two days after you decide to do it. They have this healing chamber in the Bohemian Forest. When you decide, we tell Gabriel and he emails his colleague in the Czech Republic. Depending on the time there, it's set up for the following day or the day after."

"I'll grasp at any straw, even one as implausible as this. And since it's you, and your skin and your mole and your earlobes... Let's tell Brie we're leaving and see your disappearing act."

They went back to Brie's room.

"Honey, I have to go with Eva for a little bit. It's important. I'll be back very soon."

"OK," Brie replied with lackluster nausea.

"Brie, I love you," Eva said strongly.

Brie looked up and into her eyes. Both Roz and Eva could see something shift. Brie looked a little more alive.

"Thank you, Eva, that was impressive, too," Roz said, as they made their way out of the building, "maybe more impressive than disappearing."

"You're welcome. I'm doing that for everyone I can."

She dug her phone out of her purse and rang Jimmy.

"Hi Eva," Jimmy chirped.

"Hi Jimmy, I'll be there in a minute or two."

"I'm here, goddess."

Eva laughed.

"You're a treasure, Jimmy."

She disconnected.

Roz watched as Eva looked at each person and saw how some looked away and some were transformed.

They walked into the building and got in the elevator.

Eva punched the button and they were there.

Jimmy was opening the door when they walked around the corner.

He looked up and smiled.

"Jimmy this is Roz, Roz, Jimmy."

"I'm pleased to meet you. She won't go through."

"Of course not. I just want her to see."

"Very well. You're the boss."

"Jimmy, you know better."

"I know a Cleopatra when I see one."

Eva laughed again.

There was a flutter in the doorway.

The light appeared.

Roz looked from it to Eva, eyebrows raised again.

Eva walked through the door and disappeared.

The light disappeared.

Roz could see the whole utility room.

No one was there.

Eva was gone.

"Well that's something you don't see every day."

"I've been seeing a mighty lot of it."

"I guess you have. You've gone through?"

"Yes, ma'am."

"You've been healed?"

"Yes ma'am, of everything that could ail the mind, body, heart and soul, wounding, scars and all."

"Truly?"

"Yes, ma'am."

"My daughter has cancer."

"I'm sorry to hear that, ma'am, but not so sorry as I would have been in the past. They can heal her."

"You're certain?"

"Yes ma'am, they grow back lost limbs or parts that didn't form right at birth. Fat and skinny people come out just right."

"No."

"Yes."

She looked into his eyes. They seemed infinite pools of wisdom. There was not one iota of dodginess in him. Roz prided herself on being a shrewd judge of character. This man had character that few souls on earth did. She was becoming convinced.

"OK," she sighed. "How long will she be gone?"

"You got me. She's one of a kind."

"How so?"

"She's the only one to go through twice. And the very same day. This is new to me."

"Really?"

"Yes, ma'am."

"Are there any chairs down here?"

"There are two in my rest area."

"Do you mind bringing me one?"

"Not at all."

At that moment Eva reappeared in front of the door, no light, no flutter, just her.

Roz gasped.

"How long was I gone?"

"Just a few minutes."

"Wow, it felt like a few days. How'd you like the parlor trick?"

"I liked it just fine. And this fine gentleman mightily reinforced it."

"Oh, thank you Jimmy, truly. Has Gabriel ever taken you out for a meal?"

"No, ma'am."

"Well what's wrong with him?"

"Why nothing, ma'am."

"Yes I know, but still. I think he and I will be taking you to dinner very soon. I imagine you have a question or two."

"I'll say I do."

"Excellent. I look forward to answering them. Let's go, Roz. I want to work on you."

They were soon back in Brie's room.

Her appearance startled them.

"Hi honey, is there anything you need?"

"No, mommy."

She looked like a different girl, astonishingly better. She was sitting up quite bright-eyed.

Eva knew something had happened. This was far more than she could do with a glance.

"Roz, I think we can speak freely in front of Brie."

Roz looked at Eva and then Brie.

"You can," Brie said. "The angels came and told me they would heal me. I feel so much better."

Roz looked at Eva. Eva smiled.

Roz turned to Brie.

"Did you see them, honey?"

"Kind of. But just as some kind of light. There were two of them and I heard them as clearly in my mind as I hear you. They said, 'we love you. We'll heal you very soon.'"

"Well who am I to argue with God and the angels? Call Gabriel, Eva. I'm ready to lie down in front of that bus."

Eva pulled out her phone.

"Two for tomorrow, Gabe, if at all possible. Otherwise two for the next day."

"Right on, superwoman, does this change your evening plans?"

"Yes, email Cyril but stay on the line. I'll be right back. Brie, do you think you can come out to dinner with us?"

"Yes, I'd love to get out of here. I'm feeling good for the first time in forever. I don't know how much I'll be able to eat but who cares?"

"Roz?"

"If she's game, I am."

"Great, Gabe?"

"It seems like this was already in the works. They're on for nine AM tomorrow."

"Fabulous. Call Jimmy and invite him to dinner. Then make reservations at Candle 79 for five of us."

"Yes, ma'am."

"I love you, Gabriel."

"I love you, superstar. Maybe you're the accelerator."

"Maybe I am. We'll be there at five-thirty."

"Great."

Chapter 9

Is This Stuff Really Real?

Eva looked at her watch.

It was a little after one.

"Brie honey, your mother and I are going out to lunch. You look wonderful but see if you can sleep. You haven't gone out for a while. If not get up and play with the kids or do whatever you want. We won't be too too long. Roz, you OK with that?"

"Yes, I could use some better food than they have here. Brie, do you want anything?"

"No mommy, I'm good. Take your time. I may sleep a little."

"Have you been to Up Thai?"

"No, I don't go anywhere."

"Good, let's go there."

They walked the sidewalk hand in hand.

Eva blessed whomever she could.

When they got there, Eva saw the same beautiful waitress as before. There was something about her that made Eva's heart and loins melt.

"What's your name, sweetie?"

"Anani," she answered, looking down.

"Anani, please look into my eyes."

At first she hesitated, then she did.

And the shift occurred.

Eva could tell she perceived it and was surprised.

"Anani, my name is Eva Dunn and this is my friend, Rosalyn. Are you Thai?"

"No, I'm Laotian."

"Lovely. I think you just noticed what happened when our eyes met, yes?"

"Yes," she said, no longer hesitant and gazing directly.

"What happened was good and permanent. And it's possible that much more good could happen. I want to talk with you."

"Oh good, I want that, too."

"Perfect. Do you remember the drink my friend and I ordered the other night?"

"Yes, it was brilliant. You were the first to do that. A few of us here have been drinking it since."

"Beautiful, that's all I'm going to have. But my friend will be ready to order very soon. Please put that order in and come back in a minute or two."

"You're not wasting any time, are you?" Roz asked when Anani had gone.

"She's special. Tell me how you're doing."

"I'm a bit dizzy."

"I know dear, I was, too."

"Is it really true?"

"Yes."

"I can't believe it. I've been so desolate and helpless just sitting there day after day and watching her *die*!" Roz burst into tears.

Eva reached out and took her hand across the table.

Roz quietly sobbed. Then her tears and shudders subsided. She dug a hanky out of her bag and dried her eyes.

"Sorry sweetie, all this has been a bit much on me."

"I know, love. You've been through so much and this on top of it. You needed a little cry."

Roz ordered. They ate. They spoke. Eva answered her questions.

When it was time to pay, Eva gave Anani her business card.

She looked into Anani's big, beautiful eyes.

"Call me, darling, we have so many wonderful things to talk about."

"Oh I will, I will."

"Good girl."

They returned to Brie.

She was asleep.

Eva decided to go to Gabriel's, take a shower and luxuriate.

She motioned Roz out of the room and told her how to bring Brie to the consulate by five-thirty.

Then she took a cab to Gabe's and thoroughly enjoyed herself.

She had postponed her bookings till next week.

Work was the last thing she was concerned with now.

Five-thirty saw Eva, Brie, Roz and Jimmy gather in the common area outside Gabe's office.

Jimmy had shaved.

He looked magnificent, like some wise, ancient, Nubian king.

But his demeanor still belied that.

Alena was there and she and Jimmy had greeted each other.

Eva introduced Roz and Brie.

Alena then looked back at Eva.

"You look wonderful."

"Thank you, Alena, I can't recommend it enough."

"I can't believe you did it so quickly."

"Yes, well, we all have our priorities. Roz and Brie will be going tomorrow."

Alena looked at them and back to Eva.

She paused for a moment.

"I was brought up to deeply mistrust anything spiritual that wasn't done in the name of Jesus."

"What about simply in God's will?"

Alena was silent for a moment.

"You believe they're doing God's will?"

"I know they are. They shared their world, experience and wisdom with me. There is nothing in them but God's will."

"Satan can deceive you."

"Look at me, look at Jimmy. Look at Gabriel. Is this Satan's work? May I tell you what I believe?"

"Yes."

"This may not help, but I believe they're cleansing us of all Satan and helping us truly become the little Jesuses we really are. This is love and life and divinity, Alena, it's not evil."

Gabriel had just joined them.

Alena looked from Eva's eyes, to Jimmy's and then to his.

Something finally softened within her.

"OK Gabe, email Cyril."

"Thank you, Alena," Eva said. "This truly is a gift of God."

The five of them took the elevator and piled into a cab.

They were soon at Candle 79 seated at their table.

Their waiter was singular. He was very short and very pretty—sensitive, androgynous and very aware. He had a mop of curly red hair, beautiful lips and both a twinkle in his eye and a sadness about him. He handed them menus and took their drink orders.

When the drinks arrived, Gabriel raised his glass.

"I'd like to propose a toast."

Everyone raised their juices and waters.

"To Eva Dunn, miraculous force of nature that she is, with whom I'm totally in love and without whom we wouldn't have gathered here this evening."

"Here, here, to Eva, we love you!"

Eva laughed and drank.

"Thank you, my divine lover and all of you. Let's also drink to the far more miraculous thing that's finally happening in our world now and the devas who are the instruments of bringing it about."

They all drank quietly.

"Jimmy," Eva continued, "I'd like to know more about you. What's your last name?"

"Handy."

"Oh really? Are you related?"

"He was my grandfather."

"Wait a minute," Roz cut in. "You're W.C. Handy's grandson?"

"Yes, ma'am."

"Then you're a celebrity."

"No, ma'am. My grandfather was a celebrity. I'm a janitor."

"Jimmy," Eva cut back in. "Do you have a bank account?"

"No, ma'am. I use a check cashing service and spend the cash."

Eva looked at Gabriel.

He looked thunderstruck.

"God, where have I been? Jimmy, I'm so sorry!"

Jimmy looked puzzled.

"Jimmy," Eva continued, "if you were to open a bank account and our friends were to put in a million dollars, could you put that money to good use?"

Jimmy paused for a moment.

"I believe I could."

"What would you do with it?"

"Well, I know a lot of folks in need, relatives, friends, just some folks in the neighborhood. I could use a nicer place to live. Maybe, somehow, it would help me grow bolder about letting folks know about the door."

"How many people have you told?"

"Fifteen."

"How many have gone through?"

"Fourteen. One died first."

"Jimmy, I want you to go and open a bank account tomorrow. Use TD Bank. They're Canadian and the best one in New York. Most of the others are all crooks."

"I know, ma'am. That's why I didn't want to use them."

"Well you need to now. And the TD people aren't crooks. Do you want me to help you with it?"

"No ma'am, I think I can manage."

She looked at Gabriel.

"Don't beat yourself up, darling. Divine orchestration. Divine timing. It wasn't meant to happen till now. This is a small part of what's happening. It's the beginning of the acceleration."

"Is that what you learned the second time?"

"Partially, we'll get to that."

"Who's W.C. Handy?"

Roz cut in again. "He was a landmark in American Music, a great blues man and scholar. He brought the blues into the mainstream."

Gabriel couldn't help but marvel at how he had made Jimmy like a piece of furniture because of his job and his color.

"Jimmy, I truly do owe you an apology. I'm deeply sorry for not being able to relate to you as a human being. Please forgive me."

"Why thank you, sir. I forgive you. It runs deep in our world. It's the way of things. You're not alone. It's you and a few billion others. And we play into it. Listen to me with all my sirs and ma'ams. You're helping to heal that right now."

Somehow, everyone could feel that. They felt the energy, the change, the depth of something happening, the tingling of their skin.

They became aware that the waiter had been standing there.

"Are you ready to order?"

"No, darlin'," Eva said. "We need a few more minutes."

He flushed and left them.

"Jimmy, what would you like to ask?"

"How come you get to go through when you want?"

"Only three of us asked them questions and invited them into our minds before the chamber. Everyone else was buzzing about the strangeness or thinking about themselves. They're ready to give information to whoever wants it but only if they're ready. I was ready. That was more important to me. The three of us can communicate with them whenever we want."

"You're one of *them*."

"Well, not quite. But in a way, yes."

"Thank you for getting Gabriel to invite me tonight and for making me a rich man."

Even now, Gabe recoiled a little at Jimmy's use of his first name while he had worked on Jack so long to get him to do that. Old habits run deep.

"You're welcome, Jimmy," Eva replied. "It's they who'll be changing those numbers and it's God who's doing it all. But we're a team. You're a very important member. Now let's get down to business and order our food."

The meal was a great celebration.

They talked and ate and laughed.

The waiter seemed to hover around their table a bit more than necessary.

They didn't bother about it, nor did they censor whatever it was they were saying.

At one point, Roz said, "If this works there are three RM women I'll want to tell."

"Of course," Eva responded, "you can tell anyone you want to."

"And I want to tell one of the other kids," Brie piped up. "He doesn't have any parents."

"No parents?" Roz asked.

"No, just an aunt. And she can't be there much."

"Yes, dear," Eva said, "you can tell anyone, too."

Somehow, the content of her second visit never came up.

After the meal, the waiter brought the bill.

He just stood there for a moment without relinquishing it.

"Can I ask you guys something?"

"Sure," Eva answered.

"I'm sorry, I couldn't help but hear some of your conversation. And, to be honest, I did as much eavesdropping as I could. Are you guys doing some kind of sci fi movie or is this stuff really real?"

"It's really real. Would you like to be healed of everything within you?"

"Yes, please, more than anything," he said, tears coming to his eyes.

He put the bill on the table and said more tearfully, "Please help me," and rushed away.

Eva looked at Gabriel.

"Of course."

He took out his phone to email Cyril.

When the waiter returned he had composed himself.

Gabriel had put his credit and business cards in the bill folder.

The waiter went toward him to take it.

Gabriel withheld it.

"What's your name, son?"

"André, sir, André Atkins."

"My business card is in here, André. Keep it and guard it with your life. Call me tomorrow and be ready to come to that address the following morning. I'll try to answer any questions when you call tomorrow."

He handed him the folder.

"Thank you, sir."

"You're very welcome, in every sense of the word."

André left the table.

Eva beamed at Gabriel.

Brie chirped, "Mommy, can we sleep at home tonight?"

"Of course, baby, let's do that."

They went their separate ways.

Eva and Gabe went their united way back to his apartment.

In the cab, Gabriel asked her about her second visit.

"I wanted to know about other civilizations. They said there are lots of them. They showed me a few—malevolent, benevolent, mixed, animal-like, robot-like, human-like, insect-like, angel-like. There's this one that's more powerfully benevolent than they are, stronger, bigger, greater light. They're the big guns and sometimes help with the heavy hitting.

And I wanted to know more about the acceleration, if I would have a role in it. It seems I do. They called me a vehicle for the acceleration. The other two don't seem to be. They just want more knowledge. They showed me this vortex around me and how it would draw people in. They said they'd need more like me around the world to help them shift into high gear. They showed me things I don't really understand and I'm trying to sort out. It's very big and wide and unfathomable. There are different ways it can go. There's darkness and light. But they showed me it would go in stages. I didn't have much time. Roz was there waiting for me and I wanted to convince her to do it. I'll go back soon and get some more. I can only absorb so much at a time. It's all somehow being taken care of. There's only so much we can know till it's time to. Things will come and then we'll know. I can't really say much more about it."

"Did you go to the forest?"

"No, I went to a room in one of their ships. There was just one of them there and it was just light. Nothing human about it. The room looked a little like their chamber but the light was different, more white, less color, less activity in the floor, walls and ceiling. Not much in that room, either, nothing I could relate to. A few funny shaped things I didn't think to ask about. They did say the ship was about a light year away. So they have some way of instant relocation. I guess kind of like Einstein's spooky influence at a distance. They can transcend the laws of nature we're usually constrained by.

I also asked them why they made a doorway of light to get you there and sent you back without it.

They said they need to get you in their field. Once you're in it, they can send you anywhere. Then you're out of their field again. I guess they can send their field anywhere but it's easier to have a fixed place. I don't really understand it."

"If they can take people to their ships, why bury a chamber in the Bohemian Forest?"

"It's like I said, they're working with earth energies, too. But it's more than that. There's so much to it it's impossible to express it all. But it's like they had to start by lovingly planting a seed in the earth, like impregnating a woman. Then watering it a little at a time by healing a few people there, then more people, then more. Each time they healed a person that miraculous energy fed the earth and her energy veins. It had to come from some magical place within earth, herself. I guess there was no better spot than beneath a great tree in the Bohemian Forest."

She paused.

"Anything else?"

"There *is* more but I haven't gotten it clearly enough and now's not the time."

"Force of nature doesn't do you justice, darling."

She poked him and said, "Now come on, let's not get carried away."

They arrived.

Jack opened the door for them.

Eva and Jack's eyes met for the first time since her healing.

The shift occurred.

"Jack, I'm going to need to speak with you soon."

"OK."

"What are your hours?"

"Lately they've been quite varied."

"That's what it seemed like. Are they overworking you?"

"Yes, of late, because we lost someone."

"Let's talk tomorrow. Do you know your hours?"

"I have the day shift. Six to four."

"Are your shifts usually ten hours?"

"No, eight."

"OK, let's arrange something tomorrow."

"I'll be here."

They went in and entered the elevator.

"Tomorrow's Friday."

"Yes."

"You don't work the weekends, do you?"

"No."

"And Monday is Memorial Day. Do you work then?"

"No, we celebrate with our host country."

"Good, I may want you all to myself."

"I usually work out Saturdays and Wednesday evenings, though I skipped yesterday. I could skip Saturday, too."

"So no one goes through on the weekends?"

"Only once. She was leaving the country. Jimmy came in to let her in."

They spent the evening schmoozing, cuddling and walking in the park.

This time they slept without sex.

Chapter 10

I Want You So Much

The alarm rang at six-thirty.

They embraced.

"Get up and shower and make us breakfast, darling. I need to think."

He did.

In all the activity, she hadn't thought about work or her own bank account.

"If Gabe and Jimmy, why not me?"

She got up, got her phone and got back in bed.

She went online and checked her account.

They had added five million dollars.

That more than freed her to do this full time.

What could be better?

Gabe had finished his shower. She got up and took hers.

When she was finished, she got his robe and went to the kitchen.

He was putting breakfast on the table.

She sat and let his robe fall open.

He sat and smiled and gazed.

"I wanna give up my apartment and move in."

"Superb. I couldn't be happier."

"They gave me five million dollars."

"Wow, that's more than me."

"I'll be doing this full time."

"Of course."

"I love you."

"I love you, too. I can't wait till tonight."

They ate their breakfast and Gabriel left.

She cleaned up after them.

On her way to the bedroom, she saw light filling the guest bedroom doorway.

She walked through it, naked in Gabe's robe.
She was in a similar room to the last one, but different.
There was one angel in a robot suit.
He held out a ring.
It was a fine, slender, simple, white gold metal band.
She followed the image in her mind, reached out and put it on her left pinky.
She didn't wear rings.
This would be her only one.
She could hardly feel it. But it empowered her and felt wonderful to the touch.
A flood of images came into her mind and body.
This ring was a field carrier.
She could come through anytime from anywhere.
She could bring any number she could see with her just by deciding.
She could pick and choose among a crowd who would go.
She could bring ones without even speaking with them if she knew they were ready or would augment the acceleration. There was no longer a one-day rule.
She could bring through anyone she knew no matter where on the planet they were.
She could disappear in plain sight and take as many with her as was called for. Disappearances were part of the plan.
This field was them. It carried their capabilities.
Wearing it, she could do anything they could under similar circumstances.
She was the first to receive one.
Only ten others would.
Eleven would be needed for the global thrust.
Then she was in the hallway again.
She went to the bay window and looked out on the park.
She took a few moments to feel the ring and assimilate this.
Her life experience kept ascending to higher levels.
She was feeling like a different being.
She got dressed and went to the entrance to find Jack.
"Jack, can you give me a few minutes at four when you get off?"
"Yes."
"Great, could you hail me a cab?"
She went home and booted up. She composed a thirty-day notice letter to her landlord and emailed it. She sent messages to all her postponed clients and referred them to her boss. She gathered all her little treasures and packed up her computer and as much as she could. She hauled it downstairs and hailed a cab.
Jack helped her bring her stuff up.
She went down with him and he hailed another cab.
She took it to Village Design.
She walked into her boss's office.
"Ethel, I'm sorry, but I must quit without notice."
Ethel eyed her.
Something shifted.
"Well, that's not convenient."
"I know. I hope you'll soon understand. Maybe Roz will help you. I think she'll

be coming back sooner than she thought. That'll help. I'm very grateful to you for giving me the job. Thank you. But this is too important. Please forgive me when you can."

Pause.

"Has something happened with Brie?"

"Let's let Roz tell you."

Ethel looked at her for a moment.

"Very well, goodbye."

"Goodbye, Ethel."

There was nothing there for Eva to retrieve. Almost all her work was out with clients.

She walked outside and looked at her watch.

It was ten-fifteen.

Roz and Brie would be coming back around eleven.

She just started walking along the sidewalk looking at people, drinking in the world that was Greenwich Village, New York.

She began to notice their energies, their carriage, the qualities of their souls in ways she had never perceived before.

She began to realize how she could see who would help the acceleration, who was ripe for the picking.

She took the ring off and put it in her purse.

She could still see many of these things, but not as strongly or as clearly.

She took it out and put it back on.

Then she became aware of a presence off in the distance.

It was masculine but very different from Gabe's.

It was menacing, jubilant, powerful, like a jungle cat.

She kept walking towards it.

It kept approaching.

Then he came into view, a gorgeous, tall, strong, swaggering black man. He looked like a cross between a gangster, a Zulu warrior and a movie star. He was probably twenty-eight. He was clean-shaven, with very short, nubby hair looking almost like a skullcap with three tasteful, fine, expanding javelins shaved into one side of his head. He wore a stylish, gangster-like, shiny suit of dark metallic blue. His skinny, purple tie and slate blue shirt complemented it beautifully. He looked like he owned the world. He ran his eyes up and down Eva as soon as he saw her. Before he passed, he looked into her eyes and winked.

Eva kept on walking. She had seen, unmistakably, how powerful a force he could be for the acceleration.

"WHOA, BABY," the man yelled, "STAAAHHP!!!"

His voice was strong and commanding. It could probably be heard a block and a half away.

She could easily have walked on but she didn't. She turned to face him.

He approached her.

"What did you DOOO to me?"

"I healed a little of your soul."

"I BEELEEEEVE you DIIID!"

"How does it feel?"

"MEELLOW, FFREEE, but MEEllow could get me KILLED. It took my EEDGE off. I NEEEED my edge. It cuts through EEEEEVERYTHING. You are BEEYUUUTIFUUULLL!!!"

"Thank you, so are you. Maybe it's time you started fixing everything."

With that, they disappeared.

Eva briefly saw the inside of a chamber and the astonishment on the man's face.

Then she was back on the sidewalk in a slightly different position.

She stepped in the street to hail a cab.

Two hours later, the man appeared in his own apartment. On his left pinky was a fine, white gold ring. He could barely move from wonder.

A few people had seen the disappearance. They shook their heads and blinked their eyes.

Later, one man said to his wife, "I thought I saw two people disappear today."

She replied, "Well what do I say to that?"

Eva arrived in the basement of the Czech Consulate about two minutes before Roz and Brie's reappearance.

Jimmy just had time to tell her, "I opened that account this morning when they opened at seven-thirty."

"Great Jimmy, look at the balance in a day or two and tell me what it is."

"I just called the automated line. They put in two million."

"Fabulous, you've certainly earned it. Now let's see what you do with it."

Then mother and daughter were there and stood looking at them with wide, divine eyes.

"It's alright, there's no need to talk. I'll lead you outside and we'll go somewhere to eat."

She stepped between them, took their hands and led them to the elevator.

They looked so wonderful and Brie had more than peach fuzz on her recently bald scalp.

When they were seated at the same diner table Gabe had taken Eva to, Roz managed her first words, "Oh, Eva!"

They had their glorious meal.

Eva told them of her new capabilities.

They decided to go straight to Ronald McDonald.

As soon as they got there, they got busy.

Eva went to the higher ups and secured a small meeting room. She donated a thousand dollars for it. She knew RM would soon be obsolete but she didn't know how soon. And they had done wonderful work.

Roz went to gather her friends. They were all there. She got the two who still had husbands to get them to come by saying it was an emergency. The sight of Brie in her robust magnificence with a delicious matt of hair on her head was enough for them to want to hear more and have their husbands hear it, too.

Brie got her friend to call his aunt and tell her it was an emergency. She simply had to come. She was the hardest but she finally relented.

When they were all gathered, Eva said, "If I could snap my fingers and completely heal you of every ailment in you heart, soul and body, would you object?"

There was silence. They just looked at her.

"Object now or hold your peace."

One man complained, "What's this about? I object."

They all disappeared but him.

Instantly, Eva appeared in her condo and Roz and Brie appeared in their room in the facility. They gathered together their few remaining possessions.

Roz looked at Brie, "I can't deal with trying to check you out. They'll want to run tests, consult doctors, the whole nine yards."

There was a pad and pen on one of the tables.

Roz wrote a note, "Sorry, we have bolted. We and this room are free. Brie is my daughter. I have decided. Thank you so much for everything. You're all wonderful," and she signed and dated it.

They went to the curb to hail a cab.

"Wait!" the man from the meeting room yelled as he rushed up to them.

He had sat there, too stunned to move. He didn't know what to do. Eventually he got up to leave.

"What happened in there?"

"They were all sent to heal," Roz answered.

"What about me?"

"You objected. Your loved ones will reappear, probably at your place, in about two hours. They'll be perfectly healed. Be as gentle as you can with them. They'll be too filled with wonder to speak. And then they'll be very hungry. Your time will come."

A cab pulled up and they left.

Two hours later, each person appeared where they needed to be, magnificent, sound and whole.

Eva started unpacking her things and putting them away.

Halfway through, her phone rang.

"Eva Dunn?"

"Yes."

"This is Anani from Up Thai."

"Beautiful."

"I want what you and your male friend have."

"Perfect. Can you come here now?"

"Yes."

"Take a cab to 900 5th Avenue. I'll reimburse you. Tell the doorman you're here for me. Come up to 1812."

"I don't have the cab fare."

"That's OK. The doorman will pay it or I'll come down. Just get in a cab and come."

Eva looked at her watch. It was two-thirty. She called downstairs.

"Jack?"

"Yes?"

"Are we still on for four?"

"Yes."

"Good. A young woman is coming to see me. Her name is Anani. Could you pay her cab fare and I'll reimburse you?"

"Yes."

"Great, thanks. Please just come up at four and ring the bell, OK?"

"Sure, I'll be there."

Eva went back to unpacking and finding the perfect spot for each of her things. Where her laptop would go would have to be worked out with Gabriel.

Fifteen minutes later the doorbell rang.

Eva went and opened the door.

Anani stood there looking an impossible, irresistible combination of demure, eager, bold and shy. Her head tilted slightly downward. Her eyes looked up into Eva's.

Eva's heart leapt to her throat. She reached out and took her hand, pulled her inside, shut the door and took her in her arms.

"I love you, darling," Eva whispered into her ear.

"I love you, too," she whispered back.

"Press your hips in, sweetie."

Anani complied.

"That's good, now press your pussy right into mine."

Anani did.

"A little stronger, sweetheart."

As Anani pressed in, a lightning bolt shot from Eva's pussy into Anani's and up through her body.

"Oh my God," Anani whisper moaned.

"You're so good, sweet pussy, I want you."

"Oh, I want you, too! I can't believe what you just did! It was so powerful! I want you so much!"

"Good girl, are you off today?"

"Yes."

"And tomorrow?"

"Yes, Friday and Saturday are my days off."

"Anani, we're going to go somewhere now and everything will change. I want you to come here tomorrow at noon. You don't have to. You don't have to let me know. Come if you want to. Don't come if you're not ready. Gabriel will be here. I want you to be with both of us. Do you think you'd like that?"

"Oh yes, I want what you want."

"Beautiful. You're my perfect pussy. Do you understand?"

"Oh yes! I want more than anything to be the most perfect pussy I can for you!"

"Good girl, my perfect girl, my perfectly darling, lovable girl. There may be a few other people here as well. Can you consider that?"

"Oh yes. I want everything you want of me! I want to throw myself at your feet and do everything you tell me to."

"Perfect. I want you so much, your heart, your body, your soul, your willingness, your wide open, hot, wet pussy, your mouth, all of you. Do you understand?"

"Oh yes, I'm yours."

"Good girl. I can't wait."

She pulled herself away, took Anani's hand, kissed her on the lips and they disappeared.

Eva reappeared and finished unpacking.

She put her luggage away in the storage closet.

Four soon arrived.

Jack rang the bell.

Eva opened the door.

"Hi Jack, is there anywhere you have to be in the next few hours?"

"No."

They disappeared.

Eva reappeared, closed the door and took a nice, long bath in preparation for Gabriel's homecoming.

Life was good.

Chapter 11

You're Ishtar, Darling, the Goddess of Love

Gabriel soon arrived.

She greeted him at the door with a kiss and embrace.

"Welcome home, darling."

"What a joy to be welcomed by you in this way!"

"Yes, everything is truly wonderful."

"Been busy?"

"I'll say. Let's eat in. I didn't go food shopping or look in the fridge. Do we have enough?"

"Oh yes. I usually eat in and we've been going out. It'll be good to use up some of it."

"Are you hungry?"

"Not so much. I will be in an hour or two."

"Good. I want a powwow. There's a lot I want to talk about."

"OK. I'll go change."

She waited for him in the living room and thought.

He soon arrived and settled in.

She held up her hand and showed him the ring.

"There was light in the guest room doorway this morning. I walked through and one of them dressed as a robot gave me this. It carries their field. I have it everywhere I go. I can go through any time. I can bring anyone I want. I can yank you from your office or anywhere in the world and pull you to me or through to them.

The one-day rule is off. I can disappear in the street right in front of people's eyes and pull anyone who's right for this with me. I'm the first one to get the ring. The other two are just for gaining knowledge. I pulled a man I saw in the village through. He's the second one to get one. Only eleven of us will get them worldwide. This is the first stage of the acceleration.

Anything they can do without the chamber, I can do with this ring. So I can dissolve pregnancies. I have to go back to learn all the things I can do with it. I know they left it to me to ask. I sent Jack, that pretty waitress from Up Thai and four cancerous children with most of their parents and one aunt. Roz and Brie, of course, are fabulous. I quit my job. I gave notice to my landlord. I brought some more things from my flat. I love you."

"Jesus, my head is spinning."

"I know. There's more to come."

"Give me a moment."

"Take as many as you like."

It took him a few minutes to assimilate it all.

As she had spoken all this she had the thought, "Now why did I tell Anani to take a cab? I could have just pulled her here. I have to get used to all this."

Gabe was ready.

"How can you pull me if I'm not in their field?"

"I know you. Just by thinking of you a bit of my energy goes to you wherever you are. With the ring, enough of their field comes with it to lock onto you. I can probably send you anywhere I want. I can do the same with anyone in my sight whether I know them or not. I can pick and choose people from a crowd."

"How do you pick and choose?"

"I can see. I can see like never before. I can see without the ring but I see better with it. The ring strengthens my vortex energy, too, so the right people are drawn to me. I see their energy, their light, their soul, their readiness for this, how helpful they might be to the acceleration."

"Are you going to pull your parents and siblings through?"

She paused.

"God, I haven't even thought of them! Thank you for reminding me. I suppose I will. I love them, of course. But somehow I'm not that attached. What a concept! Can you imagine their surprise! This brings it home and makes it personal!"

They sat in silence for a moment.

"I have to get used to the idea. Alena and André should come here. There's no need for Jimmy to go in tomorrow. I'm sure I know them well enough to pull them through from wherever they are. But let them prepare and come. Sometimes I need to take it a little more slowly, too."

"OK. I'll let them all know."

"Let Alena and André know. I want to talk with Jimmy anyway."

"OK."

"Let's get that out of the way. Why don't you go into your office and call Alena and André. I'll call Jimmy from here. We need to decide where to set up my computer."

"I'll make space in my office unless you want your own. Let's do everything together as much as possible. But let's be free to take breaks whenever we want. Do you need privacy with Jimmy?"

"No, come back when you're done. I just don't want two conversations going at the same time. I like the idea of sharing an office. Let's do that. I won't need much space. Tell them to come at ten instead of nine."

He got up and left. She called Jimmy.

"Hello Eva darlin'"

"Hello darlin' Jimmy."

"What's up?"

"They gave me a ring. I can send anyone anytime. I'll be doing this full time. I'll be sending the two tomorrow. There's no need for you to go in. We've entered the first stage of the acceleration. You're days there are numbered."

"Oh no, I like being gatekeeper!"

"I know, like the usher to the gates of heaven. You get to see them before and after. And you get to be in that energy. But you've come up in the world. There's something better for you now. They gave you that money for a reason. You've been part of this since the beginning. Now you'll be part of the acceleration. You're more than a janitor, Jimmy."

Gabe had returned in the middle of this.

"I know. I just ain't been ambitious. What's next?"

"I don't know. That needs to come from you. If you want me to send you to talk to them, I can. But you should think on it first. You don't have to quit till you want to. But you won't be doing much gatekeeping."

"OK, I'll give notice now. I don't have to think on that much. But I will on what I'll be doing. I'd mighty much like it to speak with them. I love you, Cleopatra."

"I love you, too. Bye."

"Bye, bye."

"He's out of a job?"

"Yes. They gave him two million dollars. That means they want him for something else. We're good for ten?"

"They both said it was better."

"Good. There's something more we need to talk about."

"OK."

"It's harder."

"OK, I'm ready."

"I'm not sure you are."

He looked at her.

"Darling, I want us to say anything there is to say to each other. Absolutely anything. We need total, open communication. I don't care how hard or scary it is. Please feel totally free. I want to know everything you're willing to tell me."

"Good. And ditto for me. OK, here goes."

She took a breath and a moment.

"I love you. I'm in love with you. I'm your woman and you're my man. I'll marry you, have your children, probably do anything you want. I won't do anything that will hurt you. I won't do anything that will jeopardize what we have.

But they healed my libido. Or they jacked it sky high. I don't know. Maybe it's part of my vortex thing, attracting people who will help with the acceleration. You said you weren't interested in anyone who wouldn't be the real thing. But you and I *are* the real thing. And I cream just looking at Anani, that waitress. I'm in love with her. Not like you. Nothing else will be quite like this. But I really want her, bad.

I used to despise virility. I really did. And I'm glad. But no longer. That man in the village was like a tall, black, Zulu gangster god. Probably the most virile man on the planet. I could feel him from three blocks away like you, though his presence was very different. You're virile, you're plenty virile for me. But I was drawn to him before he was healed and was probably a drug-dealing murderer. I'm curious. I'm attracted. And I'll probably want to be with Roz.

I've only been with two men and you. You're my heaven. You're my life. But I want to experience more and it goes far beyond that.

I wouldn't want you going off and being with other women or men. That would hurt me. And I wouldn't want to go off with any of these people. But I'd love to bring Anani into our bed and lick her pussy and watch you fuck her and do all the things my libido is coming up with. And do it with our precious, sweet, powerful love. I know this sounds odd, but I'm sexually attracted to the people who will most help the acceleration. Could God possibly work that way?

So I'm saying we do these things together, fully, consciously, lovingly, joyfully, sexually. We know we're all perfectly healthy. We know I can dissolve pregnancies. I believe we're meant to do this, to create joyful, sacred, sexual light. To help pour it into our world. To make love and fulfill pleasure and create joy that radiates out into Earth's veins. Sacred, loving sex. Golden, loving families. Making beautiful love with a few right people. The radiance could just pour out of our condo and light up the world. We could be a beacon of freedom, love and life! So I do believe God *is* working this way.

I don't really know how much I'll want to do this. Maybe we shouldn't. Maybe the actuality won't come close to my imagination. Maybe if we try it'll be terrible. But I know it won't. I know it'll be wonderful. I want to try. You and I are solid enough that we'll weather anything. And I'd rather try and find out I'm delusional than never try and never know.

And how could I be delusional in this perfectly healed state?"

She looked at him.

He smiled at her.

"You are jacked up, aren't you? You're a vehicle of the acceleration. I'm ready."

"Really?"

"Yes. Remember when I told you I loved you more because you and Roz were thinking of loving each other?"

"Yes."

"I meant it. I wouldn't want you going off with other people, either. That would kill me. I'd want to be there, part of it. I'd want to watch or engage. With the right people, it could be wonderful. I'd love to see Anani naked."

"Even with the Zulu?"

"You say he has the ring. That makes him a god. I might not let him stick his cock up my ass. But I want you to receive all that you wish for. If you want to experience the most virile, god-like man on the planet, why would I possibly want to stop you?"

"Really?"

"Yes."

"Even with Alena?"

"Why not? If she'd consent. You know how religious she is. But she needs lovin' bad. She's a beautiful woman. I'd love to see her naked, too. I'd love to watch you lick her pussy and her yours. That would be stunning. She and I have been wanting each other since we met. But I couldn't complicate my life with the wrong thing. This is different. Everything is different. Now that I have the real thing, I'm willing to share it. I like the idea of bringing other people into the circle of our love. You're Ishtar, darling, the goddess of love, sex and war. This condo is our love altar. Perhaps this is why they wanted me to buy it. I'm ready. Nothing will shatter what we have."

"Boy, did I fall in love with the right man! We're already three. Anani's in. She's coming at noon tomorrow, fully healed."

"At the speed of thought!"

"Yes."

"Good."

They ate their dinner and made marvelous love, more passionate, exciting and fulfilling than ever.

Chapter 12

About the Dark Side

Six-thirty came and went, the alarm blessedly silent.

They slept in till eight then showered, prepared breakfast, ate and cleaned up together.

Then they got dressed and started creating Eva's workspace.

Jack called up from below.

"Morning guys, Alena and André are here for you."

"Send them up, Jack, and let's talk soon."

"Yes, please. Thank you for this unbelievable miracle!"

"My pleasure, I still owe you cab fare."

"Forget it."

"No, debts must be paid. When are you off today?"

"Four again."

"Let's see if that works."

The doorbell rang.

She looked at Gabe, "Let's see if this works."

She opened, smiled at them and said, "Bon voyage."

They disappeared.

"It worked."

"What?"

"Before, I'd go through with them and they'd send me back. This time I just sent them. It's funny how they let you learn, they let you grow, they let you figure it out. But when you ask, they tell you. I guess it's part of divine orchestration, each person going at their own pace. They don't want to overload you, to give you anything you're not ready for. They leave it up to you and God. But they give you everything you ask. I think I know how to use our two hours."

"How?"

Eva's cell rang. She held up a 'one moment' finger.

"Hello?"

"Hello, Eva. This is the man from the sidewalk. They branded my brain with your name and number."

"Perfect. Did they give you my address?"

"No."

"It's 900 Fifth Avenue, 1812. Can you have your black ass here at noon?"

"Yeeees."

"Good. What's your name?"

"Lakane. But I'll be changing it."

"See you soon, Lakane. Looking forward to it."

She looked at Gabe, "It's perfect. We'll be seeing a lot of perfection. That was the Zulu. His name is Lakane."

"Tell me."

"It's like we already have this golden family for being all over each other and loving in every imaginable way, for just walking down the street and blowing everyone's minds to the moon, for learning and growing and love and fun, for drawing people to us and enhancing the acceleration. I think. We'll see.

Maybe God wants us to have fun and be happy and show people how. You and I will always be the core no matter who may come and go. We'll probably have people like Roz or even Jimmy—see? Even I say 'even' when it comes to Jimmy. I guess because of his age. Lakane is black. That didn't give me a moment's hesitation. Maybe it's Jimmy's personality. But people like him and Roz who will just quietly be with us, the three of us, maybe lots or only once. I don't know. I can't say I'm that attracted to Jimmy, but I just love him. I don't know why but I trust my love. He has something very special in him that's been under a bushel all his life. I want to do something magnificent for him. I want to give him something glorious. Heaven, that's it. I want to bring heaven here, to generate heaven through love. Wait a minute. I think I'm getting this. Could you hand me my phone, sweetie?"

He got up and brought it to her.

She rang Jimmy.

"I love getting calls from you!"

"I love calling you! It's time for you to stop playing small. Are you ready to speak with them?"

"Am I ever!"

She hung up the phone.

"You just pulled him through?"

"Yes, another first. He's still holding his phone. I believe this is all divine orchestration. We'll always go with that, no matter what it may be. Anyway, if I'm not mistaken, our first golden family will be you, me, Lakane, Alena, André and Anani."

"Wow. Six of us. What a glorious group! And what possibilities for glorious pairings. André and Alena will be newly hatched."

"I know. We'll go to lunch first."

"No grass growing under your feet."

"No, we're speeding up. There's so much synchronicity. This is part of enlarging my vortex and hastening the global thrust. See? Listen to me! Even those words are sexual—enlarging my vortex, the global thrust. I don't think it's happenstance. It's meant to be. This is the love phase of the acceleration. The world is so fucked up about sex."

"For the global thrust, I'll do anything."

"Fabulous, me too. How could we not?"

"And now?"

They both disappeared.

They were in a white room with a few odd objects and one light being.

They both began receiving.

Eva asked what she could do with the ring.

She could heal people significantly like they did with Brie before the chamber. She could relocate anywhere and the ring would generate a field to protect her— the moon, the sun, the bottom of the ocean, the planets, a distant star, anywhere on Earth. She could bring people with her, up to about thirty. All she had to do was consciously decide to be there and she would. Random thoughts or dreams would not trigger this. The field would 'know' true intention over dreams, considerations or whimsies.

She could transmit and receive thoughts, ideas and images to anyone she knew no matter where they might be. She could read minds and deliver thoughts to anyone or any number whose location she could pinpoint, including any room, building, block, city, country or the entire world. The thoughts of others would not intrude until she consciously decided to receive them.

At her request, they perfected her ability to do all these things.

Then she asked them to show her the opposition.

An onslaught of images and data came in that nearly overwhelmed her but they always protected her from too much. She saw the forces of control and disruption, those who wished to own the world, those who wished to destroy good, the Greys, civilizations that were worse, the Illuminati, the wealthiest families, the greed, power and dominance-possessed and the Satanic energies that drove them.

"Why can't we just put them all in the chambers?"

"They consciously oppose God and their healing. You'll encounter a few that you cannot send to us. There is no forcing anyone. It's only when enough love and healing have touched and reached them that it finally melts their resolve and they join us."

"Could we lose?"

"Yes, we lose some worlds. We win some worlds. If the balance of the world's energy is on their side when we reach the critical point, the world is theirs. It's not really losing. It's meant to be. If we can shift it enough to love and God, the world is God's. This world feels like God's. But we cannot know. We do what we can."

"What is the critical point?"

"When they are about to destroy large parts of the world and large numbers of beings and those who might protect them are not ready. To circumvent that, we relinquish the world to them."

"So you monitor them?"

"Yes, and they monitor us. But we understand the unfoldment of this process better than they. We have done this many times. For them this is new."

"Could Gabriel and I become targets?"

"They know of you. They don't wish to kill you. We will do everything we can to protect you. And you have the ring. They know they would not gain by killing you. You would just be replaced. And they'd have to find the new ones."

"Could you resurrect us if they killed us?"

"Yes, if we could find any part of you. If they completely destroy all of you then no."

"You can't just keep our DNA somewhere and make us from that?"

"No. That would obviate God's will."

"If they burn us could you still resurrect us?"

"Yes."

"Would we be as we were with all our memories and everything intact?"

"Yes."

"Then I want you to resurrect us."

"Ask Gabriel to tell us this and we will."

"Can they kill you?"

"No. We go home or on to the next world."

"I have a gun. Can I kill one of the opposition?"

"Yes, to protect yourself or others."

"But if I couldn't send them and knew they were opposition, could I just kill them?"

"You could but that would be helping them."

"So you never try to destroy them?"

"No, they are God's creation and part of God's plan."

She reappeared in their living room. She had reached her saturation point. Gabriel was already there.

He looked at her concerned.

"There's a dark cloud on your countenance."

"I asked them about the dark side."

"Ah, and they showed you."

"Yes. Let's talk about that tomorrow. I want to enjoy today as much as possible. But there's one thing. They know of us. They also know it wouldn't serve them to kill us. They would rather keep tabs on us than have to find someone new. But if they kill us, our friends could resurrect us and we'd be just as we were. Would you want that?"

"In this life, of course."

"Me too. If they could only resurrect you would you want that?"

"That would be harder but yes again. I'd want to see as much of the acceleration as I could and the end game if at all possible."

"Me too. Let's go tell them."

They disappeared and reappeared in about three seconds.

"So now the good part."

She transmitted it all into his mind.

He looked at her in astonishment.

"Wow, what a partner I have!"

"Yeah, something, isn't she? What did they tell *you*?"

"Very little, really. I asked them what I could do in the acceleration. They told me what I already knew, to support you as much as I could. I asked them if I needed to stay at work. They said no but to find someone in concert with all this. I asked them about your group idea. They said all those with rings would have one."

Eva broke in, quite excited, "Oh darling, how glorious! Then I'm not delusional and it can work! I'm thrilled! Now why didn't I think of asking them? Maybe because I'm afraid I'm a naughty, sex-crazed girl. This means it's good I'm a naughty, sex-crazed girl. How luscious! Find your replacement, Gabe, I want you all in with this. What a prince you are! What a godsend all this is! What else?"

"I asked them if that's why they wanted me to have this condo. They said yes. And I asked them if they knew it was going to be you. They said no, they never know. They just heal whoever comes and God takes care of the rest. That's about it."

She stood up and stretched before him quite luxuriantly. He thoroughly enjoyed her opulent display.

"God, I've been so busy. I need a walk or some exercise. Today's your exercise day."

"I hope to do some exercising in the prone position this afternoon."

"Ha ha, very funny. Would you massage my shoulders a little?"

"Sure, sit on the ottoman."

"Wait, we need to make reservations for six at a wonderful restaurant we can walk to. What do you think?"

He paused.

"Italian?"

"Oh yes, that'll be fun!"

"For this occasion, I would say Caravaggio. It's a four block walk."

"Perfect, call them, will you?"

He did.

She sat on the ottoman to wait for him.

He returned and began. His hands were quite skillful.

"Oh, that's wonderful! You're so good!"

"Conscious love, my dear, speaking of which, I hope I can get it up this afternoon. I'm so fulfilled from last night."

"Oh, I think Alena or Anani could think of things to help. I have faith in you, darling."

"Thank you, my love, that means a lot to me."

When they were done, they still had an hour to kill.

"Let's walk in the park! I haven't done that here during the day and it's gorgeous out!"

Eva got a hundred dollar bill and they went downstairs.

"Wanna cab?"

"No, we're walking in the park. Jack, you look fabulous, like a different person! Something must have happened."

"Something indeed. How could I ever show you my gratitude?"

"No need for that but maybe you'll get to. Here's the cab fare and a tip. Listen, we're expecting a few folks. Just send them up."

She handed him the folded up bill as they stepped into the street.

"You got it. Hey, this is too much!" he called out as they crossed.

"I'm a big tipper," she yelled back

They walked in the park holding hands like children in wonderland. Everything was so amazing and people lit up as they walked by. Eva picked a few appropriate minds and sent the ones who wouldn't be needed for two hours.

But mostly they took their little vacation.

It was almost time to go back.

"I think I'm ready to send my family. I want them to be living this."

"Go for it."

She put what she was doing into all their minds and sent them through.

"A little gift from little old me."

Then she giggled like a little girl.

"Let's go home."

They called her over the next few days. It was lovely. But she knew with a little poignancy that they were complete. She would see them sometime, she was sure. But they were, as if, from another life.

Chapter 13

Arm in Arm

It was about ten before noon. No one was there yet.
Jimmy rang Eva's phone as soon as they got in.
"So watcha gonna do?"
"Go Martin Luther King one better."
"Beautiful, Jimmy, this is more like it."
"They said you'd show up and empty the church."
"And so I will. Perfect, Jimmy. Perfect, perfect, perrrrfect! I'm thrilled! I'll mostly show up as you finish. But I want to hear you a few times, especially the first. I want to see the real Jimmy."
"OK, goddess, though the first might not be my best."
The doorbell rang.
And there were Anani and Lakane.
Eva took Anani in her arms and held her for a few moments. Their hearts and loins stirred.
She whispered, "I love you," in Anani's ear.
Anani did likewise.
"Go inside, dear. Make yourself comfortable."
She looked appraisingly at Lakane, running her eyes up and down his body and then winking at him.
He burst out laughing.
"I guess I deserve that."
"God knows what you deserve, Lakane. Some people might think you didn't deserve what they gave you."
"And they'd be right. But if it's been given, then somehow it must be deserved, no?"
"Yes. So I guess you deserve to be here. You two introduced yourselves?"
"Oh yes. What a magnet you are!"

"It takes one to know one. Come in, Lakane. I'm not ready to hug you yet."

"Will you ever be?"

"Oh, quite possibly very soon and more. It depends on how greatly you repel me."

He laughed again and they headed towards the living room.

Alena and André appeared behind them.

Eva swiveled to look at them.

"Don't try to speak, darlings, Gabriel and I will lead you to a restaurant. You'll get very hungry very soon. Gabriel, would you come and take Alena's hand and lead the way?"

Gabriel did and Eva took André's and followed.

Alena glanced at Gabriel, flushed a little and looked away.

Lakane gestured Anani out and closed the door. They piled into the elevator.

Jack smiled like a lighthouse as they all passed.

When they got to the sidewalk, Eva turned back to Anani and said, "Sweetheart, come take my other hand."

Lakane was left alone behind. He skipped ahead of the three of them and fell in beside Alena.

Eva watched him walk. It was totally different than before. It was feral, graceful and dignified and carried his power far more subtly. It was quite beautiful and inspired her libido.

"Hey Lakane, can you still saunter?"

He went back to his old walk exactly as she remembered.

Anani chuckled.

Eva said, "I like the new one better."

"Me too," Lakane replied.

They walked the rest of the way silent, loving everything about everything.

Lakane opened the restaurant door for all of them and they were led to their table.

"OK," Eva said, "Gabriel to the far end, Alena to your right. Me at this end, Anani to my right. André to my left."

Leaving Lakane to Gabriel's left and Anani's right.

A waiter came to the table with menus, "Can I bring anyone drinks?"

"Not yet, please," Eva said.

He was a decent man but not Godsent.

"OK everyone," Gabriel said. "This is on me, though actually, it's on our divine friends. So totally indulge and have everything you want without holding back and with absolutely no concern about price. This is a major celebration for all of us. Please all out indulge."

"May I get it?" Lakane's powerful voice gently inquired.

Gabriel looked at him then to Eva.

She shrugged, "Why not? Lakane has some heavy-duty karma to pay off. What better way to start than by feeding *us*?"

She looked at Lakane.

"Did they augment your net worth?"

"I don't know."

"You probably don't need it."

"No, probably not."
She took Anani's hand, "Honey, have you checked your bank balance?"
"No."
"Could you do that now?"
She pulled out her phone and did.
Then she looked up to Eva with eyes of wonder.
"They added a million."
"Beautiful. Let's order."
They perused the menus and placed their orders.
In the lull that followed, Eva looked at Alena to see if she was ready to say more than 'Rigatoni.'
Alena returned her gaze with eyes of love.
"Thank you, Eva. God knows how long it would have taken me without you."
"You're so very welcome, my sister, thank you for joining us. I love you."
André piped up, "And me too! I can't tell you how grateful I am that you came to Candle and took pity on my bawling. This is beyond anything I could ever begin to conceive of. I was so wanting to die!"
"We're so glad you didn't, André, and that you're with us," Gabriel said.
"Is there any point in looking at my balance?"
"Probably not," Eva answered. "Anani's taken a step you haven't taken yet. But you never know what tomorrow may bring. You're welcome to look if you like."
He did.
"Nothing," he said.
"Like I said, dear boy. Anything can happen. We don't know what role you might play."
They feasted, talked and laughed and laughed and laughed.
Lakane managed to startle the entire restaurant with one particular booming roar. And somehow, it was perfect. The rest of the time he was the most perfect gentleman.
At one point Eva asked him, "So Lakane, you must tell us, drugs and murder?"
"Yes, drugs. Murder only when truly necessary."
"Did you run women?"
"No, that didn't appeal to me."
"Good. Anything else?"
"Some extortion on some folks who were crying out for it."
"And that's it?"
"That's it. I broke the speed limit all the time."
"Well, I hope that continues. So you were a prince among drug dealers?"
"I tried my best."
"Did you use a lot?"
"Very little, on special occasions. I liked to have my wits about me."
"What did you do with your stash?"
"I had very little. I dealt in huge amounts. I unloaded almost everything the day before you saw me. So I was very cash rich. That added to my saunter. The tiny amount I had left I gave to a few people on the street."
"Have you sent anyone through?"
"About thirty-five."

"Wow, far more than me. You got busy."

"Yes. I had my hands less full than you."

"Granted. Have you found anyone you couldn't put through?"

"No. Will I?"

"Probably, we'll get to that. Why the name change?"

"I'll spend a little more time here cleaning up the city. I know certain sectors of its underside quite well on both sides of the law. Then I'll go to Ghana, the place of my ancestors. My one ancestor was a great chief. They killed him and took all his children here. Lakane is my gangsta name. I'm no longer a gangster. I'll take a Ghanaian name. When in Africa…"

"Excellent. They gave you a ring. I knew they would. We're brothers. I forgive you."

"Thank you," he gazed into her eyes. "Truly."

When they were finished, they walked back arm in arm. Gabriel, Alena and Lakane in front. André, Eva and Anani behind.

Eva slipped her arms around Anani and André's waists. She gently started stroking them and moved her hands around and onto their bellies. Then she let her fingers lovingly and consciously feel their way downward to cover and caress their deltas. She watched Lakane as he walked. The three of them were getting aroused. Alena felt it and turned her head back to see what was going on. It gave her the courage to put her arms around Gabe and Lakane's waists. She didn't go as far as Eva but she allowed herself to feel the strength of their movement as they walked. It was magnificent. It made her dizzy. She had been so male and touch deprived. And one of them was Gabriel. Lakane started getting aroused. The six of them made a startling, magnetic display. Nearly everyone rubbernecked as they passed. A few people behind them started getting aroused. Three people disappeared by the time they got to Jack. Then they disengaged.

"Jack, this is Alena and André. You've seen Anani and Lakane. Any of them may be coming by at any time. Just send them up. No need to call. Even if you know we're not here. If you don't hear from me, today won't work. You and I can speak tomorrow."

"Thank you, my savior."

Eva laughed.

They piled into the elevator.

"OK, group hug. Me in the middle." Eva sang out.

They all laughed and swarmed around her.

"Oh yes!" she shouted as the elevator door opened.

Gabriel punched the numbers.

And they were home.

Chapter 14

The Perfectly Accessible Goddess

The living room was an expanse of couches, chairs, tables, lights and ottomans. Beneath the bay windows was the long line of armless couches. They could easily hold five people and more.

As soon as they were all inside and the door was closed, Eva announced, "Could everyone please sit on those couches by the window? There's something I want to talk with you about."

When they were all seated, she looked at them joyfully. They were so beautiful, wonderful and radiant. They all fully appealed to her every side.

"I am so thrilled to have you all here and see you arrayed before me like this. It's a miracle to top all the miracles that have been given to us. I love you all.

Gabriel and I are very lucky. We have found each other. We are a unit, a team, partners. We'll probably marry. Nothing will come between us. We have a circle of love around us that binds us together and will always be there. I'm his woman and he's my man.

I believe this circle of love has power and effect in the world, that the beauty of what we have radiates outward and touches people and draws the right ones to us, that it flows into the energy channels of the earth and helps our cause. And, of course, our healing and this ring greatly amplify this."

She held up her hand to display it.

"They gave me this. I was the first to receive one. I ran into Lakane in the Village and sent him off. He's the second. Only eleven will receive them in the whole world, enough to bring about the final thrust of healing everyone. But there is opposition and the outcome isn't known. I don't want to talk of it now but you should know for reasons that will become clear.

I believe with all my heart, my soul and my love that Gabe and I are meant to do more, more with our union, more with our circle of love.

I believe we are meant to invite in others, a few precious others, and expand

and amplify the power of our circle to make it a greater force of joy, pleasure, fun and fulfillment in our dear, sick world. I believe you are the appropriate people that divine orchestration has brought us for this.

I see us as a sacred, golden family that can be beautifully and happily all over each other so we can have all the love we could possibly want or need and blow the minds of the people who see us who would be very well served by having their minds blown. It's what we just did walking back from the restaurant. I see this as part of healing our puritan strangulation. But it's also something I simply want for myself. I want to experience a wide variety of love. Neither Gabriel nor I want to do this by going off with other people. We want to invite you into the field of our love.

I have already invited Anani and she has accepted. So now there are three of us. We have not done anything yet. This afternoon will be our beginning. But we're inviting the three of you as well.

I'm speaking for us because this is my baby, my vision. I have spoken with Gabriel and we're in total agreement. Anani has given her consent. It may be a total disaster but we want this. We want to see if it's everything I believe it will be.

Just today the devas told Gabe that each of us with a ring will have a group. I didn't ask them. I was going ahead with it. But to me that means it's part of the divine plan. Before that I was concerned about being a sex crazed delusional. But even then how could I be? We are truly healed and we know it. And I still wanted to try.

For me, I am asking you to embark on something very sacred. I believe it's totally in God's will. God wants us to be happy and fulfilled and to receive everything God has to offer. Otherwise I wouldn't be doing this. I only want our highest good.

Gabe, is there anything you want to say?"

"Eva is my love and we're in total accord. I totally trust her and the healers. I feel the joy the six of us have already created. I believe our intimacy could be wonderful."

Eva continued, "There is an opposition. If you join us, they will know. They are not benevolent but they know killing us will not help them. They would rather keep us in their sights than lose us and be forced to find our replacements. I choose to give them no power over me and to continue doing everything that will help the acceleration. I believe this is one of those things. And I want to have all the joy, beauty and fun I can to celebrate God's creation and what is now happening through us.

This ring gives us superpowers. I can read any mind anywhere and send my thoughts to one or many. I can take us all to the moon, the core of the sun, the bottom of the ocean, anywhere on Earth."

Lakane raised his eyebrows. He hadn't yet asked.

"It can create a field that will protect us anywhere. I can send anyone through anytime to gain information if there's good reason. I can heal a lot but not totally. I can also dissolve pregnancies.

Our friends and the fundamentalists agree on one thing. Life is sacred. But it's not a combination of cells that constitutes life. It's a being in a body. They know that no soul should come in unwanted. That is where they put their sanctity and they are the servants of God's will.

We're all perfectly healthy. If you get pregnant, you can have the baby or not. There will be no trauma if I dissolve your pregnancy though you might regret or grieve it. Know your own mind. We are free to enjoy divine and human love in all the ways we wish. At least that's what I believe, that God wants us to, especially now. I don't know if I'm right. But I invite you to find out with me.

Gabe, Anani, anything more?"

"I love you and I'm all in," Gabriel said.

"And I, too," Anani echoed.

"So I'm twenty-three. They say I'm a great beauty. I didn't care much about that before except for the doors it opened. I despised men. I despised virility. I don't anymore. In some ways I'm like I was. In some ways I'm very different. I've only been with three men in my life. I want to be with all of you. I invite you to partake of our beauty and love. And I ask you to give us yours. I seem to want to shock people, to jolt them out of their cages. I seem to be more like a male dominant now than a woman. I don't fully understand it. But I'm loving it. And I'm guided not to hold back. It seems necessary. It seems important.

The Sumerian culture is the oldest known to man. They wrote of the Perfectly Accessible Goddess. To you, I want to be the Perfectly Accessible Goddess. I want to stand here before you and take off my clothes and let you enjoy my beauty, at least visually to start with. I feel like a healthy exhibitionist. I want to display myself. This is my way of inviting you. Does anyone want to leave?"

Eva knew all along she totally had Lakane and André. On the one hand, this was all for Alena. On the other, it was for her own pleasure. She reveled in her healthy selfishness, in God providing the means to satisfy all her desires. She looked at their faces. They were looking at her with love and delight. They were thrilled with everything she'd been saying, including Alena. Lakane, especially, was exploding with light. But Alena had a huge holdout. She knew only Alena might leave. She gave her time to do so. No one moved.

"Beautiful! I love you all."

Gracefully and straightforwardly, she unbuttoned and removed her blouse and threw it on the couch behind her. Her bra came next and then her shoes and socks. She unbuttoned and unzipped her jeans and pulled her panties down with them. All her clothing was gone.

She stood there before them perfectly naked, her body perfect as a body can be. The hair of her delta was a little darker than the hair of her head. Her breasts were full and round with the perfect, indefinable beauty only perfect breasts can have. They were a marvel of symmetry. Her thighs and belly, her arms, shoulders and hips were exquisitely shaped and enticing. Her face was gorgeous. Her feet were small, narrow and fine boned, the ultimate feet, no hint of any protrusion or corn, with slender, beautiful toes. Her hands were exquisite. She was ultimately desirable.

Lakane's pants were bulging.

She raised her arms and stretched. She put her feet wide apart. She took in the deepest breath she could and lifted and thrust forward her magnificent chest. André and Gabriel's cocks began to respond. She released her breath. The sexual energy in the room was rising. Alena's pussy was getting warm. Anani was beginning to moisten.

Eva took a quarter turn to her right. She repeated her breath and her lift. She took another quarter turn and faced away from them. She placed her feet wide apart and took her breath again and held it as she thrust. And then she released.

Very slowly, holding her back ramrod straight, she began to bend forward. She continued this very gradually and deliberately until she could go no further. Then she allowed her back to curve and bent over completely. Her cheeks were wide apart. Her legs were wide open. Her pussy and anus were completely revealed, perfectly displayed to those sitting on the couch. They were beautiful. They were sacred. They were precious. They were raunchily, humanly sexy. Eva held her position.

"Oh my God," Lakane said with genuine revelation, "the Perfectly Accessible Goddess!"

"Yes," Eva said, her face upside down now facing them from between her feet, "and all this time you thought she was nothing but pussy.

Men crave and despise her just as I used to despise them. They want to own her, go back to her and stomp her into the dirt. I want you to elevate her, to love her, to worship her with your tongues and your lips and your hearts."

And so they were doing, at least with their hearts and their eyes.

All three men had to shift and adjust themselves to accommodate their growing members. Anani longed to lick her. And Alena was starting to cream.

The divine, sexual energy in the room was growing, radiating outward and pouring into Earth's energy rivers.

Gabriel was feeling a special kind of poignancy that couldn't be described.

Eva slowly unwound her position and stood erect.

She turned again and took her deepest breath.

Then she turned to face them.

With her feet only slightly apart, she began to rapidly jiggle her knees, alternately forward and back. This caused not only her breasts to bounce and shake, but all the flesh of her body. It also stimulated her pussy and anus and heightened her arousal... and theirs.

There was something about this primal sight that was ultimately fulfilling.

She ended by bouncing both knees a few times.

This caused both breasts to jump up and down quite dramatically.

"Anani, darling, come to mama."

Lakane and André chuckled.

Anani smiled and arose.

Eva held out her arms and she walked into them.

Eva's lips caressed the skin of her ear as she whispered, "I love you, Anani."

"And I so love you, my goddess."

"How old are you?"

"Twenty-one."

"Beautiful. Will you allow me to take off your clothes? Will you stand with me before these people?"

"Yes, I'll do all that you want. There's nothing I won't do. Just tell me and I'll do it. I'm yours."

"Good girl. You are so beautiful. You're exactly what I want."
She slowly undressed Anani, throwing her clothes on top of her own.
Anani stood naked.
Her body was very different from Eva's but very beautiful. Her breasts were smaller but perfectly shaped. The hair of her delta was black, as the hair of her head. It stood out starkly from her pale skin. She had slender, shapely hips. She was perfectly proportioned, a stunning model of that special oriental beauty. Eva knelt before her and kissed upward into the nadir of her delta. Anani pressed a little into her and softly moaned. Eva got up and turned her towards the others. She stepped to her side and held her hand.

The men's desire was pulling them. Alena was rapt with eyes of love.
"Gabe, will you join us?"
Gabriel arose and removed his clothing.
"Stand by Anani and take her hand."
This put him directly in front of Alena. She looked at him, his face, his body, his hard, erect cock. She longed, as she always had, to kneel before him, to pleasure him, to give herself to him, even more now that he was standing like this before her, so beautiful, so strong, so within her reach.
"Who else will join us?"
Lakane was off the couch and out of his clothes in no time flat. His cock was full on engorged, rock hard in total erection. It was quite a sight.

Eva reached her left hand towards him. He turned to face Alena and took it.
His hand was powerful but gentle. Eva knew he could crush her but he held her lightly, consciously. It was more erotic than anything else he could have done and a pulse of hot love shot through her pussy. Alena could feel it and looked at her.

André took a little longer. His erect cock couldn't match Lakane's but it was more than sufficient and beautifully shaped and proportioned, clean, chiseled and perfect. He was adorable, androgynous, unique. They couldn't help but love him.
"André, stand to Gabe's right and take his hand."
The five of them stood before Alena.
"Alena, just look at us all for a few moments."
She did.
Gabriel could see that she longed to stand and join them but that she couldn't. She was immobilized.
André could see her barrier almost as if it were a physical wall. Something started to build within him.
Lakane and Anani looked at her beauty.
Finally, Gabe let go of Anani and André's hands, stepped forward and knelt before her.
He looked up into her eyes.
"Darling Alena," he said, "you and I have wanted each other for so very long. I have always wanted you. But I knew as a couple we couldn't last. Now I have my truest partner but I still want you. You are a precious, beautiful woman. You don't have to join our golden family if you don't want to. But this afternoon, you and I can love each other in all the ways we have wanted to. I know Eva won't

mind if you decide when you're ready. I won't make love with you without Eva's presence. But she is here. Stand up and allow us to see your beauty. Then you and I can fulfill the love that we've had from the day that we met."

Alena looked at him, kneeling before her. She looked at the others, especially Lakane. His startling erection had not diminished one iota. She thought of that inside of her. Her pussy longed for it.

Then she looked at Eva. She wanted her almost as much as she wanted Gabriel.

"You don't mind?"

"No dear, I love you. I want to fulfill you however I can. I offer you Gabe lovingly and freely. Please let yourself have what you've always wanted."

Alena looked at her and started to tear. She looked back to Gabriel and something cracked within her.

She let out the most painful, desolate, tortured wail anyone could imagine and burst into uncontrollable sobs.

Along with her, André did the same.

The two of them sobbed and cried and wept in total, impossible abandon.

The sexual love charge in the room alchemized into compassion.

Gabriel rose on his knees and put his arms around her.

She clung to him and wept.

Eva went to André and helped him lie down on the carpet. She coaxed him into the fetal position and lay down and held him as he cried.

"Give them your love with your hands and bodies," she said to Anani and Lakane.

Lakane went to Alena.

Anani came to André.

They touched and stroked them.

Anani lay down behind André and pressed up against him. She gently placed her hands on his head, shoulders and arms, moving them from time to time.

Lakane sat beside Alena and put an arm around her and his hand below her throat.

She wept for her longing, her desire, her unfulfilled love, for the five long years of seeing Gabriel every workday, the torture of wanting him so much and never being able to have him. She wept for the impossible agony of eternal longing, lostness, aloneness, isolation, withheld, blocked and chopped off love, for all the pain of unrequited ardor. She wept for the sternness of her upbringing, the stone heart of her father, the beaten down repression of her mother, the hatred of the world. She wept for her loss of innocence, the barriers between people, the rigidity of her stance, her broken wholeness.

Her heart had cracked open and shattered. It was now melting. She wept for all the pain of the world.

André wept for the terrible abuse, the whippings, the beatings, the sexual torture. He wept for the vicious attacks that were heaped upon him every day. He wept for the terror, the mortification, the frozen, petrified fear, the unendurable horror he had continually endured. He wept for the loss of his mother, the loneliness of his childhood, the other children's malice.

He wept for the desolate, the unwanted, the abandoned, for the loss of innocence, purity, love and God. He wept for the starving, the maimed and the wounded. He wept for the loss of wholeness and the agony of the world.

Their weeping began to subside. The love that was being given began to seep in. The deepest wounding they had forever sustained more fully healed. They finally became quiet.

There was a growing feeling of divine peace in the room.

"Please help me stand," Alena said.

Gabriel backed away and Lakane lifted her to her feet.

"Thank you, everyone," she said, "let me go to the bathroom and wash my face."

"We have two," Eva announced.

"Oh, please help me too!" André pleaded.

Eva and Anani helped him up and he bolted out of sight.

Alena sat to pee and thoroughly cleansed her face.

André sat on the throne and passed the most humongous turd of his life. He emptied his bladder and sighed. For the very first time, he felt thoroughly safe. For the very first time, he felt wanted and happy. He marveled at the feeling of being home with his family. He marveled at the feeling of being utterly content.

He cleaned himself, washed and returned to the living room. His face and body were radiant. Alena had not yet returned.

Eva came to him and took him in her arms. She was a little taller than he. His head fit perfectly in her neck.

"Welcome to our family you dearest boy," she murmured.

"Thank you, mama, I'm finally home."

"Yes, my darling. You are so wanted here."

Then Alena emerged. Her face without makeup was as stunning as with. But it made her more tender and vulnerable.

She smiled a bit shyly. It lit up her face. She stood there the only one clothed.

"I guess I made a spectacle of myself."

"The most beautiful spectacle I've ever seen," Eva said. "You just helped heal the world in ways you haven't begun to imagine. You've been carrying a very heavy burden for a very long time, my love. It was beautiful to see you drop it."

She held out her arms and Alena stepped into them. They held and hugged for several moments and then Eva disengaged.

"And you, my precious puppy," she turned to André. "What a prize you are! The pain you've endured! You have done the work of titans! I'm so very proud of you!"

André stood up tall and straight and gave her his biggest smile. It made him want to cry again. A few tears did come to his eyes. It also healed him even more.

"Thank you, mama, I'm not used to being loved."

"Well here you are and will be."

Eva turned back to Alena.

"Tell us what you want, my darling."

"I want to join this family."

"Well, ALLL RIIIIGHT!" Lakane boomed.

Everyone laughed, hooted and applauded.

Alena laughed along with them.

"But you have to do penance for being such a holdout," Eva admonished. "Let's all sit on the couch," she said, taking the middle.

"Gabe," she patted to her right. "Anani," to the left. "André," she thumbed to her right. "Lakane," she pointed to the left.

They all sat.

"You're penance is to stand before us, take off your clothes and do everything I tell you. Then you have to kiss me three times on the lips. After you've done this you'll be totally absolved and free to go about your love and pleasure as you wish."

"With your permission, may I kiss your other lips three times as well?"

"Ooooweee," Lakane sang softly and sweetly.

They chuckled and laughed again.

"With my permission and delight."

Alena removed her clothing and stood before them.

She was magnificent.

"Kneel," Eva said.

Alena dropped to her knees and sat back on her heels.

"That's kneel down," Eva said. "Come up on your knees."

Alena complied.

"You saw me stand with my legs apart. I want you to kneel with your knees apart. Find that magical position where they're as far apart as they can be but you can still hold the position for a long time."

Alena spread her legs almost to the maximum.

"That looks like a strain. Could you hold that for long?"

She brought her knees in a little.

"Find the best possible position."

Alena edged her knees a tiny bit closer and finally felt the position. It felt good. She could hold this. Her pussy stirred.

"Beautiful. Perfect. You can feel it, yes?"

"Yes," Alena said throatily. "It feels good."

"Good girl," Eva replied in kind. "Hold that for us, sweetheart. You're breaking my heart. Look at her! Don't you want to lie on your back and lick it?"

And indeed they did. The sexual energy in the room was rising again.

"This is 'kneel.' You can feel it. Remember it, all of you. Do this for me when I say 'kneel.'"

"You're the Alpha Goddess, darling," Lakane said dryly.

"Just for now, hot shot. I'll get tired of it. Then we'll all be equals. Give me this now. It's time a woman was in power. Let's redress the imbalance. Our vortex needs a locus and I'm it. This is turning me on."

"You're right. I defer. I surrender. It's about time I did. I just felt my testosterone rise. Forgive me. There will be no competition here. Old habits die hard."

"Indeed they do," Gabriel murmured.

"You're forgiven, Apollo. Just watch it. Three strikes and you're out. This is temporary. You'll soon have a harem in Africa. Here you're mine or gone. Everyone can say no. Always. I'm really just playing here. But I'm playing serious and you're a special case. So special I'll probably enjoy commanding you the most."

She turned back to Alena.

"OK, sweetie, sit back on your heels."

This brought more of her pussy into view.

"This is kneel down. I want you all to remember these positions so I just have to say a word or two and you know what I want. Jawohl?"

"Ja!" A few of them chorused. But they all got it.

"Kneel."

Alena came up, her knees fixed wide.

"Kneel down."

Alena obeyed.

This aroused and fulfilled them all. They began responding as one.

"Kneel."

Alena came up.

"Now feel the angle in the inside of your knees. It's as ninety degrees as it can get. Your thighs are perpendicular to the floor. Try to keep the lower part of your body exactly as it is and come down onto your elbows for me."

Alena obeyed. Her breasts hung down gloriously.

"Keep your knees where they are and bring your torso a little forward. You sat back a little as you came down."

Alena inched her upper body forward.

"A little more."

And she did and felt it. Her bottom was as high and open as it could be, everything between her legs spread apart as beautifully as possible. A wave of shakti shot from her pussy.

"Good girl! Everyone felt that, right? This is shakti, feminine power. Anani felt it shooting from my pussy into hers and up through her body. Sometimes it can be so strong you can see it. Bring your head down, sweetheart. Bring your forehead to the floor. Place your hands flat touching the top of your head. Put your thumbs and index fingers together."

Alena complied. She complied perfectly.

"Look at her," Eva said. "Have you ever seen such a masterpiece?"

And was she ever. The stunning image of her beauty in this position of worship, obedience and surrender appeared to be the most beautiful thing our Earth could offer. They were all entranced. And Alena's wide-open crotch and body were creating waves of pheromones wafting into the air.

"Such a goddess you are, my perfect, beautiful pussy. My perfect slave. This is 'bow.' Remember it. We'll all be surrendering to each other but I want you all to surrender to me. I don't know why. This is totally new to me. I would never have behaved anything like this in the past. But it's coming to me quite strongly and I trust it. In usual circles this might seem quite sick. But feel the Eros in the room. I believe we're creating something magnificent here."

"Let your seat come down to your heels, sweetie."

Alena sank down.

"This is bow down."

"Bow."

Alena came up and found her position.

"A little forward."

She edge into it perfectly.

"Bow down."

And she was there.

"Just one more, darling, then you can kiss my lips. Kneel."

Alena came up into it.

"Now turn around and kneel with your back to us."

Alena did.

"This is 'kneel away.' Now bow."

Alena found it perfectly.

"Beautiful. This is the same position but look at what it reveals to us."

"The Perfectly Accessible Goddess," Gabriel said.

The loving way he said it, coupled with the fact that Alena knew he was seeing and adoring every part of her, caused another bolt of shakti to fly from her pussy directly into his face. It was so strong they could see it as faint energy.

"Oh Alena," Eva said. "You are so very good at this. All that repressed love can now fly out of you. You're my Perfectly Accessible, Obedient Goddess. This is what I want of you. Do you understand?"

"Yes."

"Are you willing?"

"Yes, I'm willing."

"Good girl. That's what I want, you're willingness."

Everything between Alena's legs was spread as high and wide open as it could possibly be. Her anus stood forth and shined, preciously, beautifully. Her pussy was magnificent.

As Eva enjoyed this display, the thought came to her, "Jack and Alena, yes."

"Alena," she said, "you are precious and perfect and good. Every part of you is sacred and right. There is nothing wrong with you anywhere. God loves you. God loves your pussy and your anus. He made them for you and gave them as a great gift. This is 'two.' Open position number two. It's the same as 'bow' but for orientation. It's very hard for us women to fully reveal our genitals. This is one way. You can imagine 'one.' When I say 'two,' this is what I want, male or female. Remember these positions. I am now your dominatrix. I'll never use whips or ropes or induce pain. I have no interest in that. I want your love and willingness, not to force or bind you. Make it easy for me. I want to teach you many things. Your surrender is the most beautiful thing you can give me. Now come and kiss me you impossibly gorgeous thing."

Alena came up and out of her position and knelt before Eva who opened her legs for her to come in close. They brought their lips together, closed mouthed, lips puckered, and held it for a moment. They pulled apart and moved back a little to look into each other's eyes. Eva licked her lips. Alena did the same. They brought them together again. This time Eva slipped her tongue slightly into Alena's mouth. Alena responded in kind. They felt each other's tongues for a moment and then disengaged. They pulled back to gaze. Everyone gazed at them with pleasure. They were all showering the totality of their attention on their budding intimacy.

The third time they tilted their heads, opened their mouths and sealed their lips together, fully extending and taking turns sucking and licking their tongues. It was ecstatic and delicious. The added awareness of their loving witnesses created a gestalt that amplified the experience. Finally, they gave a few touches and licks and came apart.

"I love you, Alena, welcome to our family."

"Thank you. May I love your other lips?"

Eva paused, looking into Alena's eyes.

"You truly want to?"

"I truly want to."

"Say 'please.'"

"Please."

"Say 'please let me lick you.'"

"Please let me lick you."

"I'll worship you there whenever you want."

"I'll worship you there whenever you want."

"And that's true?"

"Yes."

"So good, my precious pussy. That will give me great delight. Let's all get up and stretch a bit first."

They all stood.

Eva hugged Alena and whispered in her ear, "Alena, my darling, I can't tell you how glad I am you allowed yourself to heal and join your love with us. You're a perfect treasure. I want to feel your face in my pussy and see your love for Gabriel and all of us totally fulfilled. And I believe there's something coming even more wonderful. Surrender to God's bounty. You've been deprived for so long. Yes?"

"Yes."

"Good."

They disengaged.

"Gentlemen, could you put those two ottomans together in the middle parallel to the window?"

And it was done.

"Beautiful. Everyone gather round."

She sat on the edge of one of the ottomans and lay back. The two together were long enough to leave a little space above her head. She lifted her legs, knees bent, and spread them wide. She placed her arms out and up, elbows bent.

"This of course is 'one.' Open position number one. *The* primal position. Alena, darling, I want you to extend your tongue out and down and with the full, wide flat of it, as much as possible, lick my pussy from the bottom to the top with a long, firm stroke."

Alena masterfully did it.

"Oh God, yes" Eva said as the pleasure filled her. "That's 'lap.' When I say lap that's what I want. Now lap it three times in a row."

Watching this aroused and delighted them all. And it gave both Eva and Alena great pleasure.

There was so much beauty, the two heartbreakingly beautiful women in such gorgeous positions doing such pleasurable things to each other.

Only Lakane had seen this before. His women could be sexy and beautiful. But nothing could compare with this. Alone, each woman was a masterpiece. Together they were beyond words.

"So very good you are. Now lick my labia and clit."

Alena very consciously loved and licked Eva. This was a profound act of worship. With the tip of her tongue she sought and found the most sensitive pleasure nerve endings and stimulated them with endearing, searching motions. Then she licked and lapped fully and lushly all around and pressed into Eva's clitoris with her upper lip-cushioned teeth.

"Mmmm yes, so beautiful," Eva murmured, melting.

"Now press deep into my pussy and bless what you find."

The three men were quite hard. Anani was longing to join Alena or suck Eva's nipple. Eva read her mind and sent her a command to do so. Anani didn't hesitate a second. She knelt and pleasured and sucked it.

"A little harder and gently with your teeth," she mentally commanded her. "Suck my nipple, my perfect cunt. *Yoouu'rre* going to lick my *aaasss.*"

"Oh yes, yes, yes," Anani thought back. "Make me your slave. Please. I want it more than anything. I'll do anything."

Eva sent a message to Gabriel. He knelt and sucked her other nipple. She reveled in the joy of the three heavenly things all happening at the same time. The perfect pleasure rippled out from those three points and filled her entire body. She moved and arched and ran her fingers through Gabe and Anani's hair.

André and Lakane looked on rock hard.

"When will I get to stick it in?" Lakane thought.

"Soon my darling, yours in mine," Eva thought back.

She had been feeling the lust of all of them through their bodies and minds. For her, they were one love/lust animal with six bodies.

Lakane looked into her open eyes staring straight at him, loving him. He melted.

"I'm learning by the minute," he thought to her, "Please help me."

"I am but you don't need my help. You can go ask them anything anytime. But you do need my help on the human level. I'll help you all I can if you'll help me back."

Then, "Oh God," she said out loud. "This is what a golden family can DOOO! OK my loves. Alena has paid her penance. She's a full-fledged member. I release my hegemony over everyone but Anani. You're free to follow your desire."

Alena looked up to Gabriel. He came to her and helped her to her feet. They lay down on the couches by the window in each other's arms.

Gabriel put his lips to her ear and whispered, "I love you."

She curled up and snuggled in closer.

They both knew his allegiance was to Eva.

But they knew he could love her as well.

And he knew Alena loved him.

They were content.

They slowly began the process of knowing each other intimately. It was gentle and quiet and precious. They had all the time in the world now.

Eva got up and went off to a smaller couch with Anani. It was just the right length for the two them. They embraced and continued their journey.

This left Lakane and André.

Lakane looked at the boy-man's face and body. Their cocks were still hard. They looked down at each other for a minute. Then Lakane looked around the room and chose two easy chairs inclined towards each other but also towards the window.

"Let's talk," he said.

They went and sat down.

They looked in each other's eyes for a moment.

"Are you gay?"

"No, I'm perfectly balanced right down the middle, fifty-fifty bi."

"Really?"

"Yes."

"You have no preference."

"I love them both, certain members of each sex. I love beauty, health and goodness."

"That's very rare."

"I know, in the normal world. Almost all the bis I know have a preference. But look at Eva. She's acting pretty bi. Maybe it's healthy."

"Maybe. You must be important to them for good reason."

André looked at him. Important. Me. It was a new thought to him.

"Does my type appeal to you?"

"Oh yes, more than almost any!"

"And me in particular?"

"Oh yes, more than almost anyone."

"Have you been with anyone like me?"

"Yes, once. One man took a liking to me. But he was nowhere close to *you*."

"How was it?"

"It was OK. He wasn't very nice."

"You know I've never let a man anywhere near me."

"Yes, I would assume so."

"I'm trying to wrap my head around it."

André had nothing to say to that.

"You sure have pretty skin and a pretty mouth."

"Why thank you sir!"

"I could imagine that mouth around my cock."

"I could too!"

"Why don't you check your bank account? Maybe you're rich, too. Come back and tell me."

André went to his phone and checked. He came back in wonder.

"They added a million."

"Excellent. Wanna go to the moon?"

"Sure!"

They disappeared.

Chapter 15

The Heavenly Choir

Lakane and André hung naked in space about five miles above the moon. They looked at each other and then back down.

"What do you think?" Lakane thought into André's mind.

"I can barely comprehend it."

"It does stretch your boundaries doesn't it?"

In a blink they were standing on the surface. Their bare feet felt a powdery dust. They felt no iota of cold or lack of oxygen.

"God, what technology!" André mind-exclaimed.

"I'll say."

Next they were far enough away so it looked like a big house.

"What a trip we're on!" André exclaimed again.

The next thing he knew they were on a tiny, tropical island with a lot of sand and three palm trees.

"LEEET'S GOOO FOOR A SWIIIIIIIM!" Lakane bellowed at the top of his voice and bounded into the ocean.

They hooted and howled in the mild ocean surf and laughed and laughed, giddy with the thought of what they were doing and all the things they could do. They felt like seven year olds in toy paradise.

"How's this for some bonding experience?"

"Thank you so much brother, it's beyond anything I could express."

"You're welcome. Let's get some sun."

They swam ashore and walked onto the beach.

Lakane gauged the angle of the sun and got into a version of position two so the rays could bless his anus.

"Visuals only for now. You can look at me as long as you like and join me when you wish. This is Daoist thing. Very nourishing for your asshole, colon and sex drive. Don't block the rays."

André looked and looked and looked. It was an amazing sight this man's wide-open crotch lit up by the tropical sun. So many colors, so many textures, so many folds and wrinkles. He wanted to lick and nibble and suck and hoped it wouldn't be too long before he could. His cock began to lift upright.

"Mind if I enter your mind?" Lakane asked.

"Not at all, please."

Lakane felt his arousal, his longing and desire. He could see himself through André's eyes and how attractive he was to him. It created an erotic feedback loop colored and augmented by a bit of narcissism. His cock hardened in response.

"Maybe brother," Lakane thought to him. "Maybe soon."

André got into 'two' beside him and they soaked up the rays.

Then they lay on their backs for a while.

"One more dip and then a shower," Lakane said.

They ran into the ocean.

"Swim out with me!" Lakane shouted

He was far the stronger swimmer but he held back and André did the best he could to keep up. They got pretty far, stopped, turned around and tread water.

"Nice vacation, huh?"

"Nicest one I've ever been on."

Lakane pulled them to an isolated, private waterfall he knew in Hawaii.

He held them in the middle of the stream and turned them in slow somersaults and twists.

All the salt was washed away.

Then he took them high in the sky to air and sun dry, far enough to be specks from the ground.

He put himself in two again, anus to the sun, and put André about two feet under him to form 69.

The direct sun beating on him felt divine.

André's privates so close and aligned with his face were interesting. He was fully erect. There was a kind of beauty to his cock and balls. He imagined himself sucking.

What would be the harm, his macho image?

Most of that seemed to be draining away anyway.

He floated André a little closer.

The next thing he knew they were back in the condo on their feet.

Eva had pulled them in.

"Hi guys, havin' fun?"

"I'll say," André answered. "Doin' things no man has ever done."

"And some things they have."

She was back on the ottomans in position two with Anani kneeling on the floor behind her licking her pussy.

Gabriel was seated on the couch and Alena had him straddled. They were in coitus.

The sexual energy in the room was very strong.

André and Lakane got even harder.

"Anani darling, I want you to service André. You've been utterly perfect. I love you."

Anani backed away from Eva and stood up, her mouth smeared and filled with Eva's cum. She looked at André with a smile. He was red from the sun.

"Hey, where have you guys been?"

"Oh," André said, "I'll tell you when I'm inside."

"I can't wait to hear," she giggled.

"Apollo," Eva thought into Lakane's mind, "I want your cock inside me. If you spread your legs the height should be perfect. Enter gently at your own risk."

Lakane laughed into her mind. "I hear and obey, my goddess. There's nowhere in the universe I'd rather be."

He took his cock in his hand, bent his knees and bent over a little to point it directly towards her and to run the tip along her labia and slightly inside to lubricate in preparation for entry. Eva liked it just fine. It gave her waves of pleasure. She was so wet from the delicious blend of her own cum and Anani's saliva that his giant organ slipped right in. He pressed in firmly, hips to butt, cock head to cervix.

"Oh yes, my Nubian god," Eva thought to him. "This is what I love you for."

It felt stunning to her.

Lakane smiled in her mind and extended his legs outward to straighten them. He found the perfect position where he could thrust and move standing fully upright. He looked down at her beauty and felt fully home for the first time in *his* life. He gave her the vision of his cock inside her beauty and the feelings in his heart and soul. It melted her towards him and created a feedback loop of erotic love.

While thus fucking, they began an inner conversation at the speed and ease of thought. It formed a new order of intimacy.

"How beautiful you are! Can we drop Lakane and call you Apollo till you find your Nubian name?"

"Yes please, I'm quite tired of it and I like Apollo."

"Beautiful. Do your thing, sir. Don't hold back. I'll let you know if it gets to be too much."

They made love with their bodies and the united experience of their images, concepts and feelings, hearts, minds and souls. It was the most total experience they had ever had, each fully in every part of the other, two enhanced, godlike ring bearers in total union together.

At one point Eva thought, "What's going on with me? I've never been anything like this. Do you think I'm siphoning off some of your dominance?"

"Yes I do. I had the same thought. And it's a relief to have less of it. You took some in our very first encounter."

"But where do I get 'position number two' and the rest of it?"

"I'd have my women get into every position I wanted and to move and shake on command. We had black culture codes like 'walk the dog' and 'strut it harder.' But I didn't give positions or tongue strokes names or numbers. That's brilliant. Speak a word and they obey. Maybe you're just smart or it's from another life."

Something opened in Eva's subterranean psyche and she got a very strange image. She let it go for now.

"Have you ever said, 'Suck my cock, cunt, you're going to lick my ass?'"

"Oh yes."

"That power thing really jacks it up doesn't it?"

"Oh yes."

"Do you like having your ass licked?"

"Oohh yeeeesss."

They were all making love now. No one had come. Apollo was jerking and thrusting a little harder, moving around in different, delightful ways. He would change his angle to press and stimulate all the different surfaces of Eva's exquisite, smooth, slippery, warm vaginal canal. He would give rapid-fire, repeated, little, short thrusts and magnificent, powerful, body-shaking, long ones that slammed his hips into Eva's bottom causing all the delectable flesh there and in her breasts to bounce and shake and ramming her cervix sending shock waves through her womb, fallopian tubes and ovaries.

Eva found it all transportingly, intensely pleasurable. He would just come to the point where it was a hair too much and then he'd pull back. He was a truly masterful lover.

"Ohh your goood! Maybe we should call you King Kock," she thought to him.

"I do my best, sweetheart, in all things," he chuckled. "Maybe that's why they gave me the ring. But I've never been this good. You and the healing have brought it out in me. I wasn't so concerned for the woman's pleasure, only my own. I'm a different man."

"Or the very best version of the man you always wanted to be. Do you think we could find the hypothalamus and the nucleus accumbens and enhance our orgasms?"

"You know more about it than I do. You lead, I'll follow."

They scanned and touched and prodded Eva's brain together. They tracked the neural pathways.

"Hit me harder, baby, make it start."

Apollo started moving into high gear.

"Oh yes, that moved me towards it. Did you see those two parts of my brain light up?"

"Yes."

"Those are they. Go find them in Anani and André and you stimulate them in the three of us. I'll take you, Gabe and Alena."

"OK everyone," Eva thought to them all, "Let's start going for it now and build it up over the next few minutes. I want to try something."

They began to thrust and move more strongly, to quicken the pace, to increase the stimulation.

She held her mind in all of them and located Apollo, Gabe and Alena's come centers. She could see that Apollo was with hers, André's and Anani's. She had him hold those places and extend his mind to them all as well. She was able to modulate their ardor slightly dampening Gabe and Alena and amplifying André and Anani. They all began feeling what they all were feeling. It was astonishing to directly perceive the similarities and yet the different flavors. And it was all pleasure. Three couples and six psyches were all fucking each other.

"I love you guys," their minds perceived. "All together, nooooowwwwwww."

She and Apollo pumped their love, joy and pleasure into all of them. Their pooled ardor shot to the sky.

"Now," she thought to Apollo, "prolonged, multiple orgasms wherever possible."

They all started to come in a tidal wave of nearly excruciating ecstasy. As Eva suspected, multiple orgasms were not wired into the male apparatus. But she and Apollo could create a semblance of that by amplifying and prolonging the men's release. All three women had the three most powerful, mutually shared orgasms of their lives. Eva could see the marvelous contractions of all their wombs and could enhance them directly as well. It was staggering. All their brains were firing like the Fourth of July. And they were sharing their experiences as one in an over-group mind/body experience none of them would ever have conceived of. It brought them together like nothing else could. They were one, big, loving gestalt bonded to the core, six people becoming one over-soul.

They remained in each other as the tsunami subsided.

Finally, the three couples slowly extricated themselves.

Eva turned on her side and thought to Apollo, "Bring your cock here, lord, I want to taste our cum."

He came around to her.

"Bring it down to mama."

He bent his knees and found a way to put it in her mouth without her having to lift her head.

"Mmmmmmhhm," she half hummed, half murmured as she sucked in her cum from his surface and milked a few drops from within.

"Mmm, very good," she said out loud. "Gabe darling, how do we all lie down together?"

"I guess we get sheets, blankets and pillows and put them on the carpet."

"Could the men go gather a nest for us queen bees? Bring all the blankets."

They were soon situated all over each other with just sufficient cushioning beneath.

"So now you all know what a controlling bitch I am. Anyone want to bail?"

Everyone laughed. They knew that nothing else on the planet could come close to this. They also knew they were central to the healing of humankind. None of them would have left for the world. They were totally blissed out.

"We're calling Lakane Apollo now. Apollo, darling, show them what you did with André before I yanked you back."

Utter silence then hoots and shouts, "Oh no, when do we get to go!"

"Let's recover from this first, darlings. And then let's shower and go out. Or should we just stay in and have delivery?"

"Stay in, delivery!" everyone wanted.

They all laughed and bounced on each other's bodies. They felt like the happiest of eight year olds but with the best perks of maturity.

"I did want to say something about my dominance. Apollo and I think I'm siphoning off some of his. I can't imagine this'll be my personality for the rest of my life."

After a moment of consideration Gabriel offered, "I think we've all been balancing each other out. Alena and I experienced that in our union."

"André and me, too" Anani said. "I've been all out Sappho. That boy's making me positively bi."

André flushed.

"Oh good," Eva said. "I can blame Apollo."

"You can blame me for anything, queen, as long as you let me put it in you again."

"Oh yes, no fear on that account. But I think André is next."

André laughed, "Oh please, please, pleeeaaase."

Apollo and Eva laughed.

"OK, what's the best delivery?"

"Portable Chef," Apollo offered.

Everyone else was silent.

"Yoouuu'rrre the one who knoooows?"

"Why not? I know a lot of things no one else knows. Who knew that Dao thing?"

"I did," Gabriel and Anani both said.

"Ah, saved by my darlings. Gabe and Anani are still my greatest loves. Sorry, mamas have favorites. But boy is my heart larger than it was this morning."

They all knew what she meant. They all felt it too.

"I do believe we have a golden family. I'm so STOOOOOKED!" she roared more mightily than any of them would ever have thought possible.

They looked at her, all quite startled except Apollo.

"Let's tone," André offered.

"Say what?" Apollo said.

"I thought you knew everything."

"No, just some things most others don't."

André sang out the most beautiful, high pitched, ringing note and held it.

The others began to join in.

They played with tones and harmonies for five minutes. It became deeply rich and moving. They all had beautiful voices and good ears. A heavenly choir. Apollo, of course, had a powerful, rumbling bass, basso profundo really, Gabe a warm, rich baritone, André a sweet, high tenor, Alena a strong, evocative contralto, Eva a happy, lilting alto and Anani the clearest, most touching soprano. Eva had a thought. Her phone rang. They stopped. The phone stopped.

Jimmy wasn't surprised when he perceived Eva's mind within him telling him to stop the call.

"I always knew you could do anything, goddess."

He directly perceived her mirth.

"I love you, Jimmy. Wow, the Riverside Church. Start at the top I say."

"I have an in and they had a cancellation."

"Wonder how that could possibly happen. There'll be six of us and we'll sing before I make them all disappear. Call us the Heavenly Choir."

She smiled at her family.

"We're going to sing for the congregation of the Riverside Church tomorrow. We'll arrive at eleven-fifteen wearing anything we want semi-suitable for church. I want them to love us, not be shocked. We'll sing for as long or as short as we want. They'll call us the Heavenly Choir. And I'll send them off as soon as we're done. This is what it's about folks. Bringing heaven here in every way we can.

Bringing on the looovve. So how do we order from Portable Chef?"

Gabe went to get his phone and laptop for its bigger screen.

"Shall I read the menu?"

"No, give it to our Nubian waiter. He'll take orders."

He passed his laptop to Apollo who put the contents of the menu in all their minds. He registered all their desires and toyed with the idea of putting the order into the mind of someone there.

Eva mind spoke to him, "Maybe that's overstepping. We don't want to give anyone a heart attack. Better safe than sorry."

Apollo looked up, "Gabe, please hand me your phone."

He called in the order and gave them his memorized card number.

And then he said, "Jeffrey Jackson, j e f f."

They all looked at him.

"My, myyy," Eva said.

She already knew from being in his mind. But it was the perfect thing to say.

"Has anyone seen As It Is In Heaven?" Alena finally spoke.

"Oh yes," André replied.

No one else had.

"They sing like us at the end only more of them. The protagonist dies to it."

"Lovely," Anani said.

"Actually, it is, quite beautiful."

"No, I meant it literally. A lovely way to die."

"Yes of course, sorry."

"What's wrong, baby?" Eva asked.

"Oh I don't even want to say."

"We're your family. Say."

"It was so beautiful with Gabe and all of us together. The thought of leaving is making me sad."

"Don't leave. Spend the night here with him."

Eva checked internally with Gabe.

He mentally responded, "I miss you but tonight, yes."

Then out loud to Alena.

"Stay with me, darling. We deserve it after all this time."

Alena went from downcast to radiant in the blink of an eye.

"What time is it?"

Apollo checked Gabe's phone.

"Six-ten."

"So we had a four hour orgy."

"Give or take."

"Will you spend the night Apollo?"

"No honey, Saturday night in the city is prime time. I be workin'."

"When do you need to leave?"

"About nine."

"Good, I want a powwow. Who else wants to spend the night?"

"Oh me!" Anani and André ejaculated together.

"Oh good! Two for me. We get the master bedroom."

She winked at Gabe. He totally understood. It was perfect.

He smiled warmly.

"So we all powwow after dinner, dressed. I believe we'll have a guest. Anani dear, come help me shower."

On her way she thought to Apollo, "Do you think there's a way we can instantly know the time? I'm getting that it'll be critical."

"I don't know. I'll think on it. Our way of keeping time is so arbitrary. It's not part of the natural world."

"I know. I'll ask them. I'm sure they have a way."

Chapter 16

We Are the First

Eva held Anani close as the water poured down on them through their magnificent showerhead.

She united their minds in the totality of fullness so they experienced and perceived every aspect of each other.

They were one being with two bodies and two beings with the full experience of all the other's thoughts, feelings and sensations. It was delicious.

Eva disengaged and had Anani soap, scrub and brush her. She guided Anani's hands and fingers onto every part of her body—her belly, her back, her legs and her feet. It was wonderful, as if she had a second body to wash her but in the form of another beautiful person. All the places she couldn't reach were so easily reached. She had Anani's hands linger and squeeze perfectly on her breasts and nipples. Since she was directing it couldn't have been done better.

Eva had her lovingly and carefully clean every part of her pussy, moving, massaging and pleasuring every lip, fold and crevice as she cleaned her with the viscous, sensual body gel.

Last was her anus.

She had Anani run the length of it and massage it with her fingertip, gently rub around it and slip her finger just inside. It was surprisingly and delectably fulfilling.

She thought her thoughts into their united mind.

"Good girl, love and adore my asshole for me. Clean it beautifully. Your luscious tongue may soon be worshipping me there."

"I'm ready my goddess. I want to. I beg you. I long to lick you no matter what may be there."

The image from Anani's mind of her drinking Eva's piss and licking in shit from her asshole, shining and cleansing it with her tongue, slipping it deep inside to pleasure and cleanse as completely as she could, taking some in her mouth and swallowing it down, sent a wave of radical pleasure and relief through Eva's entire alimentary canal and body.

This shocked and surprised her.

It was at once ultimately fulfilling and revolting.

"Where do these desires and pleasures come from? Are we slipping into the satanic side?"

"No my love. Everyone has them deep inside, hidden away, bottled up. Some people express them on the street. Where I live you hear, 'Lick my ass! Eat my shit! Drink my piss!' It's always men, of course, trying to be more dominant than other men. But it's the crudest men with the least inhibitions that are most in touch with such things. We have them within us, too."

"And you'll do this for me?"

"Yes. I want to fulfill everything within you that wants to be fulfilled. I want to love and heal everything."

"But isn't it sick?"

"No, it's sickness healing. You know that millions of people in India drink their own urine every day. They go up to cows in the field and drink theirs. Many in Laos are similar. We don't have the horror and aversion your culture has. We believe it gives our bodies direct feedback on its imbalances and helps correct them. But doing it for another person brings about the deepest surrender. It's like sharing water. You know what golden showers are for gay men. Piss in my hair. Piss in my face. Piss on my belly and pussy. We could love that, too. Shit is harder. But shit is shit. We all have it. We create it out of the precious food that supports and sustains us. It's good to move beyond our horror of it. I won't be able to take a lot in. But I'll take some if you ever want me to. I want to show you how much I love every part of you, every aspect, every function, even your shit. How many people say holy shit? They're expressing their unconscious needs and desires—to move beyond their disgust and more. And in a way, it's true. We're wired to be repelled by it. It can be harmful. You have to be careful. But a little won't hurt you. Especially us. We're perfectly healthy. And if something did occur, you could heal me or send me to a chamber. Aren't they opening people up surgically and putting other people's shit in there now, probably the surgeon's? That's the stupidest thing I've ever heard of. Just find the right probiotic.

Don't be afraid, my love. Love and surrender are great sublime powers. They have no judgment, no disapproval, no rejection of anything that is. My love accepts all that you are without resistance. The more we love everything, the more we perceive our identity as love. At least let me lick you any moment you might want even if you're not clean. I want to. I'm yours. You said it to Alena. Every part of you is sacred. There's nothing wrong with you, anything of you. I love everything of you. I surrender to everything of you. I'll eat your shit. I'll drink your piss. I'll be your toilet girl. Let my mouth be your toilet and my belly. Piss in my loving open mouth. Shit in it. I'll swallow it down for you. It is part of who you are and how you function. You have loved it in your mouth and it's been through you. I'll love it in my mouth and take it through me. I'll do anything you ever may want. It's love transforming horror and disgust to acceptance. It's the ultimate act of surrender."

Something welled up from the deepest recesses of Eva's hidden psyche. For the first time in forever she remembered the terror she felt as a toddler when her mother first tried to teach her to release her effluents into the toilet. It felt like she was sitting on a cliff and would fall through and die. She remembered the visceral waves of her mother's annoyance, impatience and revulsion hitting her like a sledgehammer. She remembered how dirty it made her feel, like some kind of terrible, hideous monster. She broke out in sobs. Her body shook and she wept aloud. Anani was feeling everything of her from within and was crying, too.

They wept for themselves and the human condition. They wept for the collective and the world. They wept for all the children throughout history who were made to feel dirty. They wept for all people who were made to feel that their sex and bodies were dirty. They wept for all the blocked desire and passion, the frustration, the impossible longing, the history of the distortions of mangled, suppressed, hated love, the degradation heaped upon all that was good and happy. They wept for the supreme insanities of mutilating and sewing up little girls' vaginas and binding their feet. They wept for God on Earth. They let the water wash away their tears and pain. They returned to their love.

"Who taught you to be so accepting, so willing?"

"I taught myself. And it's my nature. Somehow my life has been meant for this. It's all I thought about, wanted and studied. I have other sides, of course. But this has been my life. I understand both, the fulfiller and the fulfilled. We need both. You will want to fulfill me. But I don't need that so much in this life. It is divinely given that I am here to serve and fulfill you. You are the one who needs it now. You are the vortex for the world's healing. You've been telling the others how they've been healing the world. We just did our little part. And you have so much more to do. You are my mistress. I have found you. I am here to serve you. We are doing the most important thing that anyone has ever done. We are the first. This is my role. I augment your vortex. I was made for this. I am yours."

"My partner, my lover, my handmaiden."

"Yes, and your dasi—your adoring and willing acolyte and slave. This is not dominance. Dominance is forcing others to your will. This is divine play. This is sublime. Surrender to this Eva, as I surrender to you. This is what is needed now. This is what we both want. Ultimately, in whatever life it may be, we all surrender to God. This human experience of command and surrender is a beautiful gift, a precursor of what is to come. You are my living, breathing, utterly desirable Goddess. I have never seen anyone I have wanted so much. I'm in love with you. God has brought this about for very good reason. You need satellites revolving around you. I am infinitely grateful that your gravity has pulled me in."

"And you are my treasure, my love, my oracle and healer," she whispered with her lips caressing the orifice of Anani's ear as she gently disengaged mentally and then physically.

Eva didn't know if she would ever have Anani go that far but it made her feel strangely delicious to know that she was willing. It was settling, calming and empowering and made her feel more like a goddess than anything else. It also softened and humbled her.

She thought to herself of doing it for Anani or Gabe. It brought forth her revulsion.

"If I have such aversion perhaps I *should* do it for her."

She kissed Anani's lips.

"Wash yourself, dress and come to me. Your deepest surrender is a great blessing. I can't convey the relief and gratitude you give me. Perhaps it will save my life."

"You have my deepest surrender. Perhaps it will save all our lives."

Eva stepped out of the shower, took her towel and entered André's mind. He was in the living room waiting for a shower to become free.

"Come get in the master shower with Anani, my darling. I want you all washed and dressed as soon as possible. Do you want to serve me, too?"

"Oh yes, more than anything. Please take me. There's nothing I won't do!"

"Perfect, my love. I accept you totally for as long as it lasts."

She could feel the heavens rejoicing in his soul. His smile and body were radiant as he passed her in the bedroom on the way to the shower.

Eva sent her mind to Jack. He was at home alone. He wasn't that surprised to perceive her in his mind.

"Jack, are you free? There's someone I want you to meet more fully."

"Oh yes, quite free. Is there anything you can't do?"

"Yes indeed, a few things here and there. Spruce up and come here. Have you eaten?"

"No."

"Call Portable Feast and add your order to Jeffrey Jackson's. Tell them to charge it to his card."

"I'll get there as soon as I can."

She noticed commanding was easier now. It felt softer and stronger at the same time.

The hard, Lakane-like edge had been mellowed.

Apollo had given her what she needed.

Anani had healed, softened and empowered her.

The healing, growing process continued after the angels' work.

She knew that all healings everywhere helped the whole world.

But these particular healings were working a new and different kind of wonder.

She and her pod were alchemizing dominance and submission into perfect leadership and followership. No hitch. No hesitation. Command, obey—convey, complete—hear, do—know, actualize.

She was surrendering to God and they were surrendering to her.

The coordination of their unit had to be flawless.

What a way to learn!

They were all dressed and ready when Jack arrived.

Since he knew all the doormen, the bell rang.

André let him in.

"He looks amazing!" Eva thought.

And he did, like a different man. He always had a handsome face. And there was something about him. But it had been almost completely covered over. Before he was likable but masked and broken. This man was powerful, rugged and confident. He had a charisma and power that bespoke the best the military had to offer.

"Of course," Eva thought, "we need a soldier, a love warrior. We'll soon lose Apollo."

"Jack, that doorman's hat and uniform don't do you justice. Maybe it's time you lost them."

Jack smiled at her, "My sentiments exactly."

He looked around the room.

What an eyeful!

Every person looked radiant and fulfilled, irresistible, languid, cheeky and blissed out.

His glance lingered on Alena for a moment as their eyes met.

When he looked at Apollo there was a palpable charge of recognition, appreciation and testosterone, the respect of two warriors glad to be on the same side.

The doorman rang from below, "Portable Feast with your food."

"Send them up," Gabriel called out.

Eva glanced at their octagonal dining table. She knew she had loved it from the first. Now she knew what it was for.

They were soon eating and enjoying their feast.

Eva let them all take their time and chatter as they would.

It would soon get serious.

There was a lot of laughter, banter and love.

At one point André sang out 'All You Need Is Love.'

Gabe and Alena chimed in with dat da da da da.

The others all joined and they sang together for a few minutes quite impressively. Jack had a fine singing bass as well.

Alena and Jack kept catching themselves looking at each other.

Eva started calling him out.

"Jack, you reek of the military."

"Yes, I was a Green Beret in Iraq and Afghanistan."

"Ouch. Did you begin at eighteen?"

"Yes."

"So you're thirty-one now."

"Yes."

"You were wounded."

"Yes, unmentionably. I stepped on a mine in Afghanistan."

"And it blew your genitals away."

"Yes, and my toes and part of my feet and thighs."

"And now you're healed."

"And now I'm healed thanks to you," his voice breaking a little on his last words and a tear almost coming to his eye.

Eva left it at that.

They were all soon replete.

They pitched in for the cleanup and it was done in no time flat.

"OK chillen, powwow time. Let's make the best circle we can in the living room. Gabe, it's amazing how divine orchestration came right down to this dining table."

"I know. God is wise."

They mostly used the living room furniture. Eva didn't want a perfect circle of dining room chairs. They decided three could sit on the bay window couches and four would create a horseshoe-like arc facing them.

They stood and surveyed their work.

It was as good and comfortable as it could get.

Eva sat down in the middle of the couch.

She patted to her right, "Gabe," to her left, "Anani."

She pointed to the chair nearest Gabe, "Alena," to the one nearest Anani, "Jack."

To the one next to Jack, "André," to the one next to that, "guess who?"

This generated a gentle wave of mirth and love.

Jack could feel it. He marveled at its quality and universality. It seemed to come equally from all of them at once.

As soon as they were seated, Eva pooled their minds into one gestalt. They started sharing all their experiences one by one. She went counter-clockwise starting with Gabe. It was like nothing before experienced on Earth.

They all marveled at their similarities and differences.

The loving, healthy simplicity of Gabe's parents. The amazing smoothness of his life from its beginning to now. The devastating pain of the loss of his wife as the one major exception. How minor and few his other difficulties had been.

"The perfect person for the inception phase," Eva's thought interjected.

Alena's strict and stern upbringing. The suppression, repression and rigidity informing her personality and the rest of her life. Her rape at the age of fifteen. The horrors of guilt and self-inflicted abasement she had undergone as a result of it. Her fleeing her country to get away from it. Her fondest hopes of being with Gabriel. Her new hopes of what Jack might bring.

Apollo's development in the urban jungle. The horrors he had surmounted to attain a pinnacle in New York's crime empire. His judicious murders and extortions. The things he would have his women do—lick his ass, drink his piss, eat his shit, lick its residues off a plate—for the explosive sensations of kinky lust, ego empowerment, mastery and self-inflation it gave him, sensations that were both true and false. As a child of God he partook of God's grandeur—an eternal grandeur that needed nothing to inflate it. As a wounded man he needed to mask his unhealed terror, pain and helplessness with distortions of power, control and grandiosity, the story of hatred and violence the world over. But the amazing outcome of how he surmounted it all and come out as good as he had. And what he was now.

The tortures André had undergone almost non-stop from birth. His titanic longing to die that was with him so much. The beauty and pleasures he'd been able to eke out of his existence.

The wholesome, Kansas upbringing Jack had been blessed with. The zeal to serve his country, bond with his fellow soldiers, be a hero, make his father proud. The utter devastation of his disillusionment in seeing what his country, its institutions, policies and wars really were. The trauma of murder and battle and how it drowned his light in misery and nearly did him in. His determination to do his duty no matter what. The mine blowing his toes and genitals to bits. The beauty of his pristine, perfect body coming out of the healing. His joy in where he now was and his pull towards Alena.

"You'll be crying like a baby in our arms soon," Eva thought to him, sharing it with them all. "The healing continues, ours and the world's."

Jack felt close to crying now.

The miracle of Anani's birth in Laos. The death of her loving mother and her coming here. The mission of her soul to love the feminine, cultivate surrender, elevate the goddess in women and make up for their suppression over the millennia of the Patriarchal Age. Her joy of finding Eva.

And then the brilliance of Eva's parents and the emphasis on the mental. Being the object of the lust of so many men. Despising them. The unconscious determination to do something magnificent for the world. The special, magnetic power that could rise like Everest around her. The love she had for them and they for her. Her communications with God's minions and her knowledge of the opposition.

It was all revelation.

They now knew each other better than almost anyone knew anyone. Even after a lifetime most couples knew less of their spouse than these seven knew of each other, their highest and lowest moments. There were no secrets nor need of them, no egocentric barriers or judgment capable of remaining within them. They knew with a directness available to few.

"Pod," Eva thought to them all, "let's call our unit a pod. We *are* a loving, golden family. We *are* a pod. Apollo will always be a pod member but as you saw, he'll be going off to Africa to form a pod of his own. I'm sure we'll all visit. Dolphin pods love meeting and playing together in the freedom of their ocean home. We have the freedom of the universe.

Jack, you weren't here for what you saw in our minds but we saw you want to join us. And we saw what you and Alena want. You're all caught up. You know everything we know. When you get through my initiation you'll be a full-fledged member.

Apollo will improve our city, our pod will initiate you and you and Alena will be together in bedroom three tonight. The more we do these things in conjunction from this love nest the more love we generate for the world.

Gabe, looks like you lost a partner. There will be another good time for that. We'll all get to be with every one of us to our hearts' content, at least if we win.

André, it's our turn but I don't think any of us are in need of more coitus tonight except for Jack and dear Alena who's been so deprived for so very long and is being newly inspired by Jack. And I'm missing my main man. So I think it'll be me and Gabe sleeping in one and you and Anani sleeping in two.

Alena, this is your gift from God for remaining so true. Gabe and Jack within several hours.

OK my loves, ask them whatever you wish."

And they vanished.

Chapter 17

They Are the Fulcrums

They were in a room new to Eva and therefore to all of them.

It seemed halfway between the forest chamber and the white rooms.

There were no objects. The colors of the floor, walls and ceiling were similar to the chamber but of a lighter hue so the room was brighter though dimmer than the white rooms. It was larger than the chamber and similarly shaped. And like the chamber, the colors moved and shimmered creating flashes of every other color but more subtly, less compellingly. About thirty people could fit. There were two light beings there.

Eva had brought her pod in with minds and experiences united.

She didn't know what would happen on this side but the devas left that intact and worked with them all together allowing all to receive what they delivered.

It began with a bridge of love uniting the light beings and the humans.

It started out gently but became stronger and stronger reaching the point where it felt to the humans like their bodies, hearts and minds would explode. It held at that intensity for several moments and then subsided.

"We enhance your containers for holding and radiating love. It is love that will transform your world. It is love that will protect you. Create and transmit as much love as you can. Living love on Earth will help your world heal. Moving in and through love will save you from destruction. Love turns everything sacred. You are ultimately nothing but love."

They showed them how the opposition was ruled by fear, power and greed.

They showed them that the human, Grey and Lizard opposition couldn't read their minds.

They showed them that if they moved too quickly or not inspired from within by love, they would frighten the opposition who would destroy to maintain their grasp on the world.

They showed them how to build the love slowly in accordance with divine orchestration, that any mass, arbitrary action would be counterproductive. It had to grow naturally like the living being it was. It couldn't be manufactured or forced.

They showed them how there would be eleven pods around the world surrounding eleven leader vortices each wearing a ring.

They showed them the third in Beijing newly healed, just returned, standing in wonder in his small apartment, the ring on his pinky.

Déwei, a lovely, sensitive man of thirty-five.

They linked their mind with his.

They amplified the love among them all.

Anani's response to him surprised her—such strong desire inspired by a man! They all of course felt it, their love for him and the strength of Anani's desire. It all enhanced their bond.

They left him to continue his recovery.

Then the colors became more active.

They became aware that this chamber was for the purpose of helping them know and connect more deeply with their own world.

Eve led but they all contributed.

They saw the world's fluctuating patterns of darkness and light, the pockets and streams where the opposition was most concentrated and held sway, the parts of the earth that needed love the most, the hidden centers of power from which the most important, secret directives came forth into the world.

At Eva's request she saw how the ring bearers could tap into the world's atomic clocks so that no matter where on the planet they might be they could instantaneously know the time and coordinate any necessary synchronized operations.

Eva and Apollo were also given an internal, three-dimensional map to help them locate and jump to any place on Earth they might want or need to be with or without others.

They were shown how certain key individuals could be bridges or liaisons between the benevolent and malevolent, people who could help swing the balance because they were deeply connected to both, people who were of the opposition but becoming disinclined. Not diplomats of state, but diplomats of love and control, healing and destruction, the God-charged and the Satanic, people who knew both but were coming back to the light.

"These we call balance points. They're already moving back towards God. They can be won and left unhealed. Then your love can move through them and soften their colleagues unaware. Each ring bearer will need to unite with a balance point. This will help us greatly. They are the fulcrums that will tilt your world back towards God."

Eva and Apollo were shown how they could jump to a chamber like this at any time to gain more knowledge or the status of any present moment.

Jack asked, "How do we fight?"

"We don't fight. We love and you circumvent their tendency to destroy."

"But if they're about to harm us or others?"

"Then yes, with any means at your disposal."

Gabriel asked, "Do I remain at the consulate?"

"Only if you wish. For our purpose you may leave any time."

Apollo asked, "When do I go to Africa?"

"Soon, when readiness arrives. At that time you will come to a chamber like this to learn more of your new area. You are almost done in your current environment."

They briefly showed him the world and history of his ancestry. From this he chose his new name, Nyame.

Anani asked, "Will I go to Laos?"

"Yes, your love will draw you there."

Jack asked, "Will we visit Iraq and Afghanistan?"

"Perhaps. Another pod will focus there."

André asked, "Why me?"

"Each soul is precious. Each has its time line. Yours is more precious than most."

Alena asked, "Do I stay at the consulate? And what of Jesus?"

"Like Gabriel, you may leave. Jesus is enshrined in your heart. This is beautiful and of your world. Most peoples choose one of their own to be their perfect God."

This was part of what they experienced and absorbed.

They reappeared in their love nest with much more.

They sat looking at each other for several moments.

Finally Nyame rose.

"Time for me to work."

They gathered around him and hugged him.

"Knock 'em dead," Eva said.

They chuckled and he left.

They took a drink and pee break. Then Eva had them all strip. She seated all but Jack on the line of couches.

"Initiation time soldier. Front and center."

Jack stood naked before them.

They all looked at him.

He looked at them.

The temperature and his cock started to rise.

"Stand."

He spread his legs.

"Kneel."

He sank to his wide open knees.

"Kneel away."

He turned around.

"Two."

He brought his shoulders, forehead and palms to the floor finding the position perfectly.

"Good boy, hold this for us."

Pause.

"Isn't he something?"

His cock was full on erect. His balls hung beautifully. His precious cheeks and anus were spread wide open, twinkling at them.

They could see his magnificent torso below.

They all remembered the image of his mutilated manhood.

Eva entered his emotional and energy bodies and found his grief center and remaining shadow and its link to the collective shadow of the world.

Jack began to feel something too big welling up within his heart and his soul.

Eva said, "I am so proud of you my perfect son, of everything you have ever tried, of everything you have ever done. There is nothing wrong with you anywhere. You have done nothing wrong. You are forgiven for everything. Everything now is as it's meant to be. You are so very perfect. You have our love. You are breaking our hearts."

In that moment, Jack's tidal wave broke forth. He wailed a quiet, desolate wail and broke into sobs.

They arose as one and helped him into the fetal position.

Eva and Gabriel lay on either side of him and held him. The others stroked, touched and lay hands on him.

He cried for the violence, murder and death all over the world. He cried for what he had seen and done. He cried for the mutilation of his body. He cried for its resurrection and perfection. He cried for his ignorance and the ignorance everywhere. He cried for those who could see but do nothing. He cried for his lost buddies and those who would soon die. He cried for his guilt over killing civilians and armed enemies in countries he had invaded. He cried for all the violation and trauma endured on Earth. He cried for all conflicts everywhere. He cried for the collective pain of the universe.

He cried till he was finally cried out. Then he settled into the peace, love and healing that saturated every one of them and spilled out into the pathways of the world. They helped him up and off to the bathroom. He emerged washed and clean.

"You're all spending the night here. Everyone is free to do as they wish. Tomorrow is Sunday. We sing at the Riverside Church. We have till eleven-fifteen. Gabe, let's retire. I may call any one of you at any moment. Till then you are free."

The three couples retired to their respective bedrooms. They all began to cuddle and whisper, laugh, sigh and cry for joy.

Eva and Gabe agreed all six of them should live together.

Within twenty minutes soft cries and moans of orgasm came from Jack and Alena.

"Good girl," Eva whispered into Gabe's ear and the minds of all her pod members, "your fourth come of the evening with no help from little old me. Jack, so glorious the return of your precious manhood."

Their gentle laughter and mighty love poured out of their bedrooms into the dark sky and rivers of light of Manhattan's upper east side feeding the world with more of the best of what it so very much needed.

They all slept like babies.

Chapter 18

You Are a Child of God

In the morning they showered in pairs, made breakfast together, ate, cleaned up and dressed.

Then Eva called for a powwow.

They sat in their living room horseshoe.

Eva spoke out loud.

"Anani, André and Jack, do you give notice or quit?"

They all said, "Quit!"

"Yes, that was my choice. The importance of this pretty much trumps everything. Go ahead and quit. But we know Gabe and Alena must find and train replacements. Gabe and I want you to move in as soon as possible. Do any of you want to keep your own place?"

André said, "No!" The rest were silent.

"Good, give notice and move in now. Does anyone have anything they want to ask or say?"

"Can we bring Déwei here and initiate him?"

A few loving chuckles.

Eva went silent and grew distant. Then she returned.

"Yes darling, it's lovely to see you interested in a man. We're set for eight tonight. You'll strengthen our bridge of love with him."

"I'm still yours."

"Yes my love. We have room in our hearts for great desires and great loves. Your desire for him is part of God's plan. I want you to offer your pussy and loving body to him as fully as you can. Surrender to this as you've surrendered to me. In so doing you are serving me. Your naked, open, arching body will be the bridge from our pod to his. You are drawn to him but I also send you. You will serve whoever I want. What better person than someone you want? I love you. You are mine and you are free."

In saying this Eva entered into every cell of Anani's body. She glorified them with love enhancing her attractive power and charisma. This would feed back and amplify Eva's as well. Though Eva shone far more brightly, the two would be like a binary star creating greater pulls of loving gravity. This she was simply moved to do from her love within. It's as if she didn't even have to think, just to respond to what arose before and within her. She was understanding and becoming like her deva allies more and more.

"Anything else? Good. Go and quit, give your notices and pack all you can for now to bring here. Go to your banks or ATMs and withdraw whatever cash you might want or need. Jack you should have been given a million, too. I will start you off by sending you there. Think of the branch or ATM you want to go to. Be ready at eleven-twelve. From wherever you are, I will pull you here or to the church."

Anani, André, Alena and Jack disappeared.

Gabriel and Eva were left alone.

It was ten o'clock.

Gabe smiled at her.

"Now what?"

"You got me," she smiled back. "What do you want?"

"I think I want to work out but to work God's plan whatever it may be."

"Beautiful. I love you darling. Why don't you move in that direction and see what happens?"

Anani had appeared by her ATM in Alphabet City.

A huge, fat, black woman slightly jumped and said, "Good lord child, where did you come from?"

"Heaven," Anani replied looking straight into her eyes.

Deep within the woman a sublime shift occurred.

Eva started moving towards a jog in the park.

As she did she began to have a sense that she had an appointment, some meeting, something important that she had to do.

She found her sexiest, black thong panties and put on her skimpiest, grey nylon running shorts split up the sides. This would allow her to flash the bottom of her bare cheeks if she so wished. She put on her slightly push up running bra and a brief halter cut off at the solar plexus to show the maximum amount of bare midriff, arms and shoulders. She completed with her running shoes and her lowest socks to keep her ankles bare.

She was ready for her appointment.

She sent a mental note to Jimmy letting him know there would be seven.

Then she willed herself straight to the park's nearby running path.

***

At the highest level of the topmost secret echelons was a small group above the law, above presidents, beyond the reach of any but themselves. They called their clearance Omega. No one else knew what they did but it opened all the other clearances to them. There were twelve of them. All were of the opposition. One was having doubts. The others didn't know he wasn't fully with them. He

101

didn't know himself. His name was Tom Stanton.

He was thirty-five, a true-blue, all out, all American patriot, ready to do or die for his country no matter what it might want of him. He had a beautiful, all American, twenty-nine-year-old wife named Ellie. She was petite, blonde and blue-eyed, wonderfully shapely, deeply devoted to her husband but more and more troubled by her desires for women which she was having more and more trouble suppressing. More and more she would pleasure herself to the thoughts of them. More and more she would be drawn to the beautiful ones on the street.

They had just had a cherub of a newborn baby boy they named Peter. Peter was born with a cleft palate. This, of course, deeply affected them both. But it was having an especially strange effect on Tom. It was adding to that which troubled him about his work, something that had been going on for some time and was becoming more and more difficult for *him* to suppress. Deep in his subconscious, he linked his son's harelip to the inner qualms he was having over his job. Specifically, he was beginning to feel that he wasn't working for America. He was working for some strange coalition of alien and foreign power brokers who had somehow taken over America. It was both implicit and often repeated that they were doing what was in America's best interests. But Tom was feeling more and more uneasy about this. He was liking his band of henchmen less and less. He was good at keeping up a solid front. The thought of in any way failing in his duty was unthinkable to him. There were two huge forces within him beginning to war. He wasn't yet consciously aware of this and the first real skirmish had not yet occurred.

They lived in Langley and he worked at CIA Headquarters as the liaison between Omega and all the other echelons. Though he didn't know it, he was the balance point for North America.

The Omega Group had come into existence in the late nineteen-forties shortly after the Greys had quietly begun to make themselves known to a few select men of power. The atom bombs dropped on Hiroshima and Nagasaki had drawn the first Greys to reveal themselves to the first humans they chose. In exchange for advanced technologies, they began to consolidate their connection to the power centers of the world. The opposition now consisted of a loose affiliation of ET Greys, Oranges and Lizards, small top secret groups around the world and the Illuminati and most of the heads of the oldest, wealthiest, human power families associated with them. Most of the ETs were renegades and pirates coming to adventure far from the galactic core. There were also a few of the ancient Annunaki who were not really of the opposition but were working in concert with them for reasons of their own. The ETs were both cooperative and competitive. This helped them all but also created weaknesses. There were chinks in their not quite monolithic attempt at Earth hegemony.

After Peter's birth, Tom and Ellie began doing their research. Peter would need a tremendous amount of care, special treatment and, of course, surgery. After extensively educating themselves and gathering information, they decided to use The New York Center for Facial Plastic Surgery. Its location was 990 Fifth Avenue just south of 77th, six blocks away from Eva and Gabriel's love nest.

Peter was now one month old. Tom had sent Ellie to bring him to their first appointment. His duties were keeping him in Langley and they knew this was just exploratory and informational. Nothing major would be done till Peter's third month. The real surgery would occur between nine and twelve months. Mostly they would learn how severe Peter's condition was and what they would need to do as he grew.

Tom had splurged and booked Ellie into The Mark, an upscale hotel within a block of the center. Ellie had decided to take Peter for a walk in the park before their ten-thirty appointment. She was in New York by herself. She felt strangely free and adventurous. She had great concern for Peter but she was happy to be on her own. She so rarely was. It was an utterly glorious day. New York's Central Park, what could be better?

With a quiet sense of excitement, she made her way out of the hotel, down and across the street and into the park. She held Peter in a baby halter on her breast. She walked into the park and along its pathways till she found an empty bench facing the asphalt track. She sat down to watch the spectacle of the runners and bikers and skateboarders and the ambling gentry of the big apple passing by. She felt like a little girl and a grown woman. She had some time before her appointment. She was content to sit and watch. Across the pathway from her was another empty bench. Everyone was on the move but her.

Eva had begun jogging this path downtown. But she soon began to feel she was distancing herself from her appointment. So she jogged a little uey and headed uptown.

She got lots of smiles and waves, winks and whistles. She mostly just responded to a few of the girls, waving back or smiling as she felt to. She did look into every eye she could. She entered a few minds, male and female, and disappeared a few people. She felt herself approaching her rendezvous.

When she got to Ellie's bench, she knew she was there. She faltered to a halt and went to stand behind the opposite bench as an excuse to use it to stretch. This placed her directly facing Ellie. She began a beautiful, evocative, slow, deliberate dance of stretching her legs and body using the back of the bench to rest a hand on to steady herself. She gently entered Ellie's mind.

As soon as Ellie saw Eva, her heart leapt and began pounding in her chest. She had never seen such a beautiful woman. She thought Eva must be some movie star she had never somehow discovered. She watched, more and more entranced, as Eva opulently displayed her body.

Eva started with the usual bending of the knees, lifting and pulling in each foot behind her. But she was soon stretching in ways few people do. She extended one leg wide to the side and raised the other to the max, bending the knee, spreading it out to the other side and placing its foot atop the back of the park bench. This spread her pussy as wide open as it might go. She made a play of stretching and flexing her leg muscles and tendons as she displayed herself to Ellie's stare as opulently as she could. The crotch of her running shorts was quite narrow. It exposed a wide swathe of the poignantly beautiful contours the black lace fabric of her panties tightly covered. Ellie gazed on them with a heartbreaking longing. Then, of course, Eva switched this beautiful, elaborate dance to the other side. Ellie savored everything she could, as did several of the passersby. The rest quickly averted their gaze. Ellie and Eva were spared any boorish advances. Somehow everyone sensed this was a sacred, private affair.

Then Eva turned around, spread her feet wide and bent over, first straight-backed and then fully, to place her palms flat on the ground and hold them there, stretching her back, her hamstrings and her cheeks wide open all the time monitoring Ellie's sensations, thoughts and emotions, enhancing her desire and plumbing the depths of her and, through her, her husband Tom for absolutely everything there was to know.

The sight of Eva's wide-open pussy, the exposure of the bare flesh of her bottom, the play of her breasts and the beauty of the flex of her bare midriff, arms and shoulders made Ellie want to cry. All she knew is that she had never seen anything so beautiful as this and had never wanted anything so much. Eva partially dissolved the rigid, Puritan block Ellie had to ever actually doing anything about such desire. Then she stood erect, turned around, looked directly into Ellie's eyes and smiled.

She knew this was not the time to send Ellie and Peter anywhere. She knew all that Ellie didn't about what Tom was doing in the world. She knew she had found her balance point in no time flat. She knew that he was the chink between the human race and the opposition. She knew the acceleration was accelerating. She knew she would need to visit her friends to learn more of how to proceed. She knew there was no hurry in this, that whatever she was to do had to be done in the very best timing with the greatest amount of love and finesse. She knew she could find Ellie, Tom and Peter anytime she wanted and that the three would be coming again in two months. She knew it was time to jog back and get ready for her appointment with Jimmy and the congregation of the Riverside Church.

She turned downtown and jogged out of sight. Ellie followed her with her eyes until she could see her no more. She knew, somehow, her life had changed. The vision of Eva was seared into her soul. Something had shifted deep within her. She sat there in star-struck reverie replaying all the images of Eva's beauty now so deeply imprinted in her mind and libido, now enshrined as the epitome of what she was so much wanting but could never have. Then the gentle movements of her waking baby returned her to the present. She had ten minutes to make her appointment.

Eva, for the very first time, had the thought of mind melding with the devas without going anywhere, like she could mind meld with anyone she knew without going to them. As she jogged she sent her mind out to them. At first she sent it to the chamber in the Bohemian Forest. They weren't there and this didn't work. Then she just thought of them and loved them. She found her awareness within their overmind. She perceived they each had whispers of individuality and full awareness of their oversoul. Eva shared everything she had just learned with them. This seemed, somehow, to help—them just knowing she was now connected to North America's pivot point.

All Eva got was, "You already know. Be aware. Move forward. Love everything. God's plan will bring what you need. Readiness will provide the answers. Do the next thing before you. It will all unfold."

Eva was satisfied. This is all she needed for now. And she could commune with them at any time. No need to go anywhere. She entered the building and their beloved condo in the usual way, got a little snack and got dressed and ready for church. Her little jog had hardly worked up a sweat.

Gabriel was soon home preparing as well.

It was eleven-twelve.

She sent her mind to her pod members and Nyame. They were all ready.

She pulled them in with all their luggage.

They all stood in the living room.

She put her new experiences and knowledge in their heads.

They looked at each other in awe.

It was good to see Nyame again.

They left their luggage where it was.

She spared the congregation the sight of their appearing out of thin air by pulling them to the basement of the church.

They walked up and settled into the seven chairs in the front row Jimmy had saved for them.

He was being called up and introduced by the female pastor.

"It's my great pleasure to introduce my dear friend Jimmy Handy, grandson of the great musicologist and bluesman W.C. Handy. Seating themselves now are his good friends the Heavenly Choir. They will be singing for us a unique sound of sacred music. Jimmy is not a pastor but he has something of profound beauty to share with us. I look forward to hearing what it is myself. He's one of my dearest friends and I know the depths of his generosity and wisdom. Let's give a warm welcome to Mr. Jimmy Handy!"

They all shook the rafters with clapping, hoots and whistles.

Jimmy stood before the congregation beaming like a lighthouse. His gentle demeanor and mighty presence soon commanded utter silence.

He began to speak with a direct, heartfelt simplicity. His voice was rich and resonant. There was a very sweet light coming from him.

"You are a child of God. God loves you and wants everything for you. He wants you to live all the fullness and glory of what you truly are.

A year ago I would not have done this. A few weeks ago I would not have done this. And here I am speaking God's message to you.

There is something happening in the world, something new under the sun, something that will take your life and transform it beyond your wildest imagination, something that will bring you into God's grace and perfection more than all the things you have ever wished for.

It's a kind of rapture. Not the rapture that so many people have been wanting where they're the chosen few and everyone else but them and their friends gets left behind. This is a rapture that will include us all. It will exclude no child, woman or man. It will miraculously bless every human being on earth. And this will bless our world beyond measure.

You are a child of God. The time has come for you to start living it. It is my greatest blessing and honor to be a part of this occurrence, this miracle revolution, this brand new gospel. This is the second coming. But it's like nothing we ever could have imagined. We thank you, we love you, we bless you. Please come forward O Heavenly Choir and bring about your miracles."

When he started, there were a few yeses, lords and amens. But something about his words and message didn't support them and utter silence soon prevailed. His words both touched them and brought forth a rising concern. The pastor, especially, wondered where he could possibly be going and grew afraid that she had misjudged him and made a mistake in allowing him to speak.

The pod rose to take their place and turned to face their audience in total silence. Their beauty and light stunned the people and dissolved their uneasiness.

André began with the purest tenor note. And the rest joined in to fill the full, resonant range of rich vocal beauty.

They sang no words. But they sang from the beauty and depth of their souls, hearts and being.

Their tones and harmonies were deeply moving and tears were welling in many eyes while several voices joined them from the congregation and members of the church choir. Manhattan's Riverside Church was truly filled by a heavenly choir, more so than ever before. And that was saying something. It truly felt like heaven on Earth.

The power of it spilled out of the church, filled the streets of Harlem and poured into Earth's energy pathways.

Then Eva gathered them all as one and sent them on their way. She could just see them all standing in a grand cathedral chamber.

The church was now empty of every living soul but the seven of them and Jimmy. They walked into each other's arms and felt the divine love and blessings of what was happening on Earth comingled with their love of each other.

Eva pulled them all home.

They laughed, loved and touched and took deep breaths of utter fulfillment. What jobs they all now had!

Chapter 19

The Womb of the Mother

"That was awesome," Nyame finally said. "Let's jump from church to church and make 'em all disappear."

"Nice thought but you know we can't. That would be us coming up with our own strategy and rampaging through the world with it instead of following the divine path continually unfolding before us, arrogating the way instead of tracking it, trashing divine will instead of living it. We can co-create to some degree. But mostly we allow God and the world to lead us. If we did what you just came up with, it would probably scare the opposition into doing something catastrophic. When readiness arrives I'm sure they'll have a much better way. Divine orchestration, baby. You understand this, don't you?"

"I guess so. I'm so used to making things happen."

"Well you can't do that here. This is important. It's not about our acting on our own bright ideas. It's about sensing what the mysterious, invisible realms are guiding our way as the next perfect thing for us to do. It's discerning which of our ideas are in divine will and which aren't. I mean it literally. We're tracking a subtle, divine path and divining where the water is, divining our next God given move, not jumping in with something arbitrary of our own. The last thing we need is for the opposition to really discover what we're doing before we want them to and that could do it. Get it?"

"Yes, I believe so."

"Good. Maybe you've been hanging in the gutters of New York too long. I do believe the time is coming for you to plow deep furrows in African soil. What's your sense?"

"Any day now or any moment. Maybe I was just waiting to hear this."

"Maybe you were. OK, so eight hours till Déwei initiation time. Why don't the four of you unpack and get settled in. I can take you on pick up runs whenever you're ready. Let's get you all moved in as much as possible. We'll sit here and converse."

They hauled their luggage into their respective rooms and begin unpacking. Alena and Jack were thrilled to be moving in together. André and Anani were like two kids or loving siblings getting to share the same room. And they were quite liking their intimacy. They were the team that served Eva. In this they were one.

"How much more to prepare for Ghana?" Eva asked Nyame.

"I'm mostly done. I need to go there and open a bank account and find where I'm to live, buy some local clothing, that type of thing."

"Why don't you do that and return when you're ready? Go to the Earth room first. It's four-eleven Ghana time. You should be able to accomplish quite a lot."

With, "Love you, brothers," Nyame disappeared.

"Tell me Jimmy, what have you been doing for sex?"

"Oh I've been celibate now, honey, for twelve years. When I was younger I was quite active. It's been that long that nobody I want wants me and the few that do, I just can't see it."

"And how has that been?"

"I can live with it. It's better than the alternatives. I could never buy it. And I haven't been inspired to go out looking."

"You're sixty-seven. Men still have babies in their eighties. Would you like to be with me and Gabriel or Anani or André or all of us together?"

"Well, ma'am, I wouldn't begin to presume but that would be the greatest pleasure earthly life could afford. How could I not want such a thing?"

"We'll all be engaging this evening along with a certain Chinese gentleman. Will you do us the honor of joining us?"

"If I'm truly invited, nothing could keep me away."

"You're truly invited. I'll send you home and get you at eight."

Jimmy disappeared.

Eva gazed for a moment into Gabriel's eyes.

Then they were in Eva's old apartment.

"Let's go through my stuff and see what's left to bring."

It didn't take them long, some more of her clothing, a few knick-knacks and books, the rest of her favorite kitchen items and toiletries. They could fit it all in a few boxes she had there and draped on their bodies. They took it all home and put it away. Then they helped their other pod members do the same.

With Eva transporting them individually and en masse, they all ended up helping each other and finishing by four.

They were all in.

Gabe got on his laptop and did a little research. Together with the others, he engaged appointments with a donation collection service called Housing Works to go to all their places and pick up everything that was left. Then he engaged Wizard of Homes to clean all their empty apartments.

They would just have to meet them and let them in at the appointed times. Then they could meet with their landlords for inspection and deposit retrieval. Their miracle move was pretty complete.

It was coming on to four-thirty.

"Let's all meditate," Eva announced. "Anani, we know from our communions that you usually do. Is there anyone who never has?"

"I've prayed and contemplated," Alena offered, "but I've never really meditated."

Everyone else had tried it. Eva only did it once in a while. It always made her feel better. And she was drawn to have them all do it together now.

"Tell us your experience," Eva said to Anani.

"I've been doing it since I was sixteen, at first twice a day and now three times. You guys have been a bad influence. I've been missing more than I ever do. I recently found this new one. Someone gave me a little book called *What We Can Do*. It's utterly simple, so simple it's deceiving. I like it better than the other six or seven I've tried. I've been doing it about six months. If you really want to do it right, I suggest you read the book. It's very short. But it's so simple I can teach it to you now. If we're going to meditate together, it's probably better that we all do the same thing. Of course each of you can do anything you want to."

"No you can't," Eva said, "this feels right. Let's all do the same thing together. One pod in unison."

"OK, so it's a mantra meditation. You just think the same thought over and over again. But think it lightly. Don't pound it. And don't feel you have to keep it continually going. Just think it easily and effortlessly and don't worry about making anything in particular happen. Think it like it has no meaning, just the sounds, repeating the words, forgetting the meaning. And just step aside and let your higher wisdom take over. Let the words disappear when they do. Then think them again when you remember. Just be easy with it all, accept everything as it occurs.

The mantra is 'I love you and forgive you.' According to the book, love and forgiveness are the two most healing energies. You let yourself go deep by not trying to make anything happen and you bring the healing with you and let your inner knowing do the work. It's a deep, healing meditation. If 'I love you and forgive you' starts to feel too long or hard, just think the word 'love' over and over, even rapidly or at any pace that works for you."

"I love you I forgive you," Eva said.

"They recommend using the mantra with only one 'I.' You want to step aside from your small self, not emphasize it."

"OK," Eva said, "I love you and forgive you."

"Yes, or just 'love.'"

"Beautiful, we can do that right? Let's try. Anything else?"

"Yes, don't worry about your experience. Just keep doing it as easily as possible. Let everything else take care of itself. If you have a lot of thoughts or feel bored or restless, just let it be that way and keep going as gently as you can. Let yourself have and feel your restlessness or whatever is there inside."

"OK, let's close our eyes. I have an idea."

Eva pooled their consciousness. Alena was the only one with qualms but she knew better. She deeply loved and trusted Eva and was ready to go with this and see what it was. She wanted to be one of them. She *was* one of them. And wasn't Jesus for love and forgiveness?

Eva had Anani begin as she usually does and they all experienced what she did.

She took a deep breath or two and then just simply began thinking 'I love you and forgive you' at a smooth, easy pace.

Eva then gave them all the experiences Anani had had in her past meditations so, instantaneously, they were now as experienced as she. They all saw and felt how deeply into an altered state Anani would often go and that, at other times, she wouldn't go so deeply and that was just fine. They all experienced how she would always come out refreshed and how it smoothed and released the roughness of daily living.

Knowing that Anani meditated was one thing. This was another, to focus in on her experience and absorb it all and make it their own.

Eva let them go and be unto themselves. And they all now did what they knew how to do. They were separate but there was a pooled energy that Eva was in no way bringing about. They began to go deeper and the energy in the room shifted into more stillness and peace.

And there were moments when all thoughts stopped.

Somehow the silence in the room rang out louder. They were in a deep, vast ocean of sublime eternity.

This went on as they come out into mundane thoughts and went deeper into the meditative state, individually and as a group. Forty-five minutes went by. It felt like fifteen. Eva gently called them back into the room. They opened their eyes and looked around at each other in wordless delight.

"Well," Eva said, "that's something we'll do again."

They silently agreed.

"That's almost as good as our sex," André offered.

"In some ways it's better," Eva replied. "It fills the airwaves with an even deeper level of love, healing and peace. Let's do this on a more regular basis. Gabe, is there food enough for all of us?"

"Yes, just enough. Let's use it all up."

They went to the kitchen. He got out his biggest pot. And they made a feast of a stew with everything he had left including all his veges and roots, roasted macadamias and raw walnuts, mushrooms, onions, garlic, ginger root and scallions and cubed chunks of fresh lamb and fish. Towards the end, he put in some coconut oil and a can of coconut milk and some Herbamare and spices. At the very end he turned off the heat and stirred in his last three eggs sukiyaki style. Then he covered the pot to let it steep and blend.

They all got bowls and spoons, forks or chop sticks. It was delicious, hearty and fulfilling and just enough for all of them. They were quite happy as they cleaned up together.

Then some took showers. Some took baths. Some lay down and snoozed. And the time went by till it was seven-thirty.

Nyame popped in and took a shower.

All was right with the world.

They gathered in the living room around ten minutes before eight.

"Let's start out naked. Everybody strip, put away your clothes and come prepare our big bed on the floor."

As she undressed, she reached out to Jimmy and Déwei.

They were delighted with the dress code.

Déwei let her know he had found his first pod member, a beautiful, nineteen-year-old girl named Liu with long, silky, black hair. They had just finished her post-healing meal. Eva entered her awareness, introduced herself and gave her and Déwei a lot of her pod's experience. Though newly hatched, her soul danced at the invitation to join them.

Eva pulled them in.

Ten gorgeous people, nineteen to sixty-seven, stood there enjoying the sight of each other. To them all, but especially to Jimmy, it was a wonder beyond words. The mix was stunning. No matter where they looked there was beauty. They would have been content to stare for hours.

"Let's put our guests in a triangle in the center," Eva thought to their minds.

Liu spoke no English, Déwei very little. But Eva wasn't transmitting words. Her concepts and images transcended language. She directly gave them total understanding. It was seamless and effortless.

The three stood in an equilateral triangle, facing outward, shoulders and arms against each other.

"Anani, press up against Déwei, Nyame, Liu and I'll take Jimmy," she communicated as she walked up to and into her man. "Guests, please put your arms around us. Everyone else pile in and around wherever you can."

They were all thrilled. Liu's response to Nyame was even more startling in its intensity than Anani's to Déwei. The rings, of course, enhanced both men. It added to their luster, their charisma and the power of their energies, sexual and otherwise. For Anani, her desire for a man was novel. And this man awoke some ancient love she could barely remember. For Liu, Nyame's virility and magnificence were beyond comprehension.

Everyone started laughing, bouncing, pressing, creaming and erecting.

They got quite giddy and then hysterical, the laughter almost hurting. The plethora of sex, love and gorgeous body parts was staggering. They went to their big, prepared bed on the floor and lay laughing all over each other till they got weak with it and the laughter subsided.

"OK," Eva thought to them all, "deep breaths everyone."

They all fully expanded their lungs several times.

"This was our initiation. Be with whoever you're drawn to. Go anywhere in our pod home you would like to. Except the master bedroom. That's for me. Let's turn down the lights and light our candles."

Alena and Jack arose and went to their bedroom. They wanted deeper exploration of their newfound love.

Nyame took Liu's hand and headed for the nearest couch.

"Take André and Anani's bedroom," Eva thought to them. "You'll be more comfortable."

They gladly obeyed.

Anani and Déwei created a love altar by putting the three ottomans together. It was the perfect length and made the entire body of whoever was lying on it totally accessible from every side and angle.

And Eva drew Gabriel, André and Jimmy into the master bedroom.

She put all her command codes into Jimmy's mind and said, "Jimmy, if I'm Cleopatra, tonight you're Mark Antony. But now I really want you to be Jimmy in all your glory and tell us everything you want of us. We're all here to serve you."

She stepped into his arms, pulled him in close and whispered in his ear, "We're yours, darling Jimmy, command us all to do whatever you want."

Jimmy took a mighty breath and let out a sigh. He disengaged and took a few steps back surveying the three of them and the room.

"OK darlings, I surrender. Gabe and André remove the duvet and put it on the floor by the wall for easy access. Let's just have the bed with its fitted sheet as a platform. Then light the candles and we'll turn out the light. Just keep that little lamp on the bed table lit as low as it can go. Too bad you don't have mirrors on the wall and ceiling."

"My sentiments exactly," Eva thought to Gabriel. "Let's have some put in."

"Of course, my queen, I am your slave," he thought back, his ego slightly hurt at all that was going down.

"And you are my prince and my love," she thought back to him with a wave of love so great it helped to dissolve his last vestiges of jealousy, ownership and wounded pride.

The room was ready.

"Thank you, all of you," Jimmy said quietly from the bottom of his heart. "This is what I've been dreaming of for twelve years. I thought I'd only be dreaming for the rest of my life. And this is beyond what I even could dream."

The love welled up strongly within them all along with a few tears in Jimmy and Eva's eyes.

"Two, my love, knees on the edge of the bed."

And Eva assumed her position.

"Gabe, you're the witness for now. Enjoy the beauty with your eyes and your love. All our love and awareness will join together and fill the room and beyond. You and André stand on either side of the bed for now and watch."

They all just stood in awe and admiration.

What a thing of beauty she was, especially in this position.

Their hearts, eyes and bodies loved and adored her.

The room got warmer.

Their cocks began to stir.

"How lovely," Eva thought to herself. "Three men for little old me."

She was quite happy to hold this position for them as long as they might want.

Jimmy knelt before the Perfectly Accessible Goddess.

He brought his face in close and examined her minutely.

The vision of her wide-open pussy and anus, the variety of all the colors—light and dark reds, pinks, greys, purples, browns, beiges and all the gradations of skin color—the expanse of the wrinkles, folds, shapes and crevices, the entryways and sliding planes, the ins and outs of her, were compelling, fascinating and utterly delectable.

She began to moisten.

Then he began a process he knew could lead to miracles, a process of command and repetition that could bring Eva to the deepest levels of her opening, offering, being and surrender, the most profound flowering of her womanhood, the greatest fulfillment and consummation of her feminine power and glory. A long, slow process of incremental steps to the utter release of all contraction, tension and resistance within her, all holding back, all unconscious reticence. The more she became the perfect vehicle of willingness, the more potential there was for perfect completion.

"Pulse," he gently commanded.

Eva read his mind and began to squeeze and release her sphincter muscles in a grand, sedate, rhythmic pattern, the Kegel exercise, perfectly suited to display her beauty.

Jimmy backed away a little saying, "Gentlemen, come around and see this."

They knelt at his sides.

All her parts danced and twinkled like the most adorable little animals.

They were entranced by the beauty of her womanhood.

Jimmy stood up and stepped back indicating for the men to return to their places.

"Why have I never thought of this?" Gabriel thought to himself.

"Oh my God," was all André, in rapture, could think.

Jimmy's fine and sizable member was half engorged.

He knew if they had mirrors it would be rock hard. He loved seeing the images in mirrors. But he had many ways to get there.

He walked up to Eva.

Her pussy was too high. He knew exactly what he wanted of her.

"Move down a little towards 'beg.'"

Eva perceived the image in Jimmy's mind.

Beg was 'bow down' with knees fully bent but more fully up on elbows with head up as well. At his command, she had dutifully moved a little towards it, not fully into it.

He put his hands gently on the highest part of her back and butt.

He pressed a little and said, "Come back and down a little more."

Her open pussy descended closer to his cock.

He pressed again, "A tad more, sweetheart."

And there she was in the perfect position for him to slip it in, stand comfortably and move around in all the ways he might want.

"Perfect. My perfect pussy. You're my perfect pussy, Eva. This is 'six.' Position number six. Six for sex. Your pussy's at the perfect height. When I say six, this is what I want. Feel this and remember it. You're my perfect cunt. Do you understand?"

"Yes."

Giving and receiving such commands was now quite thrilling to her. Just being told what to do, not having to think, knowing all she had to do was surrender was a comfort, fascinating and arousing. Hearing the crude, hard edge of those iconic words turned her on. He spoke what he wanted and she wanted to fulfill him. On the one hand it was that simple. On the other, the element of erotic rule jacked up the juice. She reveled in it.

"Perfect... One."

She moved up the bed and flipped over on her back raising her legs wide apart, bending her knees and moving her arms up and out with her elbows bent.

"Now reach up to the corners of the bed and pull yourself smack into the middle of it."

She did this and reassumed her position.

"Perfect. This is 'one.' Gentlemen, look at her."

And they did.

There was nothing on Earth as beautiful as this.

"Honey, you're magnificent. The dreams of a lifetime surpassed. I can't tell you what this means to me. Six, pussy girl, put your body in six. Show me how good you are."

And Eva was there.

"André, I want to see your pretty mouth and lips worship her pussy. Get it all nice and wet. Prepare it for me. Start with five nice long laps. You're my cunt lapper. Do you understand?"

"Yes," André answered, being commanded like this thrilling him as well, especially to doing something he so much wanted to do.

Gabe began to feel like he wanted to be commanded by his ex-janitor, too.

Jimmy loved seeing women lick pussy. In some ways this could be even better. The prettiest of boys doing his bidding.

André got into place and lapped his laps.

Eva softly moaned and spread her crotch a little wider.

"Good boy. Now with the tip of your tongue, lick her lips all around then press into her clit and urethra."

When André pressed into her, Eva had a little urine in her bladder. She released it into his mouth. He gladly took it in and swallowed it down. They all perceived this.

"Good boy. Say, 'Thank you. I'll do that whenever you want,' to Eva."

"Thank you. I'll do that whenever you want."

"Please feel completely free with me. You can do anything."

"Please feel completely free with me. You can do anything."

"Please piss in my mouth. I'll drink in as much as you want."

"Please piss in my mouth. I'll drink in as much as you want."

"Perfect, now press in deep and give her all the pleasure you can with your full tongue."

And he was there. And Eva was moaning and sighing and softly grunting and whispering, "Good boy, good boy, such a good boy."

And oh how she meant it. The feeling of releasing her bladder into André's mouth and him taking it in and swallowing it down gave her a feeling of the deepest contentment. It felt like everything in her body settled in more than it ever had. And the knowledge that both he and Anani were ready to do these things gave rise to a number of different delectable ideas within her. This augmented the pleasure he was now giving her and made him even more deeply precious to her. She was very, very pleased with him.

"Now my pretty, perfect man, your nose is about one inch from her asshole. I want you to keep your tongue in her pussy and press downward. Rub your nostrils up and down her asshole. Breathe in deeply. Sniff it in good."

André obeyed. The outrageousness of Jimmy's commands jacked up the intensity of their desires and sent a delicious thrill through Eva. All three men were now rock hard. It was startling to watch André rubbing and sniffing Eva's beautiful anus. It was humorous and erotic. The more you watched, the more you liked it.

"Good boy. Retract your tongue and tilt your head so you only touch her anus from now on. You must be absolutely careful not to get anything from her asshole into her pussy. Don't go near there again. That was 'brown nose.' That's what you do when I say 'brown nose.' You're my perfect brown nose. Do you understand?"

"Yes."

Each 'yes' André spoke got a little breathier, a little more sultry. Like Eva, he was reaching deeper levels of surrender. It heightened his arousal and felt divine. He was sexually melting.

"Good boy. Rub your nose in it again for me, long and lavishly. And keep sniffing it in."

They watched, utterly fascinated, as André did this so very perfectly.

"So good. So very good. Now lap her asshole."

And he did, five times.

"Good boy, you're my ass licker, my brown nose, my piss drinker, my cunt lapper. You took in and swallowed her piss, yes?"

"Yes."

"And you rubbed your nose in her asshole."

"Yes."

"And you lapped it with your tongue."

"Yes."

"Perfect. You'll do this and more whenever I tell you. Look how beautiful her anus glistens, wet with your mouth water. Gabe, come closer and see."

André moved back a little and Gabe came around. He was delighted to obey. They were ecstatic at how much they could love her anus, how beautiful it could be.

"You are perfect and good, Eva. Everything about you is divine. There is nothing wrong with you anywhere. We love your asshole and every other part of you. Do you understand?"

"Yes."

"Good girl. OK my precious André, lick around the lip of her anus with the tip of your tongue and then slip the fullness of it right on into her as deep as you can."

André obeyed.

Jimmy knew this was more of a man thing, that many men truly loved how this felt. But he also knew that women could enjoy it as well and how erotic it was to watch. He had loved having his ass licked when he was younger. But as he aged, he developed the problems that organ is heir to making it impossible to enjoy. With his healing, all that was gone. His anus and rectum were as clean and healthy as a newborn babe's. How nice it would be to have this beautiful man or Eva or Gabe give him that pleasure again. But that could wait.

"Now press your face into her cheeks and your tongue up into her as far as you can."

This was very interesting for Eva. It didn't give her the intense pleasure that having her pussy licked did but she was enjoying it. And just having it done somehow both empowered and softened her. It actually did make her feel like a Pharaoh with slaves ready to satisfy her every desire but also like a kitten having its belly rubbed. And she could feel it opening things deep inside her and making every part of her alimentary canal happy.

"Beautiful, now take your place at the side of the bed."

André cleared the way and Jimmy stepped in and slipped his cock all the way into Eva's pussy, pressing his hips against her butt.

She sighed with a feeling of contentment and relief.

They were in union.

"What time is it?"

"Eight thirty-three," Eva answered.

"Beautiful. Penetration occurs at eight thirty-three. Let's remember that."

He moved around and in and out and got them both used to his being inside.

Then he came to rest fully but gently inside her.

"I love you, darling. You're going to do things for me you've never done for anyone. Do you understand?"

"Yes."

"Good girl. I'm going to say 'do you understand' and 'good girl' a thousand times. I love to say them. It turns me on. And your job is to turn me on. Do you understand?"

"Yes."

"It's really a code phrase, a command. The command to say 'yes.' I love to hear you say 'yes.' And I love using that question to prompt you. Each time you say yes, you can sink deeper into the state of surrender. It gives you the chance to say the more perfect 'yes.' A woman can say 'yes' and it's ten percent yes and ninety percent no or fifty-fifty or seventy-thirty. Everything I'm doing is to move you closer to the perfect yes, to get you to open and surrender a little more. Do you understand?"

"Yes."

And she could feel it—her willingness, her 'yes,' going deeper and deeper and with it her womanhood opening and flowering even more. Even her voice got a little deeper.

"Surrender is an infinite continuum. It has no limit. You can always surrender a little bit more. The deeper you go the better it gets. The more chance there is for miracle to occur. 'Good girl' and 'do you understand' can bring up resistance and rebellion or deeper surrender. Allow them to help you surrender even more. Do you understand?"

"Yes."

"'Good girl' means you are pleasing me. You're doing perfectly. Just keep going in the same direction you're going. Allow yourself to take pleasure in my praise. It's the highest praise. It's saying 'you're perfect.' Let it help you want to do even more. Do you understand?"

"Yes."

"Good girl. Now I want you to love yourself for me. Loving yourself is like masturbating but better, more sacred. Masturbating can get mechanical, even violent. They don't call it beating off for nothing. That's more men but women, too. Which hand do you use?"

"My right."

"Beautiful. I want you to reach down with your left hand and love yourself.

Give yourself as much pleasure as you can. Find new ways to stroke and please and feel yourself."

Eva brought her left arm down between her legs and began to touch and press her divine clit. She tried different strokes and found new, surprising ways of producing pleasure. Jimmy's cock and energy inside her enhanced it. André and Gabe's attention did as well. She did this for several moments.

Then she got the idea of pooling their consciousness so that the men could directly experience her pleasure and she theirs. This allowed her to see herself and the glamor they cast on her through their eyes. And this made them direct participants in her pleasure.

"Now try both hands. Get as comfortable as you can in this position."

Eva reached down and turned her face to the side so that her shoulders and face supported her. She found ways to love herself with multiple fingers she had never come close to before.

Jimmy allowed this to continue.

"Good girl. Now use whatever hand or fingers you want. Give yourself all the pleasure you can. Keep loving and stimulating yourself more and more to the best orgasm you can. It's something you know very well how to do. But it's a whole different world with me inside you. I want you to bring yourself to come for me in this way. Don't wait for me. Don't hold back. Don't send out your energy and make me come with you. I don't want to come now. I want you to come for me as fully and ecstatically as you can. Don't resist anything. Do what works best for you. Think any thoughts you wish to. Let this be a supreme act of loving yourself in union with me."

Eva brought her left arm up and got as comfortable as she could. Then she began rubbing her clit with the tip of her right index finger. She started slowly moving it around. Then she began that long, loving stroke along the side of her clit she knew so well that gave her so much pleasure, that brought her to come. More and more she felt herself stimulated. More and more she felt herself closer to coming.

Jimmy began to move a little more inside her. He pulsed his own sphincter muscles, which flexed his cock and jerked it up and down. This increased her pleasure and excitement. Till, finally, she was at her threshold. She arched her back and pulsed her muscles and came with one of the mightiest comes of her life. She came and moved and felt herself and Jimmy's cock inside her. Her womb tilted and deeply contracted. And she let the waves of her orgasm sweep her away.

It was sublime, magnificent, powerfully releasing. She came and came until the pleasure subsided.

Jimmy's cock and energy, Gabe and André's love and their combined awareness all helped peak her pleasure and fulfillment.

"Oh Jimmy, that was maarrvelous," she breathed.

"Yes it was, my precious come girl. Do you understand?"

"Oh yes, oh yes, oh yes, yes, yes. I truly understand."

Jimmy moved his hips in and out and around for her.

"I love you, Eva. You're the world's most perfect pussy. And I believe I just taught you all something. Have any of you ever done this?"

They hadn't.

"Really, it's a trick, a sexual trick. But it's a good one, one of the best on the planet. Many women have never come with a man inside. This could help pretty much all of them. It's not fail safe. It depends on the energies of the man and the woman and other things. But it's one of the most sure fire ways for a woman to have a magnificent orgasm, even the most powerful one of her life. It's obviously clitoral. But with a man inside adding his love and energy, it brings about a great one. Where I hope we're going, though, goes far beyond trick. In my world, we're about to begin the world's highest form of sacred tantra. Are you up for that, sugar," he asked, thrusting a few times to help her decide, "or are we done?"

"Oh no, I'm up for it, I'm up for it. Bring it on, darling Jimmy. You're my man."

"Ohhkaay. In a moment or two I'm going to slip out of you. Then I'll have you do some magnificent things for me. Then I'll say 'now.' When I say it, I want you to flip over on your back, reach up and grab the corners and pull yourself into 'one' smack in the middle of the bed. Do you understand?"

"Yes."

"Good girl."

He moved some more then nearly all the way out and all the way in with a few heart-rending thrusts.

Then he slowly and gently slipped out completely and knelt before her.

"Pulse," he said and "come see this," to André and Gabe.

They came by his sides and watched as she squeezed and released her beautiful muscles for several minutes.

"Now come up on your hands and dance your hips in circles and slants and forward and back and every which way you can."

She pushed up on her hands and began to swing, jerk and rotate her hips.

"Oh yes, so good. This is position number four, on all fours, the best one for dancing your pussy. Move it for me stronger and faster, make it deliberate... Good girl, exaggerate... Jerk it hard and fast, forward and back... So good. Whip it, darling, as fast and as hard as you can... Beautiful... Now slow and languid all around, arch and stretch your pussy and anus even wider... Look at you, my perfect pussy, my perfect asshole, my perfect, supreme Goddess.

Now down on your shoulders and face. Reach down with both hands. Fingertips on labia. Stretch them apart. Open your pussy wide."

Eva pulled her lips apart.

"A little more, Goddess."

She stretched her flesh wider, opening up more of the beauty of her vaginal canal to them all. He let her hold that for a few moments as all the men enjoyed the sight and Eva experienced their delight.

"You're exquisite. Now fingertips on your anal lip. Both sides. Pull your asshole open for me."

And she did.

"Magnificent, open it wider, sweetie."

The pink of her rectum broke their hearts.

"Good girl. Say 'My pussy is yours.'"

"My pussy is yours."

"I'm your perfect pussy."

"I'm your perfect pussy."

"I'll do anything with my pussy you tell me to."

"I'll do anything with my pussy you tell me to."

"My asshole is yours."

"My asshole is yours."

"I'm your perfect asshole."

"I'm your perfect asshole."

"I'll do anything with my asshole you tell me to."

"I'll do anything with my asshole you tell me to."

These last few statements also inspired their risibility. And there were a few internal and external semi-chuckles. But Jimmy didn't want Eva to lose this ineluctable pose or the group to lose their powerful sexual charge.

So he said, "Your asshole is precious, beautiful and good. It's such a joy to see you open her like this for me. We need to name her and your other beautiful parts. None of the usual names are good enough. She is Aina. Sweet, adorable, wide open Aina. Your pussy is Uma. Your clit is Sita. And everything between your legs is Clarinda, cla for clit, ri for pussy and inda for anus. My cock is Siva. If I say Siva, you say Uma. If I say cock, you say pussy. Do you understand?"

"Yes."

"And I so know you do, better than any other woman on Earth. Say 'we love Clarinda.'"

"We love Clarinda."

"I present her to you."

"I present her to you."

"I open Aina wide and present her to you as perfectly as I can."

"I open Aina wide and present her to you as perfectly as I can."

"There's nothing I won't say."

"There's nothing I won't say."

"There's nothing I won't do."

"There's nothing I won't do."

"I promise you perfect sexual obedience."

"I promise you perfect sexual obedience."

"Again."

"I promise you perfect sexual obedience."

"Three times in a row."

"I promise you perfect sexual obedience. I promise you perfect sexual obedience. I promise you perfect sexual obedience."

"Beautiful. Release Aina and come back into two. All this is 'pussy dance.' When I say 'pussy dance,' you dance your crotch and body in all these magnificent ways, in any sequence, whatever occurs to you next, everything you can think of, everything you can do.

Tune in to your own erotic muse and find the movements that arouse you the most, that give you the most pleasure. Then follow your own erotic river. Make it a high art of erotic display. Let magical inspiration take over. Go into a trance dance. Come up with the most astonishing motions you can. Do you understand?"

"Yes."

"Good girl, say 'please.'"

"Please."

"I'm your pussy dancer."

"I'm your pussy dancer."

"I'll dance it when you tell me to."

"I'll dance it when you tell me to."

"I won't be lazy."

"I won't be lazy."

"I'll perform for you as perfectly as I can."

"I'll perform for you as perfectly as I can."

"I'm your pussy cunt fuck."

"I'm your pussy cunt fuck."

"I'm your goddess bitch whore."

"I'm your goddess bitch whore."

"I'm completely and totally yours."

"I'm completely and totally yours."

"Good girl. This is how I want you, as perfectly obedient and surrendered as you can possibly be. Do you understand?"

"Yes," she said, with the deepest 'yes' she had ever spoken.

Everything he was doing expanded her surrender. It was sublime. Each yes, each statement, each act of obedience melted her more. It felt very complete.

"Perfect... Now."

Eva moved up to flip on her back. She pulled herself to the middle and opened up wide.

"Beautiful," he said kneeling on the bed, coming down onto her and slipping it up inside her again.

All Jimmy and Eva had been doing, all the words and the sight of her had kept all three men fully aroused and totally hard throughout.

Now he was lying on top of her with his mouth close to her ear. This was much more intimate. He half spoke and half whispered so they could all easily hear.

"You're so very good. Where's my cock?"

"In my pussy."

"What are we doing?"

"Fucking."

"Good girl, three times."

"Fucking, fucking, fucking."

"Good girl, you're fucking me."

"You're fucking me."

"I am, indeed. So by definition, while I'm fucking you, you're my fuck. There's no way around it. I'm your fuck and you're my fuck. Do you understand?"

"Yes."

"As long as I'm in you or soon to reenter you're my fuck. Until we're done tonight you're my fuck. But as soon as I slip out for good, I've lost you. You're no longer my fuck. Unless you promise me one more fuck. Do you understand?"

"Yes."

"If you promise me one more fuck then until you've fulfilled that promise, you're still my fuck. When you're fucking Gabe you're my fuck. When you're shitting and pissing on the throne you're my fuck. When you're washing your pussy in the shower you're washing my pussy. Until you fulfill your promise. You're my dedicated, promised fuck. Do you understand?"

"Yes."

"Good girl. I want you to think of all the orgasms you've had in your life before this week, all your prior experiences. And I want you to put all the orgasms you've ever had, whether alone or with a man, on a scale of one to ten. The most powerful being ten, the faintest wisp of a mini-orgasm being one. Do you understand?"

"Yes."

"This orgasm we just gave you, was it more powerful than any of them?"

"Oh yes."

"So it's a ten-and-a-half or eleven or fourteen. I want you to rate it as accurately as you can. How far out should we extend our scale?"

"Fifteen."

"Beautiful. So it was half again as powerful as any orgasm before this week?"

"Yes, maybe sixteen. It felt more than just half again."

"Good girl. Say 'I beg you.'"

"I beg you."

"Now say it with the 'p' word."

"Please, I beg you."

"Please, I beg you, I'll do anything."

"Please, I beg you, I'll do anything."

"Three times."

"Please, I beg you, I'll do anything. Please, I beg you, I'll do anything. Please, I beg you, I'll do anything."

"Good girl. Remember this. This is your mantra, your surrender mantra, your sex mantra. When I tell you to say your mantra, this is what you say. Do you understand?"

"Yes," more breathily and deeper than ever.

"Thank you for that magnificent sixteen."

"Oh, Jimmy, thank you so much for that magnificent sixteen. It was stunning."

"Good girl. Are you willing to promise me one more fuck?"

"Oh yes, more than one."

"Not yet, sweetheart. Just one at a time. One more?"

"Yes, I promise you one more fuck."

"Again."

"I promise you one more fuck."

"Now three times with the 'p' word."

"Please, I promise you one more fuck. Please, I promise you one more fuck. Please, I promise you one more fuck."

"I absolutely promise you one more fuck."

"I absolutely promise you one more fuck."

"I swear a sacred oath."

"I swear a sacred oath."

"I make this sacred vow."

"I make this sacred vow."

"One more perfectly obedient fuck."
"One more perfectly obedient fuck."
"Good girl. You're mine till you fulfill your promise."
It was like he was mesmerizing her but this was not hypnosis. It was much more than that. All the yeses and repetitions were truly helping her drop more deeply into the most sublime state of surrender possible. She could feel it, each little step, doors at the deepest level of her being opening, moving into new realms of letting go, obedience and willingness. He was right. It was an infinite continuum. To keep moving into its deepest reaches was enticing, compelling and divine.

"So beautiful," he said, feeling it, too, "the depth of your surrender and you the greatest Cleopatra of our time, the most beautiful woman on Earth glorified into a goddess by an angel ring promising me one more fuck. I can't tell you what this means to me. You're so precious, so perfect, so good, truly, you're the Perfectly Accessible Goddess and more. You're my pussy, my lover, my come girl slave. Do you understand?"

"Yes."

"Now we leave the realm of glorious, human sex and approach divine union. Thank you so much Eva for fulfilling my desires. This has made my life. What a miracle this is! What a miracle you are! What more could I ask for? I can die a happy man. The most fulfilled man on the planet. But there *is* more. And yet *more*. Unbelievably, miraculously more."

He came off and out of her and lay on his left side below her across the end of the bed. Then he moved in and put his right leg through her legs and his left leg slightly under her slipping his cock back up her pussy.

He had her lift up a little and pushed his left leg further beneath so they were perfectly situated for his cock to be fully inside her, their bodies perpendicular.

"Beautiful. Now lower your legs on me and completely let go. Loosen and relax all your muscles, relax everything. We'll lie here together in union with me all the way in, my cockhead kissing your cervix.

This won't take long.

All this talking I've been doing, it's for many reasons. One, I hope, will soon become clear.

This position is the best one to help it come about.

I love you, Eva.

I love you more than I've ever loved anyone.

I know you belong to Gabriel. And that's as it should be.

And I know you love him and Anani the most and all of us and, really, every human being.

But I love you the most. And I want you to know that. You are our savior and Goddess more than anyone now. I somehow knew that the first time I saw you.

My love is no burden on you. It adds to your glory and your power.

This night is really all I need.

Another fuck would be glorious.

But I love you and what we're doing and God. And I invite God into our union.

When a man and woman lie together like this something can happen after half-an-hour.

It can happen in other positions, too. But it takes time. What time is it?"

"Nine-fifteen," Eva said instantly.

"Beautiful. We've been mostly in union for over forty minutes. This won't take long. So let's just lie here and see what happens. Men, do whatever you can to make yourselves more comfortable."

They had, to some degree, been doing that all along. Sometimes they would stand, sometimes kneel and then get back up again. Now they took the two chairs in the room, brought them to the sides of the bed and sat.

After only a few minutes something started to happen.

"Oh my," Eva said.

"Yes."

"It's our energies."

"Yes. It takes this long for most of our energies to find each other and unite. It's a deeper level of union, more sublime, richer, more wonderful. After this happens it helps the man, especially, relax more deeply into it. It makes it easier for him to do all kinds of things without coming. Before this happens, he can all too readily come too soon. And most folks around the world are done long before this happens."

Their awareness was still united. They were all getting to experience this directly. Jimmy and Eva's energies were flowing together like two rivers having joined.

It was beautiful.

Jimmy let this go on for several moments.

Then he said, "Lift your legs."

He pulled out and away and came back onto and into her. It didn't disrupt the combined flow of their energies.

"And here's the utmost. Gentlemen, move the chairs back and lie on your sides on the edge of the bed facing us. The world won't end if you touch up against us or put your hands on us but don't do too much of that. It might get distracting. Mostly get as comfortable as you can and listen up.

The first part was easy. The second part was a little iffier. This is the hardest and the best. It might not work the first time. This is sacred tantra, not a sexual trick. We ask God to fully join us. Arrange your hips or thighs so Eva can rest her feet on them. Hold your legs up, sweetheart, till you get tired. Then place your feet on the two of them."

They nestled into position.

"We all have energy barriers between our chakras. We all have all different kinds of energy. We can send some of our energy all over the universe. A lot of Eva's energies have already united with mine. But we have what I call life force energy that can't leave our bodies. It sustains us. It almost never moves beyond our skin.

Eva, darling, you have an energy barrier in your cervix. Every woman does. Your cervix is like the guardian of your womb. It's there to close and protect and open for the baby. My cock is in your pussy. So my life force is in your pussy. That's part of what makes sex so delicious. But my life force energy can move up into your body. If you allow it, things can get even more delicious.

These things are unconscious. We don't know about them until we do. Then we can consciously bring things about that normally don't happen.

So I want you to bring your awareness into your cervix just above the head of my cock. I'll attend to her, too, and Gabe and André, you do likewise. And Eva, just gently and lovingly have the intention and ask your cervix to surrender her barrier, to soften and open, to allow my life force energy to rise up into your second chakra area. This is an energy thing. It's subtler than the physical. But it's more powerful and beautiful than what has already happened. It's extraordinary when it comes about. A man's life force energy can rise up and fill the woman. It's the highest love a man and woman can experience together. Just open and relax. Talk to your cervix. Let her know that everything's alright. That you want her to do this. That she can."

They all got quiet and poured their love into Eva, into her cervix, into the energy barrier therein.

A few minutes went by.

"Tell her you love her. Thank her for the great job of protecting you she's been doing. Ask her to show you how she can open her door."

Eva knew she could bring this about with her powers. But she didn't want to. She wanted to see if it could happen without her using them. She knew she would use them as a last resort. But now she just loved and coaxed that precious part of her body.

"Send your energy into the heart of her. Love her. Encourage her to open."

Eva was finally able to do this and, in a moment, everything changed.

The barrier in her cervix dissolved. And Jimmy's life force energy moved upward and filled her second chakra, her womb, her fallopian tubes, her ovaries and every fiber and cavity of her lower abdomen area.

"Oh my God," Eva said.

It was like heaven had entered their bodies.

A whole new universe had opened up.

They were transported to a different realm.

The unity of their other energies that had previously occurred was wonderful.

It took them deeper into fulfillment, togetherness and a natural ease and confidence.

But this was something else altogether.

"This is amazing," Eva half whispered.

"I know, darlin'. There's nothing like it."

Ripples of bliss were washing through Eva's reproductive organs and radiating out to her entire body.

She was feeling heavenly sensations in all her erogenous zones.

The levels of her pleasure were rising within her.

It was as if Jimmy's life force was able to stimulate her all over, all at once.

Jimmy was in heaven loving her with everything he had.

This went on for about fifteen minutes.

They were in rapture.

Time was meaningless.

And Gabe and André were experiencing this as well.

"OK," Jimmy finally said, "we did it. We did the first step of this sacred tantric love. See how wonderful it can be?"

"Yes," Eva said. "This is totally new for me. It's astonishing. I love it. Divine energy love."

"Exactly. And this is only our first level together. There are many more. The higher we go the better it gets. Every step is another level of heaven. These are the levels of heaven the ancients wrote about. We have moved from the root chakra into the second chakra. Each chakra level is like a universe. You have another energy barrier at the top of your womb. Opening that door will allow us to move higher. As we rise, it gets more and more divine. Shall we continue?"

"Oh yes, please."

All this time Jimmy had remained fully hard within her. All this time his life force energy had been in her pussy. Now it was in her pussy and her second chakra world. Eva was feeling a new kind of fulfillment. She knew this could lead to another kind of orgasm altogether, a vaginal orgasm, a whole body orgasm, a body, heart and soul orgasm. Gabriel and Anani were her true loves. But this man was giving her something she had always wanted but never even knew existed. She felt a mighty love for him as a mentor, a friend, an ally and a man.

"Now let's all love that place at the top of your womb about halfway up your lower abdomen, a little above your delta. Envision her, the sacred chamber of life, small and contracted as she is with nothing inside to stretch her. There's an energy wall right at the top of precious her."

They all allowed their attention to come to rest there.

"Talk to her like your cervix. They're all protecting you."

And internally, she did.

In a few moments that barrier dissolved and Jimmy's energy rose to her diaphragm filling her entire abdomen.

The effect on them went beyond words. It filled Eva with a love, beauty and pleasure she had never known. It was ecstasy both earthly and divine. His energy was working its wonders in every cavity and organ of her lower torso. It stimulated her pussy and her clit. It stimulated, fulfilled and pleasured every organ. It flowed out into every part of her body and every particle of her being.

Tsunamis of joy washed through her, swept her away, carried her beyond the shore. She began to come in a way she never had. Everything within her rose in unison and swelled into a rapture of pleasure. It was like her whole body was tilting, contracting and expanding in unison with her womb. She was transported into a cosmic come. Every cell was coming. She was a fountain of love and heaven.

And her three men were directly sharing her experience with her.

And somehow, like several women synchronizing with the alpha's cycle, everyone around her had synchronized with her lovemaking.

Even while Jimmy had been hard inside her for over an hour, the others had been doing other things and were now in coitus close to climax.

Déwei was supine on the ottomans straddled by Anani.

Alena and Jack, like Jimmy and Eva now, were in mission position.

Liu was on top of Nyame jerking her pussy and pressing her clit hard against his pubic bone.

Somehow, miraculously, without Eva consciously controlling them, they were moving along the same energy lines towards orgasm.

Eva, Déwei, Anani, Liu, Nyame, Alena and Jack all came at the same time.

Eva's orgasm was unearthly. Afterwards, all she could do was cry in relief, wonder and joy. This had fulfilled her womanhood like nothing else had. It was of a higher order than all the glory she had recently experienced. This was, indeed, divine love, the sacred marriage, God participating in their lovemaking. She held Jimmy and Jimmy held her and Gabe and André pressed against and stroked them.

Her rapture continued, softening and transporting her.

The most fulfilling cry of her life tapered off and ended.

She felt beautiful and complete.

"Oh Jimmy, thank you. This has made me a different woman."

"Oh Eva, thank you. You are the queen of all women."

They lay for a few moments quietly.

"Where did you get all this? Did you do it with all your lovers?"

"Oh no, you're the first. Men are wired to think about sex. At least I am. So for all these dry years I had a lot of time to think. Once, when I was active, I got the idea of having this beautifully surrendered girlfriend of mine love herself to orgasm when we were in the right position for it. She told me it gave her the most powerful come of her life. I was born with a deep love of the sacred power of surrender. It's been a lifelong theme with me and many of my experiences reinforced it. And the tantra thing was innate as well. It surfaced during one long, lovely fuck with a woman conducive for it. We just got to her second chakra. I got the half hour thing and sideways position when I was a teenager from a book called *Sex Perfection and Marital Happiness* and then verified it for myself with a few women. Interestingly enough, it came out the year I was born. I've been wanting to combine everything with the right woman for years. It had to wait for the supreme moment and Goddess, you."

"Thank you for waiting and having this wisdom. I'm so grateful to be the one to receive it."

"My supreme pleasure. You are so worth waiting for. God is wise. She formed and shaped me to bring it to you at this most important time in our evolution. This is how she pushes things forward."

"God is female?"

"God is both and more. We just don't have a pronoun for that. When I'm in church I say He for them. Now I say She. The power of Her feminine side has been dismissed for too long."

In this moment something happened and the four of them reached a deeper level of awareness together. The depth and breadth of it held them in quiet, sublime vastness as if they were in the womb of the Mother. It also rippled the tingles through their skin. Somehow the subtle, mysterious ways in which God works revealed itself to them. They floated in the sanctity of it all for several minutes.

Then Eva said, "You're still hard."

"Yes."

"We're still fucking."

"Yes."

"I am so your fuck," she said laughing a little. "What now?"

"Prolonged eye gazing would be magnificent. But not tonight. First tell me. Put all your orgasms on a scale of one to ten, including this week, including our last one. What number would you give this one?"

"I can hardly rate it. It was more like a quantum leap. Thirty."

"Beautiful, it's so fulfilling to fulfill you. So fulfilling for both of us. And that was only three. Less than halfway to the top. What might it be getting to your heart and above? Three was so much more than two. It's hard to imagine four through seven. What's now is to come or not to come. That is the question. And the decision is yours."

"Mine?"

"Yes."

"You don't have a preference?"

"They each have their plusses and minuses."

"You don't have a preference?"

"I want to fulfill you as much as possible. I want to fulfill your preference. I'm totally blissed out and grateful either way. This is my fulfillment of a lifetime. I couldn't be a happier man."

"Come."

"Are you sure?"

"Yes, I want it all to be as complete as it can."

"Yes ma'am. You're the boss."

"And don't you forget it."

They chuckled and Jimmy began to move.

"In this position?" Eva asked.

"Yes, in this position."

Up until now almost everything Jimmy had done was for bringing Eva to where he had brought her, her ultimate surrender, pleasure and fulfillment. He had satisfied all his desires in so doing and had loved every minute of it. But it was also geared for her.

Now he could focus on his own simple pleasure, the pure, visceral joy of fucking. He had brought Eva to her completion.

He placed his hands by Eva's sides and straightened his arms, raising his head and upper torso so he could take in her beauty with his eyes and move more effectively. Then he started slowly, moving deeply in and nearly all the way out, feeling the sensations, the tactile wonder of it, allowing his entire being to become one with the pleasure. Eva again pooled the awareness of her four-person pod. After her orgasm she had let it lapse as they spoke out loud. They were again all sharing in Jimmy and Eva's experience. And this enhanced it. It was particularly fascinating for Eva as they all savored every delicious, pleasurable love sensation the warm, wet, slippery friction of her perfectly caressing vaginal glove poured forth upon the innumerable ecstasy and joy receptors blessing the significant length of Jimmy's warm, engorged, moving, blissed out member.

Then, over time, he picked up and varied the pace. Fast and rapid, slow and strong, hard, jerking, flesh jiggling thumps, high speed whipping it in and out, all the ways to give him satisfaction till he began to approach his own threshold.

Then he thought his thoughts, which they all perceived.

"André, I won't command you on this one but how do you feel about licking my ass?"

"Oh Jimmy, you're amazing. I want to. Two supreme beings in one night! Command me. Please."

"You'll be my cunt?"

"Oh yes, please, I'll do everything I can to be the most perfect cunt I can for you."

This increased Jimmy's arousal and brought him even closer to his threshold. He had always been thoroughly straight. But now he found it thrilling to have André, with his pretty boy body and his male genitals, to command for his own pleasure.

He spread his knees and cheeks wide apart.

His cock was throbbing and wanting to come inside Eva.

"Lap it three times."

André came around behind him and gave him his three best tongue strokes.

"Good boy. Now press in hard and extend your tongue as deep as you can."

André obeyed magnificently.

"So goooood," Jimmy breathed.

It felt exquisite to him and fed every part of his being, his cock in Eva so close to coming, André's tongue up his ass moving, caressing and giving him such deep satisfaction.

And Eva could feel how it gave Jimmy so much more intense, sexual pleasure than her though it had felt very good to her.

He moved gently in and out so André had no trouble moving with him. Then he made a few subtle, shorter, similar motions. He spread his cheeks to the max so André could push in a little deeper. Then he pulled his cock almost all the way out arching his back and opening as wide as he could. He commanded André to slowly move his head and tongue out and all the way in five times. Then he had him withdraw and stand at the foot of the bed.

He was ready. He gave a few long thrusts and came, pressing insistently deep into Eva and spurting, rubbing and pushing his cream into her cervix with the head of his cock. He moved a few more times in a few more ways and then slumped down onto her with his full weight. They were complete.

This, too, had been amazing for Eva. She had loved it.

She almost felt she might come again. But that would have been too much.

Nothing could have been more perfect than this was.

He lay on top of her remaining inside for several minutes as his penis slowly went limp.

Then he slid out and rolled off onto his side facing her.

"What time is it, darlin'?"

"Ten-oh-three," Eva said letting her legs come down. She had only rested her feet on their witnesses several times briefly for leverage and movement.

"Beautiful. An hour-and-a-half to the minute. When was the last time a man was inside you that long?"

"Never. Not even close."

"Well no shame cast on anyone. Like I said, I've had over a decade to fully assimilate my lifelong experiences. Very few men on Earth would know this. Glad we did?"

They all laughed but could hardly do so.

Eva could barely move.

She managed to turn on her side towards Gabriel, back into spoon position against Jimmy and pull Gabriel towards her.

"Can you fit on the bed, sweetheart?" Eva asked André.

"No, I don't think so. I'm good. I'll get some floor bedding and lie down on a couch."

"Put our duvet over us and blow out the candles, darling, your mouth in me was magnificent."

His heart and soul swelled. He did as he was bid and was gone.

He, Anani and Déwei made a big, comfortable pallet on the floor.

They all slept like babies the entire night.

Chapter 20

May We Soon Have a Warless World

In the morning they relieved themselves and freshened up. Then they wandered into the living room in varied states of dress and undress.

They didn't concern themselves with sitting in a circle or a horseshoe.

When they all gathered, Eva unified their consciousness.

"Happy Memorial Day. May we soon have a warless world," she generated in their mind. Then she pooled and shared all their experiences of the previous night so they all got to feel, see and taste everything each one had. It was a beautiful, deeply intimate form of group love they relived together.

Regarding Eva's experience, only Nyame had used Jimmy's trick a few times.

No one had come close to experiencing the tantra.

But now they all knew how and what it was like.

Internally they loved, saluted and bid farewell to Déwei and Liu who gathered the rest of their clothing and winked out to Beijing. They could reunite in the blink of an eye.

Nyame had one last thing to do in the city. Then he was ready to leave.

They all got up and put him in the middle of a group hug.

Then he winked out of sight, accomplished his errand and was in Accra in fifteen minutes.

The rest of them, with Eva's help, ordered their breakfast from Portable Chef.

Eva sent Jimmy to his place to shower and change. She would retrieve him for breakfast as soon as he was done.

The rest used their two showers two at a time to prepare to meet their day.

The Portable Chef delivered, Eva pulled Jimmy back and they ate their breakfast at the octagonal table.

When they were done, they cleaned up and sat in the living room.

"What now?" Gabriel asked.

"I don't know, food shopping?"

They all laughed and laughed.

It was all too much.

Jimmy was well stocked and didn't need anything. So Eva sent him back to his place.

The rest of them went shopping and had the blast of a lifetime.

A few places were closed but the important ones were open.

What fun they were having, this golden family!

What life on Earth could be when lived like this!

From the stores they visited, Eva winked them back to their kitchen one by one protected from the view of too many eyes. She didn't want to draw too much attention.

They were soon well stocked, in the living room and wondering what to do next.

Eva's phone rang once and stopped.

She pooled all their minds into Jimmy's.

"They want me at a big gathering at St. John the Divine tomorrow night at eight."

"Good, we'll be there but not for the talk. We'll come when you're done and sing. Let about ten minutes go by and see if you can call out to me with just your mind."

She looked at her pod, first into Anani's eyes long and deep, the love simply pouring back and forth between them.

Then André, "Sweet André, did you feel deprived last night?"

"Oh no. I was in heaven!"

She poured love into him.

Then Alena, "Dear Alena, let's sleep together soon."

"Oh yes, I'd love that," her eyes and lips lighting up like a Christmas tree.

Then Jack, "Jack, Jack, Jack, dear Jack, you know Alena can't keep you all to herself forever."

"Yes ma'am, I belong to you all as well."

"Good boy, don't forget it."

And finally Gabriel, "Boy, have I been neglecting you."

"You're a busy woman," he smiled in the fullness of his love, feeling far more love, admiration and genuine humility than neglect.

"How do you feel about these black gods I've been sleeping with?"

"I can't say I'm perfectly devoid of bruised ego but I also feel privileged and deeply humbled. Seeing Jimmy in all his glory, learning what I've learned from him and thinking of how I could hardly perceive him as a human being so incidental and beneath me. What an arrogant fool I was!"

"No my love, diminishing yourself is its own kind of arrogance. That was the way of the world then. This is the way of the world now. I love you, Gabriel. You're my prince of all princes."

She let the love flow beautifully between them for several moments.

"You haven't cried yet, have you?"

"No."

"Anani and I cried in the shower. They all cried in front of us. Perhaps it's your turn."

"Perhaps it is."

"Or maybe since it's been a year for you and your life was so smooth, you don't have the need. Do you think you fully grieved Lada?"

"I think so but who can know? There's probably more. Having you has healed a lot."

Eva could feel Jimmy calling out to her with his mind.

She let him know she had received the call.

"Let's see what divine orchestration brings, my love. This doesn't seem to be the moment for it."

She looked at André.

"I think it's about time we did what you and Nyame did."

They found themselves hanging in space before the moon.

It filled about a quarter of their field of vision.

They gazed for several moments.

She turned them about.

The number of stars they could see was staggering.

She turned them about again and pulled them in to a distance where the moon filled half their vision.

They gazed some more.

Then to where it filled nearly all their vision.

It was stunning.

Then to where they were close enough to see boulders and hills and mountain ranges.

Then she landed them on the surface.

They laughed.

They felt like children, free in the universe.

They took their first steps.

They started hopping and skipping and then jumping and bounding as they got used to and thrilled by the lesser pull of gravity.

They laughed and shouted and hooted.

They couldn't hear a single thing but Eva had their consciousness pooled so they could internally.

They ran and raced and jumped, soared and floated.

They couldn't be giddier.

Eva thought of Jimmy and he was there.

They didn't tire of this.

But after about fifteen minutes, Eva pulled them to the opposite side, the dark side of the moon.

They couldn't move because they couldn't see a thing. But they could look out at the sky.

It was unbelievable, so many more visible stars. And just knowing where they were!

She pulled them to a place in space directly over the dividing line between light and dark.

They could see half the moon in darkness, half in light.

And off in the distance, Earth, so much bigger and prettier than the moon from there.

She took them to Saturn and showed them the surface and the rings from many different distances and angles.

It was dizzying and full of awe and splendor.

They went to Jupiter and watched the swirling gases. She jumped them to the center of the great red spot. It was a stunning blend of swirling clouds and wind with a hole to the sky at the center of the vortex.

Then to Neptune to enjoy it's beautiful, deep blue color.

Then she took them straight to the face on Mars. They circled and viewed it from every angle. It seemed clear it had been fashioned and formed by other than the whimsies of nature.

It was deeply eroded. If it had been built, it was many eons ago. But the base foundation was too uniform, too sculpted, too perfect to not have been shaped by the hands of sentient beings.

Eva sent her mind beneath the structure searching for any telltale clue.

Then she found it, a cavern deep under the ground protected from the elements containing artifacts, statues and some huge, strange, metallic mechanism whose purpose was about unearthing, bringing forth and revealing something, what it was she could not see.

She was thrilled and excited but as she thought to pull them there, she got, "No, not yet. The time will come for that."

Instead she took them to the surface and they walked the red dust of Mars looking at the structure before them and all around.

This was a desert world.

They briefly visited Venus and Mercury and then to that part of space best suited for facing and viewing the sun.

As they hung there gazing on the spectacle of our fiery father, seeing the titanic storms of plasma spewing from the surface and the seething, unimaginable heat of its orb, Eva marveled at the miracles their friends and the tiny ring on her pinky could bring forth. And those other, more powerful, benevolent beings, the gods to their angels, what could they bring forth?

But we are God's children are we not? What miracles could not be wrought by God? How little of our true nature have we truly been living? That we could be here and not rupture or freeze, that we can gaze at the sun with no discomfort, that I can blink us anywhere in the universe that I can conceive of, what is reality? What is not?

She took them to the center of the galaxy. They could see the super-massive Great Central Sun. They could see the Council of Twelve, the twelve stars surrounding their father. They could see how crowded with stars and worlds the core of our galaxy is. They could see our most massive vortex, the Great Central Yoni, our greatest black hole, the mother of us all.

Eva took them right up to its event horizon but it pulled on them in a way she felt could irrevocably change them. She pulled them back a few hundred thousand miles and they watched things disappear into a mouth so big and powerful they could barely comprehend it.

They had reached their limit. They could absorb no more. Eva took them home.

They just sat there silently. No one had any thoughts or words to share. Eventually, André got up in search of food. The others followed and they prepared their lunch and ate it.

Eva looked at Gabe and then Alena.

"Work tomorrow."

Alena replied, "Yes. We'll find replacements soon."

"Please do."

They finished their lunch, cleaned up and congregated in the living room.

Eva took them to the Taj Mahal, Angkor Wat, Machu Picchu, the sky above the Eiffel Tower, the top of Cape Town's Table Mountain, the Great Wall of China, Victoria Falls and the Acropolis.

In some places it was night in some, day. It didn't matter. They could enjoy the beauty and thrill of knowing where they were.

In Paris Eva slowly rotated them in the sky 360 degrees so they could fully take in the panorama of the City of Love's twinkling night lights from a vantage point above and to the side of her so very famous tower.

In most places they landed. In some they didn't. But she kept them in each place long enough and gave them enough different vantage points so they all felt they had truly been there.

She brought them to their living room, dropped all their clothes to the floor and whisked them away to the tiny island in André's mind.

Again they laughed like children and ran into the water cavorting, splashing, laughing, arcing back into the luscious, gentle surf.

They spent time getting direct sun on their assholes, sunning their genitals, rotating their bodies on the sand, washing it off and coming back out. Eva took them back to Victoria Falls to get wet in the foam and spray, to Nyame's Hawaiian waterfall to wash themselves clean and flew them high and fast in the sky for a quick air dry. Then she put them in the best positions to get more sunlight on their crotches and then their whole bodies, slowly twirling them like multi-angled rotisseries. Then they were home.

"OK," she smiled, "Now we're more than even with André and Nyame, not that I'm counting."

"Oh no, never!" a few of them intoned.

Then she saw them all with their clothes on and they were magically dressed.

"Let's meditate."

They drank in the depth, love and peace of diving deep into the layers of their infinite being.

More and more they were loving this form of being one together.

Then they were done.

"What shall we do about dinner?"

"New Orleans?" André offered.

"South Miami!" Alena exclaimed.

"How about Rio?" Anani smiled.

"Oh, Rio!" a few voices chimed in.

"Sounds like Rio gets it tonight. Hopefully we'll have many nights to go everywhere we want. Will their restaurants take American money?"

"Oh I'm sure."

"Jimmy what do you need?"

"Send me home, darlin', there's something I need to do with some neighbors. I'll be moving into my new digs tomorrow."

"Call out if you need help," and he was gone.

"Let's dress up!"

They all loved it.

Their boundaries were definitely widening.

Eva cast her mind to Rio and asked to be drawn to the best Brazilian restaurant for her personal taste. That's all she needed to do. She could be her own search engine now. She had somehow assimilated much of what the Earth Room could do though she knew she'd go back for the intensity of it. It could still extend her reach. She was being given and learning more of her capabilities without having to ask the devas. More and more she was feeling omniscient and omnipotent. This wasn't grandiosity. It wasn't ego. She knew the powers resided in God and the ring and the more she was able to utilize them the better.

She thought of the benevolent beings greater than their friends. She tuned into them. They were extraordinary, like gods to the angels that were helping them. She realized that through the ring, she was tapping into their power as well. She moved through the ring into their realm and began to meld her energy bodies into theirs. The might of their world, their bodies and their god-like souls expanded the substance of her body and her own being to the bursting point. She held the maximum she could for several moments. She couldn't go beyond that. This went beyond orgasm. It was God incarnate. It felt like she would burn to a cinder. Finally she had to retreat.

She began to come to.

Someone was saying something to her.

It was Gabe, "Darling, are you alright?"

She looked at him to help her refocus into the present moment.

"Yes love, I seem to be growing. Everybody go get ready. I just need to sit here a little longer and set things up."

She returned her mind to Rio and then, specifically, to the mind of the maître d' of Aprazível and placed the highest priority reservation for six under 'Eva' there. They were, of course, booked but Thiago had contingencies for such things and within minutes there were two cancellations.

Eva wanted another shower. She joined Gabriel who was already there and let him soap and massage her. When they were done, she let him dry her. It was good to be pampered and free to assimilate all that was happening. Gabe somehow knew not to converse.

They were soon on the street by their restaurant in beautiful attire. They entered, greeted Thiago and were seated at their table. Eva read the waiters' minds and shared the detailed knowledge of everything on the menu with them including the correct pronunciations. When their waiter came she put all their orders in his head and left him to deal with that in his own way.

They savored the delicious food as it came to their table. They savored and loved their beautiful company. They savored the simple delight of being in Rio.

About halfway through the meal, Eva felt someone approaching the restaurant. He was like Lakane, the Lakane of Rio.

"Oh good," she thought. "Another ring wearer. Odd we have two crime figures."

She sent her mind into his before she saw him.

"Now why didn't I think of this with Nyame? I'm getting better at this. Oh right, I didn't know I could yet."

Comando Vermelho, the Red Command. The major drug gang that ruled much of the city. This was one of their top lieutenants. There were only a handful of bosses above him. He had a few henchmen and two beautiful women with him. His name was João.

They were seated at a table not far from Eva's.

She continued downloading gang information from his mind.

He noticed the beautiful six of them and especially her. He had his own private thoughts of semi-raping her. She didn't so much care for his desires to overpower her. But she did enjoy the knowledge that she could completely overpower him with no physical harm to anyone. She realized it was probably good that she hadn't gotten into Nyame's mind before healing him. Knowing the unhealed version too well wasn't enticing.

But she soon knew everything of his gang, its rival and their police allies and adversaries that she needed to.

The ten major cell bosses of Rio's Comando Vermelho and Terceiro Comando simultaneously disappeared from their various locations.

Eva had just neutralized most of Rio's gang warfare.

She then decided to send the city's ten top policemen as well. One was quite decent. The rest were varying degrees of corrupt. João knew the players well. Eva wondered how many policemen Nyame had sent. She reached out to him. Twelve.

She expanded João's bladder giving him the sensation he had to pee. He got up to make his way to the men's room. She disappeared him before he locked the door.

She noticed her pod was silent and looking at her with concern.

"Did someone say something to me?" she asked aloud.

"Yes dear," Gabriel replied. "You seem to be disappearing more. Need we be concerned?"

"Oh no, my loves. I've just majorly cleaned up Rio's crime and police world."

She transmitted to their minds all of what had just occurred.

"I'll be engaging in all kinds of things from time to time. Maybe I'll bring you with me. Probably I'll just do it on my own. Please watch over and protect me. There's no need for concern. If there ever is you'll immediately know. I also need to assimilate how fast I'm learning and growing. It's a bit much to keep up with. I need to keep silent now and do some of that. Maybe I can eat and do it at the same time."

They were nearly finished with their entrées.

She could think and enjoy her meal.

"So," she thought. "What about ISIS, Al Qaeda, Hezbolla and the leaders of Israel? What about Joseph fucking Kony though I think his health has already neutralized him. What about Boko Haram and all those girls? They could sure use liberating. And what about Obama and Putin?"

But she knew she couldn't go rampaging around the world sending people off according to her will. She knew it wasn't time for that. She knew they would all be taken care of. She was getting too big for her britches. Better tone it down. Her path was being laid out before her. It had led her here. It had led João to her. Through him it had led to what she had just done. Her job was to simply follow it and do what arose to do. This was more than enough.

João's party became concerned at his prolonged absence. One of his henchmen got up to investigate. She disappeared him. The two women grew concerned. They went off to the ladies room just to check it before fleeing. They disappeared. She left the final henchman to do what he would. He calmly sat there and resumed eating.

"Good boy," Eva thought to herself. "I'll leave you to João."

She was finally ready to return her attention to her own party.

"Sorry babes, mama's been busy. This desert is delicious!"

She took them to Lapa. They found a club and danced. People disappeared right and left. She took them into the skies of Rio, to the Christ statue, to the top of Sugarloaf, cruising over the entire city, landing at places they were drawn to.

Finally they walked Ipanema. They took off their shoes and stood in the ocean. They were content.

She winked them into the skies and found a pristine mountain lake. She dropped their clothes on a big rock on the shore for skinny-dipping. This time they were happy to feel like adults. But it was chilly!

She winked them to the tropical skies of the Seychelles to dry in the sun, their clothes in tow like banners. She flew them fast for the wind to quick dry as the sun warmed their naked bodies and hearts.

Then they were home, their clothes in their closets, naked together to do as they wished.

As one they all just decided to sleep.

Needless to say they all slept well.

Chapter 21

They Call Us Creamies

The alarm went off at 6:30.

"Oh God," Eva moaned, "Why hast though forsaken me?"

Gabriel smiled and kissed her on the cheek.

She just lay there and went back to sleep.

Alena had also awakened for work. Gabriel and she showered together in the guest bathroom. How delicious it was, the joy of seeing and feeling their soapy, slippery skin, her breasts and nipples, his cock and balls, his ass, her anus and every other wonderful part! The things they could do with each other now that they couldn't before—that they had always wanted to do! Then they had their breakfast together and left to walk arm in arm to work, an extraordinarily beautiful, happy, perfect but otherwise normal looking couple. So much better than the five years of coming to work alone!

They were totally in love with each other and with all kinds of other people. They could revel in their newfound intimacy in the haven of their pod. Alone they would never have made it. They both realized this. They both thanked God for what they now had, the divine bounty and wisdom of this gift! The contrast from before! How much their work and everyone who touched them would be blessed by the love they now shared! They both smiled with ultimate fulfillment.

Their pod members began getting up at their own pace.

André wandered out first and headed for the kitchen.

Anani and Jack soon joined him.

They began preparing a meal for four in earnest.

When everything was ready Eva emerged.

She'd been monitoring from afar.

"Thank you, sweeties, life is bliss," she flashed them a smile.

They munched and chatted aloud.

Sometimes talking happened. Sometimes it didn't.

When they were finished Eva wondered, "Well, we've done Rio, where next?"

"Vientiane," Anani said with a gentle but decisive tone that didn't leave much room for alternatives.

"Beautiful, my love, I hear and obey. But there's a bear of a time change."

"Yes, eleven hours. If we leave at nine in the morning it'll be eight pm."

"Or we could get there at sunrise or later. I'd like us all to go unless we wait till the weekend."

Anani inclined her head in deferment.

"Let's leave it to God, darling. I so do love you. Take off your pajamas for me. I want your pussy for dessert."

It was so delightful to see her undress. There was a time for instant and a time for leisure.

They were still seated at their kitchen table for four.

"Come here to my right and put your left foot behind my chair leg. Good. Now put your right foot up on the table."

Anani could just do this with one hand on Eva's shoulder to steady herself.

This stretched her pussy beautifully open right in Eva's face.

"So glorious," Eva murmured letting them all feel her love and pleasure.

She licked her a few times and then slipped her tongue in deeper. Just enough to get her smell and taste.

Then she turned to her men.

"Jack, Jack, Jack. Why do I keep saying that? Jack, Jack, Jack it. Jack it up, Jack. Jack it up good."

They laughed a little.

In an instant he was standing naked facing her on her left.

"Whoa," he said, feeling exhilarated surprise. "That was something!"

With her seated and him standing, his genitals were just below her face.

She slumped down and took his cock deep in her mouth. It had begun to stir at the sight of her licking Anani. She began sucking and caressing the full length of it with her tongue and cheeks and held and caressed his balls in her upturned palm. He was soon quite hard. She slowly slipped her lips down the length of him and licked his undertip with the tip of her tongue.

Then André was naked in his place and Jack was up next to him.

She did the same for André.

They stood erect side by side.

She turned back to Anani and surveyed her beauty.

Then to the two engorged cocks on her other side.

"Oh my," Eva said, "how lovely. Two cocks, four balls and a pussy. Isn't it divine, Jack, the miraculous regeneration of your genitals? So whole and so perfect! What a breakfast I'm having! What shall we do with these lovelies? I'm truly thrilled to have them all standing so proudly displayed before me and at my disposal! Aren't I just the most terrible thing on Earth? Where do I get this stuff? Oh well, I'm just a crude, controlling lust monster so happy to see Anani wide open and you two hard. Maybe I'm relieving the world's repressed lust. Maybe I'm siphoning off its testosterone-driven desires. Whatever it may be, it's totally delicious. Thank you, darlings, I love you. I'm tempted to see one of these wonderful cocks slip into this gorgeous pussy. But I think we need to take stock. I wonder if I can do instant cleanup."

She saw in her mind's eye everything before them pristinely clean and put away.

And so it was.

They all looked at each other.

"God, the possibilities! What's next, instant feast? Wasn't there an Indian guru who was supposed to be able to manifest things? But that turned out to be sleight of hand, didn't it?"

They went to the living room.

"So Gabe arranged for us to let in Housing Works and the cleaning people throughout the day, yes?"

"Yes," Anani informed her. "But darling mama, you're not a terrible monster. You may be siphoning off the world's testosterone but it's not only that. We'd *all* love to have our desires fulfilled, to just get to do anything we might think of. We'd love to have our objects of desire ready to do everything we want. And we've all been living deprivation. You're the one who's *meant* to get them all fulfilled. It's perfect for us. We want to fulfill you. Just like children, mama, we love your attention. Don't even think about holding back with us."

Eva looked at Anani for a moment and then to Jack and André.

"Absolutely," Jack affirmed simultaneously with André's, "Yes!"

Jack went on in heartfelt words that nearly ended in a tear, "My cock and balls are yours, Eva. Without you I wouldn't have them. My life is yours. The life of a PTSD eunuch was barely a life at all."

"I love you, Jack. You're perfect and good and the best conceivable addition to our pod. So I needn't feel guilty or apologize?"

"Right!" and "No, you don't!" they chorused.

"I can just keep telling you what to do?"

"Yes!" they said and Jack added, "You're our General. That's what Generals do."

"Alright," she gave a big sigh. "I'll keep working on it. So let's get ready and I'll send you there."

They went off and Eva was left alone. They dribbled in and she sent them to their old homes.

Of the four of them, Eva's first appointment was last. She had some time.

She winked out to the Earth Room to cognize the world of man.

She started with Vientiane. Such a relaxed, graceful city!

She could see its entirety almost as if she were there high in the sky. But she could sense and feel things ordinary humans could not. She could feel the beat and flow of the energy, the qualities of the different places and peoples, the heart and soul of the vibrations that drove the city's life.

She soon located a ring wearer, a diminutive, seventy-five-year-old woman who lived mostly in solitude. She had the fiercest light, like a laser or Siva's infinite pillar. She had hardly used it in her life. It felt like it could burn another human to a cinder or shine with divine glory and uplift everything around her. Her name was Konane. Eva realized, with a start, that she could simply send her from here. Intellectual knowledge of new powers was one thing. Using them in the real world was another.

"So what's to stop me from sending everyone on Earth?"

She already knew. Those who consciously opposed. She couldn't send them. And if she sent large numbers of others they would react with fear-driven violence. This had to happen slowly enough to soften them. She couldn't function from one iota of grandiosity. God's grandeur. God's love. God's time and generosity. God's gentle touch.

She could, though, send Konane.

And she did.

"How will we send so many?" she asked and was answered.

The deva's could deploy ninety-nine chambers in far, deep space. Each could hold a million people. Ninety-nine million souls every two hours. A hundred and fifty hours for everyone. Six days plus to do every human on Earth.

How fitting.

But that was a long time. The opposition could wreak havoc.

The human race would be vulnerable.

The contras would have to be neutralized beforehand or early in the game.

She cradled Earth in her awareness like a fragile egg.

She saw her energy rivers, the template that held her current patterns, all the beings she sustained. She saw her pristine places still nearly untouched and the swarming masses of humanity with all their peace and all their turbulence. She focused in on Nyame in Ghana and saw his little pod growing. Then Déwei in Beijing and João in Rio. One of the beautiful women at dinner was his second pod member. The other wasn't.

Then she focused in on herself, her pod members, Jimmy. The light around them was amazing. But her light was far different than Konane's. Eva's own could be laser-like. But it was more a magnificent mountain, Everest standing majestically around her. She saw the tendrils of energy connecting her with her family and Roz. She saw similar tendrils reaching from her pod members. She saw how healing the beings they were most connected with could strengthen her unit and its influence.

"Ah yes, the next thing for me to see."

Then she focused in on the contras.

She could see Tom and, by extension, Ellie and Peter. Ellie knew nothing of the devas or their opposition so she could be sent. Tom would resist. She could see the Omega group and other top secret cadres dotted around the world. She could see all the power pockets of those who consciously opposed. They idolized force and control, self-aggrandizement and the drive to own everything. They feared and hated the devas and those 'turned' by them.

"They call us creamies," Eva thought with a smile. "How funny, as if they despise pussy juice, the weakness of women, the weakness, in their eyes, of love and the love of God. I guess Satan *is* alive and well. What shall we call *them*? The darkies? No. The inkies? No again. Oh I know, the creepies! The creamies and the creepies, what could be better?"

She saw the controlling ETs, the Greys, the Oranges, the Lizards and some other frightening, amorphous dark cloud beings. She saw the Greys monitoring her own pod's comings and goings from afar.

She saw the human families who had for so long controlled the money supply, the ebb and flow of world wealth, and who had amassed the great bulk of it. She saw how they feared the loss of all they thought they had. She couldn't help but pity them. Did they have one one-millionth of the joy and happiness that her pod did? She could see they didn't—the scheming and maneuvering they were forced to do to retain and bloat their holdings, their grandiosity masking their fear, their ruthlessness and hatred for all things truly precious, how they knew so many things that few others did and guarded their secrets so viciously.

Then she saw the dolphins and the whales, the elephant and the jaguar, the lion and the lamb and all the animals of earth, sea and air who poured so much love into and around our world.

And Earth herself, her oceans as living worlds, her atmosphere and tectonic plates and the assault upon them from the works of man.

What a miracle it all was! How warped and distorted so much had become! How beautiful and supportive all things could be!

And last she saw how the devas depended on the ringed ones to expand their capabilities for the acceleration. They could do so much but so much and more had to come from within the human race.

"It is we who will make our destiny."

So here too, she was being asked not to hold back, to move forward fully and completely, to stretch her capabilities and love to the max, to become all that she could.

She came back to her living room crying. She lay on the couches and let herself weep. When she felt complete, she saw herself perfectly clean, dressed and in her old apartment.

She arrived fifteen minutes before her first appointment.

She cognized all her things that still remained.

A few items reappeared in her new home.

She was ready to let go of everything else.

She let in the retrievers of second hand items.

"Please take everything and thank you."

She returned to her living room, pulled her phone from her bag and auto-dialed Roz.

"Hi love."

"Hi honey, are you working?"

"I just finished with one of your clients and I'm on my way to lunch."

Eva cognized the time. It was 12:11.

"Mind if I pull you here?"

"I'm not in the Village, sweetie."

Eva saw where she was and then she stood before her.

Roz looked at her for a moment with her mouth open.

"Whoa, that was exhilarating! Doing more than just disappearing now?"

"I guess so and that's just the beginning."

"But really honey, I was on the sidewalk. People just saw me disappear!"

"I know. That's part of it. They're supposed to. It helps blow our minds in preparation for what's to come."

"OK," Roz looked around. "This is Gabriel's? Pretty swanky. And overlooking the park!"

"Ours now and more than ours. There are six of us."

Roz shot her a glance, "Six!"

"Yes, remember that luscious waitress at Up Thai? She's one."

"I knew you had the hots for her. I'm jealous. Who else?"

"Mind if I download?"

And she did, pretty much everything except for any more about the opposition than the fact that there was one.

"Holy fuck!"

"Yes."

Eva was realizing she could download with any degree of realism. She had given Roz the Imax version. So it was almost as if Roz had lived it all herself.

"God, the center of the galaxy."

Eva just looked at her giving her time to assimilate.

"And Jimmy. I knew he was amazing but bring him *on*."

Eva smiled.

"And your *doorman*. Well, I've seen a few I wanted to jump... And *I'm* seeing your clients."

"Sorry Roz, someone's gotta go on living."

"No honey, what *you're* doing is living."

"Yes, it *is* hard to argue with that."

"But I can't complain. You know how wonderful it is to feel and look the way I do now but especially to see how Brie is. She's my life really and I'm utterly thrilled and grateful. If you hadn't helped us she'd be dead or nearly so. And *I'd* be wanting to die. I owe you my life, my love. And she's still my highest priority. I can't be running around doing all the things you guys are doing."

"I know. Maybe I can take you and her on a little vacation sometime. When's her birthday?"

"It's coming up June seventeenth. She'll be seven. That would be stunning."

They looked at each other for a moment.

They both knew without telepathy what the other was thinking.

"No honey, you're out of my league now. Better we don't get started."

"Yes, that's probably the wisest. Still, maybe a one night stand sometime with Gabriel or one of the others. It could be pretty amazing to fulfill our desires. Maybe you could end up with Jimmy or Gabe or Jack and André together. Just think of all of us naked doing whatever pulled us the most."

Roz laughed, "OK, I'll keep my options open though more quiet with you and Gabe might be more to my liking."

"Good, whatever you desire, my love. And if not, I understand. What's the most wonderful meal you could think of for us both to celebrate right now?"

"Oh that meal I had at Colombe D'Or in the south of France. They had this cantaloupe they somehow grew to be the most delicious thing on Earth. And the rest was marvelous, too."

Eva took the experience from her mind and manifested two full course meals on the kitchen table, plates, place settings, napkins and all.

For the duration of their meal, they were in heaven going into ecstasies over their identical gustatory experiences and speaking and laughing of then and now.

When they were done, Eva sent Roz on to her next appointment and sent back the remains of their meal to wherever it had come from.

It was good to know there might be more to come.

It was interesting how different people were ready for more or less at different times.

She jumped to her old place to let the cleaners in. She knew she could make it instantly cleaner than anyone could but this had been arranged so she let it be. She also managed to reach her landlord. When the cleaners were done, she met him there and got her security deposit back.

It was good to complete this chapter of her life.

Then she went out for a real jog. She felt the need to clear her mind and truly exercise. She jogged for an hour and only several people disappeared.

Then she winked herself back and took a shower.

Today was the day for ending the old and learning the new.

Jack and then André and Anani wandered in and then Gabriel and Alena with big smiles on their faces.

She put "Shower and put on a robe or something," in all their minds. "We'll dress after supper. First we powwow then meditate then eat. Then we go to Jimmy and then Vientiane."

When they were gathered, she decided to speak out loud. Sometimes she just liked using words and hearing the sound of her own voice.

"It isn't just arbitrary," she consoled herself. "I'm fulfilling the whole world. I really *do* have to rid myself of all my compunctions."

The latter she knew was true.

"You can all call me directly with your mind no matter where you may be. I want you to do that now, exclusively, every time it will save us time and effort. No more cabs. I know they're fun after all those subways and buses but the more we use our capabilities the better for what's to come. We can walk and be leisurely when we want to but we now use our powers whenever it's convenient. I'm rapidly expanding my capabilities and realizing I'm not to hold back. Before I was thinking the devas would do it for us. But that's not the case. We're the ones to do it, we ringed ones and our pods. They're helping us but it ultimately must come from us. So don't hold back either. The more we expand what we can do the better chance we have of the outcome we all want. You're all on alert. Use me to the max. Call out to me from wherever you are. We're transitioning from love mode to combat mode, nonviolent combat. How's that for a concept? We'll still love but we'll make ready for what's to come. I'm you're mama and your general. But no wasted time on sirs or ma'ams or permissions to speak. Simple, instant and direct. As fast as the speed of thought can go. We need to become the most well oiled combat unit the world has ever seen. Got it?"

Gabe, Anani and André shot a mental "Yes!" into her mind. Jack and Alena nodded in assent.

"Beautiful! Those three shot me mental yesses. That's more of what I want from you two as well. Jack, you were the soldier ready to salute, speak words and act. All those proscribed ways of doing things. Set yourself up some speed of thought drills and get back to me with them. Practice with me whenever you can. And Alena, you've been holding yourself back all your life. I want you to fly forward now with a vengeance. Any questions or suggestions?"

"Mental maneuvers," Jack shot to all their minds.

"Perfectly conceived and delivered! We'll do it. I'm going to be relying on you to help me as much as you can. I'll say it a million times. Don't hold back. Maybe the closer we get, the more the field of the ring will expand to give you powers directly. Don't hesitate to try things.

But now to our loved ones. It'll help us to heal our near and dear and even our close enemies if we have any. We can be as connected to them as we are to our friends. I want you to think of all those who are close enough so that you'd be relieved to have them healed, the ones we're most bonded with or antagonistic to."

They all did.

And Eva sent them all.

"That fast," she thought to them.

Gabe had only two, Lada's sister and mother. Anani had four, her sister, brother, grandmother and friend. André had two as well, a friend he grew up with and his father, his main torturer. Jack had eight, his parents and brother, three war buddies and two superiors, one an enemy and one a role model. Alena had four, all in the Czech Republic, her father, sister, pastor and friend. And just for good measure, Eva sent her longtime girlfriend from Madison and her main harasser all through college. She didn't feel that connected to either one but they came to mind.

Her unit felt a deep, wonderful wave of relief. Consciously or unconsciously they had all been wanting this.

"Good my lovelies, we're that much more prepared now. Anything else?"

"Can we send a beloved pet?" Alena thought to her mind.

"Good girl. You sent that just to me. Now send it to all of us."

Alena did.

Eva tried. No dice.

"The animals will come later if we succeed. There, more motivation."

"Someone else has come to mind," Jack put in all their minds.

"Anyone else," Eva thought to them?

She sent off Jack's beloved aunt.

"Good, each thing as it comes. Our minds will allow us to do things as we're ready. Don't hesitate if something comes up for you. Let's meditate."

For twenty minutes, their peace, well-being and relief were nourished and deepened.

They felt the love on the inner planes.

They came out a more unified whole.

Eva whisked them to their seats at the table. The octagon was so much better than a rectangle. The space that held their legs was about as perfect as it could be, plenty of it and identical for everyone. And there was room for two guests.

"We're going to dream up a dream meal together. We'll be doing this often so we'll all get turns. And then sometimes we'll all get whatever we want individually. But this is the first time. I want us all to enjoy the same few things. It can be things you've had in the past or have thought of or dream up now. We're playing the dream food game. Who's got an appetizer?"

"I do," Gabe laughed.

No one else did. Eva thought of Roz's cantaloupe but that was for another time.

And she had just had that with Roz.

"I guess we're not an appetizer crowd. Think it for me, love."

"I've never had it but I've been wanting to make it."

And there it was in his mind.

A creamed soup of asparagus, artichoke heart, shiitake mushroom and roasted macadamia nuts made utterly delicious the way only the French can. Not totally pureed but partially thick, rich and grainy with hearty, bite-sized chunks of all four ingredients. Maybe too much going on but there it was.

And there it was on the table in fine, porcelain bowls with elegant, silver spoons and soft, linen napkins in front of each of them steaming warm, the perfect temperature, on a stunning, embroidered, high quality linen, cream colored tablecloth.

"Be careful what you ask for… I'll say grace. God bless you, all around you and all such everywhere. We thank you. We love you. We forgive you."

As she said this slowly, they realized she was saying it directly to the food, everyone and everything around the growing, gathering and delivery of it and all the like, living ingredients worldwide. They could actually see the energy of her love blessing every artichoke in the world and everything else they were about to imbibe and forgiving all the humans who could be cultivating, harvesting and distributing them better. They knew this food was different. It was divinely manifested super food that came to them in its most pristine, powerfully flavorful form. But they also knew the grace was meant for the mundane world as well. And they could also see how the blessing further sanctified even this food. They spoke their amens all around.

Then they tried it.

It was utterly delicious, the thick, richly textured creaminess of the liquid, the crunch of the macadamia nuts and the supernaturally succulent taste of the mushrooms, asparagus and artichoke hearts—not like those awful things that come in bottles, only chunks of the freshest, thick, grey artichoke meat coming from the middle devoid of hair and leaf. They were thoroughly thrilled but they did agree it was a bit much, maybe one or two less ingredients or the nuts with each one separately. But it was one of the most delicious things they had ever had. And they all got to experience it together.

When they were finished, everything but the napkins and tablecloth disappeared.

"Who's got an entrée?"

They all did and she saw them all.

"Ah well, darlings, I'm afraid my favorites win again. You know I love you all. But I just can't help it. There truly is enough love in my heart for all of you but there are still gradations. Why is it that way? I'm not *really* your mama. Can you live with it? Does anyone have an objection to fish?"

They all contributed, one here, one there, for all to mentally perceive, "Let's see, we each got a million dollars. We're all experiencing the most amazing love humans can experience. We're being taken to the most amazing places on Earth and in our galaxy. We're living greater and greater magic. We all love you and each other. We all have our favorites. We're on a mission to fully heal and perfect everyone on the planet. If we die tomorrow, so be it. In these few days we've lived more than any human ever has. And what a cause we'd be dying for! Yes, we can live with it! And no, bring on the fish!"

And Eva could live with it, too.

Laos is landlocked but Anani had gone spearfishing off the coast of Vietnam with some English lunatics who had nearly gotten them all eaten by sharks. They had speared a few fish that were hanging on their cables and bleeding in the water. Ten or so big greys began circling up from below and started to go into a feeding frenzy. One of the Brits let loose his spear into one that was getting too close. It swam away bleeding with the nearest one after it. They relinquished their fish to the rest and did what they preferred not to. They went to a place where there was easy fish for the taking, a kind of dodo fish they didn't like depleting. When a local girl pan-fried it with her magical spices, it was one of the most heavenly things Anani had ever eaten.

This, with perfectly cooked, oiled and seasoned white rice and an incredible mélange of mixed vegetables appeared on plates before them all. For each portion of fish, there was a little bit of skin and not one bone or scale.

It was exquisite. The taste sensations were indescribable. It was just as Anani remembered. They were all transported.

"This is it," Eva thought to them. "Heaven on Earth. This is how we are meant to live. This is what we are meant to bring here. This is what humankind will live if we succeed. How can we not succeed? This now, or ten thousand years of hell on Earth. Let's succeed."

"Amen," they all thought as they made their way through their most stunning, succulent meal.

And when they were done, "OK, dessert."

They all had one in mind.

They all got their wish.

"Enough of only one," Eva thought to them.

Chocolate mousse with a small amount of fresh, not too sweet marzipan evenly mixed throughout, perfect gulab jamun, the most delicious cut spears of mango, papaya and pineapple, a pomegranate honey flan that managed to be both delicate and pungent at the same time, its real, fresh pomegranate juice having the most intense, wonderful flavor that fruit could ever offer, a Swiss, melt in your mouth lemon fruit tart and, complements of Jack's early childhood, a small icebox cake with gourmet, homemade cookies better than any store bought ones could ever be.

Eva manifested six long, elegant iced teaspoons and issued the mental command that they feed each other small mouthfuls of each dessert.

To clear their palates, they had water from the purest, clearest streams high in the Himalayas.

They were further ordered to fully focus on the delivery of each mouthful making sure the spoon came in lovingly, slowly and straight and then pouring all their love and consciousness into the lips, mouth and pleasure sensations of the recipient, watching the nuance of every minute oral motion and how the recipient's internal responses played out on their mouth and face. The recipients were commanded to utterly and consciously prolong the enjoyment of every mouthful to the max. They were pushing the envelope of the art of sensual, gustatory co-savoring to new human heights.

All their mouths were watering and the flavor of the room became decidedly erotic.

Everyone was spoon fed all the different desserts they wanted to try, which was pretty much all of them for everyone.

At the end they all focused on Eva as Anani gave her the last taste of Eva's own favorite, the chocolate mousse.

They all watched as Anani lovingly gathered the final remnants onto the spoon and slowly raised it to Eva's mouth, making sure it was angled perfectly to come in straight. Then they watched Eva open her beautiful orifice to take in the intense, sweet custard she knew she so loved. Her lips were wet. She pursed them around the spoon and took it all in. Her mouth was in heaven as they watched her gently masticate, tongue love and savor the blending, transforming substances therein. She swallowed the first small bit of it leaving most of it still there.

She pooled their awareness and gave them all the direct experience of her food mouth love. She had closed her eyes but now she could see herself through their devotion. It was amazing how much they all truly loved her. Their total attention was completely and fully with her. She held her tongue in the middle of the perfect blend the mousse and her mouth juices made and took in the luscious feel and taste of it from every side as more of her mouth water poured forth. Even her saliva seemed to be transforming into some kind of soma, some kind of ambrosia, amrit, divine nectar. She swallowed her second little mouthful down and continued loving and savoring the rest.

This was better than any erotic food movie scene. All that love and bliss on her face and in her mouth and the shared experience of her paramount pleasure nearly made them all come at the dining table.

Finally, she swallowed down the last of her mouthful and then caressed her mouth with her tongue to enjoy the last residues and aftertaste.

They were now all melted and done.

She opened her eyes.

"Wow, how could we beat that?" one of them thought, who it was they weren't even sure as they were all wondering the same thing.

"Oh, I think we will. Imagine all the variations. One never knows what a different moment will bring."

The remains of their meal disappeared.

They got up and hugged and went off to get dressed for the Cathedral of Saint John the Divine. There was a special event on 'What's Spirituality, What's Religion?' The featured speaker had been called away on a family emergency. The Riverside pastor convinced her cohort to allow Jimmy to speak.

As they went off to their respective closets, Eva put the thought in their minds, "Maybe we should change tonight's subject to 'Sex and Salvation.'"

They all chuckled, got dressed and gathered in the living room as each became ready.

Chapter 22

A Deep, Rattling, Silent Cry for Mommy

"You guys look happy," Eva said to Alena and Gabriel.

"Oh, and we are," Alena sighed. "Just to experience the difference at work with how we are now and how we were then. Just to be able to go and be there as lovers. It's a great blessing. There's so much love!"

"Indeed there is, an unending infinitude."

Jimmy called out to her.

They appeared beside him in front of everyone.

The audience gasped and a few applauded at the trick in delight.

André started them singing.

When Eva felt the time was right, every single soul but Jimmy and one man seated toward the center disappeared.

If any of the Riverside healed were there, they were probably home now.

Eva saw the remaining man go for his gun.

In the blink of an eye, it was out of his briefcase and in her right hand pointing directly at his left eye.

For good measure, she pulled her own Beretta from her drawer at home into her left hand and pointed it at his right eye.

They stared at each other for a moment, Eva down the barrels of two guns.

Then she waved his pistol in two casual, come hither circles.

He didn't budge.

The others all looked from Eva to him and back.

"Come here puppy, I want to take a good look at you," she thought into his mind.

She raised him to his feet and walked him stiff legged and against his will to her. When he was about six feet away, she stopped him. He had no control of his body.

He flushed and spoke out loud, "Stay out of my mind, bitch."

"No, I think not."

With the guns still pointing at each eye nice and close now, she read him like a book.

His name was Arnold.

He was visiting New York from London.

He had been dragged to the meeting by his cousin.

She couldn't send him but he couldn't withstand her power or her mind.

She could see everything.

It wasn't pleasant but it wasn't so evil, either.

A lot of fear.

A lot of hurt and wounding.

A lot of posturing and bravado.

Anything to prop him up and make him feel safer and stronger.

He was enamored of the Bilderbergers.

He wasn't one of them but he knew a few.

The one who had befriended him was a thorough creepy. And Arnold was indoctrinated.

Eva could see what Arnold couldn't. The Bilderberg group was very mixed with some in the opposition but most only pursuing a world better suited to their interests without knowing of the larger struggle. They weren't as important or powerful as this man made them. But he was strongly identified with his one admired friend. Arnold was on the outermost fringe of the opposition. His knowledge had little to offer her. But she could now locate his friend.

She couldn't send Arnold to the devas. But he couldn't stop her from taking him elsewhere.

"Shall I do this?" she said out loud to him. "One bullet in each eye? Is this what you wanted to do to me? How brave you are. You should be ashamed of yourself."

He looked at her with a momentary doubt. He slightly shook his head.

His thought was, "I just wanted to protect myself."

He didn't say a word.

Eva checked with Jimmy. He wanted to stay with this.

Then they were all in their beloved living room.

The seven were lined up seated on their long set of couches.

There was just enough room for all of them.

The man was standing before them.

They were all naked.

There were no guns in sight.

Arnold's eyes nearly popped out of his head both from the change of locale and what was before him.

He became aware of their utter beauty.

He became aware of his unattractive paunch.

He shifted his weight and grasped his fingers.

He started to sweat.

His cock didn't stir but their beauty began to get to him.

He felt very uneasy.

He could see their utter calm.

He could feel their eyes on him.

Somehow he began to feel their love.

There was something about standing naked in front of seven gorgeous gods and goddesses pouring their love on you that changed you.

His eyes had long since met Eva's and she was working her deeper wonder in him as well, healing his soul as the devas had significantly healed Brie's body before the total healing of the chamber.

The longer he stood there feeling small and unattractive, viewing the beauty before him, the more he began to doubt the arrogance of his certainty, the more he began to think there was something more precious than his desire for wealth and importance, the more he longed to be one of them.

He began to shake a little and his hatred turned to the feeling that he wanted to cry like a baby, that he wanted their love more than any power or material thing on Earth. This somehow evoked in him an image of himself as a vulnerable baby on the floor feeling the loss of his mother's love for something he was or did that he couldn't comprehend. His resistance and resentment metamorphosed into a deep, rattling, silent cry for mommy and he covered his face with his hands and burst into tears.

His conscious refusal to be touched by the creamies faltered, shattered and melted away.

They all got up and held him. They lay him down in the fetal position. He cried and cried as they held and stroked him. He quietly opened his mind to being healed and perfected. He snuffled a bit and became quiet.

Then he disappeared.

Eva thought to them, "His name is Arnold. He was weak and alone and on the fringe. He only had the confidence of one of the opposition. This was easy for us. There are others that are far stronger and determined who won't be. But they all have the same weakness. They're masking their fear and pain with the trappings of power. And we'll have to deal with the malevolent ETs who won't be attracted to us at all. God knows if we could do anything whatsoever to heal them."

She went silent and tuned in to the wisdom of the angels.

Then she returned.

"No, thank God, only the humans. We don't even have to think about healing the others. Our job with them is to stop them from harming us."

This new knowledge brought her great relief. It made everything far simpler.

Now Eva had a direct link with two of the opposition and, through them, many more—Tom and his Omega group through Ellie and Count Fursten and his creepy friends through Arnold.

She knew she could locate all human members of the opposition in the Earth Room and perhaps even without it. But she knew that couldn't be her path. God and the universe had to bring those she was meant to start with and unfold her path before her as they had.

She thought of reaching out and reading the Count.

She knew it wasn't time.

It would all unfold.

It was nine-eleven, eight in the morning Vientiane time.

Eva checked with Jimmy and sent him to his new apartment to continue settling in.

"This will be a short visit, I think. We can always return."

They were high in the sky above the city and dressed.

"You lead, darling," Eva thought to Anani.

Eva followed Anani's image and they all stood on a large, flat plateau by her favorite waterfall. She then pulled Anani's four loved ones there.

About four hours had elapsed since their healing.

They had all fully recovered and eaten.

Her pod watched Anani hug and chatter with them and took in the beauty of their surroundings.

Anani introduced them all. They did a long, wonderful group hug and Eva sent them home.

Then she pulled Konane there slightly apart from them.

Konane stood facing them. She pierced them all with her bright eyes.

She was tiny.

But what power and magnificence there was in her perfect posture and gaze!

Her aged beauty and white hair held dignity, grandeur and simplicity.

But the power of her eyes and energy was immense, in some ways stronger than any of theirs.

This went on for several moments.

There was intense love and recognition but no need to hug yet.

Eva pulled in the other ringed ones and their pods.

They all stood on the plateau gazing on one another, hearing the beautiful song of the waterfall.

Nyame had three with him, all black, two beautiful women and a powerful elder man slightly younger than Konane.

Déwei and Liu were there along with a third, a beautiful Caucasian woman slightly younger than Déwei.

And João stood with the one beautiful woman from dinner and a very powerfully built man about his own age.

Five ringed ones, seventeen altogether.

They stood in their pods in a large, rough circle all facing each other, Konane all by herself.

Eva took them all to a higher flat plateau in the mountains north of Vientiane.

She created seventeen large, beautiful, throne-like chairs in a big, perfect circle.

They were all seated, ringed one toward the center of their pod, Konane alone.

"You're a match for us all," Eva thought to them and more directly to her.

Konane flashed her a radiant smile filled with laser-like shafts of love, gratitude and a streak of intense hilarity.

It hit them all and they burst out laughing into a long, riotous laughter fest. It finally subsided. Their love was titanic.

Eva pooled all their worlds and they all learned all they knew from each other.

They became one greater being, more than the sum of their seventeen parts, fully grokking all they all knew.

They noticed that Nyame had ventured more deeply into the world of the opposition than Eva had.

"Yes," she thought to them, "my time is coming."

They communed like this for many moments for the sheer joy of it.

Then they all arose and pressed into the center, worming their way through the throng, feeling every other body with their own.

With this complete, they shouted and whooped to the skies and all but Eva's pod and Konane returned to their places.

Then the two Laotians took them to all their favorite places, the temples, the boulevards, the surrounding power spots and places of beauty. They fully experienced the delight of it all together. Then Eva took her pod home to bed.

Konane went straight to the Earth Room and became her greater geographical area, that huge South Asian peninsula, Laos, Vietnam, Cambodia, Thailand, Myanmar, Malaysia and Singapore. She perceived the teeming humanity of all these places as a tenuous ocean of sand.

She began to perceive one grain here, one grain there as shining with a special brightness. She plumbed the depths of each grain that drew her, coming to know that soul and body profoundly.

One person from each country but Laos winked out of sight. And they all found themselves standing in a magical chamber large enough for ten.

Konane had her pod.

It would consist of seven souls.

The other ringed ones had likewise completed their pods as Eva's group had gone sightseeing.

They all had pods of six or seven.

As Eva drifted off she thought, "The time will come when we probably won't sleep for long periods of time. So nice to sleep now…"

Chapter 23

And the Best Was Soon to Come

At six-thirty the alarm sounded.

"Oh God," Eva moaned.

Gabe turned it off and nuzzled her cheek.

"I love you dearly, but sleep with Alena on the weekdays now. I'll take one of the others to bed. This isn't helping me."

"Of course, darling. That will be lovely. And since you're our master, you keep the master bed in the master bedroom."

"Till you feel like having it. Then let me know and I'll demote myself. I could traipse around to their beds. Musical beds. I could live with that. Especially since we all sleep so well now."

It was arranged.

Eva lay there but found she wasn't sleepy.

She began thinking.

Nyame's forays into the camps of the opposition had emboldened her.

She reached out to Ellie asleep in her bed in Langley.

She saw that Tom was off for a few days on opposition business.

Through Ellie she could sense his disquiet.

"Lovely," Eva thought, "but something else first."

She imagined her mouth, armpits and entire body immaculately fresh and clean.

And so it all was, that morning taste and smell utterly gone.

She went to the Earth Room.

She was realizing more and more that it depended on her and the ringed ones. Their healing was God given and miraculous. But it was now the humans who had to bring it all about. There was no one else to wait for. And their wait was coming to an end. She knew she could now do this.

She became one with Russia and all her surrounding countries. A young

Siberian man named Ilia was the best one possible to wear the ring. Then India, so many to choose from, a woman saint of fifty-five in Uttar Kashi named Sati. Then all the European countries, Capucine, a compelling Parisian sophisticate similar to Eva in many ways. Then Indonesia, the Philippines and Japan, another female Tokyo sophisticate, a beautiful, thirty-three-year-old artist named Kumi. Then to Australia, New Zealand and the southern islands, a Maori warrior shaman named Taanga. Then the Near East, a lovely, twenty-two-year-old, Qatari peasant girl named Cyti.

And that made eleven blanketing the world.

She was ready to send them all. She gave them the means to return to her living room. But she stopped short. Something signaled otherwise.

What she had known all along crystalized in the forefront of her mind.

She knew they were being monitored. She knew the opposition knew of her and Gabe and, therefore, her pod and Nyame and Déwei. But did they know of João and Konane? Why give them the instant knowledge of six new ringed ones?

She felt into it more deeply.

She could see that they monitored the condo more than her individual movements.

And she could see they barely paid attention.

They lost track of her when she materialized elsewhere.

They could find her if they wanted to but they weren't yet concerned with her.

They were blinded by their arrogance.

They were concerned with the dominant.

They had no understanding of the power of the unknown individual to influence the whole.

If Eva started creaming the rich and powerful of the world, the well-known villains or the opposition, that would alarm them.

But by divine orchestration, Eva's movement was grassroots.

They weren't following closely.

It was like they were video recording the comings and goings of their pod home and not even watching them.

But if Eva brought Ellie here, that would alert them.

They knew Omega thoroughly.

They would know who Ellie was if she appeared here.

They didn't know Eva and Ellie had already met in the park.

Eva now understood what she could and couldn't do in their condo.

With a start she realized how risky it had been to bring Arnold here.

But again, she was protected.

They had no knowledge of Arnold.

He was a nothing. He wasn't one of them.

He had only been indoctrinated by one of them.

But the wife of one of them was noteworthy.

And all the powerful around the world.

They only respected power.

Control and power were their main motivations.

They hadn't even seen Eva sending the groups from Riverside or St. John.

They had no idea how truly powerful she was becoming.

As long as she moved in accordance with divine will, she was still protected, as long as she followed the path of what unfolded before her and didn't do anything that would be obvious to them.

But now she was more alert and knew how to proceed with herself, her pod and all those she sent.

She scoured the South Pacific and the Indian Ocean for a beautiful, uninhabited island larger than the one they had used. She wasn't ready to try to manifest one, though, "Why not?" she thought.

But she knew better. That would alert them, too.

"How ridiculous. I can't start manifesting new landmasses," she thought to herself with a laugh. "The display of that much power would draw them like flies. Watch it, silly. Don't get cavalier."

It was a fine balance between not holding back and going too far.

But she really did know the difference. Maybe that was a thought for the future, her own brand new island under no jurisdiction but hers.

She found one off the Vanuatu chain. It was magnificent and large enough to have a small lake and waterfall but small enough to have no single human.

She went there and created the most beautiful Samoan fale with an oval, wooden floor, slender, wooden pillars on the periphery holding up a thatched palm roof and no walls.

She could have created anything. But this was perfect.

She gathered up her new ringed ones and sent them off with the knowledge in their minds to be sent here when they were done. The devas would see it.

It was six fifty-seven New York time. They would arrive just before nine, midnight Vanuatu time. Beautiful. It was near full moon. It was ten here now, a gorgeous tropical night in the depths of the South Pacific.

Eva manifested the most beautiful bed in the center of the fale with the finest fitted sheet and two pillows and pillowcases.

Then she checked with Gabe, "Darling, I know we agreed not to go off with anyone but I'll need to be with a few people from time to time alone or with the others."

She gave him all the knowledge of what she was about to do.

"Of course, my love, beautiful. Always do everything you need to. I am yours and Alena's and whoever's. It's all perfect and I'm totally good. What you're doing can save us all. I totally trust in your knowing what needs to be done. Totally enjoy it, darling, guilt free. No need to check with me in the future. But thank you for doing so this time. Just tell me after the fact. No secrets, OK?"

"Absolutely. I love you, darling."

"And I love you more than anything or anyone."

Eva reached out and cleansed the mouth, armpits and body of sleeping Ellie and brought her naked to their tropical bed without disturbing her sleep. Peter was sleeping in his crib as well and she placed him nearby.

Then she crawled onto the bed directly over Ellie. She entered into Ellie's mind and soothed all her panic centers. Then she lowered her mouth and began sucking her left nipple.

It was lovely and with it came a little milk.

Very slowly she allowed Ellie to awaken to the pleasure of it, giving her a dream of what was actually happening and the knowledge of who was loving her.

Ellie looked down and saw in the moonlight the beauty of Eva's hair, forehead and nose and her puckered lips around her nipple.

She knew her thoroughly as the woman in the park.

"Am I dreaming or in heaven?" she murmured.

"Both," Eva answered as she released Ellie's nipple, smiled and scooted up to kiss her on the lips.

"How did this happen?" Ellie asked as their lips parted.

"I brought you here to love you and to heal you and Peter. I love you, Ellie, you're my perfect pussy. Do you understand?"

"Yes, I understand. It's what I want."

"Good girl, now I'm going to bring my pussy to your mouth and you're going to lick it for me. I want my cum in you when I send you off to heal."

Ellie was ready. She wouldn't fight the fulfillment of her heart's deepest desire.

Eva crawled up, put her hands on the headboard and pulled herself upright. She brought her pussy to Ellie's mouth and Ellie caressed it with her tongue. She licked her long and lovingly in all the different ways she could think of. And Eva gave her a few ways of her own. Eva grew wetter and wetter and more and more loving.

When they finally had their fill, she sent Ellie and Peter off. They would return here shortly after the ringed ones.

A good morning's work.

Then she was jogging on the track in Central Park for the joy of feeling her body run.

She knew she could tone her muscles and lungs to whatever degree she wanted whenever she wanted. But nothing could beat the simple pleasure of experiencing the real thing. She hydrated herself with the purest of vital water as she ran. She disappeared a few people here and there. When she was done, she appeared naked in the shower to enjoy that experience. Then she joined her four pod members for breakfast at their kitchen table. Without her presence they had made her one. She was thrilled to eat it.

***

Tom was as riven in two as the palate of his newborn, cloven-mouthed boy.

He knew of the creamies. He knew they could make his son perfect and whole. He knew it would do nothing to his son's innocence or personhood, only enhance it. He knew it would cause no harm to anyone. But he knew it would make him a traitor. Or would it? A traitor to what?

He knew the ETs his country had allied with were giving them technology and making them more powerful. But more and more it seemed to him that it was they who were holding the power, that his beloved USA was being run by them. All these wars! They were the invader again and again and again. And none were cleanly won. And who were these wars against? And what was their real purpose?

He was coming to a crisis of conscience. Peter was pulling him hard away from his cadre. He had informed none of them of his son's condition. For all they knew, he was a normal, healthy boy. They never socialized though a few of them had met Ellie.

Tom was coming to the decision of his life on his own.

His balance was tipping away from them though his façade and demeanor were perfect.

None of them could see the crack in his soul.

He was the perfect soldier through and through.

Would he fight for his cadre or would he fight for his son?

Would he fight for the ETs or would he fight for his country?

More and more it became less and less of a question.

His allegiance was sacrosanct.

Love and the sacred were pulling it away from the sinister energies he had long been feeling in those he served.

Becoming his own man was becoming more important than his vows of obedience.

About halfway through Ellie and Peter's healing, something snapped within him.

He was fully theirs again and fully his country's.

He didn't know what he'd do, but he'd do his utmost.

He knew he had some role to play.

He felt whole for the first time in years.

Eva felt it happen.

"Good boy!" she thought to herself. "How beautifully it falls into place. What help we are getting!"

She finished her breakfast and did her instant cleanup.

They retired to the living room.

Eva looked at Anani, "You'll be sleeping with me tonight. Come naked to my bed."

Then she gave all her pod what she had done this morning.

And the best was soon to come.

Chapter 24

The Perfect Size for What Is Needed

The four of them appeared in the fale a few minutes before midnight.

Eva created glow globes on all the pillars shedding a lovely, golden light.

She created a large oval table to match the oval of the fale with eleven throne-like chairs.

The six new ringed ones appeared.

They stood around the table immobile.

"It's alright, don't try to speak or move," Eva thought to them in concepts they all understood.

She disappeared all their footwear and took the hands of Kumi and Capucine. Anani gathered Ilia and Taanga. Jack took Sati's hand and André, Cyti's. They led them down the grand wooden steps of the fale's entrance at the ocean end, across the sand and into the gentle, tropical surf.

Their little walk and feet in the ocean helped ground them in their bodies and the present.

A few of them stirred their feet and felt the wonder of the sea.

A few looked at their rings and felt them.

Eva's pod led them back and seated them all at the table.

Eva plumbed their gustatory memories and gave them each the meal of their dreams.

They all looked around in wonder.

Then they began to eat.

Eva's pod stood and smiled on them.

Ellie arrived with Peter in her arms.

Eva walked them to the water and hugged them as Ellie came around.

Then she seated her at the table and manifested her meal before her.

Ellie took her first mouthful.

It was utter bliss.

Peter started suckling with his perfect mouth.

Ellie looked down at him with the glory of her mother love. This combined with her love for Eva and her gratitude for all she and her beloved son had been given.

Eva's pod sat and Eva manifested drink, fruit and cheese for them to nibble.

They all ate and gazed around in silent communion.

Eva gently downloaded all there was to download into their minds.

She held nothing back from any of them. For the first time in her life, Ellie knew her husband. For the first time, she felt like an adult and a goddess.

They were imbibing the most delicious food and the most sacred knowledge in one of the most beautiful places on Earth.

Their joy and wonder shot heavenward and filled Earth's energy rivers.

The opposition hadn't a clue.

Ellie wondered at all that was happening to her and on Earth.

Eva gave Tom her experience and the newfound beauty of his wife and child.

His soul exulted to the skies along with theirs.

He felt as if he had arrived home for the first time in his life.

He was now fully Eva's and as connected with the opposition as ever but no longer of them.

To them he was on the periphery. They knew him as the liaison between Omega and groups they needed to anonymously direct.

He served them well.

And that's what he was, their servant.

He would do his duty.

But now, in his unhealed but transformed state, he would influence them in ways they couldn't perceive.

Eva would quietly transform them through him.

He was the balance point for North America.

And the continent was tipping towards Eva.

He opened his soul to her completely.

She fully absorbed everything he knew.

Eva gave all the ringed ones in the world this knowledge.

The acceleration took a turn forward.

The other balance points would be found.

Her army of seventeen had become thirty-eight. It would soon be an army of at least seventy.

Seventy nobodies the opposition had no interest in.

Seventy humans who would save the world.

An army of love, an army of beauty, an army of non-violent combat.

An army to end all armies.

The six and Ellie all finished their meals.

They stood and the table and its contents vanished.

Eva approached Ellie, kissed her lips and whispered, "We'll soon be together again," into her ear. "Now is the time for you to love and be with Peter and Tom."

Along with the others, Ellie had been given the ability to mentally call out to Eva if it were ever needed.

"Don't hesitate, darling. You and Tom are very precious to me and the world."

Ellie, Peter and the crib disappeared.

She pulled in Nyame, Déwei, João and Konane.

She manifested three more chairs and placed them all in a perfect oval. The eleven ringed ones and Eva's three partners all sat and faced each other.

Their eyes sparkled as they gazed from one to the next.

And their hearts rejoiced in their newly extended golden family.

"Let's close our eyes and commune internally."

They became as one and grokked each other from within.

They took the time to fully know and experience every other one, fathoming each to their depths one at a time.

Eva loved every one of them as they all did every other one.

But inevitably, each was drawn to some more than others.

It would always be the way of things.

And there was something about Déwei that gave Eva pause, a hesitancy in his character, a flaw in his judgment that caused her to question.

She was most drawn to Capucine and Cyti but she was there for every one of them as each was there for all the others.

They were, indeed, the ultimate family, the ultimate team, the ultimate army, all generals of their own little squadrons to come.

Then they were complete. They opened their eyes and gazed at one another in silent knowing.

They all stood, came forward and hugged together, moving and pressing their bodies all around.

Eva disappeared their clothing and whisked them all into the ocean where the water came up to their chests.

They reveled and hugged and played in the water.

They rejoiced at everything but especially this moment, the tropical night, the nurturing ocean, the stars, their love and the sparkling beauty and sensation of their flesh.

She lifted them into the sky, thoroughly cleansed, dried and clothed them and sent the six new ringed ones to the Earth Room to locate their pods.

She sent the rest home and returned with her three to their living room.

Any of the ringed ones could have done these things but she was still mama. She had made them all but Déwei. They were all happy to let her lead. She was the commanding officer of all the generals, Mama Eva, the twenty-three-year-old knockout from Madison, Wisconsin. She who had despised men.

It was eleven-ten New York time.

They had a whole day to kill.

"Gee, what shall we do next?"

Silent pause.

"How about some mental maneuvers?" Jack offered.

He gave them his vision of Eva throwing them around the skies of the world and catching them in free fall at different times in different combinations when they called out to her—dangerous, thrilling and fun, requiring action at the speed of thought with total trust and presence of mind.

Eva laughed. They were ready.

Eva's phone rang once.

She and Roz communed.

"Brie's been harassing me. She's been saying some very strange things and demanding to see you."

They appeared in the living room.

"No school?"

"I'm giving her a break and I have the morning off. She missed most of the year. School doesn't seem that important right now."

Eva and Brie looked at each other.

Brie looked amazing, so bright, vital and healthy. She was enveloped in a great, vibrant light.

"How gorgeous you are, dear Brie. You look like an angel. I love you so much!"

"Thank you, Mama Eva, and I so love you! Mommy and the angels say you can read my mind."

"Yes, darling, and so I can."

"Please do it now."

And there it all was.

The angels had appeared to her several times since her healing as they had in the previous life that was there quite vividly in her memory. They had also come to her in several incarnations prior to that. But the one she was showing Eva was her life as the Maid of Orléans, Jeanne d'Arc.

The angels had also conveyed that she would play a part in the upcoming battle with the opposition along with her friend, Theo, the young Haitian boy healed with her at her behest. They had also visited him.

Brie looked directly into Eva's eyes.

"They said each pod would need two of us this small to help with the smallest of them in their smallest spaces."

"Well, they've told you more than me but I totally believe you. I can see within you that they have. Thank you, darling, your timing is impeccable. We were about to embark on our first maneuvers. You've been trying to tell this to Roz?"

"Yes, but she can't see what you can."

"She can if I show her."

Eva gave Roz everything she had just learned from Brie.

"I have to sit down," Roz said, plumping onto one of the ottomans.

Eva and Brie gave her the time she needed.

"Good grief, I almost lose you to cancer and now you're jumping into battle?"

"Yes, Mommy, with Eva and the angels and all the rest of them. They'll take care of me. I won't be captured and *burned* this time."

Roz looked at Eva with a look that went to the very core of her soul.

"I have no idea what's coming down the pike. All I know is that we have a helluva lot of help and we can do some pretty amazing things. We won't be fighting and killing. We'll be circumventing destruction and saving lives. But I can't guarantee we won't be dying."

"The angels told me we wouldn't die and if we did they could bring us back."

"Yes, they told me that, too, at least that they could bring us back."

Roz looked from Eva to Brie to the rest of them and then back to Brie.

"OK, darling, you win. If it weren't for Eva and the angels you'd be dead. I said it before and I'll say it again. Who am I to fight God? If you're meant to be Brie of

SoHo this time around, so be it. But she was nineteen, wasn't she? Or you were nineteen then. Now you're all of seven!"

Brie looked her mother right in the eye, "The perfect size for what is needed."

"Oh well, Eva, she's yours. Just try to get her back to me safe and sound at some reasonable hour. But I understand you may need to scoop her up at anytime. Just let me know when you do. You're her schoolteacher now and her commanding officer. Take damned good care of her."

"You know I will, darling Roz. Where should I drop you?"

"Maybe some bar somewhere. No, send me home. I need to lie down or take a bath or meditate and pray. Just you both hug me first."

The three of them hugged.

Roz enjoined them, "I love you guys. Don't get too carried away. I guess this is for us all."

"It is, darling. And we're watched over," and Eva sent her home.

Then, through Brie, she found Theo, pulled him into the living room and gave his aunt all the knowledge she needed to condone and accept this. Theo had been Joan's most stalwart supporter and co-captain. He had been killed trying to defend her from capture. This is how they were meant to fulfill their destiny.

Eva put in all their minds what she was about to do and imprinted deep within them the means to call out to her from anywhere.

Then she threw them all high into the skies of the four directions all around the world.

Anani was plummeting toward the Indian Ocean. When she stabilized, she could see the shape of the tip of the subcontinent and Sri Lanka.

Jack fell towards the sands of the Sahara Desert.

André was over the South Pacific, Brie the South Atlantic and Theo his native Caribbean.

The first thing they noticed was the cold of the altitude and the wind of free fall. They weren't protected from the elements like when Eva had taken them into space. She had just thrown them there on their own as they were.

The next thing they all noticed was how wonderful free fall was.

It was stunning to experience what most of them had wondered about.

They all soon spread eagled and felt the balance of that position in the wind.

"See if you can link with anyone."

Anani and André could in a flash. All that sleeping together definitely helped.

Brie and Theo could as well. They were now more bonded than in their previous life.

Jack was all by his lonesome and the only one headed for solid ground, not that it mattered from that height.

Eva united all their minds and created bridges between them. She could easily reach them all but now they could link with each other whenever they wished.

"Eva, darling, it looks to me like I'm getting close," Jack thought to her.

For whatever reasons, she had thrown him to the lowest altitude.

She scooped him up and threw him higher.

"Whoa!" he shouted in her mind, "that's *too* exhilarating! All my insides nearly flew out of my body! *Inertia* could kill us!"

She tried being more gentle but they each reported too much lurching.

Eva knew this was critical and that she needed to overcome it. She knew Jack's suggestion was right on and they'd be doing something like this when the time really came.

She knew they couldn't be distracted by motion sickness or worse.

She gently stopped their falls and brought them home then disappeared leaving the thought, "I need to experiment on myself."

She chose a remote part of the Kalahari Desert. She wanted to see flat, hard ground coming up at her.

She experimented with little breaks in her fall as she descended. Each time she felt the lurch.

She became fascinated by the sight of the fast approaching ground. She kept wanting to see it get closer.

But she knew she had to master inertia first.

After some major discomfort, she realized she could create a unique inertial field around her body so that no matter how abruptly she changed or reversed direction it didn't, as if, 'change.' She was her own universe and there was no lurch. She could still feel the wind and everything else but she could be going a thousand miles an hour in one direction then, in a nanosecond, be going the same speed in the opposite direction without a hitch.

She asked why this had never been a problem before.

"Instant relocation frees the body from inertia. Changing motion doesn't."

This gave her a second option. She had been changing motion. All she had to do was relocate them. She realized what she hadn't before. When it was short distances, she had unconsciously moved their bodies from one place to another. That's why they felt exhilarated or the lurch. For the long distances, that was unthinkable. The same with protection. When she took them to space there was no question they needed it. So it happened automatically. Just now when she threw them in the air, she unconsciously knew they didn't. Neither her conscious nor subconscious mind created it.

Now these things were conscious. And she could choose accordingly.

She began lifting and dropping her body towards the desert floor watching it coming at her, feeling all the sensations she felt as her body came closer and closer to splatting on the ground.

She didn't fully understand why she was doing this or how it might benefit her. All she knew is that she wanted to. It called to her. She was compelled.

She kept cutting it closer.

She tried using both the inertia field and instant relocation. They weren't that different. She felt no discomfort either way. But the sight of the hard earth, of death coming so swiftly at her, brought up all the visceral fear a body is programmed with.

She became determined to keep herself going through this. She wanted to plummet right up to the hard ground in total equanimity.

So she did, over and over, seeing the desert coming up so fast, monitoring her fear responses as it looked like she'd slam into it.

Ten feet, six feet, three feet, one foot, eight inches, four inches, three inches, two—finally she stopped herself dead within a hair's breadth of touching the ground.

It was enough, enough of this experience, more than enough.

She had achieved that eerie detachment, the simple curiosity she had felt in her one near death experience when, bleary-eyed and tired from driving a borrowed Volkswagen bug out West, she had pulled out to pass an eighteen wheeler thinking she was on a four lane highway only to realize it had become two lanes and a pickup was fast approaching her head on when she had only reached half the length of the truck she was passing.

There was no hint of fear in her at that moment when she saw the pickup driver panic, slam on the brakes and start skidding towards her even though she had pulled off the road onto its far shoulder leaving room for him to go right through.

Finally, the pickup driver lifted his foot from the brake pedal, righted his direction and passed through safely.

All Eva had felt was curiosity—would he do that in time or would the pickup come barreling into her?

Afterwards of course, she was glad he came around in time.

But there was no fear response anywhere within her she could perceive.

She returned to the living room.

The five of them were eating.

"Where did you go?"

"Sorry, I had an appointment with inertia and death."

"Glad you made it back, hungry?"

After they finished eating, Eva gave them all her experience.

"Whoa," Jack said, "still have a death wish?"

"Maybe, though I think that'll be helpful when the time comes."

"Do you think we all have to go through that?"

"No, you just did vicariously. That should be enough. Anyway, we've got the lurch thing licked."

She did her instant cleanup and threw them high in the air all over the world thinking to them, "Maybe we'll have to do something radical on a full stomach."

They spent the next few hours in free fall, being put on mountaintops, being thrown into small spaces individually, in pairs and in groups, linking, going solo, every different combination and permutation they could think of.

It got quite exciting, faster and faster, scenes and places blinking in and out. Finally, Eva used their physical bodies to snatch each other from wherever they were to some distant place.

This seemed important and they spent the last hour practicing this in every conceivable way, one person, large or small, appearing on another going at any speed or 'stationary,' arms and legs wrapped around them and plucking them from there and depositing them wherever Eva chose to send them, finally to their beloved fale.

They all ended up naked in the ocean deliriously cavorting in the early morning surf.

What a school Eva ran!

They were all in bliss.

They arrived in their condo clean, dry and clothed in time to greet Gabe and Alena's homecoming.

Eva unified their consciousness and delivered all their experiences in the highest definition. So they all gained the benefit of everything each had gone through.

Then Eva gave Brie and Theo all their experiences of meditating and they dropped into the deeper realms together for twenty minutes.

When they were done, Eva sent the children home.

"We've found our replacements," Gabe informed them. "We'll just be going in a few partial days to train them. They're ready to be healed. You can send them any time."

"Good," Eva said, sending them. "No time like the present."

For a moment, Eva shared her thoughts with her loved ones as she pondered all the unknowns, so many, so much already given.

But she knew it was useless.

When readiness arrives the action will be inherent.

Everything in its proper sequence, which no human could know.

Planning and strategy are for the mundane world.

We move forward into the unknown dealing with what arises as best we can.

Thus it is for the highest things.

Thus it has always been.

Only the world has never before seen such stakes.

Chapter 25

It All Must Come from You

They had their scrumptious magical mystery meal, each to their own desire. And Eva gave them the night off.

"Mama's gonna commune and gather data."

"Who wants to see X-Men: Apocalypse?" André chirped.

"I'll go," Anani smiled.

"It won't hold a candle to Days of Future Past," Jack intoned.

"I know, but hey, we can enjoy it, right? They're like us only we're better."

"Right, but I think I'll pass. I wouldn't mind seeing The Man Who Knew Infinity."

"I could see that, too," Gabe interjected.

They both looked at Alena.

"Sure, why not. Who knows when we'll get to see another movie? And we can all afford it, right?"

They laughed, "Right!"

"And all the women will be jealous. Two beautiful men on each arm," Eva predicted.

"And the men, too, such a beautiful woman between us."

"Alright, enough already. Get us out of here."

Eva desired to know where these movies were playing nearby and it was given. She sent them to the Loews Orpheum and Lincoln Plaza.

Trivial but handy and useful for more important things down the line.

She could have sent them anywhere. But why think an unnecessary thought?

She thought of depositing them inside the theater. On a Wednesday evening there would be plenty of seats. But that would be theft. So they landed around the corners on the quieter side streets.

Eva was alone.

She could do this anywhere in any crowd but she welcomed her solitude.

It was rare now that she had quiet time to herself.

It was good to be alone again.

She luxuriated on one of the couches for a few minutes.

Then she thought about gathering data as her own search engine.

But the Earth Room still heightened it.

So she winked out and was there.

She was surprised to see Cyti there, though there was no reason to be.

They linked consciousness.

Cyti had discovered a Mid-Eastern plot involving five ISIS cells in Afghanistan, Syria, Iraq and Pakistan. They were planning to steal a Pakistani nuclear warhead and detonate it in Washington, DC. They had secured the cooperation of two army guards and one nuclear physicist.

So far, she wasn't able to link any of those involved with the opposition.

This seemed to be a purely human affair.

This is not what Eva had come for but it took immediate priority.

She communed with the devas.

"This is unrelated to our purpose. It would be a terrible thing but we leave it to your world. These people do not know of us. If it were the opposition trying to stop us and were not circumvented, we would yield your world to them. But it is not. You are free to do as you will."

"Well, gee," Eva thought to Cyti. "We can't very well allow this to happen, can we?"

"I should think not," she thought back in her own language in her own way though there was no wrinkle in their understanding.

"Let's just watch them for now and see how close they get to stealing one. Mass healings of ISIS operatives might somehow alert the opposition. If they get it, we could always hurl it into the sun and heal them."

"OK, let's both keep tabs for safety."

"You be first point on this, Cyti, but I'll let all the others know."

And she did.

Then they got to the important stuff.

It had occurred to Eva that she could find the best possible balance points around the world like she had found her new pod leaders.

Cyti had come to find her own balance point.

Nyame had already found his but Eva didn't think the others had.

So she read their minds for this.

As with the nuke, sleeping or waking didn't matter.

Those asleep could remain so. She could deposit or extract data without disturbing them though she could, of course, awaken them if necessary.

They all had full pods but only the two fulcrums had been found.

Eva released all but Cyti. The two of them saw the mass of humanity as before, innumerable grains of sand in a vast sand desert.

Their intentionality now drew them to balance points.

One by one they came into focus.

Cyti's was a lower-ranked member of the Saudi royal family.

Capucine's a similar member of one of the great European banking families.

Déwei, Kumi and Ilia's, like Tom, were members of their country's topmost secret service.

Taanga's was an Australian atmospheric scientist who had somehow stumbled onto the existence of the Greys and had linked them up with a friend of his in Australia's secret service.

Sati's was the odd one, a member of the ancient Sarkic cult. It had a small, nearly unknown offshoot that had made its way to India centuries ago. It now consisted of a few scientists, criminals and computer hackers who had become obsessed with finding the alien civilizations most involved with Earth. They had succeeded. And they were in league with them and a few of their own secret service agents the aliens were using to consolidate more power. The one computer hacker helping them the most was beginning to have second thoughts. He was a young, New Delhi, Indian boy of eighteen. He had been helping them for six years.

João's was an Air Force pilot who had once played tag with a small Grey saucer. They had landed at a remote, abandoned airstrip and the Grey had seduced him with a few high tech toys. The pilot had introduced him to a few select friends.

Konane's was a retired Vietnamese Air Force General.

And the one Nyame had already found was a semi-retired, ex-apartheid, South African military operative.

The opposition had been busy.

They were better connected than Eva had thought.

Doing such finely detailed work in pooled consciousness, though, was more trying than doing it alone.

So Eva gave all their new information to the ringed ones and sent Cyti home. She would leave it to each of them to find the best way to turn their human entry points.

She communed with her friends.

"Can I read the minds of the opposition aliens?"

"Yes, to greater and lesser degrees."

"Can I read their minds without them knowing I am so doing?"

"You can perceive and learn some things of them from afar. You can enter into the minds and bodies of the Greys and Lizards without their knowing. You can make brief forays into the Oranges if you tread carefully and don't stay long. They are all historically more advanced though constitutionally less so than you. You carry more God, light and awareness than they. If you directly enter an Annunaki or Dark Cloud, they will know immediately."

"Please give me all the information about them that you now can."

And it came pouring in almost to the point of overwhelm but continually not.

Eva kept downloading till she could take no more.

Just before her saturation point she thought to them, "Can you simply download anything and everything that could help as I'm able to receive it without my coming to you?"

"Yes."

"Good, please do. Are all the ringed ones OK? Could I have done better?"

"All the ones you found are perfect. Déwei could be replaced by Liu. He was sufficient. She would be perfect. We can't go searching as you can. We must select among those who come to us. Ultimately, it all must come from you."

"João is OK?"

"Yes."

"Have any of the others requested what I just requested of you?"

"Nyame and Konane."

"God bless them and you and everything. Thank you!"

"And thank you."

She was alone again in her living room.

She took a long, hot bath and then a shower and crawled into bed naked.

Soon thereafter Anani joined her.

Eva pulled their bodies together.

"I love you, darling, but I'm exhausted. Let's see what the morrow brings."

Chapter 26

Every Morning They Were Born Anew

Eva and Anani slept in till after nine-thirty.

So delightful not to be awakened by the alarm clock.

So delightful for Eva to have Anani in her bed this morning.

They hugged, kissed, played with and examined various and sundry body parts for half-an-hour.

Then they got up and showered.

Life on planet Earth.

What it had become!

They soon emerged.

No one had bothered to begin breakfast.

Eva decided to use up all their fresh food.

It was still good but aging.

With a few thoughts, she created omelets and a complex vege, meat, chicken stew.

Why waste time on mundane chores?

She had barely begun pulling fresh, exotic produce from around the world.

That would be fun, perhaps even more so than simply manifesting it.

"Maybe we'll start a restaurant when all this is over. The Dream Meal Machine."

They chuckled.

"Will they let you keep the ring? Will it still work?"

"Good questions. I haven't asked. First things first."

Towards the middle of breakfast she heard Gabe call, "Pull me!" in her mind.

And he was there.

She had pulled him from the elevator.

He felt not a hint of the old disorientation.

"Cyril says they blew up the chamber. They're calling it an asteroid hit. It burnt a pathway in the forest right there."

Eva was already receiving. She spoke as she received.

"They say it's fine. They've been expecting it. It usually happens. They've hardly been using it now. It fulfilled its purpose."

"So nothing to do?"

"Nothing to do. Let them think they accomplished something."

"Great. There's a small backlog of people who want healing. Requests still come trickling in."

"Do you have a list?"

"Yes, names, email addresses and telephone numbers."

"Let me see."

He dug it out his pocket and gave it to her.

"Nine souls," she mused. "I guess Ethel's not ready. Roz would have told me if there were anyone from her side."

She found and sent them.

"Do you have to go back?"

"Yes, just for another hour or two today. Then they can be on their own."

"Give me a kiss and call out when you're ready," and she sent him back.

They finished their breakfast and their kitchen was immaculate.

The remaining stew was in a perfect container in the fridge for any who might want it.

They retired to the living room.

"How were the movies?"

"Jack was right. It was disappointing. So much violence. But it had its moments. I'm glad we saw it."

"Me, too," Anani agreed, "and I'm really glad we won't be killing and maiming."

"Amen," Eva muttered. "The murder and mutilation of any soul's body is not my idea of fun. How was The Man?"

"It was good," Jack answered. "But great movies are hard to come by."

"Amen," André concluded. "And what could beat the movie we're living?"

To that they could all silently agree.

Eva pulled in Brie and Theo and let Roz and his aunt know.

"What we ended up doing yesterday is going to be our main offense. It turns out that the ETs have implants that nullify our field. They have them in their bodies, missiles and ships. I'll be able to read their minds but I won't be able to relocate or control them from a distance unless they voluntarily disable their implants. Either there's no way for us to disable them or the devas aren't giving me that information. The aliens know we don't want to kill them and will sometimes disable them voluntarily if they realize they have no other choice.

The ring's powers have expanded. There will be a lot of aliens flying in a lot of different ships. Most of them will probably be in space. But you'll all be protected no matter what the distance. It's like we'll be one being with one mind in one field no matter how far apart we might be.

Maybe I'll figure out a way to neutralize their neutralizers. But it doesn't seem like it. Hold on, let me ask them point blank."

She went silent and communed for a moment.

"They say that on the surface of things, the devices do disrupt our field so we can't affect them directly. But on a deeper level, we're not meant to disable them, we're meant to overpower them. Something esoteric about them needing that much free will, to be able to defy God even if it kills them, but then our coming in and removing them without harm. This will be the best scenario for their evolution and our effect on all that is. I don't fully understand but it'll work. It's somehow far better this way. You'll be a field bearer wherever I send you. And with you wrapped around them, I'll be able to pluck you both away. It won't depend on your physical strength. It'll be instant and easy. You'll be like a magic ring that will overpower them, their disrupter, their free will and their tendency to kill and die. This will help tip things towards God not only here but elsewhere, too. But it means you'll be full body hugging some rather unsavory types."

"But isn't love what we all need?" Brie opined.

"And what a wise and perfect treasure you are, dear Brie. This'll be love overpowering violence and the disruption of God's will," Eva answered, wholeheartedly agreeing.

Jimmy broke into Eva's thoughts.

"I got invited back to Riverside and there's nearly a whole different crowd here. Can you come and sing right now?"

And there they were, all in appropriate attire.

André sang his note and the others joined in, followed, in perfect harmony, by Brie and Theo. And oh how they loved to sing! The Heavenly Choir was missing its baritone and contralto but had gained two of the purest, most joyful sopranos one might imagine. Anani's and the children's could make an exquisite, tripartite choir of its own.

The crowd was transported and, as usual, a few bold souls chimed in.

Then all but a handful, the pastor and Jimmy disappeared.

Those remaining had gone before. None were of the opposition. This time Eva had selectively sent all those who hadn't gone before. Last time there was an adversary to deal with alone. Funny how, unconsciously, she was somehow able to do the most perfect thing. Perhaps she had some help in these things.

The pastor looked at Eva.

"What a thing is happening in the world!"

"Yes indeed. Pray for us, mother. We can use all the prayers we can get. Jimmy, we've begun maneuvers. Would you like to join us? We could probably use another adult male."

"For this I'm in."

"Good."

They said their goodbyes and retired to the living room.

Eva heard Gabe's, "We're ready," and pulled them in.

"So now we're nine."

She changed all their attire to more conducive clothing for the task at hand.

They all found themselves in free fall, Eva included.

While falling and monitoring, she communed with Déwei and Liu.

"Ah yes," Déwei thought, removing his ring and handing it to Liu, "I believe this is better with you. I've been thinking it myself. Thank you for the nudge, dear Mama. Liu, I'm so glad I found you and you're our ring holder!"

Liu placed the ring on her left pinky.

It shrank to the perfect size.

Eva left them to it and started throwing her unit members around each other and relocating them to higher altitudes.

"Fuck this," Eva thought to them all. "It'll be better if we don't let them get anywhere near this close. Let's do it in space!"

They all started flying around at thousands of miles a minute between Earth and the moon.

They're maneuvers began to approach the speed of light, bodies appearing wrapped around bodies like monkeys on their backs or around them from the front, relocating them elsewhere and reappearing where they were.

It all got more and more blurred, more and more crystal clear, more and more flawless, more and more exciting.

Eva started manifesting big tin coffins with seats as surrogate space ships. She knew the aliens sat. Whenever possible, on their backs would be the best. But that would be rare. The pilots would mostly be sitting. The humans would have to land in their laps, legs raised, with their arms around their necks. That would startle them.

This became their drill. They were each now yanking others from inside the cans.

She paired Brie and Theo, Jimmy and Jack, Gabriel and André and Anani and Alena and had them retrieve each other from their coffins.

Then she started trading partners and ended up pairing the smallest with the largest.

They all got more and more used to plucking anyone from anywhere and releasing them wherever she sent them, then reappearing seated in the empty can.

It had to happen as instantaneously as possible.

Grab and deposit in the blink of an eye.

No time to get zapped.

Eva would have to transfer piloting skills from the minds of the aliens to her pod members. They would have to direct the vehicles out of harm's way.

This would be more time consuming. The best would probably be just to make sure they wouldn't crash into Earth by setting them adrift in space. The less time spent on this the better.

Many of the ships would probably have multiple crewmembers as well.

Eva would have to deal with them and protect her own. And who knew what unthought of contingencies might arise?

These flying cans made for quite a little spectacle.

Earth space had never before seen such a thing.

And space was big enough so they weren't perceived by others.

They were gaining greater and greater mastery at the art of enemy abduction and spaceship commandeering.

Alena surprised herself at how much she enjoyed this.

It gave her feelings of power she had always wanted but had never felt.

Eva was thrilled to learn they had no weak link.

They kept practicing and getting better.

Eva had them periodically call out to her as if it were an emergency.

In space, time becomes meaningless.

Three hours went by like twenty minutes.

They returned home in time to meditate.

During that time Liu had given the Caucasian woman and one other pod member their freedom, had gone to the Earth Room and found the three best replacements Mongolia, North Korea and Tibet had to offer, had sent them off to heal and had fed them. She now had a pod of seven.

Déwei made a fine pod member. He would stay. He just didn't have the ruthlessness to lead his pod to perfection that Liu did. His heart had a slight weakness for weakness.

The fully healed still had their own personalities and the combined total experience of all their lifetimes, accessible to their memories or not. This and more, combined with their genetic heritage, the influence of their families and cultures and the effects of day to day human existence, created the unfathomable, ineffable mix of what constituted the unique blend a human being was. Some were more suited to leadership than others. Liu was superb.

The two retired pod members got to keep the money they had been gifted.

All eleven pods were now as strong as they could be.

During the meditation, Eva decided not to risk maneuvers so close to Earth again.

She sent her awareness to Andromeda and found the perfect Earth-size planet.

From now on, they would do their maneuvers there.

She came back to her meditation with her pod.

Their unity flourished at the deepest levels of their being.

They were one.

Just as the meditation was ending, Ellie cried out to Eva for help.

One of Tom's cohorts had called on her unexpectedly.

He knew Tom was otherwise occupied. He'd come to see if he could seduce her.

Just like those creepies—a new, nursing mother! Of course for Eva it was perfect. But for him—eewww!

As Ellie was trying to get rid of him he looked closely at her skin and realized she'd been creamed.

And Ellie perceived his realization.

"Good girl," Eva reassured her. "Always call me. Mama will take care of everything."

Without physically relocating, Eva entered the man's mind, put him into a coma and laid him gently on the floor. She isolated the endangering data and locked it away so deep in his unconscious mind that he couldn't access it.

Around it she placed a solid wall of frustration that he was unable to seduce her and an irritation with her that additionally blocked his access to her new condition. Every time he would think of her, his mind would swerve away. And around that she wrapped a layer of guilt. All this would block his ability to consciously recall that Ellie had been transformed. She also took the opportunity to retrieve all his knowledge and soften his allegiance to his cause.

Then came the pièce de résistance.

She linked his mental block with his heightened desire for Ellie due to her perfected skin and body.

Ellie was now his ultimate, forbidden, longed for object.

He would obsess on her as a distant, obtainable ideal but not be able to think of her directly more than fleetingly. The tension of this dichotomy and his impossible desire would become a festering sore deep in his subconscious mind, the woman he most wanted but could never have. The woman he knew he couldn't approach again.

Her allure would draw him away from the opposition toward the delectable, despised creamies.

His craving, the inaccessibility of her sex and the buried knowledge of her creaminess would split him apart. He'd become ripe for the picking.

"That's what you get for sniffing around my pussy," Eva thought to herself as she stood him upright, awakened him and sent him on his way.

With the thought, "Do something constructive," to her pod members, she manifested the bed in the fale, brought Peter in his crib and placed Ellie, naked on her back, in the middle of it. Then she placed her naked self on all fours above her.

"Such a good, good girl," she murmured to Ellie giving her the knowledge of all she had done to the man. "Surrender to Mama. Trust in Mama. Play with my breasts and nipples, darling, and suck when I put one in your mouth."

Ellie reached up and began to fondle, squeeze and caress the beauty of Eva's magnificent tits hanging down so perfectly above her. She moved them to the right and the left and brought her fingertips from their base to their tips. She squeezed and twisted their nipples firmly and perfectly giving Eva maximum pleasure. She flapped and shook them, watching the gorgeous jiggle and shake of their ample flesh. Eva sank down a little more and placed her left nipple between Ellie's lips. Ellie gently moaned and firmly sucked and masterfully nibbled it with her teeth. Then she moved Eva's breast side to side and all around feeling the nipple on her lips, in her mouth and with her tongue.

It both infantilized and empowered her. She became the happiest combination of pre-verbal infant, able to play with her mother's breasts as no infant could, and mature, sexual woman, able to totally love the magnificent womanhood of another. And there was something about completely fulfilling yourself in ways you wanted but never thought you could have.

Her joy and gratitude for this fulfillment reminded her and combined with the most profound gratitude she had for Eva's role in the healing and perfecting of her and her son, of helping her attain her adulthood and maturity, of giving her the knowledge of her husband and freeing him from the clutches of the opposition, of freeing her to fulfill her own desires, of everything that might be in store for Earth and of all she learned in the fale along with the new ringed ones. All together, this brought her into the deepest level of love, lust, surrender and gratitude imaginable.

Ellie loved Eva with a completeness few humans have ever known.

She would walk into the fire for her.

She was a puddle of the most intense desire and fulfillment.

This sexual, soul, heart love was beyond anything she could ever have imagined.

"Such a good pussy," Eva said, feeling it and praising her, "such a good heart and mouth and soul. I love you Ellie. I love what you're feeling. I love knowing that you're totally mine."

"I'm completely and totally yours."

Eva crawled upward and pulled herself upright. Her pussy was above Ellie's mouth. She spread her knees wider and sank down onto it.

She began moving deliciously against Ellie's tongue and lips.

"Who do you belong to, sweetheart?"

"To you. To Eva. Totally to you."

"Good girl, nice and deep with your tongue and mouth. This is how you worship me. I'll teach you all the ways to worship me. Do you understand?"

"Yes, I understand. Please command me. I'll do anything, anything, anything."

"Perfect."

They loved and licked and hugged and caressed.

Eva anointed her with her cum—her nose, her forehead, her cheeks and chin.

She knew their love would soften and heal Tom even more.

He would feel the depths of Ellie's new surrender and it would melt him.

And the more he melted, the more its subtle but profound effects would work wonders in his cohorts.

They continued their foreplay till they both felt complete.

Then Eva brought Ellie to supreme orgasm. She found and stimulated the most sensitive nerve endings of Ellie's clitoris with the extended tip of her tongue. She recreated Nyame's warm, erect, living cock in her pussy to move but also to inhumanly vibrate, ripple and undulate to give her maximum pleasure. She used her powerful energies to stimulate all her body's sweet spots, the come centers of her brain and her womb and organs directly, along with her heart, mind and soul to fill every particle of her existence with rapture. No one had ever been so thoroughly pleasured and stimulated before.

And Ellie climaxed with a cosmic come like Eva had for Jimmy, a superhuman crowning point only even a further step forward, the most total such experience a human had ever had. And the completeness, resolution and extravagance of its ultimate fulfillment rippled out from this divine, feminine pair of giver and receiver goddesses into Tom and Ellie's would be seducer and through them into all of Omega and the opposition here, both human and ET, and throughout the omniverse. And all that is took the tiniest of steps forward in its endless cycle of evolution, death and rebirth.

And, like Eva, Ellie cried and cried in fulfillment, ecstasy and love.

She cried for the coming to completeness of her womanhood and the totality of what had just happened.

She cried for the love she felt for Eva she could barely contain.

She cried for the gift of perfection she and Peter had received.

She cried for the eternal impulse that moves everything forward to its ultimate return.

And Eva held her in her arms and cried with her until they felt the greatest peace and contentment humans could feel.

They took their time and reveled in the sacredness of these feelings.

They floated in ecstasy, peace and fulfillment together.

Then Eva sent mother and child home.

"Suckle you're baby, darling, and think of me and all we have done. I couldn't be happier with you. You are like a second heart within me."

She returned naked to her pod.

She was hot and wet.

She hadn't come.

Her soul was completely fulfilled but her body was filled with desire.

"Hello darlings, what have you been doing?"

They'd been practicing mind meld by playing Favorites. Each one would come up with a category like color or food or sex partner, city, place in nature or almost anything. And then each in turn would give them a living experience of their favorite.

They were all having fun and doing great.

"Beautiful. This slut's been off with Ellie and she wants it now. It's time for me to be with Gabe again. Alena, I want you with André and Anani with Jack. Hang dinner for now. Let's make love."

And so they did for the next two hours.

It was very sweet for Jack and Anani and Alena and André to finally unite.

Jack and Alena loved each other most and Anani and André loved Eva more than anyone. But they had been seeing and wanting to experience their current partners as well. This consummation came just at the right moment. André was such a pretty, loving man. Alena was a gorgeous, mature woman. Anani's exotic beauty and pheromones were so compelling. And Jack was such an all American hunk. How could they not want to sample all the pleasures each could offer?

And Eva and Gabriel felt so wonderful being together again.

Their love was supreme.

But what had happened earlier between Eva and Ellie had turned a notch in the order of things.

Something in Eva knew that at some future point her universe would change.

But that was in better hands than hers and could be left there for now.

So again, their love nest became a beacon of joy for the city of New York and the world at large.

They all evinced and absorbed the most wonderful fulfillments.

They and God were happy.

Then Eva manifested them another dream meal and they slept, Eva with Alena, Gabriel with Anani and André with Jack.

Not a one of them ever snored or disturbed the other in any way.

Their sleep was as fulfilling as their lovemaking.

They were the pod made in heaven.

Every morning they were born anew.

Chapter 27

Their Gestalt Was Staggering

Come the morning, they all played with each other for a while.

Jack had never fondled a man's genitals. It was new and exciting, something previously forbidden but no longer. It was surprisingly fun and erotic. And what man more perfect than androgynous, little André? There was something about that hard cock that was simply delightful to play with. Then he had André suck him. And that felt supreme. André was better at it than anyone Jack had experienced.

"Hmmm," he murmured, "Give Alena lessons."

Then he realized he could share this with her mentally.

Gabe and Anani were likewise delighted. Her body under his hands was like the most perfect, fine tuned, musical instrument. She was exquisite to touch, the feel of her sublime. He kept touching and caressing and marveling at the beauty of her responses. And Gabe's hands were superb. She reveled in the pleasure of his masterly play.

And Eva and Alena did all kinds of things together. Finally, Eva licked and loved her asshole for her. Alena had never experienced this and she'd been wanting to. It felt supreme to her that it was Eva to do it. It somehow healed her final pout about Eva getting Gabriel.

When she assumed position number two, the very best one for this, Eva saw a small spec of shit nestled on Alena's anal lip. Alena didn't realize it was there and Eva didn't enlighten her. Instead, she willingly lapped it in and swallowed it down.

But then when Eva slipped her tongue deep inside, they both felt a little more come into Eva's mouth and perceived her swallowing it.

This was more than a little spec, but there was no hint of revulsion anywhere within her, anywhere within either one of them.

It just felt somehow right and fulfilling.

The smell and taste reminded Eva of rotting leaves in a north Wisconsin forest.

"So perfect, darling Eva" Alena said out loud to her. "Lick my ass. Eat my shit. I totally forgive you for everything. I love you and what you're doing for me. Thank you so very much. We're even."

Eva smiled and loved her back as she give her beautiful anus a few last little sweet caresses with the tip of her tongue.

"Isn't that what we're doing," she thought to her, "making everything even? I'm so happy to do this for you. It has helped me as well."

Then she thought to herself, "It's like a mother cleaning her baby's bottom with the utmost love, care and tenderness instead of the disgust, annoyance and impatience so many of us got. It *is* healing. How lovely it will be to have Anani do it for me."

No one came.

They didn't feel the need after last night.

They knew with a deep, calm elation that the desert of dearth was finally over. They would all be coming to their heart's content.

They just loved and explored their intimate bodies however they wished.

It was all too good to be true.

But the glory of this new heaven on Earth was that nothing was too good to be true.

Not even their breakfast when they were finished with their lovemaking.

And all that simple joy and pleasure couldn't help but radiate into the world as well.

It was the miracle of creation that the opposition didn't perceive it all and blow them to bits.

But that was the way of things.

The opposition was unfortunately and thankfully blind to love.

For breakfast they had the most succulent, delicious, fresh-cooked pig imaginable. And Eva pulled the most exotic, exquisite fruit in the world fresh from a wide variety of places around it including that French cantaloupe. They had fruit they didn't even know existed with a variety of nuts, cheeses, raisins, dates and figs.

They completed with a few mouthfuls of chocolate, dark and milk, according to their predilections.

They couldn't be happier.

They were ready to take on the world.

Upon completion, their table was bare and immaculate.

Then they were on various couches and chairs in the living room.

Eva united her energy bodies with Gabriel's.

It wasn't like Jimmy's tantra where his life force could rise up her body.

Their life force energies remained contained.

But each chakra has its own energy body.

It was those she united.

It was more subtle, yet intimate, powerful and sublime.

They were two beings become one.

And synergy was.

The one overbeing they became was more than the sum of the two of them.

They were one plus one equals three or two-and-a-half or four—a being significantly more.

Then she brought in Anani and the effect was manifold.

This always happened when they united but now Eva was accentuating it, calling attention to it, bringing it to the forefront of their awareness.

She wanted them to fully know this more than they ever had.

And the three of them did.

Alena was next.

And then André and Jack.

Each addition augmented them more than that one being alone.

They felt deeply into the more they had become.

It was large and powerful and joyous.

They felt its divinity, its God-like qualities far more than they could their own alone.

For a few moments they simply sat there taking it in, feeling it, being what they now were.

This is what Eva wanted.

This was the glory and potential of her pod.

Then she reached out and brought in Brie's consciousness—Brie, Joan of Arc and the other, angel-visited beings she had been.

For whatever reasons, and perhaps the angels helped with this, Brie's past lives were far more fully available to her conscious mind than any of the others.

Eva remembered the brief image that came to her while united with Nyame. She considered trying to bring forth more but forbore. Now was not the time either.

Brie added to the group gestalt exponentially.

Then came Theo.

Only his one past life memory was there in clarity and detail. It was more than enough.

Eva pulled them physically into the room and alerted their guardians. Theo was a latchkey kid. And he wasn't going to school these days. He had been outside shooting baskets.

Then came Jimmy, his consciousness first and then his body.

They were complete.

And they were magnificent.

The depth, breadth and power of the being they now were filled them all with ecstasy.

Their eyes gazed on each other like lighthouses.

They all burst into laughter as one.

The laughter poured forth for quite some time.

Their great joy and mirth filled Earth's airwaves.

Little by little, Earth was healing.

With this within them, how could they not succeed!

At least that's how they felt.

It was eleven-twelve, three-twelve PM Ghana time.

Eva reached out to Nyame and brought in his consciousness.

What a joy to unite with him again!

They felt the expansion for a moment. Then she was ready for more.

It was time.

She united the consciousness of all the ringed ones and their pods, her entire growing army.

Some were sleeping. Most were awake.

It didn't matter.

Those asleep she gently awakened and gave their bodies the benefit of a full night's sleep.

In a moment they were fully alert and rested. She also gave them the essence of food as she had hydrated herself on her run in the park.

Such was the tiny fraction of what their rings could now bring about.

As Eva, they were ready.

Their gestalt was staggering.

It took getting used to.

They took the time to do that.

Eleven ring wearers. Eleven pods. Six of six souls. Five of seven.

Three complements to Eva's pod.

They all assimilated all their knowledge.

Nyame, Cyti, Konane and Ilia had brought in two children each.

None of the others had.

Eva called in the hearts and minds of those eight children as well.

No one besides Eva had an adult complement like Jimmy.

Eva, Taanga and Kumi had won over their balance points.

None of the others had.

They all knew they would soon have two children and loyal fulcrums.

They all knew of the plan to nuke DC and that there were no new developments.

They all knew they could call on any of the others at any time.

They were all of one accord.

"It's time for us to complete. I've been lucky. Or I've had a lot of help. We all need to find ways. Call on me if you hit a dead end. Use the Earth Room. Commune with the devas. Do what you can. We all need to do this. I love you."

They were now eighty-one, soon to be at least ninety-three.

"We will stage our first mass maneuvers now as we are."

She brought them all to her Andromeda world.

It had water and an atmosphere similar to Earth's though no discernable life.

They could comfortably live and breathe here without protection.

It was a touch warmer than Earth. They'd be fine without clothes.

Eva had placed them standing in line on a high, flat plateau looking out over a great valley of dirt and rock. There was a beautiful river in the heart of the valley.

"This is our world away from home. We can come here at any time. This is where we will stage all our maneuvers. This plateau is our meeting point."

They communed in detail about all the practice Eva, Nyame, Cyti, Konane and Ilia's pods had already done. This would be the first for the others.

They all now knew what it was they would be doing.

They all had incorporated the same experience.

They mapped out this world as an Earth surrogate. Each ringed one would oversee their own geographical area and the incoming space above it.

And their pods and complements would pluck pilots from flying cans, deposit them on this plateau and inhabit the cans in the blink of an eye.

For now they would do this in space.

They would try it fully linked and then only linking when the need arose.

Eva suspected it would be better the latter way but she wanted to experience both and see if any other combinations would be helpful.

The maneuvers began.

Forty metal coffins blinked into existence in space all around the world, three for each pod with six members and no children, four for pods of seven or six and two children and five for Eva and Konane who both had units of nine.

Eva wanted enemy ships to outnumber defenders.

All were moving at high speeds.

The leaders peopled their spaceships with select unit members. Then they threw their other members around them to pluck them from their vehicles, deposit them on the plateau and inhabit the vehicles themselves. They started recycling them faster and faster so they each got to be pilot and usurper many times.

It soon became apparent that linked awareness was counterproductive. Too much was going on. It was too much to process.

So each ringed one took charge of their own unit and sector and focused only on that. When a ship crossed a boundary, they would alert their neighbor. They soon decided to make ships cross boundaries frequently.

They began to get the hang of it.

The combatants practiced their telepathy. For this exercise it wasn't so much needed. But they wanted to be able to call out in the thick of battle.

The ringed ones learned to coordinate better.

It started to happen as if it were really happening.

Their charge and excitement amplified.

Their functioning approached the speed of thought.

They decided to compete with each other, one pod invading another's sector.

The ringed ones weren't hijacking pilots or stealing ships.

They could, if necessary, but they oversaw their sectors and deployed their forces from afar.

They soon got to two units attacking one sector.

And then three.

And the attackers became the attacked.

All this went on for quite some time.

The leaders could control these ships but they wouldn't be able to control the enemies'. Their human replacements would have to fly them. They'd have to retrieve that knowledge from the deposed ETs and give it to their unit members. This would take precious seconds. Perhaps they could do it in advance. Eva would look into it. Now was not the moment.

They were making a game of it.

The goal became crashing a spaceship into the ground of someone's sector.

They knew these spaceships would have missiles that could each destroy a city or more.

They knew the opposition didn't want to destroy the whole world but would gladly decimate large parts of it to retain control.

Points were given for hijacks and hits.

So far, Eva, Nyame and Konane were in the lead.

Cyti, Ilia and Capucine were second tier.

And the other five were trailing.

The children were loving this game.

They delighted in yanking any sized body out of its ship.

The adults knew how valuable the children were. In all the ships of tight, small quarters an adult would squash both bodies.

Konane was the one exception.

She was the smallest adult, André the next.

Eva emblazoned their sizes into the consciousness of all the ringed ones.

"We can't know all that we'll need. Any of us might encounter a unique situation. We can all utilize each other where the need is greatest. Use any of us to avert disaster. I want you all to practice. Millions of people will be depending on us. The whole world is depending on us. The omniverse is depending on us. We all need to get as good as we can. But don't call attention to yourselves. Do it here, not around Earth. If no children come forward, go to the Earth Room and find them. We each should have units of eight or nine. That's a good size. More will be unwieldy. But each of you commune with the devas and follow your guidance. We've been doing this for five hours now. It's enough. Get ready for the next session as soon as you can. Find your way to convert your balance point. Call on me or any of us who can help. Thank you. You're precious. I love you."

On their way home, Eva gave them a tour. She placed them in space at distances from Andromeda best suited to view the diminishing majesty of a galaxy.

It was stunning and mind blowing, the form a trillion stars in space would take.

Half their vision filled with it, then a quarter, then a tenth.

Then they likewise enjoyed the approach of the Milky Way.

How many light years away were they at each stop?

They could know this as well.

They were learning to appreciate God's creation as no human before.

What was one world with seven-and-a-half billion people?

As the heaven they knew it could be, well worth everything they could do to save it.

At their first stop in towards the Milky Way, it looked like a small island off in the distance. Eva held them there to gaze upon it.

Seeing a picture was one thing.

Being in the midst of it quite another.

Eighty-one of them were strung out in space. They looked at where they came from against the backdrop of our universe's myriad stars and galaxies. It deepened their resolve to succeed. They became one loving determination.

The small beauty of their home galaxy, their love for each other, their deepening knowledge of how tiny their world with all its inhabitants really was and the promise of their mission to make it so unutterably wonderful crystallized their unity.

Eleven pods with one mind, one heart and one will.

Slowly, Eva brought them all home.

Chapter 28

Earth Was a Balance Point

It was four fifty-seven.

Eva knew it was time for her to foray more deeply into enemy camp.

She hadn't been relishing it.

As a matter of fact, she'd been avoiding it.

But she could no longer.

She decided to take solace in an afternoon meditation with her pod.

She invited Jimmy.

He was game.

She loaded all their experience into him.

He had some of his own.

They went from super active and hyper alert to the calm depths of silent being.

It rejuvenated them all.

During it, Eva reached out to Arnold.

She was delighted by his transformation.

He was whole and healed and his paunch was gone.

He had decided to leave his London life and relocate to New York.

He had made brief excuses to his Count friend.

They hadn't seen each other.

She went back to her meditation.

When they were done, Eva set them all free letting them know she might be calling on them at any time but probably wouldn't be. All, that is, with the exception of Jack.

She knew that he and Tom would respond well to each other.

She wasn't in an eating mood.

So she gave Jack and herself all the hydration and nourishment they needed and left the others to fend for themselves however they saw fit.

She was on a mission.

She was no longer to be distracted.

She reached out to Ellie and Tom.

He had just arrived home from work.

It was now Friday afternoon, five-thirty, eight-thirty the next morning Vanuatu time.

She had them take Peter and go out for a walk.

When they were out of sight of their home, she relocated them, herself and Jack to the fale.

She knew if the opposition were tracking them all carefully, this little subterfuge would fall apart. But she knew they still weren't and wanted to do the minimum to protect them all.

This reinforced in her how much more she needed to know of her enemies.

She manifested four chairs in the fale and made her introductions.

Tom and Jack *did* respond well to each other, more so than anyone else Eva could have brought. And it was better than leaving Tom alone with two women. It put him at ease to be with a fellow patriot warrior.

"Just keep doing what comes naturally," she thought to herself. "Follow your guidance and we'll be fine."

Being with Eva soothed and fed Ellie's soul to the depths of her being.

Tom also responded to that and relaxed more deeply, himself.

He felt that new sensation even more—finally being home.

He knew he'd have to wait for his healing and perfection.

He was content with that.

He wanted to do all he could for the creamies, especially these creamies.

He wanted to make up for all he had done for the opposition.

Where had he been?

Exactly, he knew, where he was meant to be.

Eva read him again more thoroughly.

Any new wrinkle might help.

She also deepened his comfort and resolve.

His direct experience with the aliens was limited. There had been some but very little. His work had been with his cadre and other top secret groups, both consciously oppositional and otherwise. So he did have connections with Ilia, Kumi and Liu's groups.

She moved through him to his team members and, one by one, milked them of everything they knew.

Then she did the same with the foreign groups.

None of them had any inkling they were so thoroughly being read.

A few members of his own cadre had a fleeting thought of Tom.

The one who had come sniffing around had a fleeting thought of Ellie.

That was it as Eva downloaded all they had to offer.

Frank was the name of the man in Omega who had the most interaction with the ETs. To the degree that humans could, he had friendships or good working relations with a number of them.

The Omega group had transcended their nationality. Their allegiance was to the control of the human race. In this, Frank and his friends had a common goal.

He wasn't clear on how much he was being used or how much he was one of them. It didn't matter. He was at the heart of the workings of the power elite of the world. That fed his ego sufficiently to make him loyal. He was in the process of trying to transcend his humanity. He thought he was doing a pretty good job.

This stage didn't take Eva long.

Maybe fifteen minutes.

They had all sat there patiently knowing what she was doing.

"Thank you, Tom," she said out loud. "I can't tell you how precious you are to our country and the human race. I'm so glad for you and for Peter and Ellie's healing. Ellie is a great gem. She's a blessing to us all. Just continue helping them in all the ways they expect you to. You can call out to me with your mind. Please don't hesitate if there is something to transmit. I'll be working through you to help soften them. Shall we go for a swim?"

She didn't wait for an answer but clothed them all but Peter in bathing suits.

Tom hadn't healed yet and was still the straightest of arrows.

He didn't know what Ellie and Eva had done together, though deep inside he could feel the depths of Ellie's love for Eva and that it was more than platonic. It didn't matter.

Everything now was infinitely better than before.

He was happy and at peace.

Hell, he'd suck Jack's cock in gratitude for his liberation and what they had done for Peter if they asked him to.

And now helping to reclaim the sovereignty and wellbeing of the human race?

He was all in.

They all thoroughly enjoyed their dip.

Peter, in particular, was ecstatic as Ellie and then Tom gently bounced him into the water's surface.

When they had had enough, Eva cleaned and dressed them and sent them back to a safe distance from their home.

Then she looked at Jack for a moment and sent him back, too.

This was hers to do alone.

She decided she wanted to lay down for it.

She manifested her bed and was on it.

Her next step was the Count.

He was in Capucine's territory but Eva had the connection to him through Arnold.

He was getting ready for bed.

She retrieved his knowledge—his Bilderberger buddies, the oppositional members of England and Europe's royal families, the few he knew in the great money clans, his brief encounters with three aliens.

She reached out to Capucine and gave her all she had learned.

In turn, Capucine showed Eva her two new children.

The boy was an enterprising, Parisian street urchin. The girl was a precocious, privileged powerhouse from Saint-Tropez.

She had also found an adult complement like Jimmy.

Her unit was now nine.

Eva had the thought that all the units would end up that number, the number of completion, giving her an army of ninety-nine.

And with that thought, she knew it to be so.

"Let's make all our units nine by tomorrow," she thought to all her leaders.

They were leaning in that direction anyway.

The time for dawdling was over.

Then she had a thought that stunned her.

"Why haven't I thought this before? If they're monitoring us, why can't I perceive it and trace it back to them?"

She knew she could read the minds of the Greys and the Lizards without them knowing, and the Oranges if she was brief and careful.

"Maybe it just wasn't time so I couldn't think of it. Now must be the time. Or maybe I'm just not used to having these abilities so I don't think of them. Or maybe the angels just downloaded this thought into my mind like I asked them to. Can I know my own thoughts from theirs?"

She decided to retrieve the answer. The devas had just given her this.

"Trust, darling, trust, trust, trust... And thank you."

She blanketed her beloved condo with her awareness and felt into what pathways of surveillance she might perceive.

At first she could perceive nothing.

She got quieter, opened her awareness more and felt more deeply into it.

Still nothing.

She did perceive the standard city video cameras on some of the street posts nearby. But she couldn't perceive anything else. So she decided to delve into one of those.

At first she was swept into the urban police surveillance system and all the grunge that entailed. But then, with a jolt, she picked up some Grey energy. She followed it to a national linkup and then to a far more sophisticated off world information system created by the Greys.

It was on Ganymede, one of Jupiter's moons, the largest in our solar system.

Most of their facility was underground. They had quite a hub there.

But how crude!

They were piggybacking manmade Earth technology.

No doubt they had something better when they thought it was important.

She surrounded Tom and Ellie's home as well, just to make sure.

Same thing. Nothing but what Langley had provided.

So good, her pod and Tom were not getting any special attention.

She was enjoying the comfort of her fale bed.

But she went to the Earth Room and tried from there.

It was no better.

She had incorporated its powers. Or the angels had transferred them to the ring. It was one and the same.

The Earth Room had been for training.

Everything was geared to help them grow and accelerate.

All the ringed ones should be able to do this.

She gave them all the knowledge as she returned to her bed.

She blanketed Ganymede with her awareness.

They had two installations in place.

One was a military surveillance base.

The other was residential. It housed their loose affiliation working towards the common goal of controlling Earth.

Eva could sense the Greys, Oranges and Lizards and a few Annunaki, the most human of all, with their ancient role as gods on Earth at the dawn of civilization.

There were no Dark Clouds. They were the antithesis of the Great Lights, the beings more powerful than the angels.

They didn't need any physical facilities.

And so far they had more important things to do at the centers of galaxies.

They didn't yet know the importance their counterparts were now placing on Earth.

The opposition had no beings parallel to the angels. Or if there were corrupting angels, they weren't involved in this attempt at human redemption. Perhaps they were off helping the Dark Clouds or had become them. Eva was given the knowledge that these would be her only adversaries. If Dark Clouds came it would be late in the game. And the Great Lights would deal with them.

Earth held an importance that went beyond their conception, such a little, primitive world far from the hub of the great intergalactic struggles.

What could be grand about Earth and her pitiful humans?

Let the lowly adventurers have her.

For that's what most of these ETs were.

She was as if nothing.

"Keep thinking that," Eva thought. "The less I have to do with you the better."

She delved more deeply into their surveillance facilities.

Their sophisticated means were constantly monitoring Earth's political and military leaders with an emphasis on the latter. Their plan was to use the war machine at the time of their takeover and, yes, to significantly depopulate our world. Then they'd enslave those who remained to gather and extract our riches for themselves.

"Not a very pleasant place you want to leave us, is it? Thank God for the forces at work to save us."

Then she more deeply realized that it was our own evolution that could damn or save us.

If we healed and loved enough, it would go one way, if not, the other.

The angels had said they felt good about this world.

"Let it be that you are right."

She found a Grey pilot and learned how to pilot their ships.

The children could do it.

She tried to see if she could dismantle their field disrupters.

She knew she couldn't but had to try.

She cognized their hierarchy.

The Greys were the weakest but had their uses.

Then the Lizards. Then the Oranges.

The few Annunaki were respected and feared. Sometimes they were deferred to, sometimes not. They had their own, limited agendas.

The Black Clouds were titanic and totally obeyed. But Earth didn't draw them.

Only the Light Gods could contain them.

The devas would not become involved in conflict.

They only helped and healed to the degree that they could.

With this, Eva reached her limit.

Plumbing the opposition drained her.

She decided to survey the omniverse.

As humans had been like grains of a vast mountain of sand, now it was universes, galaxies, stars and worlds, different grains calling to her in different ways.

So many levels of being. So many havens of life.

Earth was not only off to the side. It was quarantined.

Many worlds and their civilizations lived different degrees of divine will. There was grace, harmony and balance.

Others lived different degrees of chaos, violence, corruption and greed.

Earth was a balance point. It had strains and influences of both, more so than the other worlds, which were more in one camp or the other.

What the dark side didn't appreciate was the ripple effects that would occur from Earth's tipping one way or the other.

Souls in tune with God's will had quietly come from all the universes to incarnate here for this event. The effects would flow through every one of them to the worlds they had come from. Much more than the human race was at stake here. The tipping of Earth would affect the cosmic totality in infinite, unseen ways.

"Oh how we must succeed!"

But Eva knew it could still go either way.

Then she blanketed our local universe.

One world in a far galaxy called to her.

It was a beautiful, graceful world living in profound accord with God's will.

It wasn't the highest, eternal heaven. But it carried the most divine, vibrant life.

Eva knew she had dwelt there once not so very long ago. For the first time, she perceived that this was her third human incarnation. That image she had seen was from her second. She would delve more deeply into it later.

The beings of her old, divine home were like Light Gods but corporeal.

At some preconscious level, she had always wanted Earth to be more like there.

Now she was helping it become so.

Perhaps, win or lose, she would return there.

Perhaps with some of her pod members.

Perhaps, if they won, they would stay and see what Earth became.

Eva could do no more.

She returned to her pod at bedtime.

She wanted to be with André, that sweet, young man who had been so tortured.

Learning her desire put André in heaven.

Gabe would be with Alena and Jack with Anani.

Their own little heaven held them through the night.

Chapter 29

We Are Not Demons

Eva awoke at five-thirty.

She felt quite wonderful.

She knew she could use a little more sleep but she could also give herself all the benefits of a full night's sleep.

Lovemaking with André had been so sweet, conscious and tender.

He was a treasure.

It was Saturday.

She had met Gabriel twelve days ago.

Her period was a few days late.

She knew she was pregnant.

That was fine.

She cognized the blastocyst. It was now implanting in her womb.

Needless to say, it was Nyame's.

Gabriel had been first.

But Mr. Super Virile had won out.

Nyame was a magnificent being and she did love him.

But she didn't feel he was the one she would choose to father her first baby.

And she was only twenty-three.

Being pregnant was fine till morning sickness came.

Life sans period was lovely.

She scanned herself to see if Nyame's race figured into her reluctance.

Perhaps, but that wasn't the decisive factor.

"Gabriel or André," she thought, "and not yet."

"And probably Gabriel."

She decided to dissolve it at the first hint of nausea though she knew she could moderate that as well.

Hell, she could circumvent her menses.

But that would be a good time to do it.

She had a month or so.

What had happened in twelve days?

What might the world be in a month?

André stirred.

"Did I wake you with my thinking, love?"

"Maybe, but I'm so glad. A moment in bed with you is like an eternity in heaven."

She laughed and hugged him to her.

"Dear, dear André."

They rolled around and felt each other.

He was such a precious man child.

"Oh yes" she thought to herself. "I could have your baby. But I think it'll be Gabe's. We'll see when the time comes, if it comes. Now we have a world to win."

She scanned her pods.

They all had nine and were ready.

Maneuvers first.

Within a moment, ninety-nine courageous souls were standing fully dressed, fed and slept on their plateau in Andromeda united in consciousness.

They all knew what Eva and Cyti had learned, that the ISIS cells were ready to steal a nuke from a Pakistani nuclear facility with the help of two guards. They also knew how closely the Greys were monitoring the world's military. If a nuke were stolen, the Greys would know it. So if members of Eva's army then retrieved and destroyed it, the Greys would perceive it. This heightened involvement in the world's power structures would put them all in jeopardy.

They were better off doing something now.

The opposition was scrutinizing the war machine in far more detail than little groups of terrorists here and there.

They were far less likely to notice these cells before they stole a nuke than after.

In a moment, all the members of five ISIS cells and two Pakistani army guards were standing in a healing chamber. They left the nuclear physicist. He couldn't do much without them. And perhaps he was important enough for the opposition to notice.

In the next moment, fifty-five tin cans with seats were flying through space, the atmosphere and not so far from this world's surface.

The games began.

As they practiced attacking, hijacking and protecting their territories, it became clear that the ultimate functioning was for each nine member unit to act from one consciousness.

So they practiced nanosecond maneuvers from that level.

Each unit became one mind in one field with nine bodies.

That one mind always knew what all the bodies were doing.

So why should the leader stay out of the fray?

They had moved beyond calling out to each other or the leader.

They were one awareness.

This sped up their responses.

Every soldier had perceived this higher form of functioning almost simultaneously.

Each one could focus on their activity and know what the others were doing. So they would instantly know where to go next.

They were all becoming better and better, more and more equal and one.

Their functioning was approaching perfection.

This was only their second exercise and the first for some. At the end of five hours, they already felt ready.

"So good," Eva thought to them all, "but we'll continue practicing."

All the balance points were converted but Sati's. And she was the only leader to maintain celibacy. She had found a like-minded male Sadhu as her partner. Of all the adults, they were the only chaste. Their pod members understood and respected their choice. But it did limit their options. She was also reluctant to use her pod members to seduce anyone. She made up for these deficiencies by the power of her awareness and her great, divine love. She was one of the most conscious, loving beings on the planet. That's what drew Eva.

But in this, intervention would be needed.

Her balance point, the eighteen-year-old Sarkic hacker, was already having second thoughts. But he was still loyal. His belief in the prophecies of his cult held him strongly.

Nandi was a loner, a shy, awkward boy who got tongue-tied around girls.

He was an orphan with no one close enough to use as leverage to change him.

Eva read his soul and psyche.

Both she and Sati knew what it would take. But Sati had compunctions.

Eva didn't.

The boy was strongly attracted to white women.

His fondest fantasy was to be with two of them.

He was already concerned about his current allies.

It wouldn't take much.

Eva had told them all to call on her. But Sati had held back. This was her only sticking point. She wouldn't ask her women to do this. And they weren't white, anyway. But here Eva was. And it was time.

Eva checked in with Capucine.

She was ready.

She sent all but herself and Capucine home with the knowledge in their minds that they would now practice three hours every day, that their major job was to influence the opposition through their balance points and that one pod would remain on Earth during their practice sessions to monitor Earth and alien activities. They wouldn't be leaving their home world unattended again.

Eva scooped up the Indian boy and brought him with them to the empty fale.

It was two in the morning Vanuatu time.

She had the glow globes give off the softest, warmest, most flattering golden light imaginable.

She and Capucine stood naked before him, the goddesses that they were, enhanced by the sultry, tropical air and highlighted by the sensual light.

She left him dressed and began thinking into his mind.

"We are two of your dreaded creamies.

We know your myths, legends and prophecies.

We are not demons.

We are simple human beings who have been healed and perfected and given powers to help the human race.

You are precious to us.

Deep down inside, you know your alien friends don't mean us well.

To save the human race, we are ready to give ourselves to you.

I am Eva and this is Capucine.

We know your hidden desires so we have come to you.

But let me show you what I have learned.

Will you allow this?"

If Sati had offered or tried to download their knowledge, Nandi would have resisted, disbelieved and denied.

Sati knew this and had waited.

But he couldn't fight the vision of Eva and Capucine standing before him, two women more beautiful than his imagination could produce, so close, alluring and within reach as he never believed could actually happen. His desire and the potential fulfillment of it rendered him putty in the face of their magnificence.

With his assent, Eva vividly showed him all she had learned of the ET's plan for the human race.

Nandi almost lived Earth's depopulation and her people's enslavement.

With a shudder, he was won over.

Nothing more was needed.

This knowledge was now part of him.

He was theirs.

"Dear, dear Nandi. We are yours. We absolutely promise you all the love and pleasure we have to offer but only after you are healed and perfect.

You have our vows and our bond.

But we can't heal you until we have softened your allies through you, unchanged as you are. We must return you now. And you must help us save the human race. We will give ourselves to you when we have succeeded and you have been made whole and perfect. Look at us now and remember."

She and Capucine turned very slowly, taking great breaths, lifting their arms, placing their feet apart, moving in the most compelling ways.

"You will have us very soon. This we promise. We are infinitely grateful to you for receiving our knowledge, for being our ally, for helping your friends. How grateful we will be when all the world starts to heal and become whole! Sati will work with you but I will come to you as well. We are now one team. Know the three of us will be together when the time is right."

Now all the fulcrums were converted.

And Nandi had two living focal points for his fantasies, two of the most desirable women on Earth.

He couldn't be more motivated to help the creamies instead of the creepies.

When Sati revealed herself to his mind, he was totally ready.

They began doing the work of all the ringed ones and their balance points.

Tilting their human opposition adversaries back towards the human race.

Chapter 30

Is this God's Plan?

When Eva returned home it was still before noon.

She held a brief powwow.

"Darlings, my time for you and love play will be far less for a while. You will have a lot of time to do whatever you wish. I will be working with the opposition through Tom and all those I can connect with through him. It's not the devas who will take over as we used to believe. It's we who wear the ring and you who help us. We will bring about the mass induction of the human race into the chambers and the true nature of who we are meant to be. The time is fast approaching. I must attend to this. You can always call out to me. Maybe the five of you go out in public more. Blow people's minds with your love and beauty. This alone will be helpful and healing. I'll be with you in spirit. I love you. Anything from your side?"

"We'll miss you," Gabriel said for them all.

"And I, you. Perhaps I'll need breaks and the comfort of your love. Perhaps I'll visit. But if not, you'll understand. If we succeed, we'll have a lifetime to fulfill ourselves. I must now do everything I can to make sure we do. I love you all so very much. You are my golden family. I'll see you soon."

She disappeared to lay on her bed in her beloved fale.

She might be able to do this with Anani or Gabe or any of the others in her arms but no, she must devote her totality to it with nothing to distract.

She merged with Tom's consciousness. He had the weekend off. He was home with Ellie and Peter.

Around the world, her ten leaders were doing likewise.

Nothing was more important than this.

It was the major step towards mass redemption.

It was also the dirty work.

As she entered into him, she felt Tom's gladness of it.

Like Ellie, he more and more belonged to her.

He was eager to do whatever he could to help his co-workers and the human race. But he also welcomed and desired Eva.

She poured through him a wave of pleasure. It filled his body and being.

"It's so good to be working through you, my precious Tom. What we are doing together is more important than anything. You are the perfect man to be doing this with. Thank you so very much."

This deepened his opening and surrender to her. He was ready for whatever she wanted. It fulfilled him more than anything else he had done to serve his country or his fellow man.

They were becoming a unique, magnificent team. Eva needed him and his connection with those of the opposition. And he needed her to redeem his life and soften their resolve.

This mutual need brought them deeper together.

They became one more deeply than Tom and Ellie ever had as Ellie and Eva had before.

But this would also bring Ellie and Tom closer together.

They were a pod of three.

And Eva knew it would help every human soul and body for this to deepen.

So she didn't hesitate.

She filled Tom with her entire being and dissolved all his remaining holdouts.

She helped him become totally hers, totally one with her.

Like Ellie, he would now do anything.

This is how it was meant to be.

She softened his straight arrow tendencies. And he allowed himself to open to being with her. He wanted to. How could he not?

She brought in Ellie's awareness and the three beings became a greater entity. She had the two of them share with Tom all they had done together.

The beauty, glory and sexiness of it, the love the two of them felt for each other and, especially, the total devotion of his wife to Eva melted him even more. It made Eva even more desirable. And he knew, directly from Ellie, that she wanted to give him to Eva, that she not only desired it but that it would deepen her love of him. She wanted to give Eva everything she had, including him.

Eva left Ellie there to be with Peter but maintained the wholeness of their union. They would all experience this together.

Tom found himself naked on his hands and knees straddling Eva's naked body.

A mighty wave of love and lust shot through him.

Eva reached down with both hands and began caressing his cock and balls.

He was soon as hard as he could be.

In her private mind she thought to herself, "I unite with Tom but not with Nandi. This will help our work together. It will help Sati for Nandi to have a future promise. It will help me to have Tom already mine. This is how I milk them both. And I daren't heal him any more than I have. His comrades might notice. Is this God's plan?"

But she knew there was no better way.

And in this, she would do everything she could.

Tom was more than ready.

This needn't be prolonged.

Eva *was* aroused. But she used her abilities to fully cream her pussy.

She held his cock in one hand and placed her other on the top his rump.

She guided and helped him into her.

Then she gave him total permission to move in all the ways that would give him the most pleasure.

For this union, she needn't come.

It would be for his pleasure, his come, for having this experience together with Ellie present in this way.

With this behind them, nothing would interfere in their working together. They would be one on every level. Intimacy wouldn't be an unrequited desire causing tension between them. It would be a done deal.

"Such a wonderful man," she said to him as he moved within her. "Allow all your focus to be on your pleasure. Move in all the ways you wish to. Then come as completely as you can for me."

And he did. It lasted thirteen minutes. Eva amplified his fulfillment and release and sent waves of love and pleasure throughout his body as he spurt his cum into her pussy. And she expanded their love and gratitude for all they were, for Peter and for all they were about to do. It somehow sanctified all she was doing. It somehow dissolved a lot of the shadow of all Tom was and had done before.

"Good boy," she said, holding him tightly. "Good boy. You and Ellie and I are one. I don't know how much we'll be together but we will. It's important for you to surrender to this as deeply as you can. Do you understand?"

"Yes," he breathed. "I understand. And I'm so grateful and glad. Thank you with all my heart for healing Peter, for healing Ellie, for helping me see and do everything I can, for the magnificence and beauty of this. I'm yours, Eva, like Ellie. We're yours. Use us for everything that will help. It's all we want."

"Perfect, you magnificent man. So good, Tom, this dear, sweet fuck. You're a savior of the human race. How funny it begins with fucking. But then life begins with fucking, does it not? Though it's sweeter to say it begins with love. How good it will be to love you when you're healed and perfect."

Then to Ellie, "We're letting you go, dear, to do our work together. Be with Peter. You and I will be together again soon. I love you, my pussy. Tom will return to you when he can."

She nudged Tom off and turned them on their sides with Tom backed into her in spoon position. They each had their own small, perfectly sized pillows. They snuggled and got as comfortable as they could.

Across the world, Sati was using her and Capucine to unite with Nandi. This she wasn't above doing. Eva and Capucine, of their own free will, had offered themselves to him.

She had no compunctions to use them on Nandi to help perfect and liberate the entire human race.

What a miracle that redemption could pivot on the sexual desires of an eighteen-year-old Indian boy.

Or was it such a miracle after all?

Eva perceived this and joined them for a moment.

Nandi could feel her within.

"So good it will be, dear Nandi, to be with you when we have done our work and you have been healed. We will be yours."

Then Eva left them and Sati allowed him to feel the fullness of her being. The direct experience of her divine love and profound awareness overwhelmed him and healed much of his shadow as well.

In other ways, sexual and nonsexual, similar things were simultaneously occurring with nine other ringed ones and their balance points.

This alone was quietly accelerating the human race towards its ultimate goal of healing, redemption, perfection, unification and liberation.

So different than anyone thought it might possibly happen.

So perfect that it was happening now.

Eva began her work.

Chapter 31

A Clean Kill

She started with Frank.

She entered into all the levels of his being.

He noticed a heightened sense of awareness but chalked it off to the coffee he was drinking.

He was not a pleasant man to be in.

But like Arnold, he wasn't so bad.

Didn't all human darkness come down to the same basic things—a mass of contradictory impulses, desires, frustrations, woundings, aspirations and alternating feelings of self-importance and unworthiness?

All this, of course, could now be healed. And like all others, Frank had his light side, his true nature, too.

She soon found within him the core of his division surrounding his role in the world—the somewhat complex knot of guilt, uncertainty, power hunger, fear and concern that he was betraying himself and the human race. It was largely unexamined. If he were to take a cold, hard look, the knot would unravel and he would be left with emptiness. This he unconsciously avoided at all costs. So his feelings of power, determination and self-righteousness kept on prevailing.

Eva softened some of the coils of that knot within him and strengthened some of the heart impulses he so repressed as weakness.

She and Tom were a love unit and they were now present in the deepest recesses of Frank's heart and soul. She let him feel just a little more of that love than he had for a long time. This, inevitably, brought up his pain. And that along with desolation was what Frank was determined to avoid.

She backed off for now. It was enough to start things deeply working within him.

She entered into the Greys and Lizards Frank had truck with and milked them for everything they knew. He had met one Orange and no Annunaki. Very few humans had. Eva didn't feel the need to venture into the Orange. That would be on an as needed basis.

As she experienced them directly from within, she relished, with great relief, the knowledge that she wouldn't be healing a single ET. They were beyond her purview—and her capabilities. All she needed from them was how to fly their ships, how they might respond and any other unknown thing of value that might be delivered.

Her purview was humankind. And the more the humans in opposition softened, the better their chances. This task was infinitely more doable.

She had done her work with Frank.

She had gained all the knowledge she could from the ETs he was connected with. She would plumb other ETs in the future.

Now her work was with the other humans Tom was connected to.

One by one she and Tom entered into them.

One by one she gathered their knowledge, softened their knots and infused their hearts and souls with more love.

This was their work and it was infinitely worth doing.

This would help them all when the time came. The ETs would find they didn't have the base of support they thought they did.

They continued this with every human adversary they could find.

Each one they turned, however little, tilted the world back to God.

Little by little the world came closer to embracing the healed state.

Little by little it readied itself to transform to a higher heaven.

In total obscurity eleven people with a little help from their friends were re-sanctifying life on Earth.

They nourished themselves with water, nutrients and sleep and kept on going.

Their days became a blur of three-hour practice sessions and working with every human opposition member they could find.

Some of the most important were in the military. They were the ones who could bring about the most damage. But the ETs had weapons of their own. Thankfully, they had advanced beyond nuclear and radiation. They could kill people without destroying the environment. But, hopefully, they could be circumvented as well.

As this continued, Jimmy had a few more groups to send and Gabe had a list of a few more souls.

Eva could take care of this in a split second after her pod had sung for them.

At one point she asked why she still needed Tom.

"It helps to have someone with you who was of them like it helped you with Tom to bring Jack."

This was enough for her.

The ringed ones could remain united with their balance points as they seemingly worked for the opposition. This helped soften their proximate co-workers even more on the subtlest levels of their existence.

It was going well.

More and more they were ready.

More and more they had softened the humans who would be lords.

They finally came to the point where they didn't know what else they could do. They had reached and done all they could with every human adversary they could find.

Eva went to the Earth Room. She didn't think it would help but just in case it might.

She blanketed the world with her awareness.

She couldn't find one untouched human opponent.

She blanketed Ganymede and the few ships in between.

They were devoid of humans.

She communed with the devas.

"It is now with you. Our chambers are ready. We have helped all we can. It is up to you to protect the human race and your world. You have surpassed the point we would leave to circumvent violence. We are ready when you are."

She communed with the great Light Gods.

"We are here. You have some of our power in your rings. Call on us if a Black Cloud comes and in your extremity."

Again, she expanded herself to the limit by absorbing their energies in the cells of her body. She brought herself to the bursting point and remained as long as she could. Then she eased off and returned to her fale.

"A day or two off," she thought to all the ringed ones.

It had only been a week.

It felt like several lifetimes.

She had only been with her pod for the practice sessions. This had been her life. She had monitored them briefly twice.

When not practicing they would often semi-party, going out into the world to let it see the glory human existence could be.

It was so delicious to see and feel people's reactions especially knowing they could all be living this soon.

She had given them her hearty approval.

She had given herself internally manifested nourishment and sleep.

Now she wanted the real thing.

She directed her ring-mates to similarly indulge.

She knew nothing would happen in the next half day or so.

Something within her wanted to connect more directly with the source of her nourishment and sustenance than she ever had.

She sent her awareness in an expanding circle outwards till she located a swordfish and blessed, loved and permeated it with her awareness. For many moments she reveled in feeling its great visceral joy in swimming through the sea as if its body were hers. She saw through its eyes and felt every flex of every muscle, every movement of every fin and the bliss, love, beauty and determination in its mission of plying the ocean in search of food and procreation.

It was deeply thrilling to directly experience it all.

Then with, "Thank you, I love you, forgive me, brother," she located her friend's most succulent, steak-sized part slightly towards the belly, dampened his pain receptors and carefully excised it out for herself. There would be some pain and bleeding but he would soon heal and continue enjoying his existence.

She cleansed her third of a pound slab of all its heavy metals and ocean pollutants and instantly gave it what the best pan searing in oils, herbs, spices and lime could give. Then she created a small table and her favorite sautéed veges, roots and leafies.

She sent out her love and blessings with, "God bless you, all around you and all such everywhere. We thank you, we love you, we forgive you. Please forgive us." And all such food including her free, living friend was touched by it.

Then she took her first sacred bite and it was like God was in her mouth. She fully savored her heavenly meal and then manifested her beloved chocolate mousse.

From time to time she brought forth mouthfuls of fresh, vital water and supernaturally flavorful, tropical juices.

To top it all off she produced one mouthful of the most delicious tawny port on Earth and mouth loved it for many minutes. She delighted in surrounding her tongue with the magnificence of its liquid splendor and feeling her mouth juices come forth and commingle with its potency. She didn't mind the very slight buzz it gave her either.

Then she slept for fifteen hours.

She awoke feeling more wonderful than she ever had. And that was saying something.

She flew her body through the air from her bed out to sea and took total delight in the nourishing wonders of oceanic love.

Then she went home and meditated with her pod and its complements, the nine of them in profound, spiritual union.

When they were done, she manifested them a dream meal. She knew her co-leaders were doing likewise. She took a few sips and nibbled a few items of what she had created for them.

They mostly ate quietly, introspectively. Some of them prayed. They consciously savored each wonderful mouthful more than usual. When the meal was finished, Eva wanted to give them a little digestion time and speak with Jack.

They gathered in the living room.

"Jack, we've perceived in you the desire to righteously kill an enemy."

"Yes, well, it's there for you all to see."

"I feel like I'd like to talk this through with you in the old fashioned way."

"I'd like that, too."

"How many people have you killed?"

"It's hard to know exactly. My best count is twenty-three."

"And how were those?"

"Truly awful."

"So why again?"

"I believe we all have a killer within us even after we're healed. If you threw any of us in the jungle and something came at us, if it truly was kill or be killed, we'd be happy to let our killer come forth. If someone invaded my country, I'd feel justified in fighting them. I never did with the reverse. All my life I wanted to be a true, courageous warrior fighting for a just cause. I don't believe I've ever had that. We're doing that now but I'd like to experience the whole nine yards, taking out a truly bad guy and seeing what it's like. I don't really want to be a warrior anymore but we're being called to it. This, hopefully, will be my last opportunity. Like the movie says, 'a clean kill.' I'd like one to initiate me out of my dirty warrior career."

"Do you understand that if we kill one of them unnecessarily we're aiding and abetting them?"

"Totally. That would be just another dirty kill. I would only want it if they were determined to murder and might succeed. I would never harm them otherwise."

"But no matter how murderous they may be, we do have the options of relocating them or letting them drift in space."

"Yes, that's true. In that light I would be killing them unnecessarily. What can I say? I want to blow a few of the worst ones away."

Eva went silent for a moment and communed.

"We don't condone or proscribe. At this point it will not hurt your cause. We leave it with you."

She gazed into his eyes. They continued this for several moments. Eva finally realized that she wouldn't mind doing that herself.

"Very well, get your weapons. You'll be our only armed combatant though it's our arms that will whisk them away. If I see the chance, I'll send you in harm's way. Remember, they have laser guns that can punch a hole in your brain or cut you in half in the blink of an eye."

"Yes, well please send me to a chamber if they do."

"Of course. We don't want to lose you."

He went to his room and came back wearing his ammo belt, pistol and knife.

"Does anyone else have anything they want to ask or say?"

"God bless us all," Alena invoked.

"Amen," they all said.

They were ready.

They were the perpetrators.

They could start whenever they chose.

Eva united the consciousness of all the ringed ones and every member of her human army. Ninety-nine souls became suddenly joyous. Ninety-nine souls were ready. They were about to begin the full on glorification of the human race.

The leaders amplified this within themselves and their unit members.

The children, especially, were sky high.

They all knew how deadly serious this was.

They all knew they could be attacked, defeated and die and humans worldwide could be plunged more deeply into slavery than ever.

But they also knew that the more they came from grounded joy, love and fulfillment, the greater their chance of success.

What greater calling had any human being ever heeded?

Nothing before could begin to come close.

They were the saviors they had always wanted—they and the angels and the Big Lights and God.

That was their army.

And what an army to belong to!

God had finally become tired of waiting.

And they were God's minions.

What a way to die if they must!

And they had the manifest promise of resurrection!

They were ready.

The eleven ringed ones surveyed their sectors. They all realized they had all the landmasses and islands covered but the Arctic and Antarctic. And there were patches of ocean left unattended. Yachts, submarines, airline passengers, scientists, explorers, they must leave no human behind.

"Konane, Cyti and Taanga, you have the smallest populations. Konane, take the Indian and Arctic Oceans and the Arctic, Cyti the total Atlantic band and Taanga, the Pacific and Antarctica. I'll take the few astronauts."

Everything was covered.

Then Eva plumbed all the Grey and Lizard pilots for the flight knowledge of all the different types of craft they had and transferred it to her entire army. All the humans could now drive their vehicles. She left the Oranges and Annunaki for when it would be needed.

The healers had ninety-nine huge chambers several light years away in deep space between galaxies. They were far from all other beings and totally safe. Only the beings closest to God could instantly relocate across the light years, those who had evolved beyond malevolence. The evil could transverse large sectors of space through wormholes. But that took time and there were no wormhole exits near the chambers. The Black Clouds were the one exception. They had once been close to God.

Each chamber could hold one million people.

Each leader could send nine million at a time.

When the sectors of smaller numbers were complete, their chambers would become available to the more populous ones.

The dangers would come to Eva's army and the earthbound.

They all took a deep breath in preparation.

They all took a moment to pray and love their oneness.

And then ninety-nine million people disappeared from the face of the Earth, mostly from New York, Rio, Paris, Tokyo, Beijing, Moscow, New Delhi, Sydney, Laos, Ghana and Qatar and Riyadh to completely fill every one of the ninety-nine chambers.

The ETs knew immediately and went on red alert.

It's hard to hide the disappearance of ninety-nine million people.

Eva's army would have nothing to do for two hours but to protect themselves and their world.

They would now see how ready they really were.

The ETs could communicate almost instantly with their human underlings. They issued orders but their human helpers didn't respond.

Some of them had actually disappeared and the remaining were either stumbling or silent.

The fleet of attackers had to come from Ganymede.

But they were very fast.

Two ships already close to Earth were commandeered.

Five humans appeared wrapped around the bodies of their five crew members and stranded them in Andromeda.

Their ships were set adrift at slow speeds out to space, weapons intact.

Simultaneously, fifteen attack ships circling Ganymede lost their pilots. Then seventy-nine of the first pilots to head for their ships disappeared before they got to them.

Then another ninety-nine were kidnapped as they were entering their ships or preparing to take off.

But this left eight hundred and twenty-one ships and eleven automated missiles successfully deployed, ships and missiles, small and large screaming towards the population centers of greatest disappearance just as the ringed ones wanted.

"Come to us, puppies. We're your enemies. Focus on us so we can most acutely focus on you."

And that's what they all did, focus on each other.

The missiles carried field disrupters but were small enough for a person to wrap their arms around.

Each pod sent one adult. The missiles reappeared as they were about to penetrate the sun. They were all soon plasma.

Eleven more were launched from Ganymede.

Human bodies appeared wrapped around their deployers and they both disappeared.

And eleven others embraced the missiles and released them to the sun.

Ninety-nine men, women and children were now furiously flinging themselves at the enemy pilots and weapons launchers and removing them to Andromeda.

When possible, the humans appeared piggyback, arms around the neck or head of the alien.

When the enemy was seated, they'd materialize legs up in their lap.

This was most frequent.

With any part of the enemy's body mostly encircled, the angel field would surround them and the one mind of each unit would shift them both.

The humans were prevailing but the enemy vessels were stunningly fast and getting closer and closer.

Many of them were quite small with only one pilot.

All of these kept the children quite busy.

Konane would often add herself to their ranks.

André was too big.

If a hijacked vessel might detonate or crash into Earth, the human would reappear in the pilot's position. All the others they just let fly through space in whatever trajectory they might be going. This freed humans to kidnap aliens.

Since most of the ships were headed Earthward, they had to redirect most of them. But many would take evasive measures and move away or tangentially. This was the perfect time to hijack them.

They kept on coming.

The minutes ticked by.

So far, Eva's army was all wins, no losses.

They were doing well.

The alien ships were now close enough to fire their missiles.

The first was aimed at Vientiane. Konane thought of a different way to deal with it.

She manifested a huge boulder flying at high speed directly towards the missile. Upon impact, the two racing masses of matter exploded harmlessly in space.

This left her and her pod members free to deal with aliens.

She gave her strategy to the others.

Then twenty more were shot off.

They were similarly dispatched.

The aliens realized only missiles fired at close range had any chance of reaching Earth.

Ships were being disabled right and left.

The number of incoming were dwindling rapidly.

It all continued for several minutes more.

Then there were no ships of immediate threat left with pilots or weapons personnel.

All the smaller, fastest ships had been won.

They had weathered the first assault with flying colors.

They all rejoiced and allowed themselves a slight lull.

Now were coming the slower, larger ships with their flotillas of attack craft.

Eva blanketed the solar system and her world in Andromeda and took the tally.

Eight hundred and twenty-three enemy ships drifted unpiloted in space. Nineteen of those ships had one or more non-pilot, non-combatant crewmembers on board. All the rest were empty. One thousand, three hundred and seven Greys and Lizards were stranded on Andromeda—not a single Orange, not a single Annunaki. Eighteen large vessels, some with around fifty, some with over three hundred small fighter ships would arrive within an hour.

Then something happened that chilled her to the bone.

She knew what it was immediately. And she knew she was powerless against it.

A Black Cloud had winked into existence in their vicinity.

Before it could strike, she called in the Great Lights.

They surrounded and contained it.

The feeling of this was overwhelming.

The most titanic impulse for evil contained by the most powerful impulses for good one could imagine, facing off between the moon and Earth, eyeball to eyeball, so to speak.

The standoff lasted around twenty-five seconds.

It felt like twenty-five years.

Everything hung in the balance.

Then the Black Cloud was gone.

"Oh thank you!" Eva thought to God and the universe, the devas and the Big Lights and her army of ninety-nine as she watched Brie and Theo fling themselves at two tiny Grey ship pilots that had come straggling in.

Two more ships started floating in space.

It was also time to send another group to heal.

That was the easiest.

Those piloting planes, trains and cars could wait till later.

People on ships were fine if they were far from harbor. A few hours of drifting wouldn't hurt anyone.

Doctors and patients in surgery could go. They could all be healed together. The devas could deal with blood. They were emptying all hospitals, clinics and prisons.

And it was easy to send the right numbers and to leave those who had already gone behind.

It was also easy to scan the millions and provide food for those who were unable to feed themselves.

All that was taken care of in the second tier of consciousness without much thought or attention.

So every two hours, as long as they were functional, this would automatically continue.

They could devote almost all their focus to protecting themselves and the Earthlings.

Eva penetrated the approaching ships.

Maybe this could be easier than she thought.

Maybe not.

Sixteen of the big ships were commanded by Oranges. Most of their crew were the same.

The two smaller, sleeker ones were Annunaki.

She decided to start with one of them. Hopefully, they were more flexible and enlightened.

She picked the better of the two captains.

"You should be ashamed of yourself. You helped seed us. I know you did that to make us slaves but that was millennia ago. You still want to make us slaves? Don't you know that sooner or later you must let your slaves have their freedom? Have you not evolved one iota in all this time?"

This particular Annunaki was Ra. He had, indeed, played the role of Sun God at the dawn of civilization.

He laughed.

"You've got gumption. Don't you realize you just made it easier for me to destroy you by revealing yourself to me? Do you think you can overpower me?"

"Not alone, I can't. But I have some mighty help. Is that all you can think in terms of, overpowering or being overpowered? Is your brain that small or your arrogance that great? Our friends just overpowered a Black Cloud or contained it so it retreated. They could overpower you. Is fighting and enslaving all you know? What about growing up? What about our being allies instead of your enemies or slaves? We look awfully alike. You're a bit bigger and stronger. You live longer. You have more advanced technology. But you don't seem much brighter. Do you have enough light and maturity to treat us as equals? We've grown a bit in the last several millennia, partially thanks to you. And with these rings we can do things you can't come close to. Or are you truly limited to conquering us or being conquered?"

To make her point, she sent Brie and Theo to yank his number two and three in command off to Andromeda.

Her communications were already giving him pause.

This reinforced it manifold.

"Perhaps you can overpower me."

"Perhaps our children can with the help of our friends."

He laughed again.

"OK, you win. Truly. I do believe you're right and becoming your first allies, after the healers and the Big Lights, will serve us far better than trying to enslave you again. Convincing my colleague in the other ship might take some doing. I should begin that immediately. Can I have my brethren back?"

"Is your word worth anything?"

"Indeed it is."

"Do I have it?"

"You have it. And you might consider intercourse with me. I can see you're profligate like we are. As you say, we did seed your race. Maybe your first child should be mine instead of Nyame's."

He had turned the tables on her and read her through and through. This is what convinced him. Why hadn't she thought of doing that with him?

She laughed.

"Maybe you are still ahead of us in a few other ways, as well. I'll take it under consideration. Could you outdo Jimmy?"

"Perhaps I could."

"Do I really call you Ra?"

"We can find another name if you wish. My real name is only for my brethren."

"Let's find another. Ra is too much and too antiquated. It's like you telling me to call you God in an ancient form."

"Isn't that what Nyame is telling his fellow Ghanaians?"

"In a way, yes, in a way, no. No one there would take him seriously. He wasn't Nyame in the past. And he isn't trying to be now. You *were* Ra. And it feels like you're still trying to be. You're not our God anymore. You can't be. Let's see how it is for us to be allies. Then, yes, maybe lovers. Can you really love? Could you love a human such as me?"

"Oh yes. You know of the stories of a god falling in love with a human. They were true. It did happen. And it still could."

"Good. Then maybe we can truly be allies. Just don't try to be our god."

"Aren't you Tom and Ellie's god, the god of your pod?"

"Same thing. Yes and no. I get to play alpha. We all agree to that. But we all know we're really equals. If I started taking myself too seriously, they'd just laugh or be disappointed. I revel in playing it. But we all know better. I'm not sure you do."

His two henchmen reappeared.

"We'll have to have a written treaty."

"Of course."

"Good. What happened to Nibiru?"

"We blew it up and moved to the center of the galaxy. We wanted to be more in the thick of it."

"But you two got homesick?"

"You might say that."

"Is there anything you really have to offer us?"

"Yes, and not only technology."

"And there clearly are things you want from us besides making us slaves."

"Yes, but let's put that in the treaty."

"Very well. Till later. We've both got work to do. Do you think the others could become our allies?"

"Possibly, over time. But most of these here are adventurers and pirates. We Annunaki are here because of our mutual past and our shared genealogy. There's a difference."

"OK, friend, thank you. I'm glad we're not enemies."

"And I as well. With your current help, you'd win. Till later, Eva. Call me Ron. That'll work for both of us. I look forward to it."

And they separated.

"OK," Eva thought to herself, "two down and sixteen to go. Let's see what the Oranges are like."

It didn't take long for Ron to convince his colleague. He simply downloaded Eva's entire life and their conversation into him. That pretty much spoke for itself and they were soon of one accord. This was far more in their interest than the alternatives.

Eva had won them both.

Their two ships peeled away from the coming armada and headed back to Ganymede.

This was acutely perceived by the sixteen remaining captains.

Chapter 32

This Was Their Extremity

Eva scanned the Earth. There was nothing of concern. They had done a splendid job of softening the human opposition. Many of them were ready for healing. Many were not. But they could just stew in their own juices till they were. The few military men who could do real damage had been neutralized. None of the others could, though like so many now they could go on a killing spree. But they were not that type. It wouldn't serve them.

Then she scanned the solar system.

Nothing left that she could perceive but the approaching sixteen ships.

She scanned the Orange captains. Some of them were losing heart. They had now lost the Annunaki, their first advance had ignominiously failed, the one Black Cloud that came had retreated and their human allies were not responding.

But most were livid.

One was head and shoulders above the rest.

Ron was right. A lot of them were pirates and cutthroats.

The one high quality Orange was the best representative of his race.

Their highest concern was their own self-interest. But they also carried some decency.

They thought of the humans as inferior. But they realized that in conjunction with the devas and Great Lights, they were superior.

Eva entered his field and read everything of him.

He, likewise, read everything of her.

He was alien but his consciousness was not that different from hers. She, indeed, did have more of God and light within her. Her intelligence was equal to his.

And consciousness is consciousness. It has different flavors in different beings but it still came down to what they both were and could understand. Their instincts, desires and impulses could be quite different. His knowledge and perspective were also quite different. But even those were not all that alien. They were two conscious beings assessing one another.

"The Annunaki have agreed to be our allies. We could be allies as well. Please consider this and turn your ship back to Ganymede. And convince all the others you can to do the same. You already see everything I am conveying. You will not succeed in conquering us, nor is it in your highest interest to do so. We have a lot of help. If you continue on your course, you will fail."

They shared consciousness for a few moments, neither retreating.

They both allowed this.

They both knew either could stop it at any moment.

"Very well," he replied. "I believe only four or five will heed me and turn their ships. The others are mercenaries with little to lose. They have deeply invested in your world. They don't want to lose their investment. Some will be willing to die for it. We will consider an alliance and a treaty. And we will leave you alone either way. But we can't control the adventurers who are here seeking gain. You are out of our jurisdiction till we have a treaty. And we will have to consult with our leaders before we make on with you."

"Very well, I understand. I am grateful for your wisdom and your decency. We will deal with the others the best we can."

"You have dealt quite well with our original wave. I will bet on you for this one as well."

"Thank you. That is heartening. I hope we can find mutual benefit in alliance."

"I do, too."

And they separated.

Within minutes, five ships turned back towards Ganymede.

It was now eleven plus against eleven plus.

The Earth eleven sent off another ninety-nine million souls to heal.

And the games began.

Decapitating the eleven ships was easy.

Within seconds the top five commanders of each ship and forty-four weapons launchers were standing on the plateau of Eva's Andromeda world.

The rest of the big ship weapons deployers were soon there as well.

It was the small attack vessels swarming out of and around the big ships that were the problem.

There were two thousand three hundred and twenty-nine of them, nearly all hell bent on revenge.

As one, they started screaming towards Earth.

The missiles they deployed early were easily dealt with. From a distance, there was so much time that they were easily dispatched by a human and the sun or a boulder.

These pilots, too, soon realized that only missiles fired at close range would succeed.

Eva scanned them all as she and her army continually snatched and relocated pilots.

The eleven soon realized that at the rate they were going, many ships would reach Earth and destroy many cities, including their own.

Those in the lead were the larger Lizard ships. They were the most vicious.

They were humanoid but descended from reptiles instead of mammals. Eva sent Jack to snatch the pilot of the worst of the lot. Besides him, there were three killer crewmembers. Jack returned to the ship to redirect it and deal with the others.

He reappeared with his gun drawn.

As he did, a figure appeared in the entrance of the small pilot cabin. It went for its weapon. Jack's bullet tore through its forehead. As it dropped to the floor, another figure appeared, weapon drawn.

Jack rolled to the floor as a shaft of light seared the space where he had been. His bullet went through this one's throat.

Jack listened intently as a he got up to redirect the craft.

There was silence. He turned the vessel away from Earth.

The rustle he heard coming from outside the entryway sent him hurtling off to the side and onto the floor again. Another shaft of light put a hole in the seat he had just been sitting in.

By some gift-of-God magic, his third bullet went through this one's eye.

Three enemies lay dead piled by the entrance.

It was more than enough.

Jack disappeared to snatch away more pilots.

As he did, he scanned himself.

At first he couldn't tell if he was glad or not. Then he realized that it had fulfilled some ancient need or vow he had made from a time his memory could not reach. From the depths of his being he asked the three and all he had ever killed to forgive him. He blessed them all and was at peace.

In the next moment, he and the ninety-nine realized their conflict had come down to kill or be killed.

They had neutralized over a thousand enemy ships.

But a thousand remained.

They were getting too close and time was running out.

It was a matter of survival.

They opted to kill.

Unlike their missiles, the enemy ships had protective fields that incinerated or deflected anything flying at them. Boulders wouldn't work.

Eva didn't know what would.

This was their extremity.

She reached out to the Great Lights.

They responded.

Through their rings, the eleven were given the power to dissolve matter, to vaporize the ships and any crewmembers aboard. These beings were determined to kill or die. They would be given their wish.

The eleven could do this instantly in any numbers.

They could not move or stop their ships but in their mind's eye they could see them evaporate.

All that would be left would be a puff of smoke.

They eradicated the eleven closest ships.

The others kept on coming.

They increased the numbers.

The rest didn't stop.

In two minutes they decimated half the remaining fleet.

The rest of them finally perceived this and fled back to their mother ships.

The war was over.

The big ships floated in space still moving towards Earth but leaderless.

Eva gathered all the knowledge necessary to fly them.

The eleven ringed ones appeared in the pilot seats, took control, turned them back towards Ganymede and left them to drift away.

They took a moment to take stock.

Not one human had been harmed.

"I think we've won," Eva thought to her army.

They all simply assented.

It wasn't that they weren't happy.

They were sobered and disappointed they'd been forced to kill.

But they were greatly glad that no humans had been hurt and that, in all likelihood, the healing of the human race would continue unabated to its conclusion.

But it was anticlimactic and sad that there was still such stupidity in the universe. And war and death were not joyous to them. They had their joy of anticipation. But the real thing was not a glad affair. Their joy would come later.

Now they were simply grateful it was over and they had won.

There were now nineteen hundred and seven Greys, Lizards and Oranges in Andromeda and twelve hundred and three floating in pilotless ships.

Eva thought to all her living enemies, "You will all deactivate your field disrupters, both in your bodies and your ships. Or we will destroy you or leave you in Andromeda to rot."

They all knew they had been vanquished. The ones in Andromeda now knew they were no longer in their home galaxy.

They all but a few complied.

Eva scanned them all.

One hundred and twelve still clung to revenge.

Fifty-seven were in Andromeda. The rest were in their ships. They were the only ones not to deactivate their devices. Eva flung over half her army around those still in their vessels and deposited them in Andromeda.

"Fine," Eva thought to them all, "you will remain where you are till you relinquish revenge."

All the others she returned to their ships.

To every alien in the solar system she thought, "You will relinquish all your investments here and leave. You will destroy your surveillance installations on Ganymede, Earth and anywhere else in our solar system you may have them. I will destroy any of you who cling to surveillance. You will not approach Earth without permission. If you do, you will reap the consequences. Any of you sincerely interested in true alliances can remain. We will communicate with you soon. But you must be bona fide representatives of your race. We make no alliances with pirates. You will deactivate all the devices on all the ships you have everywhere inside Neptune's orbit. Your ships will be returned to Ganymede."

They complied and she placed their ships in Ganymede orbit.

"If any of you come here intent on revenge, we will know and show no mercy. You will be obliterated. We will not give you a second chance. We wish you no harm if you leave us alone. If you come here to harm us, you will cease to exist. Go in peace. You are not welcome here in any other guise."

"I love you all," she thought to her army. "We'll celebrate later."

And they found themselves home.

Over the next six days, they completed the healing of the human race.

There were no interruptions.

Each successive day, Eva's army felt more and more joyous.

Life on Earth was becoming as it is in heaven.

When it was done, they and everyone else on the planet were truly ready to celebrate.

Every human but one hundred and fifty-one were now whole and healed.

Those remaining were all that was left of the human opposition.

They would soon be dealt with.

After a few days in Andromeda, all but seven of the aliens were ready to throw in the towel and leave.

She sent them to Ganymede or the world of their choosing.

As they approached starvation, six of the seven relented as well.

The last Orange had been uncharacteristically wealthy. He had thrown all his significant holdings towards the conquest of Earth. Most of the others had just been opportunists with little to invest. He couldn't face his total loss. He made his way down to the river and gave himself to it. Perhaps his body would give life to this world.

It was twenty-five days since Eva had met Gabriel.

All their work of healing humankind was done.

What was their world now?

What would it become?

How would it function?

Eva had some guesses.

But who could know?

It was time to commune with her brethren.

Chapter 33

Everywhere She Looked There Was Love

Eva spoke to the minds of every human being on Earth. Those too young to comprehend would hear her voice and feel her essence.

"Thanks to God, our beloved healer angels and the Great Light Beings, every member of the human race is now whole and healed but for one hundred and fifty-one who have declined.

I say to them directly, as soon as you are ready, you can be healed, too. Why cling to misery?

Eleven of us were graced with rings of power to help bring this about. I was the first and our leader.

I also found and selected the others but for China's and there I helped the former leader give his ring to his protégé for the good of us all.

It is we and our angelic friends who transported you all to the chambers and fed those of you with insufficient food.

But this is not about me or leadership.

It's about our highest good.

We eleven each have pods of six or seven. We augmented them with two children and a friend, if needed, to create eleven units of nine souls each to resist our enemies and protect Earth. I believe you should know us. We don't need or expect anything of you. But our roles should be known."

She emblazoned the knowledge of every member of her army and the jurisdictions of each leader in the hearts, souls and minds of the entire human race.

"While the first of you were being healed, malevolent ETs were trying to stop us by destroying enough of us to do so. The one fifty-one and more were in league with them. They all wanted to rule us and to make us their slaves. They already held most of us in economic servitude without most of us knowing. They were also planning massive depopulation. In other words, they wanted to kill most of us.

Thankfully, with the powers given to us by our angelic ET friends and the direct intervention of the Great Lights, none of us were harmed.

Instead of death and slavery, we have this.

We are truly blessed.

Life on Earth can now become far more wonderful than it ever has been.

We are now without sickness and deformity.

We can be without war, hunger, murder, theft, rape and servitude.

But for the one fifty-one, we are without the crippling greed for wealth and power that has so undermined the wellbeing of so many.

Is that why you cling to your misery, so that you can cling to your wealth and power?

If so, know that the rest of us will no longer allow it.

We would much rather heal you than stone you to death.

Come forward and be healed.

We know who you are.

You are a disease.

We have moved beyond disease.

We invite you to join us.

We ringed ones can read you to the depths of your souls.

We will soon be doing that and deciding what to do with you.

Decide for the good of your own soul what to do with yourself.

Decide to be magnificent instead of what you alone now are.

I don't know what will happen to governments and justice systems.

I don't know what will happen to the wealthiest among us.

The war machine is an obsolete monstrosity. The health care industry has nothing to do.

We've been told that we eleven will keep our rings.

They give us great abilities.

We will continue to use them for the good of mankind.

If any of you are damaged or fall ill, we will send you to heal.

Perhaps if judges will still be needed, we will be the world's highest court.

There's so very much for us all to do.

Our world and infrastructures need our help.

We will take care of many things but so will you.

Let's all do everything we can together.

Ninety-nine of us helped save our world.

We will commune and see what there is for us to do now.

We can perceive need anywhere on Earth.

We will do our best to fulfill those needs.

But that is your job now.

We were looking to our higher helpers to heal us all. But it turned out that we were the ones to do it, with their help, but for ourselves.

This will be the same.

Find ways to fulfill your own needs. Call out to us when you can't find a way.

Look to see how you can fulfill the needs of others.

We all must find the need and fulfill it together.

What our world becomes depends upon us.

Now is the time for you to find your way of contributing to this new world we've been given.

You are precious to us all.

Let us all now help each other and, in so doing, help ourselves.

We finally truly can.

We can now make this world the heaven it deserves to be.

Don't wait.

Begin now.

I love you all.

You'll be hearing from us."

Then she was silent.

Within moments she could feel twenty-seven holdouts call to her for healing.

She sent them to a chamber.

One twenty-four to go.

She went to her island and created a great, circular, wooden fale built on short, thick poles like a kava-kava bowl only flat. It had upper, slender poles holding up a thatched roof and overlooked the little lake in the hills.

In a moment, her army of ninety-nine stood on it in a circle facing each other.

They allowed themselves to feel the joy of the human race.

This amplified their own joy to the point of uncontainability.

Eva then placed all the children in a smaller circle facing outwards toward the larger circle of adults.

This brought them a different kind of joy. And they all burst out laughing as one, filling the skies with greathearted love and mirth.

Then she had them mill around and hug and touch each other. Nyame picked up Theo and whirled him around in delight. A few others soon followed suit.

Some adults hugged others longer than most.

Ilia's pod had a great Russian beauty that strongly drew Eva.

Her and Capucine.

There would be time for all this.

And in what combinations!

And the whole world was now filled with beautiful people, some of course more beautiful than others.

Obesity, emaciation, malnutrition, disease, all that was repulsive and imbalanced had been healed and made perfect.

"You know what blows my mind?" she thought to them all. "Except for the holdouts, Earth does not contain a single circumcised man or mutilated woman."

They smiled. They had all thought the same thing.

"And no piercings or tattoos," Nyame thought to them.

"I wonder how long that will last," Eva thought back. "Perhaps this newfound pristine perfection of our sacred human vessel will be more honored now. Look out tattoo and piercing parlors. Look out vape dens and tobacco industry. Look out drug production and liquor stores everywhere. Look out weapons works. Look out, we hope, superstition.

And this too, even more so, no need to blow anyone's mind!

All our smallness gone!

The whole world living the true nature of our divine, greathearted generosity!
What unbelievable miracles!
Let there be the healthy freedom of God."
They paused for a moment to savor it all.
"I don't think we need to dwell much on what we're to do. We can each survey our sectors and see what is needed. We can call on each other to help if help is needed.
You wonderful children, what you can do for your fellow children!
I don't know what roles you might play. But the human population is now fertile ground for all kinds of miracle solutions.
The human race has been cleansed.
Let's clean our world.
Now we must look to the fauna and flora, the atmosphere, the oceans and our waterways.
Let's dematerialize all polluting facilities and cleanse the water and soil around them.
I don't think we'll have to send all the animals to heal but maybe we will.
I have yet to commune with our friends about this.
I or any of us could do that now.
But let us have our day of rest.
We can all commune at any moment.
I just wanted to see you all.
Let's pile in together and press bodies."
And they did.
Then they all returned home and slept for many hours.
And when they awakened, they looked with new eyes on a new world.
There would be much to do.
But the most important things had been done.
When Eva awoke, she felt twenty-five of the unhealed ones calling for healing. She sent them. And now there were ninety-nine.
"There's something about that number. We will see what they need."
She let Anani and Gabriel soap, brush and cleanse her in the shower.
She manifested a feast for them all.
She surveyed North America.
Wherever there was poverty and lack, the wealthy were organizing food for the needy.
In the few rural pockets of meager resources, Eva manifested all kinds of foodstuffs.
"Find your ways to feed yourselves or go to where food is plentiful. We must all find our way. If you wish to remain here and your land is fertile, I will manifest farms and orchards. Decide and act or let me know."
Then she surveyed the world's jails and prisons.
None of the inmates had been returned to them. They had all been sent to the closest thing they had to a home.
Some of the workers had showed up for work. Then, almost universally, they left. The few who were trying to complete administrative chores soon gave up and left as well. They all knew the world was a different place.

Likewise, all hospitals and mental institutions stood empty.

Not a single clinic had a single thing to do.

Accidents would probably occur.

Births were occurring at home.

The fear of birth and death was gone.

No one wanted hospitals, clinicians or clinical settings.

With perfect health and fearlessness came far greater ease of birth.

Mostly, with support, women stood and then squatted and the baby popped out. Sometimes they chose under water. Their fetuses, of course, had been healed along with them.

It was a world holiday and for most of the world the weekend to boot.

The military was still intact but orders had been given to feed the needy.

The same for police forces.

For the first time worldwide, there was wholesale love between the peacekeepers and the people. None of the former carried weapons.

Everywhere she looked there was love.

She went back to her meal.

"Oh God," she said. "Am I dreaming?"

"Yes," Gabriel answered. "You are dreaming into existence the world we have always wanted."

And he kissed her on the cheek.

The love in the room and everywhere on Earth filled her energy veins as never before.

And Earth became the beacon of light she was always meant to be.

Our little sister of the sorrows was now our goddess of divine rapture.

It was time for humankind to undo all the damage it had done.

And it now had the love, will and wisdom to do so.

Coda

Eva brought Capucine and Nandi to her small fale. They fulfilled all his desires and, in so doing, some of their own as well. It was simple, healthy and happy. Afterwards, Nandi found himself becoming more interested in Indian girls.

She brought her ninety-nine to the great fale. They all stood naked on the circle's outer edge. Then she brought the ninety-nine remaining opposition and stood them naked in the middle.

Most of them were, indeed, the pillars of the old order and those of the world who had, for the longest time, held the most wealth and power. And they had been plotting with aliens to take total control. There were only two women among them.

They all looked on each other.

The ringed ones read them through and through.

No one spoke for a long time.

Finally, Eva said to them in words.

"Look upon us. We saved the human race from you and your alien allies. You would have murdered millions of us, perhaps billions, and more thoroughly enslaved the rest of us. You are the betrayers of the human race, the betrayers of God, ultimately, the betrayers of your very own souls. Your arrogance is staggering, your greed revolting. You are the worst of the human race.

Look at these children. They are magnificent. Their souls are precious, far more precious than yours. They helped save us from you. They have love for you and compassion and pity.

We who wear the rings have looked into your souls. We have seen all your secrets. As I speak, I dissolve your holdings. The longer I speak, the less you have. Your wealth will be used to heal our world and rebuild it, to feed the hungry.

Allow yourself to be healed. Your existence then will be far richer and more precious than it ever has been or could have been had you prevailed. I will allow you to keep some of your wealth if you allow me to send you to the healing chambers. The longer you resist, the less you become.

If you're willing to go, simply assent internally. I will know."

Thirty-one disappeared.

The two women were among them.

Sixty-eight remained.

"I am looking into the depths of your being. It is pride and fear that hold you back. It is your haughty arrogance. How important you are. How wily and clever your ancestors were. How better than everyone else you think you have always been. Do you really believe that? Yes, your great, great grandfathers were smart and in the right place at the right time. But mostly they were good at taking advantage of others, at out-maneuvering them.

Your world is dead.

God has helped us outmaneuver you and your criminal ET friends.

You are no longer important.

You are a blight on the face of the Earth, the only unhealed left.

You fear what you will be if you join the human race. You fear being judged and the wrath of God, though you deny the truth of God. You cling to your false identity of being above everyone else.

There is nothing to fear and everything to gain.

There will be no punishment.

You are your own worst enemy.

We are judging you. And we find you unworthy. This is your judgment. Return to worthiness. It's the most wonderful thing in the world. You will love your life and yourself far more healed than unhealed. You have nothing to be proud of. Allow us to heal you.

As I speak you are losing everything. Be healed and gain everything you have never had."

Twenty-seven more disappeared.

Forty-one remained.

"Go fuck yourself," one of the men said.

As one the ninety-nine burst out laughing.

It was too hilarious.

The laughter lasted a few minutes and then tapered off.

A few of the unhealed couldn't help but laugh as well.

"Why would I do that? I have all these beautiful people to fuck. Not the children, of course. We are not pedophiles as some of you still are. I can see the sickness within you, the ambivalence, the misogyny. You desire me and you hate my womanhood. You see me as weak. If I were so weak, how is it that in all your greatness you are the vanquished?

I used to despise men. In a way, I was like you. Then I was healed.

Love is precious. Fucking can be glorious beyond your comprehension. You can enjoy it far more than you ever have. Let me give you one of my experiences."

And they lived, in the highest definition, what she and Jimmy had lived.

"Why should I go fuck myself when I have Jimmy and those I love even more? Go and be healed and relinquish your pitiful lives for true humility, beauty and greatness."

Twenty-nine disappeared, including the man who cursed her.

Twelve remained.

"Let me show you something else."

She took her ninety-nine and the twelve to the center of the galaxy.

They could see the Great Central Sun and the Council of Twelve.

They could see our galaxy's Great Black Hole.

They could see the myriad stars and worlds at our galactic core.

She let them gaze on this for many moments.

Then she returned them.

"How can you cling to your smallness in the face of that? When you are healed you become one with that. All your wealth and power is nothing in the face of that. Surrender to God and be healed."

Ten disappeared.

Two remained.

"What is it with you two? Tell me. I can see that you are so deeply identified with the old order you simply refuse to join the new, that you are so identified with your position and importance you can't conceive of living without it. Your order is dead. You are a dinosaur. Become a new, glorious human. It's so much richer and more fulfilling than anything you have ever known. It's heaven. We're offering you heaven and you're clinging to hell. Tell me why."

"You can't teach an old dog new tricks."

They burst out laughing again.

"Bullllshit. Be healed and you'll be the newest trick on Earth. You'll love it. I promise. The wonder of it is stunning. The experience of being healed is the best thing you will ever know. Why deprive yourself? You can always blow your brains out if you disagree. Try it. Stop being so bullheaded."

"OK," he said and was gone.

Only one remained.

She looked at him.

"You're convinced you're remaining true to yourself. You are lying to yourself. Your unhealed self is not your true self. It's your stupid self. Your healed self is your God self, your truest self. You're disgusting. I have lost patience with you. You are the last unclean human. You see your holding out as strength. It's not. It's weakness. It's the ultimate foolishness. You cling to your smallness. You're too exasperating. I banish you from the face of the Earth. Our world doesn't agree to bear you. You are a foul spot on the face of heaven."

He found himself alone in a barren world.

"I'll visit him in a day or two. I'll keep doing that and see if he relents. I won't let him die unless he kills himself in my absence. If he never relents, I'll bring him back to live out his life as he sees fit. Thank you. Thank you. Thank you. We did so unbelievably well. We saved everyone but one. I love you so very much."

Several days later, Eva went to him.

"Will you let us heal you?"

"No."

When she returned, Gabriel asked, "Can I try? I have an idea. And maybe it'll help that I'm a man."

"Of course, darling, now?"

"No. Let's give him another day. Send me tomorrow."

The following morning after breakfast, Gabriel said to her, "Dress me in robes like Jesus might have worn."

"I could make you look the most amazing Jesus."

"No, just the robes."

"Not even a beard?"

"No."

She draped him in thick, slightly coarse, neutral-colored lengths of cotton. She surveyed her work and made a few changes.

"Sandals?"

"Yes."

He looked perfect.

She sent him to Andromeda with a bit of her awareness. She wanted to see what might occur.

Gabriel walked towards the man.

He was seated and in a weakened condition from lack of food and sleep.

The water there was quite potable. When it rained, it collected in declivities in the rock. He hadn't bothered to make his way to the river. So he'd been fasting on water.

He rose to face Gabriel.

Gabriel came to him and put his arms around him.

The man stood rigid but allowed it.

Gabe whispered in his ear.

"I have come for the last lost sheep. You are the last of the lost. Please allow me to take you home."

The man stood still then shuddered and shook a bit.

Then something finally softened within him and he allowed himself to cry.

He did it quietly with a few moans and snuffles. But it lasted for many moments.

Finally his weeping was over. And he stood in Gabriel's arms in a state of surrender.

Eva sent him to heal.

And so the last human being became whole.

All his holdings were gone but one small beach cottage and enough wealth to live out his days in comfort.

And so he did in a constant state of bliss.

The last of the mighty titans of commerce was subsumed back into the human race.

Gabriel appeared in Eva's arms.

"I knew there was a reason I loved you, my own little Jesus."

They smiled and held each other.

"Can I ask you a question?"

"Of course, darling!" she said, pulling away and looking into his eyes. "You can always ask me anything! You know that, don't you?"

"I thought I did. But your role in all this has been so titanic. I guess I'm feeling daunted."

"Please get over that, love. I'm still yours more than anyone's. You're my great love. I know I've been running around doing things without you with Ellie and

Tom and Nandi. And I know you told me to. But let's go back to our not doing anything without each other, except of course, when we sleep with our different partners. At least I will. If you see someone and want them, I give you permission. Several times. That'll make us even. Just tell me afterwards, cause I'll know anyway.

I want Svetlana and more with Capucine and Ellie and Tom and maybe Roz. And I promised Nyame and Jimmy one more fuck. Debts must be paid. And God knows who else we might meet. But only with you there from now on. That other was needed. It's not needed now.

And remember, absolutely, we can ask or say anything to each other. Don't be daunted. We speak whatever there is to be spoken. We don't need permission. Yes?"

"Yes."

"Good. So what is it?"

"Why didn't you give them the experience of being in the chamber?"

She slightly startled for a second and then burst out laughing.

"How brilliant! You'd think that would have done it in the bat of an eye! Did you think of that at the time?"

"Only after you gave them your experience with Jimmy."

"Why didn't you mentally suggest it?"

"Maybe I was daunted. Maybe I was trusting you. It didn't occur to me."

"And it didn't occur to *me*. Maybe I wasn't ready. Maybe they weren't ready. Maybe God wasn't ready. Maybe they each had to lose that much wealth in that order. All I can do is what comes to me to do, what I am given and what feels right. We do the best we can. We learn from our experience. We think of how we might have done it better. I did what I could. I did what I thought of. Maybe, for some reason we can't know, you were meant to save him, you and Jesus. What we all did seems to have been enough."

"And so very much more than enough. Every person on the planet healed. Not a single human life lost. It's unbelievable."

"Maybe it's time for you to cry."

"Maybe it is."

"Let's see about that in bed tonight."

Gabriel did cry that night in Eva's arms.

He cried for the suffering so much life had for so long been.

He cried for the great love and joy all were now living.

He cried for the loss of his beloved Lada, that she wasn't here to experience this.

He cried for the gift of Eva's love and the hurt and jealousy he felt in the beginning.

He cried for all the hurt and jealousy everyone in the world had ever gone through, the pain of betrayal, infidelity and loss.

He cried for his wonderful childhood, for the monstrous childhoods so many had lived and died and for childhood's end.

Over the weeks and months, the ringed ones manifested many farms, orchards and wells and relocated many people.

They obliterated everything that polluted earth, air and water and cleansed the polluted places.

They dissolved the mountains of garbage in the oceans and the pollutants in the air.

They cleansed the Earth of all nuclear, chemical, biological and traditional armaments including assault weapons, mines, hand grenades and the facilities for producing them.

The only weapons to remain were handguns, sporting rifles and bows and arrows.

Their use fell to near non-existence.

Science, literacy, education and the arts flourished beyond imagination.

Nowhere on Earth was stupidity prized anymore.

The devas manifested huge underwater chambers and many of the animals of Earth, sea and air were healed.

The Great Lights gave the eleven the power to vaporize all disease carrying and noxious insects and vermin.

So the tick, mosquito, most parasites and all other bothersome creatures were no more.

They had been born of the fall and the noxious in man.

The human race began to find new ways of governing, being and living.

All was becoming healed.

All was becoming whole.

All the world loved the eleven and the ninety-nine.

All the world loved everyone.

Love pods of three to seven became more prevalent.

More and more those who belonged together were able to find each other.

Units of two remained the norm.

The degree of tolerance on Earth became as it is in heaven.

Irreconcilable disputes were brought to the ringed ones and resolved. Very few arose. Loving people were able to work things out for themselves.

After plumbing the depths of Ron, Eva decided to forego his offer.

He did have more power and technology than humans. But he had less love, humility and light. He had less of God and more of arrogance.

Eva decided he had nothing to offer.

They did, though, consummate their treaty.

Ron and the other leader signed for the Annunaki.

The eleven ringed ones signed for humanity.

And so began the reconnection of the human race with the other civilizations of our galaxy.

Eva did dissolve her pregnancy.

She was too young and had too much to do and enjoy.

The time for children would come later.

The ringed ones periodically scanned their sectors and dissolved all unwanted pregnancies.

Human birthrate went dramatically down. Conception did, too. Our species' innate ability to find its proper balance had also been healed.

This was the way to depopulate. Not mass murder and incarceration.

Everything on Earth was coming back to health and equilibrium.

The ringed ones and normal folk cleaned up their world.

They dismantled and dematerialized all the horror man had perpetrated upon her.

They repaired and perfected their infrastructures.

They removed and gentrified their blights.

They created more graceful dwellings for all their brethren.

They dissolved all the wreckage of reckless humanity.

Everywhere one looked beauty and grace met the eye.

The ancient desire of so many for heaven on Earth was now manifest.

Life had become a celebration of abundance and love.

And this continued to grow and become more so.

And it lasted innumerable eons.

Earth had graduated from dysfunctional chaos and joined the worlds of divine harmony.

And on one quiet night, Rosalyn came to Eva and Gabriel's bed and they made the sweetest, most wonderful love more than humans can make.

About the Author

After devoting a lifetime to healing and awakening himself and others utilizing therapy, many meditations, energy and bodywork, 12-step programs, Rebirthing, Shamanic Journey, Soul Retrieval, DNA Activation, Sacred Spirit Healing and esoteric Hindu, Vedic, Buddhist, Christian, Jewish, Hawaiian and Native-American practices and, ultimately, pretty much giving up on attaining his goal for himself, Mark Landau was gifted with divine guidance to co-create the tool that healed what nothing else could. He has a Masters Degree in Linguistics and ordination as an Interfaith Minister and Spiritual Counselor and facilitates Highest Dimensional Healing circles and individual sessions. He worked very closely with Maharishi Mahesh Yogi, founder of Transcendental Meditation, and studied and worked with four other teachers. By 2002 he had worked with thousands of people worldwide and had a growing following as a spiritual teacher. But his inner life didn't reflect this so he stopped. On 4/29/12 he discovered the Love and Forgiveness Meditation. He has written four other books and a musical play. He lives in Santa Fe, New Mexico. For his other offerings, see www.mark-landau.com.

CPSIA information can be obtained
at www.ICGtesting.com
Printed in the USA
BVOW08*0811071116

467101BV00023B/195/P